Praise for
DAY OF THE DEAD

"J. A. Jance's latest
will keep the reader up nights."
Pittsburgh Post-Gazette

"A tale of chilling terror . . . As suspenseful as
anything I've read in recent years."
Green Bay Press-Gazette

"[A] page-turner . . . One of her most
ambitious, and certainly it is going to satisfy."
Forth Worth Star-Telegram

"Jarring . . . The fast-paced action . . . propels
the reader on a harrowing ride through good
and evil . . . Jance creates characters worthy of
our sympathy or loathing."
Sunday Oklahoman

"Ingenious . . . A harrowing plot."
Publishers Weekly (*Starred Review*)

"Jance deftly combines Indian tribal lore,
mysticism, and contemporary crime-solving.
The result is a dark, compelling, and shocking
novel that exposes clever killers and their
gruesome deeds."
Lansing State Journal

"[Jance has] formidable skills."
Cleveland Plain Dealer

Books by J. A. Jance

Joanna Brady Mysteries

DESERT HEAT • TOMBSTONE COURAGE
SHOOT/DON'T SHOOT • DEAD TO RIGHTS
SKELETON CANYON • RATTLESNAKE CROSSING
OUTLAW MOUNTAIN • DEVIL'S CLAW
PARADISE LOST • PARTNER IN CRIME
EXIT WOUNDS

J. P. Beaumont Mysteries

UNTIL PROVEN GUILTY • INJUSTICE FOR ALL
TRIAL BY FURY • TAKING THE FIFTH
IMPROBABLE CAUSE • A MORE PERFECT UNION
DISMISSED WITH PREJUDICE • MINOR IN POSSESSION
PAYMENT IN KIND • WITHOUT DUE PROCESS
FAILURE TO APPEAR • LYING IN WAIT
NAME WITHHELD • BREACH OF DUTY • BIRDS OF PREY
PARTNER IN CRIME • LONG TIME GONE

and

HOUR OF THE HUNTER
KISS OF THE BEES
DAY OF THE DEAD

J.A. JANCE

DAY OF THE DEAD

AVON BOOKS
An Imprint of HarperCollinsPublishers

Grateful acknowledgment is made to reprint "Coyote Sitting," copyright © 2003 by the Family of Harold Bell Wright. Used by permission.

AVON BOOKS
An Imprint of HarperCollins*Publishers*
10 East 53rd Street
New York, New York 10022-5299

Copyright © 2004 by J. A. Jance
Excerpt from *Long Time Gone* copyright © 2005 by J. A. Jance
ISBN 0-380-72434-0
www.avonbooks.com

First Avon Books paperback printing: August 2005
First William Morrow hardcover printing: August 2004

10 9 8 7 6 5 4 3 2 1

This book is dedicated to the memory of bestselling American storyteller Harold Bell Wright, who, in the early 1900s, realized that if they weren't written down, the ancient stories of the Tohono O'odham people would be forever lost. It is thanks to him that many of these stories remain.

DAY OF THE DEAD

prologue

November 2, 1970

It was Monday, so Benny Gutierrez was fighting a hangover—a serious hangover. He had gone to the dance at Crow Hang on Friday and then spent all of Saturday and Sunday timed-out with some of his buddies over at the Three Points Trading Post just east of the Papago Reservation boundary. Now, as he halfheartedly dragged the plastic trash bag along Highway 86 west of Sells, what he wanted in the worst way was a hit of fortified wine—the drink everyone on the reservation called Big Red. But he'd settle for a beer.

First, though, Benny had to make it through the day. He had to work. That was the deal he'd made with Robert and Doreen, his brother and sister-in-law, after Esther had kicked him out. If he'd work, Robert and Doreen would give him a place to stay—a bed, anyway—and that beat sleeping on the ground. In the summer the ground wasn't bad. Even when he and Esther had still been together, he'd slept outside a time or two—in his truck sometimes, or else on the ground. But the credit union had repossessed his pickup, and Esther had sent him down the road. Now, in early November, it was way too cold to sleep outside at night, even in a truck.

Benny didn't rush. There was no reason to hurry. The Tribal Work Experience Program didn't pay enough to make working hard worthwhile. When one bag was full, he dragged that one over to the pile he was gradually accumulating. Across the highway, Alvin Narcho's pile was growing at about the same sedate pace. If the two men were racing, it was a very slow race. And since Alvin had been out behind Three Points Trading Post all Sunday afternoon right along with Benny, he probably wasn't in any better shape than Benny was.

The sun was high in the sky when Benny spotted the cooler. A big blue-and-white Coleman ice chest—a relatively new one, from the looks of it—lay hidden just inside the yawning opening to a culvert that ran under the highway. As soon as he saw it, Benny was sure he knew what had happened. It had probably blown out of the back of a pickup driven by some Anglo returning from a trip to Rocky Point in Old Mexico. There was always a chance that the cooler would be full of once frozen but now rotting fish, but if Benny was lucky—really lucky— maybe there'd be beer in the cooler as well. Warm beer was better than no beer.

Dropping his bag, Benny scrambled down the edge of the wash. Despite his big belly, he moved with surprising speed and agility. He needed to beat Alvin to the prize. If there were two beers, Benny might be willing to share. But if there was only one? Too bad for Alvin.

Panting, Benny grabbed the handle. The cooler was surprisingly heavy. Grunting with effort, Benny pulled it out of the culvert and off to one side so it would be out of Alvin's line of vision once he reached the far end of the culvert. Only when the ice chest was safely concealed from Alvin's view did Benny reach down to unfasten the lid. As soon as he did so, a cloud of unbearable stench exploded into the air. Covering his mouth and nose, Benny staggered away from the cooler. In his rush, he stumbled and fell. His hand banged hard against the top of the cooler, knocking the lid wide open. The jarring blow caused the contents of the cooler to shift and something wet and foul slopped onto Benny's long-sleeved shirt.

The smell alone was enough to stun him. Benny tried to control his gag reflex long enough to push himself away. It was then, as he attempted to regain his feet, that he saw her. A face stared out at him. Strands of long black hair floated on top of a vile-smelling stew.

Groaning in horror, Benny lurched away. He managed only a few steps before he fell once again. He dropped heavily to the ground and vomited uncontrollably into the sand. When the spasms finally left him, Benny lay there, exhausted and unable to move, wondering if he would ever breathe again without the heavy odor of rotting flesh permeating his lungs.

Less than two years after that November afternoon, Benny Gutierrez was dead at age thirty-eight—a victim of cirrhosis of the liver and of acute alcohol poisoning. That was what his medical chart said, and it was true.

But had anyone bothered to consult a medicine man—a *siwani*, they might have learned something else was wrong. A medicine man could have told them that Benny's spirit had been infected by a ghost, a *kokoi*—by the spirit of someone who was dead. And that was true as well. Even as Benny lay dying in a spotlessly clean hospital bed, the awful smell from the murdered girl in the cooler lingered in his wavering senses. Doreen and Robert were there with him, and so was Esther, but the last thing Benny saw, swimming hazily before his eyes as he drifted into unconsciousness for the last time, was that terrible face staring blindly up at him from deep inside a blue-and-white Coleman cooler.

It was only when Benny Gutierrez was dead, too, that he managed to escape the girl in the box. Only then did she finally set him free.

one

They say it happened long ago that I'itoi, Elder Brother, came to a village to see if his Desert People had enough water after the long summer heat. As he walked along he heard a crowd of Indian children playing. He stopped for a while and watched them, listening to the music of their voices and laughter. About that time Elder Brother saw an old woman carrying a heavy load of wood for her cooking fire. Old Woman was not as happy and carefree as the children. She had no energy to sing or play.

About that time an old coyote came and stood by I'itoi. He, too, watched the children. Old Coyote's ribs showed under his thin, ragged coat. Like Old Woman, Old Coyote could no longer play and dance. His paws were too stiff and sore from just walking around in the desert.

Seeing Old Woman and Old Coyote made I'itoi sad. Because Elder Brother's heart was heavy, he couldn't walk very fast. He went to the shade of some cottonwood trees to rest. It was autumn, so the leaves on the tree had turned yellow, but they still made shade.

As Great Spirit sat under the trees, he thought about the children at play and about how different they would be when they grew old. He thought about some young *calves he had seen that morning in a field and about how they would change as they grew older. He thought about a young colt he had seen kicking up its heels with joy, and he thought about how, one day, Young Colt would become Old Horse. He thought about flowers and about how their leaves withered and their colors faded when they grew old.*

Thinking about these things, I'itoi decided he would like to have something around him that would not change as it became old. He wanted something that would not grow heavy like the cows and horses or wrinkled and bent like old men and women or dry and colorless like dead flowers. Great Spirit wanted something that would always stay happy and beautiful like the children.

As I'itoi was thinking these things under the cottonwood trees, he looked up. He saw the yellow leaves. He saw the blue sky through the leaves. He saw the shadows under the yellow leaves. He looked down and saw streaks and spots of sunlight dancing around on the ground just as the Indian Children had danced. Then Great Spirit laughed, for you see, nawoj—*my friend,* I'itoi *had found just what he wanted.*

March 16, 2000

Brandon Walker stood in front of the bathroom mirror locked in mortal combat with the stubborn strings of his bow tie. As sweat dampened his brow and soaked through the underarms of his starched white shirt, he longed for the good old days when, as Pima County sheriff, he could have shown up at one of these cattle calls in his dress uniform instead of having to put on a stupid tuxedo.

There was a tap on the door. "Are you ready?" Diana asked. "It's getting late."

"Then you'd better come help me with this damned tie," Brandon grunted.

Diana opened the door, and her reflection joined his in the mirror. She was so beautiful that seeing her took Brandon's breath away. She was dressed in a deep blue full-length taffeta gown that complemented every inch of her still slim figure. In the cleft at the base of her throat a diamond solitaire pendant hung from a slender gold chain. That single piece of jewelry had cost more than Brandon's first house. Her auburn hair, highlighted now with natural streaks of gray, was pulled back in an elegant French twist.

"Hi, gorgeous," he said.

She smiled back at him. "You're not so bad yourself. What's the trouble?"

"The bow," he said. "I'm all fumble fingers."

It took only a few seconds for her to untangle and straighten the tie. "There," she said, patting his shoulder. "Now let's get going."

Brandon picked up his jacket from the bed and shrugged his way into it as he followed his wife down the hall. "Which car?" he asked. "Mine or yours?"

"Yours," she said.

They drove east from Gates Pass and into downtown Tucson to the community center where the Tucson Man and Woman of the Year benefit gala was being held. The honorees, Gayle and Dr. Lawrence Stryker, were friends of Diana Ladd's dating back to her days as a teacher on the Tohono O'odham Reservation. Now a local luminary, Diana had been asked to give a short introductory and no doubt laudatory speech. Brandon's plan was to go, be seen, and do his best to be agreeable. But when it came to Larry and Gayle Stryker, he intended to keep his mouth firmly shut. That would be best for all concerned.

Larry Stryker sat on the dais overlooking the decorated ballroom filled with candlelit banquet tables and listened as Diana Ladd stood at the microphone and spoke about old times.

"As some of you know, in the early seventies I went through a rough patch. I was teaching on the reservation, had lost my husband, and had a brand-new baby. Not many people stuck with me during that time, but Larry and Gayle Stryker did, and I'll always be grateful for that. Over the years it's been gratifying for me to see what they've done with their lives and to watch as they've turned a single idea into a powerful tool for good."

Larry searched the sea of upturned faces until he caught sight of Brandon Walker sitting at one of the foremost tables. The former sheriff, looking uncomfortable and out of his element in what was probably a rented tux, sat with his arms folded across his chest. Their eyes met briefly. Brandon nodded in acknowledgment, but there was nothing friendly in the gesture—on either side.

Former sheriff. That was the operant word here. While Diana Ladd spoke of the good old times, Larry was free to let his thoughts drift back to those times as well. Fortunately, no one in the room—most especially Brandon Walker—was able to read his mind.

1970

Larry Stryker had no idea how long Gayle had been gone. Truth be known, he'd been half drunk when she left the house. He'd had to be before he could find the courage to tell her what had happened—what he'd done. He had no idea how she would react—hadn't given himself time to think about that. Instead, he blurted out the bad news and waited for all hell to break loose.

For a moment there was absolute silence between them, then she had looked up at him with her green eyes flashing sparks of fury. "Give me the keys," she said, holding out her hand.

"The keys?" Larry stammered. "What keys?"

"The car keys, stupid. What keys did you think I meant?"

So that was it. Gayle was leaving him, and why wouldn't she? Given the sordid circumstances, what else could he expect? Without a word, Larry reached into his pocket and retrieved the keys to his beloved Camaro. Feeling defeated and lost, he dropped the ring of keys into her upturned hand.

"Where will you go?" he asked.

"Go?" she flung back. "I'm going to clean up your mess. I'm going to take care of it."

With that, she had stalked out of the house and driven away. That had been hours earlier—sometime after school but still in the afternoon. Larry had sat there in the living room in front of a blaring television set all evening long, but he heard nothing. Saw nothing. Instead, he sat there envisioning how everything he had ever wanted—everything he had ever dreamed of and worked for—was going up in flames. The years he had spent struggling to make ends meet in college and in medical school meant nothing. Evidently his marriage was over as well. And it was all because he'd been stupid—and now he was going to be caught.

Sometime after midnight, when the Tucson TV station Larry wasn't watching finally went off the air, he got up and turned off the set. Then he sat there in the dark, brooding and waiting for whatever would happen next.

It was at least an hour after that when he heard the sound of rubber tires crunching on the gravel driveway and the grinding noise as the garage door opened. Amazed to think Gayle had come back to him, he leaped up and rushed to the kitchen to meet her. He flung open the door to the garage just as Gayle got out of the car.

One glimpse of her was enough to stop Larry Stryker in his tracks. She was covered with blood—dried blood. It was everywhere—on her face, in her hair, and on her clothing and shoes.

"My God!" he exclaimed. "What the hell happened? Did you wreck the car? Are you hurt?"

"Good," she said, wearily acknowledging his presence without answering his questions. "You're still up. Bring me a trash bag and a roll of paper towels."

"But . . ."

"Come on, Larry. Do something right for a change. And a dishpan of water, too, so I can start cleaning up."

He did as he was told. By the time he returned from the kitchen with the towels and water and the trash bag, she had started undressing. He put down the pan of water, then stood speechless and holding the bag open while she dumped in her Levi's jacket, her shirt, and bra. She followed those with her shoes, jeans, and panties.

Finally he found his voice. "My God, Gayle, what have you done?" he whispered hoarsely. "Tell me."

"What do you think I've done?" she retorted. "I did what I told you I was going to do. You had a problem. I took care of it."

She turned away from him, leaned down into the car, and removed something from the backseat. When she faced Larry again, she was holding a butcher knife by the handle. Larry saw it and knew that it was theirs—the one from the wooden block that sat on the kitchen counter.

"You'll probably want to clean this up while I go take a shower."

She started toward the door while Larry stared down in astonishment at the bloodied knife in his hand. This was a nightmare. Surely it couldn't be happening, and yet . . .

"You didn't . . ." he began.

She turned back on him. "Didn't what?" she demanded. "Didn't let you wreck everything we've worked for?"

For some reason all the muscles in both Larry's hands quit working at once. He dropped the trash bag, letting the bloodied clothing spill messily onto the floor. The knife slipped from his other hand. It fell to the concrete floor and landed on its tip. The top inch or so of the steel blade shattered while the rest of the knife spun out of reach under the car. Leaving them where they fell, Larry followed his naked wife into the house and down the hall to the bathroom.

Gayle had turned on the shower in the tub and was stepping into it when Larry entered the room behind her. Seeing him, she shook her head in resignation. "Well," she said, "as long as you're here, you could just as well come wash my back."

And, God help him, that's exactly what Larry Stryker did because, no matter what, he always did what Gayle wanted him to do. He stripped off his clothing and clambered into the tub behind her. She was waiting for him, standing under the steaming-hot cascade with little rivulets of bloodied water streaming from her hair. He watched in fascination as they coursed down her neck and across the gentle slope of her breasts.

"Here," she said, handing him a bar of soap. "You do know how to use this, don't you?"

And so he had scrubbed her clean. A pale pink sheen of blood sluiced off her body and made its way across the white porcelain tub and down the drain. She stood like a compliant child under his ministrations, letting him wash her body and shampoo her hair. All the while she watched him with those amazing green eyes of hers, eyes that never wavered and seemed somehow unaffected by both shampoo and soap. Just when Larry thought he had completed the job, she handed him the fingernail brush. It turned out she was right to do so. Close examination revealed crusted blood still lingering under her nails.

When he had finished with the nailbrush and glanced back at Gayle, she was smiling at him. "See there?" she said. "Lady Macbeth was wrong. The blood does too come off. Now it's my turn. Let me wash you."

By then the hot water was beginning to give out. Even so, Gayle worked her customary magic. From the beginning she had always known exactly what to do to make Larry wild to have her. It had been true when he'd first met the eighteen-year-old college sophomore who was two years younger than he was. It was still true now, twelve years later. Gradually the water went from warm to cold, but Larry didn't notice. He was aware of nothing but the tantalizing touch, first of Gayle's hands and later her lips, on his all-too-compliant body. It was all he could do simply to remain standing.

Finally, she turned off the water. Without bothering to towel off, she led him, stumbling and still soaking wet, into the bedroom, where, in one smooth motion, she drew him down onto the bed and into her body.

Gayle had always liked sex, but that night she was ravenous for it, wanting him—giving and taking—far beyond anything Larry could ever remember. It was only later, when Gayle was sleeping and Larry wasn't, that he realized what had happened. Rather than being appalled by what she had done, Gayle was excited by it. And by allowing himself to be drawn into her frenzied acts of fierce lovemaking she had infected him with the same excitement. She had killed for him and then come home to make love. What drug could be more intoxicating than that?

Gayle dozed off almost immediately, while Larry lay beside her, sleepless and spent. As the hours dragged by, his initial sense of euphoria disappeared as his mind tried to grapple with the consequences of what she had done. If she had actually murdered the girl—and Larry didn't doubt it—how much of her terrible crime was his fault, his responsibility?

Larry was more than willing to acknowledge that he had violated the physician's sacred creed to do no harm. He had taken sexual advantage of a patient—a helpless minor—who had been under his care. That was bad enough—bad enough to have him tossed out of the world of medicine and bad enough to make him liable for criminal proceedings as well, but what he had done wrong was a long way short of murder.

But Gayle? Not only had she slaughtered someone in cold blood using a knife from their own kitchen, she had come home afterward and exhibited not a trace of remorse. She hadn't been ashamed of what she'd done; hadn't been sorry. Instead, she had come home to her husband reveling in it—wearing the gory evidence of her crime as though it were a badge of courage or even honor. And then, by having Larry clean that evidence away and by welcoming him into her body, she had some-how made her crime his and had turned him into an accessory—a willing accessory—to murder. In the pro-cess, she had extracted something else from him as well—his tacit agreement to secrecy and silence.

Larry had always known Gayle was headstrong and ambitious, but until that night he would never have thought her capable of murder. She had been pro-voked—pushed beyond the limits of her endurance. And what had caused that to happen? Larry's actions. Larry's stupidity. And that made all of this Larry's fault. He was the one who had pushed Gayle to this appalling extrem-ity. No matter what the law said, in Larry's mind and heart he really was an accessory to murder—both before and after the fact. If Gayle went down for the crime, so would he.

He could hear himself now lamely trying to explain to some stupid cop exactly how it had all come about. Well, yes, his wife had come home covered in blood. "And what did you do then, Dr. Stryker?" the cop would ask, and Larry would have to explain how first he had cleaned Gayle up by getting into the shower with her and then screwing her brains out before finally getting around to calling the authorities. Try telling that to a jury—or a judge.

It was almost dawn before Larry finally began to come to grips with the reality of his predicament. The unspo-ken complicity Gayle had exacted from him in the bath-tub and in the bedroom was far more all-encompassing and compelling than any paltry marriage vows. Those Larry had broken time and again without so much as a second thought.

But this was something else. Ten years ago, in a church, he had promised to love and cherish Gayle

Madison Stryker until "death do us part." As dawn began to color the sky outside their bedroom window, he finally saw how those very same words now meant something else entirely. Gayle had Larry by the throat and by the balls, and she wasn't letting him get away. Ever. And maybe that wasn't half bad.

Larry had always been his mother's "good boy," not because he had never been in trouble but because he had never been caught. Growing up in a time that predated video surveillance, he had shoplifted with impunity all through grade school and high school, and he had loved it. Had loved doing it and getting away with it; had loved living on the edge where he might be caught but wasn't. He had loved being accepted as an "exemplary" student—as someone his teachers pointed out as a "perfect role model" for others—when Larry, in fact, knew better.

He had married Gayle because she was beautiful and rich, but it had never occurred to him that they had so much in common. Tonight he realized that the person he thought he had married was someone else entirely. It was like picking up a pencil and discovering, once it was in your hand, that it was actually a stick of dynamite. By doing what he had done to Roseanne Orozco, Larry Stryker had unwittingly lit the fuse. He was yoked to someone who, with a single word, could bring the world crashing down around him. He was scared to death, but it gave him a rush—an incredible rush—and he loved it.

When the alarm sounded at six, Larry reached over and switched it off. Gayle, sleeping peacefully beside him, never stirred. Throwing off the still-damp sheet, Larry crawled out of bed. Once he was dressed, he went straight to the garage. He picked up the spilled clothes and stuffed them back into the bag, then he scrambled around on the floor until he had retrieved both the knife and its broken tip. When he looked inside the Camaro, he was amazed by the amount of blood he found there. The seats, front and back, and the floorboard were soaked with it. He must have been blind not to have noticed it the night before. Now, though, there was nothing to do but go to work with soap and water and try to clean it up.

Gayle had taken care of his mess, so Larry needed to take care of hers. He was doing just that when the door opened. Gayle stood in the doorway, with a smoldering Virginia Slim in one hand and a copy of *TV Guide* in the other.

"What did we watch last night?" she asked.

"Watch?"

"On TV. If someone asks where we were or what we were doing, we were home all night long, watching television together. That means we'd better have our stories straight about what we watched, what we ate, and what time we went to bed."

Saying nothing, Larry returned to the task of scrubbing the car, but that was when he realized, once and for all, that the genie was out of the bottle. And she wasn't ever going back in.

March 2002

Maria Elena Dominguez rode the bus from Hermosillo to Nogales, fighting to stay awake and clutching her backpack all the while. There was little of value in the knapsack—only her papers and the change of clothing she'd been given earlier that morning as she left El Asilo

Seguro. Still, Maria Elena was afraid someone might try to steal her paltry belongings. Even when she dozed off, she didn't relinquish her hold on the backpack's straps.

"So," Señora Duarte had said with a sneer as Maria Elena slipped silently into her office at eight-thirty that morning. "You must be one of the lucky ones."

Fifteen-year-old Maria Elena didn't feel lucky. Her father, a leftist sympathizer, had been gunned down by a troop of soldiers four years earlier in their tiny village in Chiapas. Then, during her father's funeral, the same group of soldiers had appeared again. This time, Maria Elena's mother and her older brother, both of them screaming and fighting their captors, had been hauled away in a single armored vehicle, while a petrified Maria Elena had been carted off in another.

The driver of that one, an older man who reminded Maria Elena of her grandfather, had been kind enough. He had given her food, sharing some of his own with her. Several days later, she had found herself in a Franciscan-run orphanage on the outskirts of Matías Romero in Oaxaca. Looking back, Maria Elena realized the orphanage hadn't been such a bad place. The problem was, Maria Elena didn't consider herself an orphan and refused to stay there. Twice she ran away but was picked up and returned to the orphanage without ever making it home to Chiapas.

The third time she ran away she was caught and shipped off to another facility, a juvenile detention center in Colima. Finally, for reasons none of them understood, she and two other girls, accompanied by a guard and wearing shackles, were taken by bus far to the north to yet a third facility—El Asilo Seguro outside Hermosillo. Despite its benign-sounding name—the Safe Haven—El Asilo Seguro was by far the worst of all, and it was anything but safe.

For one thing, boys and girls were warehoused together. There were supposedly separate sleeping facilities, but curfews inside the institution were widely ignored and sleeping arrangements poorly supervised. Sexual encounters were forbidden, but that prohibition wasn't strictly enforced, either. Many of the inmates, like Maria Elena, were orphans whose crimes involved nothing more serious than running away. Others, at ages as young as eleven or twelve, were already hardened criminals. That number included two convicted killers, several drug dealers, and a band of tough-eyed gang members who carried knives and were a constant simmering threat to everyone around them.

Arriving from Colima, Maria Elena and the two girls with her, Madelina and Lucia, were smart enough to figure out that the knife-wielding boys were interested in girls for one reason and one reason only. In order to avoid being preyed upon, the girls manufactured a story about how they had been sent away from their previous institution because all three had been diagnosed as HIV positive. To their amazement, the ruse worked. It turned out that the devil-may-care gangster wannabes who weren't afraid of drugs or guns or knives or each other were deathly afraid of AIDS. The new arrivals were pretty much left to themselves. The three girls had survived by sticking together, by speaking only to one another, and by making themselves invisible.

Maria Elena tried hiding out in silence now, avoiding Señora Duarte's question and piercing gaze with a simple shrug rather than a verbal reply.

"You're wrong there," the señora said, pulling her reading glasses down onto her sharp nose. She glared through them at a stack of papers on the desk in front of her. "You really are lucky. It would seem you have a patron," she continued, "a benefactor in the States who has arranged for you to come live with him and his wife and go to school."

Maria Elena's jaw dropped. Once she had loved school. She had wanted to grow up and become a teacher, but the last time she had actually attended school had been three years earlier in the orphanage. In Colima, there had been a few classrooms, fewer teachers, and even fewer books, but at El Asilo Seguro no one bothered to pretend that they intended to reform or educate their charges. Maria Elena's heart beat fast at this first tiny glimmer of hope. Perhaps her long-abandoned dream was possible after all. It was strange that she hadn't been consulted about these arrangements in advance, but still . . .

"I have examined the papers," Señora Duarte went on. "Everything appears to be in order. You are to catch the bus from Hermosillo to Nogales this afternoon. The ticket is right here, as is your passport and identification card. You'll find some money here as well, enough so you'll be able to buy food and water for your journey. You will be picked up at the bus station in Nogales and taken from there to your new home."

Maria Elena's head teemed with questions. She had heard some of the older kids talking about passports and identification cards. Legal ones were very difficult to come by, and forged ones were obtainable only by those with enough money to pay the price. What would happen to her if she reached the border and for some reason her paperwork wasn't in order? And how would she know this person—this kind stranger—who was supposed to meet her in far-off Nogales?

"But . . ." she began aloud.

Señora Duarte's disapproving frown silenced her. "Certainly you wouldn't be so foolish as to turn down such an opportunity!" she declared.

"No, señora," Maria Elena murmured in agreement. "I would not."

"Very well, then." Señora Duarte picked up the papers and stowed them inside an outside pocket of the knapsack, which she then zipped up. "Here," she said, handing it over. "You can't travel in your uniform. Go see Señora Escalante. She'll give you something suitable to wear."

As directed, Señora Escalante had outfitted Maria Elena with two sets of someone else's cast-off clothing—one to wear on the bus and another to change into later. The skirt and blouse were too small; the shoes far too big. They flopped up and down when she walked. By the time she had walked through the bus station and found food to eat, Maria Elena had painful blisters on both heels. But none of that mattered. Her feet might be sore, but her heart was light. She was out. She was free. She was on her way to a new life.

At the bus station, she wondered briefly what would happen if she tried to trade the ticket she had—the one to Nogales—for one that would take her back to Chiapas. *But who would be there if I did go home?* she asked herself. She knew for sure that her father was dead. Most likely, so were her mother and brother. After four years, who would be left to take her in or even care about her?

In the end, she boarded the bus for Heroica Nogales. *Where will I end up?* she wondered as the blurred landscape unfolded outside the moving window. Along the way, the world outside that window became more and more barren. More and more empty. That emptiness bothered Maria Elena. It reminded her of how empty her life was. It made her wonder what her new life would be like. Who were these kind people—this man and woman—who were taking a stranger into their home? Were they hoping for a daughter to replace one they had lost, perhaps, or were they looking for a servant—little more than a slave—who would work for them for next to nothing?

Other girls had left El Asilo Seguro in similar circumstances. A year earlier, Maria Elena's friend from Colima—Madelina—had been adopted out and had gone north as well—north to what they all regarded as the Promised Land, north to the United States. There was a graffiti-covered map of North America on the wall outside Señora Duarte's office. After Madelina left, Maria Elena had often stared at the map of the United States. It had to be a huge country, and she puzzled about where in it her friend might be living. Now she wondered if she might find Madelina again. Years from now, would they somehow meet somewhere in that strange new country? Perhaps they would sit together in some nice place—a fancy restaurant, possibly, with brightly colored tables and umbrellas outside—and laugh and talk about how much their lives had changed since the old days in Colima and in Hermosillo.

Maria Elena took the papers out of the zippered pocket and studied them one by one, but they told her nothing. She had purchased some food from a stand outside the bus station, and she had eaten it all before she ever boarded the bus, savoring the wonder of eating food she had chosen for herself rather than having it slopped carelessly into a bowl by the resentful woman who had parceled out stingy servings of bad-smelling food to the inmates at El Asilo Seguro. There, Maria

Elena had always gone away from the table still feeling hungry. Today she felt the strange sensation of being full. Lulled by contentment and the motion of the bus, she fell asleep.

She spent three hours on the bus—three glorious hours—where no one told her where she had to go or what she had to do. When the bus finally reached the station in Nogales, Maria Elena was awash in a combination of anxiety and anticipation. But then she saw him standing there on the platform, watching for her. Catching a glimpse of her face at the window, he smiled and waved. In that moment she recognized him. He was someone who had come to El Asilo Seguro the summer before, a kind doctor who had treated the children there, many of whom hadn't seen a real doctor in years, if ever.

Señor the Doctor, Maria Elena whispered to herself. *That is good. That is very good.*

Weak with relief, she grabbed up her knapsack and raced for the door.

two

April 2002

Under a clear blue April sky, Brandon Walker swam his laps one after the other. He didn't bother about timing them. At age sixty-one, he was no longer interested in setting speed records, and he didn't count laps, either. What he wanted was to maintain his endurance, so he swam until he couldn't swim any longer, then he stopped. He was a little winded, but not too bad. The heated water in the newly installed lap pool was kind to his joints, especially his right hip and left knee, both of which had been giving him trouble recently.

When he had gone in for his annual physical, Dr. Browder had hinted that it was about time to discuss the possibility of hip- and knee-replacement surgery. Brandon was considering the possibility all right, but not very seriously. He'd get around to having joint replacement surgery about the same time someone perfected the art of human brain transplants. In the meantime, he'd get along as best he could without complaining. If he didn't gripe about it, maybe he could keep his wife, Diana Ladd, from setting another doctor's appointment.

The cordless phone he had carried out to the patio rang with the distinctive ringer that said someone was calling from the locked security gate at the front wall. Had he been home alone, he would have had to scramble out of the pool to see who was there and let them in. Fortunately, Diana was home and in her study, locked in mortal combat with the stalled beginning of her next book. Convinced she would welcome any interruption, Brandon kept swimming. Besides, the visitor was probably UPS or FedEx bringing some new missive or assignment from Diana's New York publishers. Most of the mail, packages, and e-mails that arrived at their Gates Pass home near Tucson these days were part of Diana's ongoing business. Years after Brandon's failed reelection bid for the office of Pima County sheriff, he had adjusted to being retired and mostly out of the loop. Diana Ladd was still working hard; Brandon was hardly working.

His wife came out through the sliding door onto the patio trailed by Damsel, a now three-year-old long-eared mutt Diana had found as a shivering, starving, and abandoned pup outside their front gate on a chilly Thanksgiving morning two and a half years earlier. Brandon and Diana had agreed that, with their daughter Lani off at school, the last thing they needed was a puppy. In the end, however, sentimentality had won out over good sense. Their Damsel in Distress—Damn Dog, as Brandon often called her, since she was usually underfoot—was now a well-loved and decidedly spoiled member of the family.

Walking toward the pool, Diana beckoned her husband to climb out. They had been married for more than twenty-five years, but in his eyes she was still as beautiful as she had been that stormy summer afternoon some thirty years earlier, when he had knocked on the door of her mobile home in a teachers' living compound near the Papago village of Topawa. He had gone there looking for Diana's first husband, Garrison, who was a suspect in a homicide that then Pima County homicide detective Brandon Walker was investigating.

By the time Brandon arrived at Diana's house, Garrison Ladd was already dead of what would be ruled a self-inflicted gunshot wound, but neither Brandon Walker nor Diana Ladd had known that then. The detective had sat across from her in the living room of a threadbare single-wide mobile home, asking tough questions about her husband's doings and whereabouts. As he did so, Brandon was struck by Diana's delicate beauty; by the hard-won poise with which she answered his troubling questions; and by her unwavering loyalty to her jerk of a husband, even though by then she must have suspected some of what had gone on behind her back.

That very afternoon, as Diana Ladd struggled to cope with the looming disaster that was about to engulf her life, Brandon Walker had longed to take the distraught woman in his arms and comfort her, but he hadn't—not then. Married at the time, Brandon had managed to maintain his professional distance then and six months later, as well, when a profoundly pregnant Diana Ladd had worked determinedly to see to it that her dead husband's accomplice, Andrew Carlisle, was sent to prison. Six years after that, when Carlisle was released from prison and came stalking Diana, Brandon Walker had once again been thrown into Diana's orbit. During those intervening years, a divorced Brandon Walker had looked at a few other women and even dated one or two, but none of them had measured up.

Brandon remembered how someone somewhere had

once asked him if he believed in love at first sight. Naturally he had laughed off the question and brushed it aside as if it were too inane to bother answering, but deep down he knew better. He had fallen in love with Diana Ladd the moment he saw her. And he loved her still.

"What's up?" he asked as she came toward the pool, holding out a towel.

"You may want to go in the back way to dress," she said. "Somebody's here to see you."

Brandon took the proffered towel and scrambled out of the pool. "Who is it?" he asked.

"An old Indian lady named Emma Orozco," Diana replied. "She's using a walker, so I left her in the living room."

"She's on a walker and drove here by herself?"

"No. Her son-in-law brought her. He's waiting out front. I offered to invite him in, but she said no, he'd stay in the car."

"What does she want?"

Diana shrugged. "Beats me. Something about her daughter."

Once out of the water, Brandon found the morning air far chillier than expected. He hurried to the sliding door and let himself into the bedroom. After dressing he made his way into the spacious living room, where a wizened Indian woman, her face a road map of wrinkles, sat primly erect on the leather sofa, one gnarled hand resting on the crossbar of her walker.

"Ms. Orozco?" Brandon asked tentatively, taking a seat opposite the old woman. "I'm Brandon Walker."

She turned to look at him and nodded. "Your baskets are very nice," she said.

Brandon glanced around the living room. Diana's collection of Native American baskets, many of them finely crafted museum-quality pieces, were arrayed around the room with wild extravagance. They had been part of the household furnishings for so long that Brandon Walker no longer noticed them.

"Thank you," he replied. "Some of them were made by Rita Antone, a Tohono O'odham woman who was once my wife's housekeeper and baby-sitter."

Emma Orozco nodded again. "I knew *Hejel Wi i'thag*," she said. "Her nephew is the one who sent me to talk to you."

Despite years of living around the Tohono O'odham, the Desert People, Brandon was still struck by the lingering influence of old ways and old things. Rita Antone had been dead for fifteen years, yet on the reservation she was still *Hejel Wi i'thag*—Left Alone. As a little orphaned girl named Dancing Quail, Rita had been given the name Left Alone in the early part of the twentieth century, long before Emma Orozco had been born. No doubt stories about *Hejel Wi i'thag* and her odd loyalty to an Anglo woman named Diana Ladd were now an enduring part of reservation lore.

Rita Antone's nephew, retired Tribal Chairman Gabe Ortiz, and his wife, Wanda, were longtime family friends. In the Walker/Ladd household, Gabe was usually referred to by his familiar name of Fat Crack—*Gihg Tahpani*. Not wanting to betray what might seem like undue intimacy, Brandon made no reference to that name now.

"How's Mr. Ortiz doing?" Brandon asked.

"Not so good," Emma Orozco replied.

This was not news. A few months earlier, Fat Crack had been diagnosed with diabetes. A student of Christian Science, Fat Crack had, in middle age and with

some reluctance, answered a summons to become a Tohono O'odham medicine man. Once aware of his diagnosis, Fat Crack had refused to accept the services of the
Indian Health Service physicians and "get poked full of
holes." Instead, he was dealing with his ailment—one so
prevalent on the reservation that it was known as the Papago Plague—with diet and exercise, along with an unlikely regimen of treatments that was as much Mary
Baker Eddy as it was Native American.

"I don't know why he has to be so damned stubborn,"
Brandon's daughter Lani had railed. Home for Christmas vacation from her pre-med studies in North
Dakota, she had heard about the diagnosis while visiting
Wanda and Fat Crack in their home at Sells. "He should
be under a doctor's care," Lani had declared. "But he
won't even consider it."

Dolores Lanita Walker was a Tohono O'odham child
who, as a toddler, had been adopted by Diana Ladd and
Brandon Walker. She had been reared by them and, for
the first several years, by Rita Antone as well. Fat Crack
and Wanda Ortiz were Lani's godparents, and Fat Crack
and Lani had always been especially close.

"You can't take this personally," Brandon had counseled his daughter. "Fat Crack has to deal with his illness
in his own way, not your way."

"But he's going to die," a suddenly tearful Lani had
objected. "He's going to die and leave us, and he doesn't
have to."

"You're wrong there, sweetie," Brandon had told her.
"We all have to die."

Brandon refocused his attention on the present and on
Emma Orozco, sitting stolid and still on the living room
couch. At first Brandon thought she was still staring at

the baskets, but then he realized she wasn't. She was looking beyond them—through them—in a way that took him back to his days in 'Nam and to the thousand-yard stare.

"But Mr. Ortiz suggested you should see me," Brandon suggested gently. "My wife said it was something concerning your daughter."

Emma sighed and nodded. "She's dead."

Brandon gave himself points. He had recognized the look on her face, and the hurt, too. "I'm sorry," Brandon said.

"It's all right," Emma returned. "Roseanne's been dead for a long time." She paused then, searching for words.

Years in law enforcement had taught Brandon Walker the difficult art of silence. There were times when it was appropriate to ask questions and probe for answers. But there were other times, like this one, when keeping silent was the only thing to do. Emptying a room of sound left behind a vacuum that could only be filled by a torrent of words. Or, as in this case, by a trickle.

"She was murdered," Emma Orozco whispered hoarsely. "In 1970."

Suddenly Brandon Walker knew exactly why Emma Orozco was sitting there and why Fat Crack had sent her. "Let me guess," he offered quietly. "Her killer was never caught."

Emma nodded again. Brandon could see that, more than thirty years after her daughter's death, Emma Orozco still found the subject painful to discuss. As the old woman struggled to keep from shedding shameful tears in front of a relative stranger—something firmly frowned upon by her people—Brandon opted to give her privacy.

"I'll get some iced tea," he said, rising from the couch. "We'll drink first, then we'll talk."

"Thank you," Emma whispered. "Thank you very much."

three

While bustling around in the kitchen, gathering glasses and ice, pouring tea, Brandon Walker remembered every word of the unexpected phone call six months earlier that had rescued him from wallowing in a sea of despair and drowning in a pot of self-imposed pity. He had been cranky and bored, tired of being seen by the world as nothing but Mr. Diana Ladd, and disgusted with himself for not being grateful now that Diana's burgeoning success had made their financial lives more secure than either one of them had ever dreamed possible.

Diana had been somewhere on the East Coast, off on another book tour. Alone with Damsel, Brandon was finishing his second cup of coffee and reading the *Wall Street Journal* in the shade of the patio when the call came in just after 8 A.M. The caller ID readout said "Private Call," which probably meant it was some telephone solicitor, but on the off chance that it was Diana calling from a new hotel and a new room, Brandon answered it anyway.

"Hello."

"Mr. Walker?" an unfamiliar male voice asked.

"Yes," Brandon growled, adopting his most off-putting, crotchety voice. The last thing he wanted to do was have to convince some slimy salesman that, as owner of a house constructed primarily of river rock, he had no need of vinyl siding.

"My name is Ralph Ames," the man said. "I hope it's not too early to call."

"That depends on what you're selling," Brandon grunted in return. He had no intention of making this easy.

"I'm not selling anything," Ames returned.

Oh, yeah, Brandon thought. *That's what they all say.*

"Does the name Geet Farrell ring a bell?" Ralph continued.

Detective G. T. Farrell had been a homicide detective for neighboring Pinal County at the same time Brandon Walker had been in a similar position for the Pima County Sheriff's Department. Geet Farrell was part of the cavalry who had ridden to the rescue when Andrew Philip Carlisle, newly released from prison, had staged his brazen and nearly successful attempt to silence Diana Ladd permanently. Brandon and Geet had stayed in touch occasionally since then, although they weren't necessarily close.

"I know Geet Farrell. Don't tell me he's gone off the rails and started selling Amway."

"I can assure you this has nothing to do with Amway," Ralph Ames said, sounding somewhat offended. "But he's part of a project I'm in the process of getting up and running. He thought you might be interested in joining us."

This guy's a smooth operator, Brandon thought. *One who won't take no for an answer.*

"For how much?" he demanded. "What kind of an investment are you looking for?"

"I'd like you to invest as much time as it'll take for me to buy you lunch," Ames answered. "I'm driving down to Tucson later this morning. Is there a chance you're free?"

"I suppose it's possible," Brandon allowed.

"Good," Ames told him. "Meet me at the dining room at the Arizona Inn about eleven-thirty. The table will be under my name."

So at least the dog-and-pony show is going to be done in style, Brandon thought. And then, because he was bored and lonely and because he was sick and tired of his own cooking, he found himself, against his own better judgment, saying yes instead of no.

"Sure," he blurted into the phone. "Why not? Eleven-thirty it is. See you there."

The rest of the morning Brandon berated himself for being such a damned fool. He was so disgusted with himself that when Diana called him from the airport in Atlanta, he didn't even mention what he'd done. Instead, he poured himself into a starched white shirt, fumbled a once-favored but now slightly spotted tie into an uncomfortable knot around his neck, and then put on a sports coat that was far more snug than it should have been—and than it *had* been—the last time he'd worn it.

Hoping to beat Ralph Ames to the punch, Brandon Walker arrived at the Arizona Inn annoyingly early—at eleven-fifteen. When he peered into the spacious dining room with its linen-dressed tables, he saw no one and assumed the place was empty. Then, in the far corner of the room, partially hidden behind a huge vase holding an enormous spray of flowers, he noticed a single occupied table. It was set for two, but only one diner was seated there—an impeccably dressed man wearing a smooth gray suit and a blazingly pink tie. Even across the room, Brandon recognized the tie for what it was—expensive as hell.

Damn! Brandon thought. *With my luck, that's got to be him. Maybe if I leave my jacket buttoned, the spot on my own tie won't show.*

"May I help you?" the young hostess asked.

"I'm looking for Ralph Ames," he told her.

"Yes, of course," she said with a smile. "Mr. Ames is already here. If you'd be good enough to come right this way . . ."

Feeling outclassed and out of place, Brandon followed the hostess's swaying hips through the room. As they neared the table, Ralph Ames rose to his feet and held out a hand, smiling in welcome. Ames wasn't quite as tall as Brandon, and he was definitely a year or two younger. His razor-cut light brown hair was combed back with only the slightest hint of gray at the temples, making Brandon aware that his own hair probably resembled an unmowed wheat field. Ames was good-looking and seemed to be in disgustingly good shape. The suit fit him well enough that Brandon was forced to conclude it was probably custom-made. Ames exuded the air and self-confidence of someone who had never failed at anything he attempted.

All right, not Amway, then, Brandon concluded irritably. *More likely a televangelist.*

"Mr. Walker, I presume?" Ames asked. As Brandon had expected, the outrageous pink tie was absolutely blemish-free, but the man's handshake was firm. *Tennis or handball, more than running a television remote for exercise,* Brandon decided. Ames's straight-toothed smile seemed genuine enough and his gaze refreshingly direct.

Still Brandon wasn't ready to drop his guard. "Yes," he allowed. "That's me."

"Have a seat. Would you care for a drink?"

A glass containing a half-consumed cocktail sat in front of Ralph Ames, along with a leather-bound menu and a thin file folder that he had closed as the hostess approached the table.

When in Rome . . . Brandon thought. "Sure," he said, taking the indicated chair. "Campari and soda will be fine."

Brandon wasted no time. He waited only as long as it took the hostess to go confer with a member of the waitstaff. If this was something he wanted no part of, it would be easier to leave after accepting a single drink than it would be after an entire lunch.

"What's this all about, Mr. Ames?" he demanded.

The man handed over a business card that said "Ralph Ames, Attorney at Law." The card listed two separate office addresses, one in Seattle and one in Scottsdale. So not a televangelist then but an attorney, which in Brandon Walker's opinion, was probably worse.

"Do you ever play Powerball?" Ralph Ames asked.

"You mean as in the multistate lottery?"

"Yes, that's correct."

A waiter arrived with Brandon's Campari. He dropped off the drink and backed away, while a courteous busboy delivered a basket of fresh bread.

Brandon sipped his drink and considered his answer. "I spent too many years being a cop to be into legalized gambling. I know a few Indian tribes are making a killing at it. The income is helping change economic outlooks on some of the reservations, but no, lotteries aren't for me."

Ralph Ames smiled. "Nor for me," he agreed. "But one of my clients was—in a big way. Her name was Hedda Brinker. She was German. Her husband, Toby, was Dutch, both of them Jews. They managed to escape Europe just ahead of the Nazis. They met on the boat coming over and married within weeks of arriving in New York. They came to Arizona and bought a dairy farm in what's now pretty much downtown Scottsdale. Toby's been gone for years, but he was cagey. He hung on to the land long enough to make money hand over fist in real estate."

"The widow had all the money she needed, but she still played Lotto?" Brandon asked.

"That's right. You may have read about her in the papers. She hit it big—a $178 million jackpot—and hers was the only winning ticket."

Their waiter made a tentative approach. Ralph Ames waved him away.

"So the lady was loaded twice over. What does this have to do with me?" Brandon asked.

"I'm coming to that. Hedda and Toby Brinker had a single daughter—an only child named Ursula—who was born in 1938. Ursula was bright, outgoing, and popular. She was a cheerleader, student-body treasurer, and valedictorian of her class. She was murdered by person or persons unknown during spring break of her junior year at Arizona State University in Tempe."

Brandon shifted uneasily in his chair. "I'm sorry to hear that," he said. "Having money isn't everything." He paused and then asked, "The case was never solved?"

Ralph Ames shook his head. "Never. It's still open even now."

"That's too bad."

"According to Hedda, Toby always believed that whoever did it was well connected—better connected than they were—and that the reason the killer was never caught was due to some kind of cover-up, but even the private investigators Toby hired—and he hired several—were never able to come up with an answer or even with a viable suspect. And they didn't find any evidence of a cover-up, either."

"If the father's own investigators couldn't solve it, you sure as hell don't expect me to do it more than forty years later," Brandon put in. "If that's what you're after, it's wishful thinking."

"Not you personally," Ralph Ames agreed, "but it's possible the case will be solved eventually. Stranger things have happened. But to get back on track—as you can well imagine, Ursula's death haunted Toby. According to Hedda, he never got over it. The Brinkers were my father's clients. When Dad retired, they came to me. After Toby's death, and since they had no living heirs, Hedda talked to me several times about the Vidocq Society. Ever heard of it?"

"Sure," Brandon returned. "They're someplace back east—Philadelphia, I think. As I remember, it's a group made up mostly of retired cops and FBI agents and forensics folks who get together occasionally and decide whether or not to follow up on some cold case or other."

Ralph Ames nodded. "That's right. Hedda saw a television program about them, and she was really interested. She tried to get them to take on Ursula's case. They took a pass."

"So?"

"She asked if I thought she had enough money to start the same kind of thing on this side of the country—on the West Coast, actually from the Mississippi on," Ames replied. "I told her I didn't think she had sufficient funds to attempt such a major undertaking."

"And then she won the jackpot."

"That's right. She didn't collect the first proceeds until after she had gone to the trouble of creating a 501 C nonprofit for the money to be paid into. It's called The Last Chance. Membership in TLC is by invitation only. We search out and encourage participation by mostly retired police investigators and forensics experts—people we believe will be motivated by the idea of helping fix the unfixable. We choose people we think share our goals and objectives.

"Investigators volunteer their services and expertise, although TLC handles their expenses, pays for laboratory facilities and analyses. TLC also supplies clerical and other support personnel. There are monthly meetings—mostly in Phoenix but sometimes in Denver—where people come and make presentations about their particular cold cases. The presenters are usually family members who understand that their local law enforcement agencies are either unwilling or unable to invest additional assets on what they regard as a dead-end investigation. Sometimes two or three TLC members will tackle a case. Other times, the group will vote to approach it en masse.

"G. T. Farrell was a young campus cop at Arizona State University when Ursula Brinker was murdered. Over the years he stayed in touch with Hedda and Toby. He's one of our founding members, and he wanted to know if you—"

Brandon Walker could barely believe his ears. Here was someone offering him a hand off the scrap heap of life—someone who thought Brandon Walker still had what it took in terms of experience and expertise to make a difference.

"Don't say another word," Brandon Walker said, finishing off his Campari. "I'm in. Next time you see Geet Farrell, tell him I owe him big."

"Tell him yourself," Ralph Ames replied. "The next meeting is two weeks from now at the Westin in Denver. I'll have the TLC travel agent contact you about flight arrangements."

Ames picked up his menu and drew a pair of reading glasses out of his pocket. "Since that's out of the way," he added, perusing the selections, "how about some lunch?"

Of course it had been a snap decision, and Brandon had beaten himself up about it later on. He had lunged at Ralph Ames's ego-salvaging proposal like a drowning sailor grabbing for a lifeline, and later wondered if he'd appeared too desperate. Brandon doubted Ralph Ames had even the dimmest concept of being cast off and ignored—how living a forgotten half-life made you second-guess everything you'd ever done.

But six months later, Brandon Walker knew that, snap decision or not, hooking up with Ralph Ames and TLC hadn't been wrong. It had given him his life back—his life and purpose, both. And now, thanks to Fat Crack Ortiz, Brandon Walker had the responsibility for a case that needed to be shepherded into and through The Last Chance.

He was surprised by how excited he felt and, at the same time, how guilty. As he carried the iced-tea-laden tray back into the living room, he was only too aware that his own rush of newfound happiness came as a direct result of someone else's long-term hurt and heartbreak.

Brandon Walker suddenly had a job to do and a case to work on—a real case. Emma Ortiz and Hedda Brinker had nothing in common but their two murdered daughters. And because of them, Brandon Walker had returned from the dead.

Maria Elena Dominguez lay naked on the bed and waited, drowning in despair. She had no way to tell time. In this darkened room with no windows and only a tiny pinprick of light over the corner toilet, she didn't know if it was night or day. She didn't know if she'd been here for weeks or months or years. All she knew was that at some time, the overhead light would flash on, temporarily blinding her. Then the latch would click, the door would creak open, and once again she would be plunged into a living hell.

She had been glad to see Señor the Doctor at the bus that sunny afternoon in Nogales, which now seemed so very long ago. She had been thrilled to think that he and his wife—the woman with the bright green eyes and beautiful silver hair—were the ones who were taking her in. And he had been so kind to her as they left the bus station behind and drove across the border at Nogales in a shiny black car that smelled of what had to be new leather. The seat had felt soft as a feather lingering against the bare skin of her legs.

There had been no question about her papers. In fact, no one had even bothered to look at them. Instead, the guard had leaned down, peered across the seat at her. He then smiled, saluted the driver, and waved them on. That was all there was to it. Minutes later they were gliding along far faster than the lumbering bus, only this time they traveled on a fine wide roadway—a wonderfully smooth highway—that stretched out ahead of them like a length of gray satin ribbon. And for the first time in her life, Maria Elena was riding in a car where the air flowing out of the vent was so impossibly cool that she shivered with cold.

Señor the Doctor had asked if she was hungry or thirsty. When she had nodded yes, he had reached behind the seat and produced a basket containing a sumptuous feast—bananas and chunks of sharp yellow cheese. When she had eaten her fill, he produced a thermos.

"Do you drink coffee?" he had asked.

"*Sí*," she said, although it had been years since she had any. She poured it herself into the top of the thermos. She savored the aroma that boiled up into her nostrils from the steam. And when she tasted it, the coffee was sweet and dark on her tongue, just the way her mother had made it. And that was all she remembered. When she awakened next, she was in this room and on this bed. And the doctor, who knew for sure that she and her friends did not have AIDS, took what she had kept from the drug dealers and killers at El Asilo Seguro. The doctor took that, and far more besides, enjoying her suffering and laughing at her when she cried out in pain.

He always brought her food—for afterward. She didn't know if he intended it as a punishment or a reward. Hoping to starve to death and put an end to her misery, Maria Elena at first had tried not eating the food and had flushed it down the toilet that sat, squat and ugly as a gray ghost, in the dimly lit far corner of the room. But something had gone wrong. The toilet had backed up, and Señor the Doctor had figured out what she was doing. He had beaten her then—beaten her with a thin, sharp strap—until she'd been left with bloody welts all over her body. After that, he watched her while she ate, making certain she swallowed every morsel.

Lying naked, shackled, and miserable on the bed, Maria Elena grieved for herself and also for her friend, for Madelina. She knew now that for Madelina, too, there had been no nice family waiting in the United States. Perhaps Señor the Doctor had simply tired of her. Or perhaps she had been lucky—really lucky—and died. There would be no meeting of two old friends at some pretty place someday. And the old times they might have discussed if they had met—the bad times in Colima and at El Asilo Seguro—had been heaven on earth compared to this.

And what of Señora Duarte? Maria Elena wondered. Did she know what would become of the "lucky" girls she was sending to their supposed patrons, their benefactors? It was a question that haunted Maria Elena. She had struggled with it alone in the dark until she had finally reached a conclusion that had plunged her even deeper into despair. Of course, Señora Duarte had known. She had known everything. She was part of it. And that was why it had all happened so fast and with no warning. Once a girl was chosen, she went away that very day, without ever going back to the other children, without leaving any hint of what had happened or where she was going with the others—the unchosen ones—who remained.

No, she and Madelina and who knew how many others had disappeared without a trace, just as Maria Elena's mother and brother had disappeared that day in Chiapas. Once Maria Elena had hoped and prayed to Mother Mary that Mama and Pepé were still alive. Now she prayed that they were dead. And she prayed that she might die, too. It was her only hope.

four

At the end of a long, sleepless night, Erik La-Grange sat sipping coffee on his patio and welcomed the sun as it edged up over the Rincons. It was Saturday morning. He didn't have to go in to work today, which meant he could put off facing the music until Monday at least.

You're only thirty-five, he told himself again, as he had countless times overnight. *Losing a job isn't the end of the world. You've got no wife, no kids, no responsibilities. You can go somewhere else and start over. So what's the problem?*

The problem was, Erik knew he'd be going job hunting with no references and with the added burden of a huge black spot on his reputation. In even the best of times, nonprofit development jobs weren't easy to come by. With corporate and private giving down, jobs like the cushy one he'd had for the past five years were now, as Grandma Johnson would have said, scarce as hen's teeth. And since he'd spent most of those five years screwing his boss's wife . . .

Grandma Johnson would have had more than a little to say on that subject as well. "You should have thought about that a long time ago" was the most likely one. Undoubtedly, she would have added something about making one's bed and lying in it.

Erik missed Gladys Johnson dreadfully—her cheerful disposition, her way of always looking on the bright side of things, and yes, even that sometimes very sharp Scandinavian tongue of hers. She had read Erik the riot act often enough as he was growing up, but he had never doubted that those scoldings were rooted in love.

Grandma had been Erik's rock. True north on his compass. The only parent he had ever known or needed or wanted. She had been everything to him—mother/father, aunt/uncle, sister/brother. And, until he made it into junior high, she had also been his best friend. He could remember riding in the car with her singing along with one of her well-worn cassette tapes. Erik's favorite had always been the one where Helen Reddy sang "You and Me Against the World." The song was supposedly about a mother and her little girl, but Erik always pretended the song had been written just for his grandma and him.

Right then, though, Gladys Johnson and her sage advice—which had grown even wiser the older Erik got—had been gone from his life for ten years. There was no way she could dose him with a firestorm of well-earned criticism for his foolishness and then help see him through to the other side of the problem. No, in this case, Erik was going to have to manage all by himself.

Down on Skyline, a car horn honked impatiently. Overhead, a noisy jet streaked toward a landing at Davis Monthan Air Force Base several miles away. The jarring background noises sliced through Erik's reverie and intruded on his thoughts.

"That's what's wrong with living in the city," Grandma Johnson had told him countless times. "With all the traffic and noise, I can't hear myself think. That's when I wish I was back on the island, where it was just me and the woods and the water. Then, all I could think or dream about was how boring it was and how much I wanted to get away. Now I wish I could go back."

Isle Royale was a long damned way from Tucson, Arizona, but remembering Grandma's voice made Erik know what he needed to do—hear himself think. Hurrying into the house, he grabbed up his knapsack. He loaded it up with sunscreen, several bottles of water, and some food—a couple of sandwiches, some cheese, and a package of dried apricots. Then he donned thick socks and hiking boots and headed out the door.

Outside, Erik paused beside his pickup and consid-ered whether or not he should drive the Tacoma to the trail-head. Even though he had the truck keys in his pocket, he finally decided against it. These days, leaving a vehicle—a company vehicle, at that—parked at a trailhead was pretty much an open invitation to have it broken into and/or stolen. Besides, the trailhead to Finger Rock was only a mile or so from the Catalina foothills home he was house-sitting for Professor Raymond Rice and his wife, Frieda, who were off on a year-long sabbatical in France.

After all, Erik thought, *driving somewhere to go on a hike seems pretty dumb. Since the point is walking, why not start from here?*

And so he did. Erik trudged off alone in the early-morning sunshine with the sky clean and blue above him. A few rock doves, a flock of quail, and a single watchful roadrunner noticed his solitary departure. So did a neighborhood dog or two, who barked briefly as he passed. In that upscale neighborhood people valued their privacy. Individual homes were set at least an acre apart and screened by carefully planted collections of native shrubbery and looming saguaros. As a consequence, none of Erik's neighbors saw him go.

Since Erik's pickup came and went from the driveway several times during the course of the day, those same privacy-loving neighbors assumed that the young man who was staying at the Rices' place was spending a quiet Saturday going in and out and running errands just like everyone else. None of them saw or noticed anything at all out of the ordinary that day. For Erik LaGrange, that would make all the difference.

Fifteen miles across town, on the edge of the Tucson Mountains, Brandon Walker, too, had spent a sleepless night. But his lack of sleep was due to an entirely different reason. For the first time in years, former sheriff Brandon Walker was excited—too excited to sleep. He had spent the entire night going over the previous day's conversation with Emma Orozco and wondering what the hell he was going to do about it.

He had come back into the living room carrying a tray of iced tea to find Emma staring up at one of Rita Antone's best baskets—a two-foot-wide medallion featuring the Tohono O'odham's sacred symbol, the Man in the Maze. Usually the design was woven onto the white yucca background in a tough black fiber harvested from devil's-claw pods. For this particular basket, however, Rita had crafted the maze by using yucca root, which, without benefit of any dye, resulted in a rusty red hue that resembled dried blood. That, of course, was what made this particular basket so valuable and so special, as Rita had once explained.

"For this basket," Nana *Dahd* had told Brandon Walker, "the yucca had to die."

Emma Orozco stared up at the basket as if hoping that

somewhere in the sacred curves of bloodred pattern she could find her own answers as well.

Brandon offered the tray of drinks. Emma murmured her thanks and daintily accepted an icy glass of tea while declining both lemon and sugar. Brandon helped himself to generous doses of both and then settled back into his favorite armchair.

He had lived with and among the Desert People for a long time—long enough to know that among the Tohono O'odham, direct questions were viewed as impolite. Rather than ask something that would be regarded as rude, he limited himself to making a single observation.

"You waited a long time to talk about this."

Emma nodded. "It was a bad time," she said. "When it was over, Henry, my husband, said we should just forget about it. It's not good to dwell on the past."

Brandon nodded and said nothing. Emma continued. "But Henry's dead now," she added. "I'm Roseanne's mother, and I want to know."

Brandon didn't look at Emma directly. That, too, would have been considered rude behavior on his part, but as she spoke, he studied her reflection in the entryway mirror. Coming here and digging up the past in the presence of a stranger and a *Mil-gahn*—a white man—besides, showed a great deal of courage and strength of character on Emma's part. To do so meant that, in both regards, she was going against hundreds of years of tradition and a lifetime's worth of teaching as well. He watched as she gripped the handle of her walker as if the plastic-covered metal might somehow help stiffen her resolve in the same way it helped hold her upright.

"Mr. Ortiz said you belonged to some kind of group that looks into old cases . . . into old murders." She stumbled over the last word.

Other people might have been surprised to hear the word *murder* stick in Emma Orozco's throat more than thirty years after the fact. Brandon Walker was not. He knew how events like that—like the death of a child—might disappear from public view after a few days of newspaper and television coverage. But for the parents of a dead child, the loss is permanent, indelible. It becomes the central issue of existence, not just for mothers and fathers, but for sisters and brothers as well; for husbands and wives and children. That sudden death is a watershed. From that moment on, life's perspective shifts. Everything dates from either before or after. This was as true for Brandon as it was for Emma Orozco; for he, too, had lost a child.

"Yes," he supplied in answer to Emma's comment. "The organization Mr. Ortiz told you about is called The Last Chance, TLC for short. It's a private organization that was started a few years ago by a *Mil-gahn* woman named Hedda Brinker from Scottsdale—a woman not unlike yourself whose daughter was murdered in Tempe in 1959."

Emma's dark eyes sought Brandon's. "Did they ever find out who did it?" she asked.

"No," Brandon replied. "That's what Hedda Brinker was hoping might happen when she started TLC—that someone would finally solve her own child's murder." He shrugged. "Maybe someday we will," he added. "But right now the stated purpose of TLC is to help other people."

"People like me?" Emma asked.

Brandon nodded. "Yes," he said. "People just like you."

"How much does it cost?" Emma asked. "I have some money. I can pay . . ."

"It's expensive," Brandon answered. "But it costs you

nothing. Hedda created a charitable organization that pays all the costs."

Emma reached for her purse, an ugly boxy vinyl one with a broken strap and brittle, damaged corners. At first Brandon thought she was going to offer him money after all. Instead, she dug out a ballpoint pen and a small spiral notebook—the same kind of notebook Brandon himself had carried during his days as a homicide detective. Emma flipped through the notebook to a blank page. She handed the notebook to Brandon, who rose from his chair to take it.

"Please," Emma said softly. "Please write down this nice white lady's name for me. Tomorrow when I go to Mass, I will say a rosary for her and light a candle."

Brandon Walker smiled to himself. He had never met Hedda Brinker. She had died more than two years earlier of congestive heart failure, but he imagined it would have come as a surprise for that "nice white lady" who was also Jewish to know that she was being prayed for and having candles lit by an equally nice Tohono O'odham lady who was a practicing Catholic.

He handed the pen and notebook back to Emma. She carefully filed both of them away in her purse. She clicked it shut, then waited for some time without speaking, staring once more at the Man in the Maze. Again Brandon Walker was the one who broke the silence.

"Perhaps you should tell me about your daughter."

Emma's gnarled fingers tightened around the handle of her walker. "Henry and I had two daughters," she said softly. "The older one, Andrea, we called *Mithol-mad*—Kitten. The younger one, Roseanne, the shy one, we called *Tachchuithch . . .*"

"Beloved," Brandon supplied without needing Emma to translate.

For the first time Emma looked at the *Mil-gahn* man—really looked at him. He was tall and well-built. His graying hair was cut short. Compared to Tohono O'odham faces, his was sharp and angular, but his eyes were soft and looked at her with a kindness she had not expected from someone who had once been a detective—and a sheriff.

Fat Crack had told her Brandon Walker was a good man—a white man who could be trusted. She knew that Walker and his wife had a *wogsha*—an adopted Tohono O'odham child—named Lani. According to Fat Crack, the girl was the spiritual daughter of the Desert People's greatest medicine woman, *Kulani O'oks,* a woman who, in a time of terrible drought, was saved from death by the beating of the wings of The Little People, the Bees and Wasps, the Butterflies and Moths. But Emma Orozco had not expected the *Mil-gahn* would understand or speak her native tongue. Her fingers unclenched. She relaxed her painful grip on the walker.

"They found her out along the highway beyond *Gi-who Tho'ag,*" Emma said softly. "Someone cut her up and put her in a box."

Emma deliberately used the Tohono O'odham word for Burden Basket Mountain. It was a test of sorts, to see how much the *Mil-gahn* knew.

"I remember now," he said, nodding. "The girl in the ice chest over by Quijotoa."

It came back to him then, not all the details, but enough. He was still working Homicide for the Pima County Sheriff's Department. When he heard about the case, he was happy the call hadn't come to him. He'd already been through one ugly reservation-based homicide. A year earlier, a young Indian woman named Gina Antone had been murdered just off the reservation. The trail had led Brandon Walker to Andrew Philip Carlisle, a professor of creative writing at the University of Arizona, and eventually to one of Professor Carlisle's star pupils, Garrison Ladd, Diana's first husband.

As the investigation closed in, Garrison Ladd had perished in what was mistakenly thought to be a suicide. As far as Brandon was concerned, Carlisle's slap-on-the-wrist plea bargain had been a less than satisfactory conclusion to the case. It had left a bad taste in Brandon's mouth. The bitter taste still lingered in 1970, when Roseanne Orozco's butchered body was found on the reservation, and Brandon had been happy to dodge that particular bullet. Some other investigator—he couldn't remember exactly who—took the call.

There were several differences between the Orozco murder and Gina Antone's. Gina had died off the reservation and at the hands of Anglos. Consequently, the investigation into her death had fallen under the jurisdiction of the Pima County Sheriff's Department. Although the actual murder site was never found in the Orozco case, it was assumed Roseanne had died somewhere on the reservation and that she had been murdered by a fellow Indian. Investigations into Indians murdering Indians on Native lands were the responsibility of either the FBI or the local tribal police.

Brandon Walker remembered that, in the early seventies, there had been a small contingent inside the FBI with the kind of corporate mind-set that preferred shooting Indians to anything else. FBI investigations into reservation murders, unless the perpetrator was Indian and the victim Anglo, were often cursory at best. People went through the motions, and that was it. "Law and Order," as the Papago Tribal Police Force was sometimes called, was summoned to the scene of the Orozco homicide. Hampered by a lack of three essential ingredients—training, equipment, and money—their subsequent investigation had obviously come to nothing, although Brandon hadn't known that for sure—not until right then, when Emma told him.

The Orozco homicide hadn't been Brandon Walker's deal. Newly divorced, he'd had his hands full in those years. Money had been short. He had struggled to keep up with alimony and child-support payments by moonlighting as a rent-a-cop on occasion and by moving in with his parents for what they had all erroneously expected would be a short time. With all that going on and with his father in deteriorating health, no wonder he hadn't kept track of the outcome of each investigation, successful or not, that had, however briefly, crossed his desk.

"Law and Order thought my husband did it," Emma said softly. Her quiet words jarred Brandon back to his living room half a lifetime away.

"Why did they think that?" he asked.

"Please," Emma Orozco said, holding out her glass. "Could I have some more tea? Then I will tell you the whole story."

Sitting in the dark at the end of the block, Gayle Stryker listened to her ringing telephone and didn't answer. Erik was the only person who had this number, and she had nothing to say to him. Instead, she sat in the car and immersed herself in rage—in unmitigated fury. How dare he toss her aside like that? How dare he think he could throw her over in favor of some little baby-producing twit who wouldn't know her ass from a hole in the ground?

Gayle couldn't help wondering who it was—somebody from work, most likely. Where else would Erik have met someone? Maybe it was the new little bitch at reception. What was her name? Denise Something. Just two days ago Gayle had caught the wide-hipped little blonde eyeing Erik and giving his body a casual once-over. Well, if Denise was it, Gayle would be more than happy to send her down the road come Monday morning.

That was Gayle's first thought. As the hours passed, that plan changed. Something better came to mind. Today—yesterday now—Erik LaGrange had been on top of the world. He'd had a good job, a company car, and a generous lover who'd taught the naive son of a bitch everything he knew. By tonight—tomorrow at the latest—his life would be hell. His lover would be gone along with his job. With any luck, he'd be in jail and maybe on his way to the state prison in Florence. Gayle wondered how Denise would react to hearing that news. As for Erik? Gayle had every confidence the guys in Florence would teach him a thing or two about screwing.

Gayle had planned to follow Erik wherever he went, but finally, as the hours drifted by, she realized Erik wasn't going anywhere. He was in for the night. Still she waited and watched. To do what she wanted, she'd need access to his house, but after five years, she knew Erik almost as well as he knew himself, and she could predict with uncanny accuracy exactly what he'd do.

Gayle knew what it cost Erik to stand up to her. He'd told Gayle time and again about how his grandmother—his sainted grandmother—had always taken to the hills whenever things went wrong—how she'd taught Erik to do the same thing. And so, as the sun came up that morning, Gayle had reason to hope he would revert to type. She wasn't disappointed.

Just at sunrise, she saw him come out of the house in shorts, hiking boots, and carrying a loaded knapsack. When he bypassed his parked truck and headed off on foot, Gayle couldn't believe her luck. Using his vehicle would make her plan far easier to pull off.

Gayle waited until he disappeared up the street, but not much longer than that. Then she drove up to the house and used her door opener to slip the Lexus past the parked pickup and into the two-car garage. It took only a matter of minutes for her to gather what she needed. When she left, driving Erik's Tacoma, none of the neighbors had yet to venture to the ends of their driveways to retrieve their morning papers.

Like Erik himself, Gayle came and went while the neighbors slept. As she drove away, Gayle could hardly wait for this new adventure to be over—so she could tell Larry all about it.

five

Great Spirit always carries a bag with him. That way, if he wants to, he can make things.

I'itoi *reached up, gathered a great handful of beautiful yellow leaves, and put them in his bag. Then he gathered some of the dark shadows from under the leaves and put the shadows in the bag. He stooped and picked up some of the sunbeams from the ground and mixed the sunbeams in with the leaves and shadows. He added some brown leaves to the bag along with some tiny white flowers. He shook the bag and looked inside, then decided he needed more yellow leaves. This time he reached so high into the trees that he caught some of the blue sky. So bits of blue sky went into the bag along with everything else.*

The children saw I'itoi *under the cottonwood trees and came to see what he was doing and to see if he wanted to play. But Elder Brother was tired with all his work. He threw his bag down on the ground, lay down, and put his head on it. And soon* I'itoi *and all the children were fast asleep in the cool shade of the cottonwoods.*

As Erik labored up the mountain toward Finger Rock, he dodged other hikers by steering clear of the main trail. He struck off on his own, heading for one of the steeper but less-traveled canyons. Once, crossing a ravine, he smelled a distinctly musky odor and knew, without seeing them, that a herd of javelina must be resting in a nearby patch of mesquite and manzanita. Unless startled or threatened, the peccaries—mostly nocturnal, boarlike creatures with coarse black-and-silver fur—weren't dangerous, but Erik was more than happy to go out of his way to avoid them. Twice he saw coyotes disappear into the underbrush, and once he narrowly avoided stepping on a rattlesnake sunning itself in an open space between rocks.

As the temperature warmed, Erik sat on a rock ledge, sipped water, mopped sweat from his brow, and watched a pair of A-10s circle lazily over the valley before settling in to land at Davis Monthan. The pilots knew just where they were going. Erik had no such delusions.

Tucson had always been home to him. His grandmother had raised him here. His mother had been a girl when Grandma Johnson brought her daughter and her disabled World War II vet husband to Tucson so he could be cared for at the VA hospital. But both of Erik's grandparents were gone now. So was his mother. As for his father? Erik had no idea where he was or whether the man was alive or dead. Erik still had a few friends in town—grade school and high school buddies who had grown up here and had never left. But with no remaining family connections tying him to Tucson, and without his job, Erik would need to find some other place to live and work. Looking over the city-filled desert below him, he felt a clutch in his gut. He loved this place and didn't want to leave. Would he be like Grandma when she had moved away from Lake Superior's Isle Royale—leave and never return?

One night when Erik was five or six, after Grandma came home from her job as a checker at Safeway, Erik had asked her about that while they ate supper. Through the years he had heard her tell countless stories about her childhood on Isle Royale. To Erik it always sounded like a magic, idyllic place—one he wanted to see with his own eyes.

"Couldn't we go back there sometime?" he asked. "Just to visit?"

"Oh, no," Grandma said. A wistful cloud of sadness wafted across her face. "It's different now—a national park—nothing at all like it used to be. No one I knew still lives there."

"But if it's a park, couldn't we go look at it?" Erik had insisted. "I could see where you used to play on the rocks and pick berries."

Grandma had put down her fork, reached over, and pulled him to her. "No," she said. "Sometimes you have to leave the past in the past. Otherwise it hurts too much."

Hunkered down on the flank of the mountain, Erik LaGrange could see how that might be true for him, too. Once he left Tucson, he wouldn't be coming back. If he didn't burn all his bridges, Gayle Stryker was sure to do it for him.

She had cut him out of the herd at a big-donor alumni function where, as a lowly junior-grade University of Arizona fund-raiser adrift in a sea of movers and shakers, Erik LaGrange had been keeping a suitably low profile.

"So who are you?" she had demanded, walking up to him with a drink in one bejeweled hand and with her other hand resting provocatively on a curvaceous hip. "I suppose you're the son of somebody important," she added with an ironic smile.

Some of the U of A's most well-heeled graduates were milling about La Paloma's glitzy ballroom. In Tucson, men seldom fought their way into tuxes, but the University of Arizona's Alumni Association's President's Ball was a notable exception. Tuxes were out in force and bolo ties banished. Among the sparkling collection of women dressed in their designer best, Gayle Stryker was the hands-down standout. Her crimson floor-length gown was set off by an emerald pendant big enough to choke a horse. A cloud of silvery-blond hair encircled a perfect face, and the woman's figure was nothing short of amazing.

"Nobody's son," Erik had stammered with far more truth than he intended. Even without benefit of her name tag, he had known Gayle Stryker on sight. In a roomful of major donors, Gayle and her husband, Dr. Lawrence Stryker, were in a class by themselves. Disturbed by the woman's unblinkingly frank scrutiny, Erik found himself trying to guess her age, but the ministrations of one or several very talented plastic surgeons made that difficult. She could have been forty-five. He would learn later that she was actually twelve years older than that.

"I work here," he murmured.

"For the hotel?" she asked.

"No," he answered. "For the alumni association, I mean. The development office."

She smiled. "In that case, since my husband already gave at the office, I don't suppose you'd mind getting a lady a drink."

"Of course not. What would you like?"

"A margarita," she said. "Blended. No salt."

When Erik returned with the margarita, he found Gayle deep in conversation with U of A president Dr. Thomas Moore himself. Not wanting to intrude, Erik tried to linger unobtrusively in the background, but Gayle had reached out, grabbed him by the elbow, and dragged him forward.

"Now, tell me, Tommy, since when did the alumni association start hiring babies to wheedle us out of our hard-earned cash?"

Damning his blond hair and fair complexion, Erik La-Grange blushed. He couldn't help it. And he had no idea what to say. Calling the wife of one of the university's major donors an uncompromising bitch wasn't an option. Fortunately, President Moore effected Erik's rescue.

"Hear, hear," Thomas Moore said jovially. "Mr. La-Grange has been with us for years, haven't you, Erik. Besides, Gayle, don't we all prefer to look younger than we really are?"

Erik was astonished. He had no idea President Moore even knew his name. The fact that he would save Erik by nailing someone like Gayle Stryker was beyond the realm of possibility.

"Touché," Gayle Stryker murmured with yet another smile as she collected the drink Erik had brought her. "So he's good, then?" she asked President Moore, all the while studying Erik's face over the rim of her glass. There was something brazenly suggestive about that look. "At raising funds, I mean," she added innocently as yet another blush erupted from the top of Erik's now too-tight collar.

"Oh, yes," President Moore agreed, giving Erik's shoulder a hearty whack. "The best. That's the only kind we hire."

Someone came up behind President Moore, tapped him on the shoulder, and led him off to another group of attendees, leaving a still-blushing Erik uncomfortably close to Gayle Stryker.

"So how old are you, then?" she asked. "I don't believe in beating around the bush."

"Thirty," he admitted reluctantly. "I started out working for the alumni association while I was still an undergraduate—"

"Studying what?" she interjected.

"Poli-sci," Erik answered. "By the time I graduated, I had lost all interest in politics. I was thinking about going to law school, but the alumni association gave me a job while I was trying to figure out what else I wanted to be when I grew up. I've been there ever since."

Gayle handed him her drink. Then she reached into a tiny jeweled purse and pulled out a business card, which she handed to him.

"If you're tired of raising money for the university," she said, "you might want to come see me. Maybe you'd enjoy taking a crack at saving the world. I'll be in the office all week. I might make you an offer you won't be able to refuse."

She had sauntered away then, leaving Erik holding both the card and a lipstick-marred glass containing a virtually untouched margarita. The card said "Gayle Stryker, CFO, Medicos for Mexico." Erik slipped the card into the pocket of his tux. Then, because he didn't know what else to do with the margarita, he lifted it to his lips and polished it off in a single gulp.

That was the beginning, Erik LaGrange thought to himself as he sat on the rock-bound ledge of the mountain. *And five years later, this is the end.*

At two o'clock in the morning a bleary-eyed Dolores Lanita Walker sat before her computer screen and longed for sleep, but sleep proved elusive this long Friday night, just as it had for days now. She knew she should be studying. Finals were coming. She didn't really need to sweat them. She'd already been accepted into the medical school at the University of Arizona back home in Tucson. But what she really wanted was to be there right now, to be home where Lani knew she was needed.

Four years earlier, her parents had tried to convince her that it would be far simpler for her to do her undergraduate work in Tucson. Her father had been especially adamant on that score. One way or another, Brandon Walker had lost two of his three sons. He didn't want to lose her, too, but Lani had stuck to her guns. Rather than stay home, she had come to Grand Forks, North Dakota, and enrolled in a program called INMED—Indians into Medicine at the University of North Dakota's School of Medicine and Health Sciences.

As an orphaned Tohono O'odham child who had been raised in an Anglo household and attended predominantly Anglo schools, Lani had wanted to go somewhere else to school, to a place where it would be possible for her to meet and interact with other Native American kids—kids from tribes all over the country, who would know what it was like to live in that uncertain no-man's-land between Anglo and Indian cultures. She wanted to spend time with people who, like her, negotiated those treacherous minefields every day of their lives.

Lani hadn't been wrong. Her three roommates in this poorly insulated rental house were proof enough of that. Margie was a Paiute from Nevada, Darlene a Rosebud Sioux, and Laura a Blackfoot from Montana. Laura, an accomplished skier, had taught them all to ski, while Darlene had helped Lani learn how to ice-skate. The four girls shared many of the same values and laughed at the same jokes. And they all shared similar beliefs that decreed storytelling to be a wintertime occupation.

It still surprised Lani to realize that her best friend, Leah Donner, who still lived in a dorm, was actually a White Mountain Apache. In the language and history of the Desert People, the word *Ohb* means Apache. *Ohb* also interchangeably means enemy.

But when Leah Donner and Lani Walker had met in a Society and Literature class their freshman year, they discovered they had more in common than either expected. Some INMED students came to the U of ND needing and finding remedial help in one or more subjects. Leah Donner and Lani were both outstanding students. Not only were they both smart, they were also orphans who had been raised in adoptive families. The two girls had been abandoned long after the practice of Anglo parents' adopting Indian children had fallen out of fashion. Leah had been raised in an all-Indian household. She was surprised to learn that Lani's parents were both Anglos.

It was to Leah that Lani told the story of the blond and black people hair charm—the *kushpo ho'oma*—she wore around her neck. It was to Leah that Lani first revealed her prize possession—the sturdy medicine basket Lani had woven for herself, making it as much like Nana *Dahd*'s original as possible. It wasn't quite as well made as that of Rita's grandmother, *Oks Amichuda*—Understanding Woman—but it was respectable enough. And it was to Leah that Lani had finally confided her worries about what was going on with Fat Crack Ortiz—about how sick he was and how much she needed to be home with him.

"I don't get it," Leah had said impatiently over dinner the night before. Months later, Leah was still smarting over the fact that Lani had backed out on their verbal agreement to spend the summer after graduation together, volunteering for Doctors Without Borders. Leah was still signed up to go. Lani was returning to Tucson as soon as she finished her last exam.

"That Fat Crack guy isn't really a relative of yours," Leah said. "If he's diabetic and too stubborn to take his medicine, what are you going to do about it? Sit there and watch him die?"

"Yes," Lani said. "If that's what's needed, it's exactly what I'll do—sit and watch him die." And that was all she said, because even with Leah—even with her very best friend—Lani Walker couldn't explain it all, couldn't tell the whole story.

six

Lani Walker stepped out of the steamy shower and toweled herself dry. As always, she couldn't ignore the ugly scar Mitch Johnson's superheated kitchen tongs had seared into her breast six years earlier. Even when the damage was hidden beneath her clothing, for Lani it was always there, just like the broken white marks Andrew Carlisle's teeth had left on her mother's breast years earlier.

In a way Lani couldn't explain—the same way she couldn't explain what she sometimes saw in the sacred crystals stored in her medicine basket—she knew that the similar scars she and her adoptive mother wore on their bodies made her Diana Ladd's daughter in a way far more profound than adoption papers from any tribal court. It was also why she kept the scar a secret from her mother as well as from everyone else, including her best friend. It would hurt Diana too much to know about it, and to tell Leah would require too much explanation.

She hadn't told Fat Crack about it, either, but she was sure he knew. He had come to her every day, bringing her a soothing salve as well as the salt-free evening meal called for during the required sixteen-day fast and purification ceremony—her *e lihmhun*—after Lani had killed

Mitch Johnson. She and Fat Crack had talked about many things during that time. She had used the salve, but they hadn't talked about it.

On the last night, Fat Crack had brought not only the food for that night's evening meal, but also his *huashomi*—the fringed buckskin medicine pouch he had been given years earlier by an old blind medicine man named *S'ab Neid Pi Has*—Looks at Nothing. After the two of them had eaten together, Fat Crack had taken a stick and drawn a circle around both Lani and himself. Once they were both inside it, he opened the pouch, took out some *wiw*—wild tobacco—and rolled it into a crude cigarette, which he lit with Looks at Nothing's old Zippo lighter. Sitting on the mountain with a beloved family friend who was not only the tribal chairman and a respected medicine man but also her godfather, Lani smoked the traditional peace smoke for the first time.

The powerful smoke had left her light-headed, so some of what they said that night had drifted away from her conscious memory in the same way the silvery smoke had dissipated in the cold night air. Other parts of it she remembered clearly.

"What's the point of the *e lihmhun*?" she had asked. "Why did I have to stay out here by myself all this time?"

"What have you been doing while you've been alone?" Fat Crack asked in return.

"I made a medicine basket," she said. "I gave Nana *Dahd*'s medicine basket to Davy because I knew he wanted it. I made a new one of my own."

"Good," Fat Crack said. "What else?"

"I kept thinking about the evil *Ohb*," she said, "the one who came after me, not the one who came after my mother. And about *Oks Gagda*—Betraying Woman, the woman who betrayed the Desert People to the Apache and whose spirit stayed in the cave along with her unbroken pottery."

"What did you decide about *Oks Gagda*?" Fat Crack asked.

Lani closed her eyes. "When Nana *Dahd* first told me the story, I thought it was just a *ha'icha ahgidathag*—a legend—like Santa Claus or the Tooth Fairy."

"And now?" Fat Crack inquired patiently.

"I know she was a real person once," Lani replied. "As real as you and me. When I broke her pottery, I freed her spirit and let her go."

Fat Crack nodded. "That's true, too. So you've put this time to good use."

"But I still don't understand why."

"Because you took a human life," Fat Crack explained. "Even though it was self-defense and justified, it's still a terrible thing for you and for your *thoakag*—your soul. You need to come to terms with why it happened and to understand *I'itoi*'s purpose in all this—why you're alive and why Mitch Johnson is dead. Tell me now," Fat Crack added, "who are you?"

"Lani," she replied. "Lani Walker."

"Who else? What did Nana *Dahd* call you?"

Lani smiled, remembering. *"Mualig Siakam,"* she said at once. "Forever Spinning, because when I was little, I'd twirl around and around like the girl who turned into Whirlwind."

"What else did Rita call you?" Fat Crack asked.

Looking at him in the starlight, Lani had realized he wasn't smiling. These were serious questions that required serious answers.

"Kulani O'oks," Lani whispered. "Medicine Woman."

Unlike Forever Spinning, this name was not a happy

one. As a child, Lani had been left alone by an elderly caretaker. After falling into an ant bed, she had nearly died from the hundreds of bites inflicted when disturbed ants had swarmed over her body. Her copper-colored skin was still mottled with faded patches from those bites. It was the ant bites and Lani's presumed relationship to *Kulani O'oks*—the great Tohono O'odham medicine woman who had been kissed by the bees—that had caused Lani's superstitious blood relatives to give her up for adoption.

"And?" Fat Crack urged, staring at her intently across the darkness.

Lani looked back at Fat Crack, studying his impassive face. She had yet to tell anyone about the new name she had given herself in the aftermath of the pitched battle in the limestone cave. What had saved her from Mitch Johnson was the timely intervention of a flying bat whose velvety wings had touched Lani's skin in passing. That brief caress had somehow imbued Lani with the certain knowledge that the darkness of the cave was her friend rather than her enemy—that by surrendering herself to the darkness instead of fighting it, she could be saved.

On Lani's final venture into the cave, where she had gone to leave her one remaining shoe as a tribute to Betraying Woman's moldering bones, she had discovered a talisman of her own—the dried, baby-finger-like bones from a long-dead bat.

"Nanakumal Namkam," she whispered hoarsely.

Fat Crack nodded. "Bat Meeter," he said. "You have met Bat and made some of his strengths your strength. That, too, is good, so taken together, what do you think all this means?"

"I don't know."

"When Looks at Nothing came to me and told me I would be a medicine man," Fat Crack said, "I thought he was crazy. How could I be a Christian Scientist and a medicine man at the same time? It didn't make sense, but I know now he was right."

He paused while Lani waited. Finally he spoke again. "You know the *duajida*?"

"The nighttime divination ceremony?" Lani asked.

"I have done the *duajida* for you, Little Bat Meeter," Fat Crack said softly. "Every time it is the same. The spirits say you will be two things at once—*Kulani O'oks*, Medicine Woman, and also a doctor."

"A doctor?" Lani asked. "As in a hospital?"

Fat Crack nodded. "It's the same thing my auntie, Rita Antone, told me long ago," he said. "And the *duajida* says it is true."

Pulling her robe on over her naked body, Lani glanced at the window. It was still night outside on the frozen prairie beyond the double-pane glass. And since the night wasn't over, it was still all right for her to do a *duajida* of her own.

For days now she'd had a nagging feeling that something was terribly wrong back home. Since Fat Crack was the one who was ill, she was convinced his condition was the source of her malaise. Because no one seemed willing to tell her what was really going on, it was hardly surprising that Lani might look to some other means of finding out what she wanted to know.

She went to the dresser and took down a small framed picture that dated from the night of her high school graduation. She stood in her cap and gown flanked on either side by Gabe and Wanda Ortiz. After retrieving her medicine basket from her dresser, she sat down cross-legged on the floor, pried off the tight-fitting top, and spilled the contents onto the rug.

There before her was everything that had been there that night on *Ioligam,* and a few things more besides. Most had come to her from or through Nana *Dahd:* First came a piece of ancient pottery with the faint image of a turtle etched into the red clay. That had belonged to Rita Antone's paternal grandmother, Understanding Woman. There was Nana *Dahd*'s sacred scalp bundle along with the shiny smooth bone *owij*—the awl—the old woman had used to weave her wonderful baskets. A few items were Lani's alone—things she had retrieved from Betraying Woman's cave—a blackened fragment of a broken pot and the delicate bone from a dead bat's wing. Last of all was the soft chamois bag that held Looks at Nothing's precious crystals.

Lani's fingers trembled as she untied the string and spilled the crystals out into the medicine basket, confining them there rather than risk losing one on the floor. Taking the photo in one hand and a crystal in another, she held them up to the light and studied the faces through the haze of rock. She focused her gaze on Fat Crack's smiling face. The first three times she did it, nothing happened. Then she picked up the fourth crystal.

After a few seconds she noticed a slight shifting in Gabe Ortiz's features. They seemed thinner somehow. *It's because he's ill,* Lani thought. *He's losing weight.*

Then Fat Crack's face changed altogether. It seemed to dissolve and then remake itself. Gradually someone else's features emerged. For a moment a blond Anglo woman's face—a face Lani had never seen before— seemed to hover there under the crystal. Then those features, too, disappeared, leaving behind nothing but a bare skull. *What does this mean?* Lani wondered. *And what does this* Mil-gahn *woman have to do with Fat Crack?*

Shaken and having no idea what the crystals had told her, Lani carefully returned them to the bag. Then she placed the bag, along with all her other treasures, back in the medicine basket and closed the lid.

With the medicine basket restored to its hiding place, Lani turned once again to her computer. Looks at Nothing's sacred crystals had left her feeling even more distressed. The old ways hadn't worked, so it was time to resort to new ones. Lani switched her computer back on and sent three e-mails in a row. Half an hour later, as the sun touched the still winter-brown landscape outside her window, Lani Walker finally lay down and went to sleep.

Maria Elena heard the click of the lock. There was a single blanket on her bed. Ashamed of her nakedness, she pulled that over her now, even though she knew it was useless. He would peel away the puny covering once he reached her. The harsh light flashed on overhead. She cringed and squeezed her eyes shut, not only to close out the bright light but also to keep from seeing his face as he came toward her. To keep from seeing the terrible greediness in his eyes as he reached out to tear away her blanket. To keep from knowing exactly when his hurtful fingers would reach out with some awful tool to probe some part of her that should never have been touched. Somehow to put off the dreadful moment when she would writhe in agony and hear herself pleading and begging for him to stop.

It was as though, by not seeing him, she could avoid or delay what was coming. By not seeing it happen, she hoped somehow to distance herself from the pain and deny its reality while she endured whatever was to come. Acceptance was not an option.

This time the doctor's approach took far longer than usual. For as long as possible, Maria Elena resisted the temptation to open her eyes. Someone had once said that eyes were the windows to the soul. Señor the Doctor had stolen her body from her, forcing her to relinquish it to him. By keeping her eyes closed, she hoped to deny him what little was left—her soul.

Finally she could stand it no longer. She opened her eyes and was amazed to see not the doctor but his wife. Maria Elena no longer thought the silver-haired woman beautiful. She was evil—every bit as monstrous as her husband.

The señora had come to Maria Elena's cell with Señor the Doctor early on, during those first awful days when he had kept her tied up most of the time. He had hurt her some before that, but only a little. As soon as Maria Elena saw the señora, her hopes soared. She was sure the woman must have come to help her—to rescue her. Surely the señora would intercede on Maria Elena's behalf. Surely she would stop her husband and keep him from hurting her.

Instead, the señora had simply smoothed her skirt under her and sat down on the steps. Rather than stopping her husband, she had sat there, strangely silent, avidly observing everything Señor the Doctor did, smiling her approval, and seemingly deaf to Maria Elena's screams.

Over time Maria Elena had learned there was a peculiar rhythm to these sessions. The doctor preferred to start the process slowly, gradually escalating the assault and inflicting ever-increasing doses of pain. By the time it ended, he would have brought Maria Elena's suffering to a howling, wild crescendo—to a point where she begged and pleaded for him to stop, even though he never stopped until he was ready. Sometimes he took pictures. When what he called that day's "little game" was finally over, Señor the Doctor would force Maria Elena to eat and drink before once again shutting off the light, locking the door, and leaving her alone.

But when the señora came to watch, things were different. For one thing, he never brought the camera along when his wife was there, but the torture was always far worse with the señora watching. At some point in the process, the señora would nod at him. When that happened, he would immediately break off what he was doing. Without a word, he would follow his wife up the stairs, closing and locking the door behind them and leaving Maria Elena alone and sobbing in the dark. Much later, he would return alone to finish what he had begun.

Other times the señora would simply disappear from her place on the stairs. She would leave so quietly that at first neither Maria Elena nor Señor the Doctor would notice. When that happened—when Señor the Doctor realized she was no longer sitting there watching—he would take after Maria Elena with such fierce vengeance that all she could do was will herself to die.

And so, this time when Maria Elena could wait no longer—when she finally opened her eyes, blinking against the harsh glare of light—she saw not the doctor but the señora herself standing alone beside the filthy cot. That in itself was unusual. Never before had the señora come any farther into the room than that spot near the top of the stairs. Maria Elena was sure Señor the Doctor must be there, too, probably standing somewhere just outside Maria Elena's line of vision.

The señora was strangely dressed. A green stocking

cap confined her mane of silver hair. Over the green headgear perched a red-and-blue baseball cap. She wore a sweatshirt over ill-fitting jeans. On her hands was a pair of rubber gloves.

At the very moment Maria Elena noticed the señora's gloves, she also saw the machete. Seeing the weapon, the girl recognized it for what it had always been—a death-dealing tool. In an instant of clarity, Maria Elena knew that the señora had come not as an appreciative audience to that day's torture but as the Angel of Death.

Maria Elena watched transfixed as the shiny curved blade rose high in the air above her. When it fell, she made no attempt to dodge away from it or defend herself. Rather than fighting the swiftly falling blade, she welcomed the blow and willed herself to rise up to meet it. Her moment of release was finally at hand.

After countless days of unrelenting horror, death came as a blessing to Maria Elena—an answer to her desperate prayers, the only possible answer.

seven

At six o'clock in the morning, with the sun barely up, a cold nose brushed Diana's bare arm. Damsel was ready to go out. Brandon had wanted to install a pet door. Despite the obvious convenience, Diana had rejected the idea. She remembered vividly how, a few years earlier, a troop of white-faced coatimundi had let themselves into one of her neighbors' house through an unattended pet door. Alone in the kitchen for several hours, the mischievous, raccoonlike creatures had trashed the place. When the woman came home, the shock of finding her kitchen alive with wild animals had caused her to suffer a mild heart attack.

No, having a pet door was absolutely out of the question. Diana much preferred being the one who got up early to let Damsel out. She padded out to the kitchen and started the coffee, then went into her office and turned on the computer. Early morning was Diana's favorite time of day. She tried to slog her way through her e-mail while the coffee was perking.

There were a dozen or so spams waiting to be discarded, a couple of e-mails from fans who had written to her through her Web site, and an invitation to appear at a librarians' convention in the fall in Tallahassee,

Florida. Finally, and most important, there was one from Lani.

Twenty-two-year-old Lani had come home at Christmas all excited about the idea of spending the summer after graduation doing volunteer clerical work for Doctors Without Borders in some godforsaken corner of the world. Brandon had put his foot down.

"Don't you read the papers?" he'd demanded. "Every week I see something about those people getting blown up or shot or worse. If you're determined to help out, surely there are less dangerous places for you to volunteer."

"What about Medicos for Mexico?" Diana had suggested, trying to find a compromise that might head off an argument between her husband and daughter.

"Who's that?" Lani asked.

"It's an organization started by some friends of mine from the reservation," Diana told her. "I'm sure you've met them somewhere along the way. Each year Larry and Gayle Stryker take a team of medical volunteers—doctors, nurses, and what have you—down to Mexico, where they provide pro bono medical care for people who wouldn't be able to afford it otherwise."

Brandon's reaction to this was as instant as it was adamant. "Absolutely not!" he growled. "No way, José. You'll work for those people over my dead body!"

"I'll work for them if I want to," Lani had shot back at him. "I'm not your little girl anymore, Dad. I'm the one who gets to decide." With that, she had stalked out of the living room and down the hall, slamming her bedroom door behind her.

Her cheeks flushed with anger, Diana Ladd had glared at her husband. "That's a nice way to start Christmas vacation," she said. "And what on earth do you have against Gayle and Larry? They're perfectly nice people."

Brandon shook his head. "Nothing," he said. "Never mind."

"I won't 'never mind,'" Diana returned. "There must be something."

He chewed his lip before he answered. "I should never have brought it up. Forget it."

"I won't forget it."

"You didn't go over the campaign-finance public disclosure forms during the last election," Brandon admitted finally, "but I did. I wanted to know where Bill Forsythe was getting all his campaign contributions. And there they were, right at the top of the list—Dr. and Mrs. Lawrence Stryker. They send us a Christmas card every damned year. I just saw this year's in the pile on the entryway table. And all the while they're making nicey-nice with you, they were stabbing us in the back—stabbing *me* in the back."

Diana was floored. "I'm so sorry, Brandon," she said. "I had no idea."

"No," Brandon agreed. "I'm sure you didn't. I wasn't going to mention it because I know they're friends of yours. My griping about them sounds like sour grapes, but the idea of Lani possibly going to work for them . . ." He shook his head. "It was just too much."

That discussion had happened the evening of the first day Lani was home. Diana had thought the summer-job issue would be a bone of contention all through Lani's stay. Then, as soon as Lani found out about Fat Crack's deteriorating health situation, all talk of summer jobs anywhere disappeared off the radar. It was all they could do to talk Lani into going back to Grand Forks to finish her senior year. She had wanted to stay home to look after Fat Crack.

Opening the e-mail from Lani, Diana found that Gabe Ortiz's health was still a major cause for concern.

Dear Mom and Dad,

Have you heard anything more about how Fat Crack is doing? I had a note from Wanda last week, but you know how that went. Wanda said he was fine, and for me not to worry, but I am worried. I've told my instructors that one of my family members is very ill and that, if he gets worse, I may have to take my exams early. Two of them said that would be fine, and they're the last two on the schedule. As for graduation, that's off. I already told the registrar's office that I'm not going to walk through the ceremony. I'm sure that's okay with you. I know how much you and Dad both love boring graduation speeches.

It's still cold here. I check Tucson weather online every morning. I'm looking forward to coming home. And staying there.

Love,
Lani

With her fingers flying effortlessly over the keyboard, Diana wrote back:

Dear Lani,

As far as we know, Fat Crack is fine. He sent a woman from the reservation to see Dad yesterday. Her daughter was murdered years ago, long before you were born. She's hoping Dad and TLC can resurrect the case and figure out who did it. If Fat Crack is well enough to be worrying about someone else's problems, Wanda's probably right and he's doing just fine. After all, Wanda has been married to Gabe Ortiz for a long time. If she says he's okay, I'm guessing it's true.

Dad's still sleeping. He woke me up when he came to bed at two. He's all excited about having a case to work on. I'm happy to have him doing something besides looking over my shoulder and asking whether or not I'm making progress.

Please don't worry about Fat Crack. Study hard and do well on your exams. I'm sure that's what he wants you to do. It's what we want, too.

Love,
Mom

P.S. I'll try to call you later on this afternoon.

After answering the remaining e-mails, Diana went to the kitchen and poured herself a cup of coffee before going out to the patio. She sat in the shade and tried to work, but the words wouldn't come. Her mind was too full of what Brandon had told her at dinner the night before.

Emma Orozco had stayed on at the house in Gates Pass for several hours. Her more-than-patient son-in-law had gone away for a time but had returned and waited for another hour before Emma finally emerged from the house and hoisted herself up into the pickup. The son-in-law closed the door behind her and stowed Emma's walker in back. Then, tipping his fraying white straw hat in Brandon's direction, he clambered back into the driver's seat and sped off. By then, Diana was dying of curiosity.

She had emerged from her study in time to see them drive off. Now she looked at her husband as he stared after the receding pickup truck, eyes alight with an intensity she hadn't seen for years.

"What was that all about?" she asked.

"Do you remember the girl in the ice chest?" he asked.

"The one they found out by Quijotoa?" Diana returned after a moment. "Sure, but that has to be at least thirty years ago."

"More," Brandon replied. "The girl—the victim—was Emma's daughter, Roseanne."

Suddenly Diana understood. "Let me guess—they never solved it."

"Right," Brandon said. "That's why Fat Crack sent her to see me. He's hoping TLC might be able to help her."

"After all this time?"

"That's the idea. Do you remember much about it?"

Diana shook her head. "I had my hands full in 1970. Davy was a baby. Rita and I had just moved in here and were trying to make the place habitable. And the truth is, I didn't really want to know about it."

The numbing combination of the murder of Rita's granddaughter, Garrison's death by what was supposedly his own hand, and the disappointment of Andrew Carlisle's plea bargain had left a heavy burden on Diana Ladd. She'd had far too much of murder. Too much heartache. She hadn't wanted to hear about anyone else's hurt because her own was still too close to the surface. Or maybe there had been so much mayhem in Diana's life that the Orozco girl's murder no longer touched her in the same way it would have once. Maybe a part of her heart had become too accustomed to such atrocities—accustomed and immune.

Even so, there had been some unavoidable talk at school. Once migrant workers, Emma Orozco and her husband had moved to Sells from *Ak-Chin*—Arroyo Mouth—while their daughters were still young. Henry Orozco worked for the Bureau of Indian Affairs. His wife became an aide with the tribal Head Start program. Andrea and Roseanne Orozco attended Indian Oasis School. Since Diana taught at Topawa Elementary, the district's other elementary school, she hadn't known either one of the Orozco girls personally.

Still, some of the gossip had penetrated Diana's emotional deflectors. "I seem to remember there was something wrong with Roseanne—that she was developmentally disabled or autistic. And something makes me think she was pregnant at the time of her death."

Diana and Brandon had gone back inside the house. The afternoon was warm. They had retreated to the kitchen, where Brandon rummaged through the freezer and found two small steaks which he put in the microwave to thaw. With Lani gone, they had slipped into an easy rhythm of sharing the cooking duties and eating dinner early.

"Not autistic," Brandon corrected. "According to her mother, one day when Roseanne Orozco was about five, she stopped talking—to anyone. Emma said they took her to the Indian Health Service doctors and even to a medicine man, but nothing helped. And you're right, she was fifteen years old and pregnant at the time of her death."

"Who was the father?" Diana asked. "Wouldn't he be a natural suspect?"

"That's the problem," Brandon replied. "No one had any idea who the father was. As far as anyone knew,

Roseanne didn't have a boyfriend. Law and Order suspected incest."

"You mean they suspected Henry Orozco of abusing his daughter?" Diana demanded. "I knew Henry. He seemed like a perfectly nice man. No way would he do such a thing."

"That's what Emma said as well. She said that when Law and Order broached the subject that Henry had done something bad with his daughter, he was really upset, and so was she. Ultimately, Law and Order couldn't prove it one way or another. DNA testing didn't exist back then. Paternity wasn't nearly as easy to prove as it is now. Henry Orozco was a suspect in the case, and although he was never tried for it, he was never exonerated, either. When Law and Order allowed the investigation to go cold, Henry was more than happy to ignore it as well. Now, with Henry dead, Emma is willing to open it up again."

"And you're going to help?" Diana had asked.

"Absolutely," Brandon had answered. "To the best of my ability."

It took time to deal with the body. Gayle had learned the art of butchering meat at her father's knee. Growing up on the family ranch north of Tucson, Gayle rather than her prissy, puking brother, Winston, had accompanied Calvin Madison to the slaughterhouse when it came time to butcher cattle. By the time Gayle was twelve, her father liked to brag to his pals that if he turned Gayle loose in the slaughterhouse, she could do the whole job herself.

And she could have, too—from beginning to end. Since the sight of blood made Winston sick, Gayle learned to love it. Sometimes, when her mother wasn't around, she'd bathe her hands in the gory stuff. Then she'd track down her baby brother, wave her bloodied hands at him, and chase him into the house. Her parents caught her doing it once. Her mother had insisted that Calvin take the belt to her, but Gayle didn't mind. Anything that tormented Winston was worth it.

But a serious butcher knife was what was needed to do the job properly, to cleave bone and flesh apart at the joints and sever them into manageable pieces for bundling and carrying. She was unaccustomed to using Erik's machete. It seemed like a clumsy tool for the job, and it wasn't nearly sharp enough.

Not only that, Gayle had to do the messy work in clothing far too big for her. Despite three pairs of socks, Erik's Nikes threatened to fall off at every step. She had to cinch his belt up tight to keep his pants from falling down over her hips, but the blood splatter would be in all the right places—on the inside bill of his Arizona Diamondbacks cap, on the outside of his sweatshirt and jeans, and on the outsides of his shoes as well. There was no faking that.

Her big concern these days was DNA. She had gathered some individual hair from Erik's hairbrush and one or two curly reddish stray pubic hairs from his bed. She left those in strategic spots where an alert medical examiner ought to be able to find them. What she didn't want to do was leave any evidence of her own presence behind.

Erik LaGrange had committed the unpardonable. He had left Gayle rather than the other way around. Gayle was no longer furious with him over it. That had passed away from her sometime overnight, leaving her determined to extract the highest possible price. For her purposes, it was just as well this was happening in Arizona.

Arizona was, after all, one of the few states where the death penalty remained in full operation. It was a place where death sentences were not only given but where they were also carried out, something that suited Gayle Stryker just fine, thank you very much. The death penalty was exactly what she had in mind for Erik LaGrange.

Brandon Walker woke up later than he had intended—well past nine. He dressed, poured a cup of coffee, and then went out on the patio, where he found Diana hard at work on her laptop. He tried tossing the ball for Damsel. Panting, she ignored the ball and stayed in the shade.

"What's up with Damsel?" Brandon asked. "Is she sick?"

Diana laughed. "She's spent the whole morning chasing butterflies and jets."

It was one of the dog's most endearing peculiarities. For some reason, from the time she had come into their lives, the dog had focused her attention on the shadows planes and butterflies left on the ground rather than on the moving objects themselves. Chasing shadows was a game she played by herself, often to the point of exhaustion.

"Dummy," Brandon told the dog, giving the winded animal a loving pat on the head in passing. "When are you ever going to wise up?" He sat down next to Diana. "I'm going out to the reservation today," he said to her. "To see Fat Crack. Want to come along?"

"I wish I could, but I'd better not," Diana said. "My deadline's actively ticking at this point." She paused. "Lani's worried about him. When you get back home, give her a call and let her know how he's doing."

"It won't be good news," Brandon said, sipping his coffee.

"You know that, and I know that," Diana returned. "Deep down, Lani probably knows it, too. She understands how serious this is even more than the rest of us. Her biggest worry is that Fat Crack won't last long enough for her to get home. She wants to be here for him."

"Just like he was for her," Brandon returned.

That fateful day on *Ioligam* was still seared in Brandon Walker's memory. By the time he had arrived, Mitch Johnson, Lani's kidnapper, was already dead. Lani had killed him. Brandon had hurried there expecting to retrieve his daughter and take her home. Fat Crack had blocked his way.

"Where is she?" Brandon demanded of his longtime friend. "Is she all right? Why isn't she here?"

"Because she killed a man," Gabe Ortiz returned quietly. "She has to stay by herself. She has to fast and eat no salted food and pray for sixteen days."

"Sixteen days!" Brandon exclaimed. "Out here by herself? Are you nuts? What the hell are you thinking?"

"It's what Lani's thinking," Gabe replied, "and that's what counts. It's what she wants to do. It's what she has to do."

Brandon had always known Lani was different, from the moment she had walked into his life as a toddler and wrapped her tiny fingers around his heart. It had hurt him when others called his baby *Kuadagi Ke'e Al*—the Ant-Bit Child, but that was the reason Lani was Brandon's in the first place. According to Rita Antone, Lani's blood relatives had refused to take her in because they were scared of her. They were convinced that because she had been singled out by *I'itoi*, she was a danger to her family members. Nana *Dahd* believed that being ant-bit made Lani special.

Brandon Walker had heard all that, but he hadn't really paid attention, and he certainly hadn't believed it. For him, Lani was the light of his life. He had adored her, spoiled her, loved her. Now, for reasons he couldn't understand, she seemed to be rejecting that love.

"Why?" Brandon had asked again.

"Because she really is *Kulani O'oks*," Fat Crack explained. "Lani is destined to be a great medicine woman. To do that—to really do that—she has to abide by the old ways."

One look at Fat Crack's impassive face told Brandon he was losing. No amount of arguing would do any good. He tried anyway.

"It's almost summer," Brandon said. "Hotter'n hell during the day and freezing at night. Where will she sleep, Gabe? What will she eat?"

"I'll look after her," Fat Crack said quietly. "It's my job, one *siwani*—one chief medicine man—to another."

"But . . ."

"Please, Brandon," Fat Crack added. "It's what she must do."

Brandon Walker had gone home empty-handed that Sunday afternoon. He had held a weeping Diana in his arms and tried to explain it to her. Although the two of them had never discussed it afterward, he suspected she didn't like this new reality any better than he did. He wondered sometimes if Diana felt as betrayed as he did to think that Lani had turned to Fat Crack in her hour of need—to Gabe Ortiz rather than to her parents.

When Fat Crack finally brought Lani home to Gates Pass sixteen days later, she was a different person. She had been a carefree teenager—little more than a child—when she was taken from them. She returned as a serious-minded young woman who was far more in tune with her Indian heritage than she had ever been before.

From then on, the relationship between Lani and her adoptive parents was forever altered. There was no blow-up—no identifiable breach or specific argument. Things were just different. Brandon was smart enough not to blame Fat Crack for the changes that had occurred. Dolores Lanita Walker was still their Lani, still at home with them. She learned to drive, got her license, and graduated from high school at the top of her class. Yet Brandon knew Mitch Johnson had succeeded in robbing him of something precious when he had kidnapped Lani.

He had stolen her innocence. No one in the world—not even Fat Crack Ortiz—could give it back to her.

"I'll talk to her about Fat Crack's condition," Brandon told Diana now, staring down into a mug where his forgotten coffee had long ago gone cold. "If I have to, I'll even lie to her about it."

"No," Diana counseled. "Don't do that. If the news is really bad, we can fly her home early. She's already canceled walking through graduation—which she figured you'd appreciate. And she's made arrangements with her professors to do some exams early."

"Which means she already knows it's bad news," Brandon observed. His eyes sought Diana's over the rim of his coffee mug. "And so do I. You're sure you can't come along?"

"I'm sure," Diana said. "I've got to work."

"All right, then," Brandon said. "See you later."

eight

At eleven o'clock on Saturday morning, Sue Lammers went into the family room to check on her husband, Ken, who had spent all morning glued to the Golf Channel watching a tournament.

"Is it over?" she asked.

"This is a different one," he said, barely taking his eyes off their flat-screen TV. "On ABC. It just started."

What Sue Lammers saw right then was red! When they had first moved to their manufactured home on Fast Horse Ranch south of Tucson, they had loved it. She and Ken both worked hard all week—she as a purchasing agent for University Medical Center and he as an economist for Pima County. On weekends, they worked on the house and the yard, gradually creating a beautifully landscaped retreat out of rough, untamed desert.

But that was before satellite TV had crept in and ruined Sue's little Garden of Eden with the forbidden fruit of unlimited weekend sports. Now, with that ugly little satellite dish perched like an overweight eagle on the roof, life wasn't the same. Football folded into basketball, into baseball, and back into football in an unrelenting cavalcade, with golf, auto racing, and the National Hockey League plugged in here and there for good measure. It was all Sue could do to get Ken to tear himself away from the tube long enough to eat an occasional meal at the table instead of on a tray. As for his lifting a finger around the house or yard? Forget about it.

Grumbling to herself, Sue left the room. Ranger, their five-year-old German shepherd, followed her down the hallway and into the bedroom. As soon as she took her hiking boots down from the shelf in the closet, Ranger went on full alert. For him, boots meant only one thing—the tantalizing prospect of a walk. Ears up, nose quivering with excitement, Ranger watched as she pulled the boots on and laced them up.

"That's right, old boy," she told him. "I may not be able to get Daddy off his duff, but I sure as hell don't have that problem with you."

Still pissed at her husband, Sue took Ranger and left by the front door without even bothering to tell Ken they were leaving. She took the whistle—Ranger was well trained and would come on the run after only a single blast from the whistle—and didn't bother with a leash. This far out in the country, leashes weren't really necessary. She let Ranger live up to his name by racing along before and alongside her, calling him back only when she saw other people coming their way—joggers, hikers, or bicyclists. Trains were another story. The power-line access road where Sue and Ranger often walked ran along the railroad tracks, and trains spooked Ranger. When he heard one coming, he would race back to Sue and cower with his head next to her knee until the noisy thing had rumbled past and out of earshot.

This morning, though, there were no trains on the horizon as Sue Lammers, still seething with resentment, strode along the rugged, rutted excuse for a road that ran under the power line. *Is this why I'm working my heart out all week?* she wondered. *So I can spend my weekends alone with a dog instead of with my husband?*

For weeks she had watched as the round flat leaves of the prickly pear sprouted buds. Now, in late April, the desert was a bright sea of yellow. Somehow, seeing the desert bloom like that made her feel better. *Wasn't that the whole point of going for a walk—to feel better?*

Ahead of her, half a mile or so away, Sue spotted a dark-colored vehicle parked on the shoulder of the real road that ran parallel to where she was walking. Seeing a parked car made her uneasy. There was no legitimate reason for anyone to be parked along there—no houses, no businesses. In the distance she could see a figure moving back and forth between a clump of mesquite and the back of what she assumed was a pickup truck.

Sue knew many people were too cheap to pay to go to the dump. They'd rather come out into the desert and use it as a personal trash heap. Meeting up with one of those lowlifes made Sue Lammers uneasy, especially when she was out walking alone—Ranger notwithstanding. She reached into her shirt pocket and pulled out her cell phone. A new tower had recently been erected in their neighborhood, making cell-phone reception better. She was relieved to see that she had a good strong signal.

She was only a few yards closer when the person who had been walking to and from the vehicle—she could see now that it was actually a dark-colored pickup with what appeared to be a camper shell—turned and seemed to see her. He jumped into the driver's seat and sped off, sending a cloud of dust spewing skyward. Relieved to watch him drive away, Sue kept walking. She had been about to lift the whistle to her lips to summon Ranger back, but with the pickup gone, she dropped the whistle and left Ranger free to explore.

Sue was still a few hundred yards short of where the vehicle had been parked when she heard the distant rumble of a train. Ranger heard it, too. The dog had been a long way ahead of her. Now he came loping back. As he drew closer, Sue saw he had something in his mouth. At first she thought it was a stick, but it wasn't a stick. It was an arm—a bloodied human arm.

"Drop it!" Sue screamed in horror. "Drop it right now!"

Ranger did as he was told, then scampered to her side as the train rumbled nearer.

Feeling faint, Sue Lammers struggled to get her cell phone out of her pocket. Her fingers felt like thick, clumsy sausages. The phone slipped from her grasp and fell to the ground. Landing on a rock, it bounced once and exploded. The plastic back fell off and the battery popped free. As Sue knelt to retrieve the scattered pieces of her phone, Ranger made another grab at his prize.

"Leave it!" she exclaimed, but by then the train was right beside them, drowning out everything. Whether he heard her or not, Ranger complied, leaving Sue scrambling on her hands and knees as she reassembled the broken phone.

It wasn't until after the freight train had passed that Sue was finally able to get her fumbling fingers to press the necessary numbers.

"Nine one one," a businesslike voice said in her ear. "What are you reporting?"

Sue Lammers took a deep breath. "I'm out walking south of Vail, south of Fast Horse Ranch," she said in a hoarse whisper. "My dog just found somebody's arm. A bloody human arm!"

* * *

Distracted, Erik gave himself permission to stop short of the summit. With his back resting against a warm cliff face in a solitary canyon well below Finger Rock, he pulled out his peanut butter sandwich and savored the first bite. It was made the right way—the way Grandma always made it—with butter on both slices of bread and with the peanut butter slathered in between.

He had traded lunches one day in the lunch room at Hollinger Elementary and had been surprised when his friend's peanut butter sandwich was hard to swallow. It had stuck in his throat, and once he finally realized what the difference was, he had asked Gladys about it that evening.

"Grandma," he said, "did you know some people make peanut butter sandwiches without buttering the bread first?"

"Yes."

"How come you always put butter on it?"

"Because that's the way you're supposed to do it," Gladys Johnson returned. "There's always a right way to do something and a wrong way. Buttering the bread first is the right way."

"Is that how your mother did it?"

Gladys nodded. "My mother," she said. "And my aunt Selma, too. It's the way everybody did it back home. Peanut butter was a lot stiffer in those days."

All these years later, even though Erik LaGrange had never met those fabled relatives he had heard so many stories about, he was glad he shared that one small trait with people who would forever be nothing but faceless names. Peanut butter on buttered bread was a tiny fragment of his own lost heritage.

It's the way I do it, too, he thought.

* * *

That fateful President's Ball had been on a Saturday night. The following Tuesday afternoon, Gayle Stryker rang Erik at his office.

"I offered you a job the other night," she said after identifying herself. "I thought you would have called about it by now."

Erik was so taken aback he could barely reply. "I wasn't really thinking about making a change right now," he stammered, sounding like a total dork.

"Really," Gayle Stryker said. "Are they paying you that much?"

That was laughable because the truth was, they were paying him hardly anything at all. "Not really," he admitted finally.

In actual fact, Erik LaGrange was someone who resisted change wherever it presented itself. For him, staying in a less-than-optimal situation was better than striking off into the unknown. It made for a stable if relatively boring life.

"How about if we get together tomorrow and have lunch?" Gayle suggested. "At El Charro downtown, say, about a quarter to one?"

Erik thought about his ten-year-old plug-ugly but still-running Volvo with its faded orange paint and crimped front bumper. He was supposed to meet the lady for lunch driving that? And what the hell was he supposed to wear? And what was he going to say to his boss? "Well, Dick, I guess I'll take a long lunch and see about getting a job somewhere else."

Richard Mathers was a guy who believed in running a tight ship. He was a micromanaging busybody who had to know where his people were at all times. He expected to be apprised of what each was doing and whether it would improve his departmental bottom line. If Erik showed up at work wearing something unusual—for Erik a sports coat and tie would definitely be out of character—Dick would ask a million questions, none of which Erik wanted to answer.

"Okay," Erik heard himself saying. "A quarter to one."

Gayle Stryker laughed. "Don't sound so worried. I'm going to offer you a job. It isn't exactly an invitation to a beheading."

But it could just as well have been. Two margaritas—blended with no salt—were waiting on the table when Erik showed up. In order to avoid rousing Dick Mathers's suspicion, Erik had left his tie and blazer in the car when he arrived at work that morning. He donned them only after pulling into the parking lot across from the restaurant.

Gayle, in a lime-green silk shirt with a pair of matching slacks, was already seated. A discreet glance at her plunging neckline left little to the imagination. She welcomed him to the table with a cordial peck on the cheek.

"So good of you to come," she murmured in his ear. The look she gave him as she resumed her seat left no doubt in Erik's mind that the double entendre he thought he'd heard had indeed been intended. Once again, Erik blushed. The bones in his legs turned to mush, and he tumbled into the chair opposite her.

Knowing Dick Mathers disapproved of what he called "boozy lunches" and hoping for something a little less volatile than tequila, Erik started to push the margarita glass away. Gayle pointed a diamond-bedecked finger in his direction and shook it reprovingly.

"Oh, no, you don't," she warned. "I didn't come here to drink alone. We're going to have a lovely lunch and get to know each other. Cheers." She raised her glass in

Erik's direction and smiled when he followed suit. "Tell me about yourself," she said after tasting her drink.

Whether it was nerves or not, Erik laid the whole story out on the table. "I'm thirty years old," he said. "My mother died shortly after I was born. I never met my father. I was raised by my grandmother right here in Tucson. I'm not married, never have been. No children, either."

Erik felt like a complete idiot. This wasn't the kind of information he should have blurted out if this really was a job interview, but he was fairly certain a change of employment for him was a long way down on Gayle Stryker's list of priorities. Her response confirmed his suspicions.

"I see," she said with a smile. "You're saying you're what could be called a blank slate?"

Several weeks earlier Erik had watched *The Graduate* on Turner Classic Movies. Poor Dustin Hoffman had been putty in Anne Bancroft's very capable hands. Somehow Erik knew at once that he was headed in the same direction.

"I guess," he replied uneasily, fingering the stem of his chilled glass.

"Well," she said. "We'll have to do something about that now, won't we."

They ate lunch. Gayle had two more margaritas while Erik had another as well. When they left the restaurant a little before four, Erik drove off in Gayle Stryker's silver Lexus, leaving his own battered Volvo sitting forlorn and forgotten in the parking lot.

She directed Erik to El Encanto, a part of town he had visited as a worker bee during top-dollar alumni fund-raising parties. Elegant El Encanto was a long way from the tiny bungalow in a predominantly Hispanic part of the Old Pueblo where Erik had been raised. After meandering aimlessly through the wheels-and-spokes confusion of the subdivision's streets, they pulled into the gate of a two-story brown stucco mansion. A copper-colored gate opened at the touch of a remote on the Lexus's visor. So did the garage door. Gayle waited only long enough for the garage door to close behind them before reaching across the seat, pulling Erik toward her, and kissing him in a fashion that was calculated to take his breath away. And did.

"Come on," she whispered finally. "Let's go someplace comfortable."

Paying only the barest attention to his surroundings, he followed her into the house and then up a curved stairway. She began stripping off her clothes as she crossed the threshold into an enormous bedroom and was standing naked before him by the time he had unfastened his belt.

"Come on," she said impatiently. "Show me what you've got."

Until that afternoon, Erik LaGrange had thought of himself as a reasonably experienced person when it came to sex, but Gayle Stryker had tricks up her discarded sleeve that went far beyond anything he'd ever considered or imagined, and her stamina was unbelievable. When she finally had her fill of him, some two hours later, she got out of bed and showered, leaving Erik lying on the bed, lost in a pink haze and unable to move.

"You'd better get going," she told him as she toweled herself dry. "You need to go into the office and give them their two-week notice."

"But . . ."

"Come on, Erik. You passed the job interview with flying colors. Whatever Dick Mathers is paying you, I'll double it, and I'll throw in a company car. Now let's head out."

And they did. It was only as he stood in the parking lot struggling with the somewhat balky lock on the Volvo's driver's-side door that he wondered for the first time where Dr. Lawrence Stryker had been that afternoon and how Gayle could have been so certain her husband wouldn't turn up at the house.

It was the first time Erik LaGrange worried and wondered about Larry Stryker's whereabouts. It wouldn't be the last.

Seated in his cubicle in the Pima County Sheriff's Department and working his way through a chorizo burrito, homicide detective Brian Fellows took the call.

"It came in about forty-five minutes ago," Dispatch told him. "Some hysterical woman called in to say her dog had found an arm—a human arm—on the far side of Vail. I dispatched Patrol. A unit just arrived on the scene. Deputy Gomez says there's a whole lot more than an arm out there. Looks like a whole body—all of it in pieces. The ME's office is my next call."

Brian stood up and flung his jacket over his shoulder. "What about CSI?" he asked.

"I'll call them, too."

Brian took a step toward the door, then he looked back longingly at the last third of the burrito still sitting on his desk. It might be a long time before he had another crack at solid food. Sighing, Brian retrieved it, then swallowed a bite as he hurried down the corridor.

He was glad to have something to do besides pushing paper. Weekend day shifts were pretty quiet because most of the bad guys were home nursing the previous night's booze- or drug-induced hangover or working on the next one. It wasn't until the sun went down that people beat up or shot one another outside bars and ran one another off the road on their way home.

Out in the parking lot, Brian fired up his Crown Vic and headed for I-10. Budget constraints in Sheriff Bill Forsythe's office now necessitated that weekend dayshift detectives work alone rather than in pairs—which was all right with Brian. He liked his partner, Hector (PeeWee) Segura, well enough, but he was happy to be on his own for a change. His early years in the department, when he'd been hassled and penalized for his close association with the previous sheriff, had made him something of a departmental loner.

Brian had first known Brandon Walker as the man who came each weekend, rain or shine, to pick up his own sons—Brian's half brothers—to take them on some noncustodial visit or outing. Brian's father had disappeared from his life when Brian was only three. For him, there was no such thing as a noncustodial outing. For a long time Brian had been left alone on the porch, watching as Quentin and Tommy rode away for their afternoon treats.

One day Brian's life changed forever. Instead of leaving the forlorn child moping and alone on the porch, Brandon Walker had opened the car door and invited him to join them. Quentin and Tommy had been outraged by their father's small kindness, but from then on, Brian had gone along wherever Brandon had taken his own sons. It was hardly surprising that Brian Fellows returned that long-ago generosity by worshiping the ground beneath Brandon Walker's feet and by following his hero into law enforcement.

Brian had joined the department as a deputy while Brandon was still in office. When a new administration came into power sometime later, Brian had more than half expected to be let go. Rather than fire him, Sheriff Forsythe elected to encourage Brian to quit by giving him crappy assignments and letting him work the cars far longer than he should have. Brian had fooled everybody—including himself—by sticking it out, keeping his nose clean, and doing a good job. Now a ten-year veteran, he had finally been promoted to Investigations. As new guys came on board and old guys retired, Brian Fellows's connections to Sheriff Walker mattered less and less.

Unfortunately, neither of Brandon Walker's biological sons had turned out to be at all like their father. Natural-born bullies, Tommy and Quentin Walker had reveled in tormenting anyone younger and weaker. On every possible occasion, they had made life miserable for their half brother, Brian, and for their father's new stepson, Davy Ladd. Later on, as teenagers, Tommy and Quentin had run off the rails entirely and turned into full-fledged juvenile delinquents. Tommy had died at sixteen while engaged in something he'd been forbidden to do. Quentin, tortured by the part he'd played in his older brother's death, had been in and out of trouble and/or jail ever since. Even now he was back in the slammer on a drug charge, which meant he'd be in prison for the better part of the next ten years.

But waging their joint defensive war against Tommy and Quentin had united Davy Ladd and Brian Fellows in a close childhood friendship that endured to this day. In fact, all of them—Davy Ladd, his wife, Candace, and their two-year-old son, Tyler, along with Brian and his wife, Kath—were expected at the Walkers' place for dinner late Sunday afternoon—just like a real family.

But between then and now, Brian Fellows had work to do. Someone had been murdered and hacked to pieces in the desert. Like Brandon Walker before him, it was Brian's job to find out who was dead—and why.

nine

After a while, I'itoi woke up. Elder Brother laughed when he looked around and saw all the children sleeping, and he thought about what was hidden in his bag.

I'itoi called to the children. When they were all awake and watching, he opened his bag and shook it. Out fluttered the big yellow leaves and the spots of sunshine and the brown leaves and the shadows and the tiny white flowers and the small pieces of bright blue sky. They were all alive. They floated in the air for a few moments, and then they danced away into the sunlight. And the children danced after them.

I'itoi stayed in the shade of the tree and was glad that at last there was something beautiful and gay that would never change and never grow ugly as it grew old.

And this, nawoj, my friend, is the story of the birth of hohokimal—the butterflies.

Speeding east on I-10, Brian dialed home on his cell phone. When Kath didn't answer, he left a message. "I'm on a call and headed to Vail," he said. "It could take time. I'll let you know when I'll be home."

Minutes later, he pulled off the freeway at Vail and

headed for the Fast Horse Ranch development. A mile or so beyond the subdivision, he saw the clump of parked vehicles. He pulled in behind a patrol car sitting with its back door open. A woman was inside and a dog—a big German shepherd—lay on the ground nearby, panting and keeping a wary eye on the people milling about. Deputy Ruben Gomez met Brian before he was fully out of the car.

"What's the deal?" Brian asked.

"It's pretty bad," the deputy replied. "Little girl, Hispanic, probably fourteen or fifteen years old. Somebody's hacked her to pieces and stuffed her in a bunch of garbage bags. The lady in my car, Ms. Lammers—Susan Lammers—was out walking with her dog. The dog ran on ahead and came running back carrying an arm. As soon as she saw it, Ms. Lammers called it in. I found the bags with the rest of the body when I got here."

"Any ID?" Brian asked.

"Not so far. I didn't want to foul things up, so I stayed away. Dispatch tells me CSI is on the way."

"Right," Brian said. "I'll go talk to the witness. How's the dog, friendly or not?"

Ruben cast a cautious glance at the animal. "She says he's fine, but if I were you, I wouldn't make any sudden moves."

Keeping one eye on the dog, Brian moved toward the open door. "Ms. Lammers?" he asked.

A blond-haired woman, red-eyed and still sniffling, peered out of the vehicle at him. "Yes," she said tentatively. "But please, call me Sue. Mrs. Lammers is my mother-in-law."

"I'm Detective Fellows," Brian said, offering his ID. "Mind if I ask you a few questions?"

"Sure," she said.

As the woman climbed out of the vehicle, Brian estimated her to be in her early forties. She wore a sweatshirt, faded jeans, and hiking boots. "I saw him," she said, brushing her short hair away with a hand that was still visibly shaking. "I'm sure I saw him."

"Who?" Brian asked. He opened his notebook.

"The guy. The one who dumped her. He was parked on the shoulder as Ranger and I walked up the powerline road. As we got closer, I think he saw us coming and took off."

"Which way?" Brian asked.

"He headed back toward Vail. I don't know where he went after that. The intersection is behind the crest of the hill. I couldn't see which way he turned."

"What kind of vehicle?"

"A pickup of some kind. I wasn't close enough to see a license or what model it was. Dark-colored. Dark blue or maybe purple. With a matching camper shell."

"What were you doing?" Brian asked.

"Ranger, my dog, and I were taking a walk."

"From where?"

"My husband and I have a place down the road. Two miles or so from here. On Fast Horse Ranch."

Brian looked around. "Is your husband here?"

"He's at the house. I haven't called him," Sue Lammers added after a pause. "We had a fight. I took Ranger out so I could cool off."

"What time did this happen?"

"You mean what time did I find the body?"

Brian nodded.

"Over an hour ago now," she told him. "Ranger ran on ahead of me. He does that sometimes, but he's scared of trains. There was one coming—a big freight train—so Ranger came back. I saw he was carrying something and thought it was a stick." Her lip trembled. "But it wasn't a stick at all," she continued. "It was an arm—a piece of an arm." Again she paused, swallowing convulsively before going on. "It was still all bloody."

She spoke with the air of one trying to forget even as she remembered. Tears welled in her eyes. Brian gave her a moment to compose herself while he mentally calculated the distance a pickup truck, traveling at legal highway speed, might have covered in the space of an hour.

Just then a van containing two members of the CSI team pulled up behind Brian's vehicle. Deputy Gomez went to meet them. He led them forward, pointing as he went. Brian stayed with Sue Lammers.

"Did you see anything that would help us?"

"No. He was too far away."

"He?" Brian asked. "You're sure it was a male?"

"Not really," Sue admitted. "I mean, it looked like a man. I saw him walk from the truck into the desert and then back again. He went back and forth a couple of times. I thought he was dumping garbage, but I worried about it all the same. I mean, I was out here by myself. The last trip he made, he must have seen me. That's when he jumped into the truck and took off."

"When you go walking by yourself like this, are you armed?" Brian asked.

"No," Sue said quickly. "I have my cell phone along in case anything happens, but that's all. I don't believe in carrying weapons. Neither does my husband."

Maybe you should, Brian thought. He said, "You mentioned the driver made several trips back and forth to the truck?"

"Yes."

"Was he carrying something each time?"

"Yes."

Brian was about to ask Sue Lammers another question when Deputy Gomez hurried up to them. "Excuse me, Detective Fellows," he said. "I think we just found something important."

"What's that?"

"A bundle of bloody clothing," Gomez said.

"You think it belongs to the girl?" Brian asked.

"It's a pretty good guess," Gomez replied. "This was in one of the pockets."

He held out a glassine bag. Inside it was a business card. Brian had to squint to read the print. "Erik La-Grange," the card said. "Development Officer, Medicos for Mexico." Brian turned the bag over. On the back of the card was a handwritten telephone number.

Brian jotted it down. "Well," he said, "at least this gives us a place to start."

Tohono O'odham tribal attorney Delia Ortiz waddled into her office. Dropping heavily into her desk chair, she rolled it close enough to the desk so she could reach her computer keyboard over the hefty mound of her protruding belly. She usually didn't come into her office on Saturdays, but with the baby due in two weeks and with her office's budget proposal expected to appear before the tribal council the week after her due date, Delia was determined to be ahead of the game.

No one was more surprised than Delia to find herself pregnant at age forty-three. She hadn't expected to be pregnant at age forty, either. She'd lost that one—a boy they'd named Adam—due to a late-term miscarriage during her sixth month of pregnancy. She had felt the baby's loss keenly, but her grief had been nothing compared to her husband's. Leo Ortiz had been utterly heartbroken. It was at his insistence and only partially because they were good Catholics that they'd done nothing about birth control. Now, here she was—three years later and three years older—pregnant again.

Wedged up against the edge of her desk, the baby—another boy—gave Delia's tummy a solid kick. Remembering how it had felt when Adam had stopped kicking, she welcomed this minor disturbance—a reminder this new child was eager to make his grand entrance into the world.

Leo had been lobbying for them to pick out a name, but Delia had resisted. She had named Adam and then lost him. She was afraid that if she named this baby too soon, the same thing might happen.

Delia browsed through her new e-mail. Midway down she spotted *Mualig Siakam,* Lani Walker's screen name, Forever Spinning, named after the young girl who had turned into Whirlwind. The subject line of Lani's message said: "How's he doing?"

Just as Lani Walker had done prior to sending the e-mail, Delia Cachora Ortiz stared at her screen for a long time before opening the message. She knew Lani was writing out of real concern for Gabe Ortiz's health. Delia was concerned, too. In large measure, everything Delia treasured in life had its origin in Fat Crack Ortiz. To a certain extent, that was true of Lani and Davy Walker as well. Delia knew Wanda and Gabe Ortiz were Lani's and Davy's godparents. Still, a surge of resentment boiled up in Delia's heart the moment she saw the listing.

What business was it of Lani Walker's to ask about Fat Crack's health and well-being? Delia herself owed her own debt of gratitude to Gabe Ortiz, but she was sick and tired of seeing Leo—her husband and one of Gabe and Wanda's two real sons—being pushed aside by what Delia couldn't help but regard as a pair of interlopers.

Biting back her anger, Delia opened the message:

> *Dear Delia,*
>
> *It's Friday night and I can't sleep. I'm really worried about Fat Crack. Would you please drop me a line and let me know how he is? It's almost the end of the semester. If he's really bad and needs me to, I can come home early.*
>
> *Lani*

That was the last straw! If he needs me? What did that mean? Did Lani Walker expect to come traipsing out to Gabe and Wanda's place and push Leo and Richard aside so she could keep her own death watch?

Delia had heard all the talk about Lani Walker growing up to be a medicine woman and a doctor. She had spent too many years in the Anglo world to put much store in all the medicine-woman mumbo-jumbo, but she had taken a serious interest in how Fat Crack Ortiz intended to turn Lani Walker into a physician. He had insisted that if Lani Walker was going to come home and serve as a doctor on the reservation, the Tohono O'odham needed to pony up the money.

Having a realistic idea of exactly how expensive sending a student through medical school would be, Delia had tried to derail the idea. As tribal attorney, she had argued long and hard before the tribal council about the fiscal irresponsibility of doing just that. Of course, the Tohono O'odham tribe needed to have home-grown health care professionals—doctors and nurses whose first loyalty would be to the Desert People—but Delia thought it was wrong to use tribal funds to educate someone whose parents could well afford to pay the tuition themselves.

Gabe had still been tribal chairman then. For Delia to go up against her own father-in-law and then lose in such a public fashion had caused a reservation-wide stir. It had also caused familial difficulties between Delia and her in-laws that lingered to this day and colored all Delia's interactions with Gabe and Wanda Ortiz.

He's dying, Delia thought, *but he is fine.* With that, she clicked the "reply" button and typed:

> *Dear Lani,*
>
> *Gabe is fine. No need for you to rush home. I'll let you know if anything changes.*
>
> *Delia Cachora Ortiz*

She punched "send" without giving herself a chance to reconsider. With the e-mail off in the ethers, Delia found she was far too upset to concentrate. Abandoning her plan to spend the morning working in her office, she switched off her computer, turned off the lights, locked the door, and left.

Out in the parking lot, she climbed into her aging Saab 9000 and headed for the little chapel at Topawa several miles south of Sells. It was the place where her mother had gone seeking refuge and comfort more than thirty-five years earlier. It was where Delia went looking for relief from her ever-present burden of guilt.

Delia knew that being at war with Lani Walker would only worsen the difficult situation with her father-in-law. Fat Crack Ortiz wasn't simply Leo's father and the grandfather of the child Delia carried. He wasn't just the man who had hired her and brought her back to the reservation in triumph years after she and her mother had fled Manny Chavez's house in Sells in abject terror. Fat Crack was, in fact, the one person who had made their escape possible even way back then. Everything else that had happened to her, good and bad, flowed from that.

Everything else.

"I'm scared," seven-year-old Delia had told her mother. "Do we have to go? Couldn't we just stay here?"

Ellie Chavez shook her head and kept on packing. "This is my chance to become a teacher," she told her daughter determinedly, pretending a bravery she didn't feel. "Sister Justine got me into this special program at Arizona State University. If I don't do it now, I never will. I'll be a teacher's aide all my life—an aide but not a teacher."

"But why do Eddie and I have to go?" Delia asked. "Couldn't we stay here with Daddy or with Aunt Julia?"

"No," Ellie said firmly. "It wouldn't work. Your father wouldn't—"

"Your father wouldn't what?" Manuel Chavez demanded, appearing unexpectedly in the doorway. He stood with his wide body blocking the glare of the afternoon sun and throwing a giant shadow that spread like a dark cloud all the way across the room.

Delia, standing a few feet from her mother, felt a sharp twinge of fear rise in her throat. Even at seven, she knew the danger signs. She could see the half-consumed quart bottle of tequila Manny Chavez held at his side, strategically concealing it behind the outside wall of their government-built house. From Delia's position, she could see the bottle plainly. Her mother could not.

"I was saying that it would be too hard on you to work and take care of Delia and Eddie all by yourself. And Aunt Julia already has her own grandkids to look after. That's why Delia and Eddie have to go to Tempe with me."

"No, they don't," Manny said. "Nobody's going to Tempe." Stepping forward, he brought the bottle into full view, raised it to his lips, and took a long swig.

Ellie sighed. She and Manny had discussed the ASU program earlier, and she had thought the matter settled. At the time they had reached what she assumed to be a final decision, Manny was on the wagon. Now he was off. That was another reason—the real reason—Ellie couldn't risk leaving the children alone with their father. There were reasons beyond that as well—painfully secret reasons she had never discussed with anyone, including her beloved auntie— *Ni-thahth* Julia.

If Ellie's parents had still been alive, she might have discussed her worries with her mother. No doubt Anthony and Guadalupe Francisco would have been thrilled to look after their grandchildren while Ellie went off to school. Unfortunately, Ellie's parents were dead. They had died six years earlier in a Saturday-night car wreck as they returned home after buying groceries in Tucson. When it came to taking care of her children, Ellie Chavez was definitely on her own.

"Come on, Manny," Ellie said reasonably, hoping to cajole her way around him as she had countless times before. "We've been over all this. You said I could go and let me sign up."

"I changed my mind," Manny said. "Now you're staying here."

"Too bad," Ellie returned. "I'm going anyway, and that's final. Sister Justine pulled all kinds of strings to make this work. She's even arranged a place for us to stay."

"A place for *you* to stay," Manny Chavez said pointedly. "I don't remember being invited." He paused and took another long swig from the bottle. "I don't care what Sister Justine did. She's a troublemaker," he added. "She's trying to break us up."

"Manny!" Ellie exclaimed. "Don't say that in front of Delia. Sister Justine's doing no such thing. She thinks I'll be a good teacher, that's all. She thinks so, and so do I."

Manuel Chavez stepped farther into the room. "We were doing just fine with you as an aide and with me driving a bus. Why isn't that good enough?"

"Because being an aide isn't the same as being a real teacher," Ellie insisted. "I want to be one of the first Tohono O'odham teachers here at Sells. It'll set a good example for our kids and for other kids, too. It's not right that all the teachers on the reservation are *Mil-gahn*."

"You'll set an example, all right," Manny Chavez muttered, taking another step forward. "If you leave here, you'll never come back, and you won't get the kids, either. I won't let you."

"Yes, you will."

To most of the world, Ellie Chavez included, those three small words, spoken quietly but resolutely, might have been considered a minor act of disobedience. With Manny they provoked outright war. He attacked her with the bottle and with his one free fist while Delia cowered in one corner and Eddie screamed from his crib. Ellie Chavez fought back. Although her husband outweighed her, he was also very drunk. In the end, that cost him.

He landed several telling blows. Delia watched in horror as her mother went down, blood spouting from her nose and lips. She landed on the floor and lay still. Manny staggered over to her. "I told you," he muttered. "Nobody's going to Tempe."

With that, Manny raised his foot and aimed a vicious kick at his stricken wife. Seeing her father raise his foot, Delia knew what he was going to do. It was more than she could stand. With a screech of outrage, Delia rushed from her hiding place. She tackled her father from behind, hitting him just at knee level. Since he was already off balance, Delia's unexpected blow was enough to send Manny crashing face-first into a corner of the coffee table. As he fell, the bottle was still gripped in his hand. When it smashed into the concrete floor it exploded, sending a spray of tequila and broken glass across the room.

Delia watched him fall and lie still. For several awful moments she expected he would rise and come after her mother again, but he didn't. Slowly, covering her bleeding mouth with one hand, Ellie struggled to her feet. Bright red blood spewed from her nose and from cuts on her upper and lower lips. A long bloody scrape stretched from the tip of her nose to the top of her forehead, where she had fallen on the side of one of three matching suitcases the nuns at Topawa had given her as a going-away present.

For a moment, Ellie, too, stood over her husband as if expecting he would lumber to his feet and renew the attack. Instead, worn out with a combination of booze and physical exertion, his breathing settled into a drunken snore. Afraid Eddie's screams might waken him, Ellie grabbed the baby from his crib and tried to quiet him. Once he settled, she examined both children to see if they had been cut or injured by that shower of broken glass, but the blood on the children had come from her own wounds.

Relieved, she passed Eddie to his sister. "Sit here and hold him," she said. "I need to finish packing."

Before Manny's attack, Ellie had been carefully folding and sorting clothing prior to packing it. Now she threw in everything that would fit and then sat on the bulging cases to force the lids shut. Once they were closed she hurried outside with two of the suitcases, only to discover Manny's pickup was nowhere to be found. Rather than bring it home, Manny had evidently hidden it. It was one more way of making sure his wife didn't leave.

Had Ellie gone searching, she probably could have found the truck. It was most likely at Manny's parents' house or else at his brother's, but there wasn't time to play hide-and-seek. Praying Manny wouldn't awaken before she returned, Ellie took the kids and trudged as far as the pay phone outside the trading post, where she placed a call to Sister Justine in Topawa.

Sister Justine came at once in the convent's nine-passenger station wagon. She looked at Ellie's bloodied face and shook her head. "You should go to the hospital," she said.

Ellie shook her head. "No hospital," she said. "He'll know to look for me there. I have to get away."

"All right, then," Sister Justine said. "Let's go."

And they did.

Arriving at Topawa in the early-afternoon heat, Delia Ortiz found only a few dusty pickups scattered here and there in the dirt parking lot outside the small adobe-covered church. She parked her Saab as unobtrusively as possible among the other vehicles and went inside. It was early enough in the day that the gloomy sanctuary, like the parking lot outside, was still relatively deserted. She didn't have to wait long before making her way into the confessional.

"Forgive me, Father," she said as she closed the door behind her. "Forgive me, for I have sinned."

ten

It was just after noon when Larry Stryker came home from a charity golf tournament at Tucson National. Luckily his foursome had drawn an early tee time. They'd finished up before the worst heat of the day, but he'd been too beat to stay on for the afternoon's festivities and the awarding of trophies. He told Al Parker he had things to attend to at home, and he did. He might be too tired to spend much time in the basement that afternoon, but he still needed to take food there. He owed the girl that much.

The spacious and solitary ranch house was coolly welcoming when he unlocked the front door and let himself inside. He had moved to The Flying C after Gayle's mother died while Gayle stayed on in their El Encanto home. It was an arrangement that suited them, allowing both to maintain a public facade as a happily married couple while leaving them free to follow their individual pursuits.

Larry pulled a beer from the refrigerator under the wet bar and then settled into his recliner—a well-worn Stickley Morris chair—in the living room. He wondered sometimes what would happen when—not if—he was no longer able to live here on his own and look after things. Considering what lay beyond the locked basement door, his having household help—live-in or otherwise—was entirely out of the question. He maintained the parts of the house he used—the kitchen and living room as well as his bedroom and bath and the basement—in reasonably good order. As for the rest of the house? He shut the doors and left it alone.

In public Dr. Lawrence Stryker was often described as a man of action. Here, in the privacy of his own home—alone except for the presence of whatever girl awaited his attentions in the basement—he sometimes allowed himself to wallow in the past and to wonder what would have happened if he had never ventured down this path.

He never knew—Gayle never told him and he never asked—just how she had managed to entice Roseanne Orozco away from the hospital that Wednesday afternoon. It was clear Gayle had done so without being seen and without arousing any suspicion. Their carefully concocted alibis for the night Roseanne Orozco died proved to be unnecessary. No one from Law and Order or the Pima County Sheriff's Department ever bothered asking either one of them about where they'd been or what they'd done.

What never failed to amaze Larry was how everything that had happened—the way his entire life had evolved—had grown out of a single misstep, one that had seemed entirely inconsequential at the time. He and the other young doctors on the reservation had regarded it as little more than a boyish prank, a well-deserved bonus for working at a dinky reservation hospital in the middle of Arizona's godforsaken desert. All of them had been in on it together, the same way they all drank beer and played poker together—card poker, that is. This had been "poker" of another kind.

Whenever one of the girls from the high school—especially one of the good-looking ones—showed up as a patient in the hospital, whoever was in charge of her care would let the others know that the game was on. During evening rounds, the girl's attending physician would administer a high dosage of a sedative—enough to put her under. Later on, one by one, the doctors would drop by her room and have a crack at her. To them it seemed like good clean fun.

The girl would wake up the next morning or after her surgery or procedure and go home none the wiser and no harm done. At least that was the way it was supposed to work—the way it had worked—for years.

AIDS wasn't even a blip on the radar back then (Gayle's brother, Winston, hadn't died of AIDS until sometime during the mid-eighties), but Larry and the others had all, by mutual agreement, used condoms. They did it as much to protect themselves from whatever STDs the girls might be carrying as they did to protect the girls. But then came the night when Larry's condom broke as he was screwing one of his own patients, a girl named Roseanne Orozco, who was due to be released the next day after being hospitalized for a ruptured appendix.

Larry felt the condom break the moment it happened, but he told no one. At first he thought everything would be okay—that he'd get away with it. Several times in the next weeks and months, Emma Orozco brought Roseanne back to the clinic complaining that her daughter wasn't getting any better.

Roseanne was a good-looking but strange fifteen-year-old, who, as far as anyone at the hospital knew, never spoke to anyone. Suspecting the worst, Larry finally admitted Roseanne to the hospital for a whole battery of tests. A pregnancy test was the only one that turned out positive.

He wondered sometimes what would have happened to him if he hadn't told Gayle that very afternoon as soon as he knew Roseanne's test results. What if Gayle hadn't taken matters into her own hands? No doubt he would no longer have a license to practice medicine, and he certainly wouldn't have spent the last twenty-five years as one of Tucson's most well-respected citizens. The aftermath of Roseanne Orozco's murder changed him forever—and it changed Gayle as well.

In the months that followed, Gayle evolved into an entirely different person. He had known she was smart and ambitious, but now it seemed some previously unknown toggle switch had been moved to the "on" position. She was at him all the time. Sex had never before been an issue between them. Now it was.

Gayle would be waiting for him in the evenings when he came home from rounds. "Did you fuck anybody tonight?" She'd ask the question pleasantly enough, the same way she once might have inquired after his day, but they both knew there was far more to it than that.

Larry always told her no. As it turned out, that was the truth. In actual fact, Roseanne Orozco had cured Larry Stryker of abusing patients, but Gayle wasn't buying it.

"Show me," she'd say. "You may be passing it out across the street, but you'd by God better have plenty left for me when you get home."

She'd take him to bed then, expecting him to perform—demanding that he perform—but the more she wanted, the less Larry could deliver. Then, after he'd done what he could, she'd drift off to sleep, and he'd lie in bed for hours, wakeful and yet aroused, wondering what was happening to him and imagining that sooner or later someone would catch on and come looking for them.

He got rid of the Camaro almost right away, within days of Roseanne's murder. Worried that some hotshot detective might find lingering traces of blood on the floorboards and seats, Larry drained most of the oil out of the crankcase before taking off, at high speed, to drive into Tucson. Not unexpectedly, the engine overheated and caught fire just west of Three Points. The charred remains of the vehicle were hauled off to a junkyard, and the insurance company made good on Larry's claim without so much as a raised eyebrow.

One day, Larry arranged to be in the hospital records room all by himself and he picked up Roseanne's file. He got a rush out of carrying it from the room in front of God and everybody. The next time he and Gayle went to visit The Flying C, Roseanne Orozco's complete medical history went into Calvin Madison's burning barrel along with the rest of that day's trash.

With those two sets of damning details out of the way, Larry expected things to get better, but as time passed, they grew steadily worse. Caught between alternating bouts of arousal and paralyzing fear, there were some scary moments when Larry thought he might lose his mind completely. By Easter break of the following year, Larry was convinced he was headed for a nervous breakdown. That was when Gayle decided they should go to Mexico for the weekend.

They flew to Mazatlán from Phoenix and checked into one of the nicest hotels on the beach. Gayle, who had learned fluent Spanish from the *braceros* and housemaids who had worked on The Flying C, told Larry she was going out shopping. Rather than accompany her, he chose to spend most of the day brooding in the bar—drinking tequila and chasing shots of Jose Cuervo with chilled bottles of Dos Equis. He was more than a little drunk when he finally returned to their room in the late afternoon.

Gayle, wearing only a terry-cloth wraparound, met him at the door. "I have a surprise for you," she said, letting him into a room darkened by blackout curtains. "Come in and close your eyes."

Larry did as he was told. After leading him into the middle of the room, Gayle left him standing there long enough to switch on a bedside lamp.

"Okay," Gayle said. "Now you can open them."

Larry did so and was astonished to see a very young and very naked Mexican girl spread-eagled on the bed. Long black hair fanned out behind her on the sheet and pillow. Her thin brown arms were lashed to the headboard with brightly colored silk scarves. Other scarves, tied to her ankles, were attached to the foot of the bed. As Larry stared at her, the girl blushed nervously.

"What the hell?" Larry demanded of Gayle.

She walked over and allowed her cool lips to graze his. "I know you haven't had much fun lately," she said. "And I thought it was time you did. It's all right," she added. "Daniella here knows what's going on, and she'll be well paid. She'll do whatever you want."

"Right now?" he asked stupidly. "With you here?"

"What did you think I meant?" Gayle returned. "It's okay. Everything's going to be fine."

Larry was half drunk and more than a little embarrassed. The last several times he'd tried to make love to Gayle he'd been totally unable to perform. For the better part of a minute he said nothing. "What if I can't get it up?" he croaked finally.

It cost Larry Stryker a lot to say those words aloud. If the booze hadn't loosened his tongue, he never would have managed to, but Gayle seemed unperturbed by this painful admission. With a shrug of her shoulder, she walked as far as the glass coffee table and retrieved a partially emptied beer bottle. Draining it in one long, graceful swallow, she returned to Larry, holding the now empty bottle in front of her.

"I already thought of that," she said with a patient smile. "Why not try this? And maybe, if I'm lucky, when you're finished with her, you'll be ready for me. Hold out your hand."

Mutely, Larry did as he was told. Gayle formed his thumb and forefinger into a small circle and then threaded the neck of the bottle through them. The glass, flecked with droplets of moisture, was cool and smooth to the touch.

"See there?" she said, moving the bottle back and forth and staring up into his eyes as she did so. "That's not so bad, now, is it."

Mutely, Larry shook his head. She was right—it wasn't bad. In fact, the caressing movement of the cool bottle felt good. But he also shook his head because he really didn't want to do what Gayle was asking. He didn't want to violate the young girl who lay on the bed watchful and waiting. Looking back, that's how it seemed to Larry now—that he wouldn't have done it if Gayle hadn't been there asking him to and egging him on. It was clearly what *she* wanted, and how could he deny her? He owed her everything. Not only was this a chance for Larry to do something for her—it was also an opportunity for him to prove, once and for all, that he was a man.

He reached for the bottle, but Gayle held it just out of reach. "Take off your clothes first," she ordered. Larry complied without a murmur. Once he was naked, she handed him the bottle. "Do it," she urged.

And he did. He approached the girl gently at first. She shrank a little when the cool glass lip of the bottle touched her body, but she lay perfectly still, offering herself to him. The tip of the bottle had barely penetrated her body when Larry encountered unexpected resistance. Feeling the pressure, the girl moaned slightly and tried to dodge, but the bright scarves held her fast.

For Larry, time stood still. He had assumed, from what Gayle had said, that the girl was a hooker or at least experienced, but the barrier blocking his entry meant only one thing—she was a virgin. Trying to come to grips with that reality, Larry looked down at the girl. Her wide brown eyes, pooling with tears, gazed back at him, imploring him not to hurt her. Not three feet away stood Gayle with one eyebrow raised questioningly, as if to say, "Are you going to do it or not?"

Larry had no choice. Abandoning all pretext of gentleness, he rammed the bottle home. The girl's body went rigid. She arched into the air, yelping in pain. Instantly Gayle was beside her. With one hand she stuffed a corner of the pillow into the girl's mouth to muffle her cries. With the other she pressed down hard on the girl's collarbone to help hold her still.

Afterward Larry had no conscious memory of how long he stood there, plunging the damaging bottle in and out of the girl's body. At some point, Gayle was beside him, whispering in his ear, "Now do me," she said.

At first he thought Gayle meant for him to use the bottle. He started to withdraw it, but Gayle shook her head. "Leave it where it is," she said. "You don't need it."

Larry knew Gayle was right. He was ready.

The unnecessary bedding Gayle had peeled from the bed lay in a heap on the floor. She lowered herself into that impromptu cushion and pulled Larry down after her.

Ignoring the girl, who still lay, weeping softly, on the bed above them, Larry Stryker buried himself in his wife's body. When it was over, Larry was convinced that not only was he a man again, he was also incredibly lucky to be partnered with Gayle, who had to be one of the smartest women in the world. And the sickest.

A little past noon, Brandon Walker pulled into the Ortiz Compound on the north side of Highway 86. The old broken-down gas station that had been Fat Crack Ortiz's place of business when Brandon Walker first knew him had been replaced by a spanking-new building—Indian Oasis Mini-Mart. Fat Crack's older son, Richard, sometimes called Baby Fat Crack, ran the mini-mart/gas station operation. One of Wanda Ortiz's nephews ran the tow-truck part of the business, while Leo, the younger son, and two helpers served as resident mechanics.

Behind the mini-mart was what people now referred to as the Ortiz Compound. Three double-wide mobile homes were arranged around a dirt-floored ramada. The interior patio was shaded by a roof made of spiny ocotillo stalks held together by a net of chicken wire. One house belonged to Wanda and Fat Crack. The other was for their son, Richard, and his wife, Christine, a teacher from the school at Topawa. The third one, clearly empty now, had once been occupied by Fat Crack's younger son, Leo, and his wife, Delia.

Brandon went directly to the front door of the house that belonged to Wanda and Fat Crack and rang the bell. Wanda Ortiz, smiling, opened the door and let him inside.

"He told me you'd be coming," she said. "He's out back. Come on this way."

Wanda led Brandon through the house to the back door. Where once there had been three steps, there was now a sturdy wheelchair ramp.

"He's down there," Wanda said, pointing.

Brandon made his way down the ramp and into a gloom of shade. Fat Crack sat in the far corner of the space, dozing in a wheelchair.

Brandon had last seen Gabe Ortiz several months earlier, when he had come to Christmas dinner at Gates Pass, leaning heavily on a walker. The wheelchair was something new. It was warm but not quite hot in the late-April noonday sun. Even so, a blanket covered Fat Crack's lap and was tucked in behind his legs.

"Gabe?" Brandon asked quietly.

Startled awake, Fat Crack looked straight past Brandon and asked, "Who is it?"

He's blind, Brandon thought. *Completely blind.* "It's me, Gabe," he said aloud, swallowing the lump that rose suddenly in his throat. "Brandon Walker."

Fat Crack relaxed. The corpulence that had given him his name was long gone. He seemed shriveled and old, with leathery skin as transparent and thin as parchment. "It's good to see you, Brandon. Sit down. Make yourself comfortable. There must be another chair somewhere."

Brandon helped himself to a plastic lawn chair and dragged it close to Fat Crack's. The shiny white surface of the plastic had been burned away by the sun. Worried that the chair might be too sun-damaged and brittle to hold his weight, Brandon tested it gingerly before settling on it.

"How come you knew I was coming?" he asked. "More of that spooky medicine-man stuff you and Lani are always talking about?"

Fat Crack laughed and pulled a cordless telephone receiver out from under the blanket that covered his lap. "Not even," he said. "Diana called. She wanted to know if Wanda had any tamales and tortillas you could buy and take home for dinner tomorrow. The tortillas aren't ready yet, but they will be. Just don't forget them when it's time to leave. Diana will kill you."

"How are you?" Brandon asked.

"As blind as Looks at Nothing used to be," Fat Crack answered with a chuckle. "Maybe that's one of the medicine-man rules that *S'ab Neid Pi Has* forgot to tell me—that medicine men are supposed to be blind." He paused. The smile on his face faded. "I'm an old man, Brandon," he added. "I'm old and I'm dying."

There it was then—all the cards laid out on the table. "Lani's worried about that," Brandon admitted. "She wants to be here to help."

"I know," Fat Crack replied. "But there's nothing she can do. She'll want me to check into a hospital and have me taking shots and pills. I'm not doing that, not even for Lani."

"No," Brandon said. "I suppose not."

"When will she be home?"

"Sometime in the next two weeks," Brandon answered. "Graduation is on the tenth of May, but she'll be home before that. She's skipping graduation and has rescheduled her finals."

"Then I'd better hurry," Fat Crack said. "If I could walk, I'd do what Looks at Nothing did and go out in the desert someplace by myself." He paused again. "I don't like being a burden," he added. "It's so hard on Wanda—harder on her than on me. But let's not talk about that anymore. It's not why you came to see me."

Fat Crack Ortiz had been Brandon Walker's friend for decades. The thought of losing him hurt like hell, but now that Fat Crack had changed the subject, Brandon did the same.

"It's true," Brandon agreed. "Emma Orozco came to see me yesterday. She wanted to know if I could help find her daughter's killer, but I'm sure you already know that."

Fat Crack nodded. "What did you say?" he asked.

"I said it's been a long time since her daughter died. More than thirty years."

"A long time to wait for justice," Fat Crack observed.

"Yes," Brandon said.

"Are you going to help her?"

"I'm going to try, but why did she wait so long?"

Fat Crack shrugged and said nothing.

"She indicated her husband didn't want her to pursue it. She waited until after he died."

Fat Crack nodded. "Some people always thought Henry did it—that he got Roseanne pregnant and then killed her because he was afraid Emma would find out. No one ever proved he did anything wrong."

"Nobody ever disproved it, either," Brandon offered.

"Yes," Fat Crack said. "That's right."

"What do you think?" Brandon asked.

"Henry Orozco was a good man," Fat Crack answered finally, echoing what Diana had said. "I know that some men do bad things to their daughters, but not Henry. You could ask his other daughter, Andrea. She's Andrea Tashquinth now. She's the produce manager over at Basha's."

"Andrea Tashquinth is one of the people I planned to see today," Brandon said. "You're right. She works at Basha's, and Emma said she'd be working today."

"Good," Fat Crack said.

"You remember when it happened, then?" Brandon asked.

"Oh, yes. I remember."

"Were there any other suspects?"

"Not that I know of," Fat Crack said, "although I don't think anyone looked very hard."

Both men were quiet for a moment, both thinking the same thing—that had Roseanne Orozco been an Anglo, more would have been made of her death and the search for her killer might well have been successful.

"Would you do me a favor?" Fat Crack asked.

"Sure," Brandon agreed quickly. "What do you need?"

Fat Crack reached under his blanket. From the same place where he had retrieved the cordless telephone, he now produced a leather bag—a *huashomi*—Looks at Nothing's fringed buckskin medicine pouch, one the scrawny old man had always worn around his thin waist. The pouch was far more threadbare now than it had been the first time Brandon Walker had seen it in the parking lot of the Pima County Sheriff's office almost three decades earlier.

Fat Crack had brought Looks at Nothing to the department and had waited patiently until Brandon showed up hours later. And there, under a mesquite tree next to the parking lot, Brandon had watched the old medicine man deftly fill and roll a homemade cigarette using *wiw*—Indian tobacco—rather than the unfiltered Camels Brandon had smoked prior to quitting several months earlier. After lighting the hand-rolled cigarette with an old-fashioned Zippo lighter that must have dated from World War II, Looks at Nothing had taken a long drag. Then ceremoniously saying the word *nawoj*—which, Brandon later learned, in the context of the Tohono O'odham Peace Smoke, means friendly gift—he passed it along, first to Fat Crack and then to Brandon Walker.

It had been Brandon's first encounter with the Peace Smoke. He had been startled by the sharp, bitter taste. Only with the greatest of effort had he managed to keep from coughing. But even then, with the smoke still singeing his throat and lungs, Brandon Walker understood that he'd been allowed entry into something special—something most Anglos didn't experience in a lifetime.

He watched now as Fat Crack once again extracted that same familiar lighter from the bag. "Would you help me? Wanda doesn't like me to do it. She's afraid I'll burn the place down."

"Sure," Brandon said. "I'll do my best."

Even though Fat Crack couldn't see to critique what he was doing, Brandon Walker felt self-conscious as he clumsily rolled the tobacco into a ragged imitation of a cigarette. "Now what?" he asked when he finished.

Wordlessly, Fat Crack handed him the lighter. The brass was worn thin. The grooves on the wheel had disappeared completely. To Brandon's surprise, it lit after only one try. He held the sagging cigarette to his lips long enough to light it, then passed it to Fat Crack. "*Nawoj*," he said.

They passed the cigarette back and forth between them several times. When it was close to burning their fingers, Brandon took it and ground it out in the dirt while the silence between the two men lengthened until it seemed to stretch on forever.

"They're all lost girls, you know," Fat Crack said thoughtfully.

Brandon felt as though he'd lost track of the conversation. "Who are?" he asked.

"Roseanne, Delia, and Lani."

"Delia your daughter-in-law?" Brandon asked.

Fat Crack nodded. "Delia's mother saved her and I brought her home. You and Diana saved Lani and are giving her back to The People. And I'itoi has chosen you to speak for Roseanne."

Brandon was taken aback by Fat Crack's suggestion. It seemed unlikely I'itoi would exhibit the slightest interest in an aging and discarded Anglo homicide detective, but the medicine man spoke with such conviction that Brandon couldn't help believing it was true.

"Someday they'll be friends, you know," Fat Crack said at last.

Again Brandon was confused. Maybe the bitter tobacco was messing with his mental faculties. "Who'll be friends?" he asked.

"My daughter-in-law and your daughter," Fat Crack replied. "Delia and Lani. They're both smart. They'll do good things for The People, and eventually they'll be friends."

"I thought they were friends already," Brandon said.

Fat Crack sighed, shook his head, and said nothing. For a moment or two he fumbled around with the blanket on his lap until he once again located the lighter. He gathered it up, along with the few remaining pieces of paper, and stuffed all of them into the *huashomi*. Then he picked up the bag and held it out toward Brandon.

"What's this?" Brandon asked. "What am I supposed to do with it?"

"Take it," Fat Crack said. "I don't need it anymore.

When Lani comes home, give it to her. Tell her Looks at Nothing and I—two old blind *siwanis*—both wanted her to have it."

"All right," Brandon said. "I will." He stood up. He knew what Fat Crack was saying, knew what this meant. "Thank you," Brandon added.

"You're welcome," Fat Crack said. "Now go find Wanda, and see if those tortillas are ready."

eleven

After a time the children and the butterflies came back to I'itoi, and the children were singing a new song. The children ran and danced as they sang, while the butterflies circled high above them.

This is the song the children sang as they danced with the butterflies:

> They are so bright, they are so gay,
> They run in the air and hide, and we
> Cannot catch them.

I'itoi *listened for the song of the butterflies, but the butterflies did not sing.*

There were some birds resting in the cottonwood tree above where I'itoi *was sitting. When the butterflies did not sing, u'uwhig—the birds—began to laugh.*

The birds had been very jealous when they first saw hohokimal—*the butterflies—come out of* I'itoi's *bag. The butterflies were so beautiful. But now, when the butterflies had no song, u'uwhig laughed and sang and laughed.*

Then I'itoi *began to laugh, too. So did all the children. For, you see, nawoj—my friend, when Elder Brother made the butterflies, he fell asleep. And all the children went to sleep, too. And so the poor butterflies were given no song. Their beauty is always bright. They do not change as they grow old, but the butterflies have no song.*

Erik had just started back down the mountain when it happened. A piece of loose rock gave way under his foot. His right ankle twisted inside his boot, and down he went. On the steep mountainside the fall might have been disastrous. Fortunately, he slid face-first into a clump of mesquite. The roots of that hardy desert-dwelling shrub were strong enough to hold his weight. He ended up with his face, hands, and arms scratched and bloody, but at least he wasn't dead. It was still a hell of a long way down the mountain, but it could have been much worse.

As the injured ankle began to swell, he loosened the laces, but he didn't dare remove the boot altogether. He could probably hobble down the trail but only with the boot on. Going barefoot wasn't an option. Neither was using his cell phone to call for help. That was one of the lessons in self-reliance Grandma had drilled into Erik's head as a boy: "Don't call for help too soon. Wait until you really need it."

Not that she had squandered any time lecturing him about it. Gladys Johnson had taught her grandson self-reliance the old-fashioned way—by example. When her husband, Harold, returned from the Battle of the Bulge a crippled and broken man, Gladys did what had to be done. She found a job as a grocery-store clerk and sup-ported both her husband and her daughter. When the doctor said that the VA hospital in Tucson, Arizona, of-fered Harold the best chance of recovery, she'd packed up her family and driven there in a '53 pickup truck, hauling her family's worldly possessions in the back of the pickup and in the flimsy trailer she'd hitched on behind the truck.

When Gladys and Harold's daughter died of cancer at age twenty-five and their grieving son-in-law had dropped six-month-old Erik off on Gladys's doorstep shortly thereafter, saying he couldn't do it, he just couldn't do it, Gladys had handled that as well. And she had done it all without complaint.

So get yourself up off your butt and start down the damned mountain, Erik told himself that sunny April morning. *As Grandma would say: "If it is to be, it is up to me."*

Wanda Ortiz came out to the ramada a few minutes after Brandon Walker drove away with two dozen each of tamales and flour tortillas packed in a foam ice chest.

"It's getting hot out here," she said to her husband. "Don't you want to come inside?"

"No," Fat Crack replied. "I'm fine."

Shrugging and more than a little exasperated, Wanda returned to the house, leaving Fat Crack where he was. The chill Gabe Ortiz felt in his bones right then had little to do with the weather. He and Brandon had smoked the Peace Smoke many times over the years. Doing so today had been Fat Crack's own friendly gift, a way of saying thank you and good-bye. But now that it was over—now that he had given away the medicine pouch and the sacred tobacco, he was left with a terrible sense of *neijig*—of foreboding.

Fat Crack had grown accustomed to having glimpses into the future. For instance, when Leo and Delia had come to the house to tell them Delia was pregnant, Fat

Crack had known at once that the baby would shrivel and die in his mother's womb. Fat Crack hadn't told Leo and Delia that dreadful news. He had kept it to himself, just as he also had not betrayed his knowledge that this new baby, another little boy, would thrive and grow up to be tall and strong.

With his old friend Brandon Walker, Fat Crack knew something wasn't right. Had the medicine man still possessed Looks at Nothing's precious crystals, even without his eyesight they might have helped him clarify in his own mind exactly what was happening. As it was, he was cursed with a sense that something was wrong without any means of preventing whatever it was from happening.

Fat Crack wondered if his disquiet could have something to do with the very thing he had spoken with Brandon about—the coming conflict between two powerful women, between Delia and Lani. Closing his eyes, Fat Crack remembered the first time he had seen them both, these two women whose power struggle might well divide the Desert People. With Lani it had been the day he and Wanda had picked the little Ant-Bit Child up from the hospital and taken her to the Walkers' place in Gates Pass. And even as they did it—even as they delivered the little Indian baby into the hands of the Anglos who would be her parents—Fat Crack had been blessed with the unerring sense that he was doing the right thing. With Delia Chavez Cachora Ortiz, things weren't nearly so clear-cut.

Sister Justine had summoned Gabe Ortiz to Topawa early that long-ago Wednesday morning. He had driven there in the old blue-and-white tow truck that had come with the business when he'd purchased it years earlier.

The truck was disturbingly unreliable. There was always a chance the tow truck would need to be towed back to Sells, along with whatever vehicle Fat Crack had been summoned to aid.

Under the Mother Superior's watchful eyes Fat Crack examined a derelict 1960 Falcon that was gathering dust in the garage behind the convent. When he emerged from under the hood and self-consciously pulled his sagging Levi's back up, he realized that someone else had joined them. Even in the shadows, he recognized Ellie Chavez and could see the ugly bruises and cuts that marred her otherwise smooth skin. Beyond Ellie, peering out from behind her mother's skirt, stood a little girl with enormous brown eyes—Delia. The child observed the proceedings with more than childlike interest, as though she understood that this discussion would impact her life in ways she could not yet fathom.

"Can you make it run?" Sister Justine asked.

Fat Crack rubbed the thin stubble on his chin. "Sure," he said. "But it'll cost money."

"How much?" Sister Justine asked.

Nervously, Fat Crack hiked his pants up again. As Mother Superior of the convent and principal of Topawa Elementary School, Sister Justine was known to drive a hard bargain. "Two hundred, maybe," he said.

When he said the words, both Delia and her mother gasped aloud. It was a sum that went far beyond their meager ability to pay. Sister Justine was undeterred.

"Two hundred maybe, or two hundred, really?" she asked.

"Two hundred really," Fat Crack conceded, knowing that if the repairs turned out to be more expensive than that, he'd have to eat the difference.

"How soon can you have it ready?"

"Tomorrow morning?" Fat Crack asked hopefully.

Sister Justine shook her head so forcefully that the stiff material of her veil snapped and crackled like jeans on a clothesline flapping in the wind. "Today," she insisted. "Registration at ASU ends tomorrow. Ellie has to get registered for school, find a place to live, get the kids enrolled in school and day care and be ready for classes to start on Monday. Tomorrow will be too late."

"Getting it fixed today would take a miracle," Fat Crack argued.

But Sister Justine had made up her mind. "You'd better get started, then," she said. "Miracles don't grow on trees, you know. They take work and time."

All that day, while Fat Crack had labored over making the Falcon run, Delia Chavez lingered in the background, watching everything he did. This was long before Fat Crack Ortiz met up with Looks at Nothing, long before the aged medicine man had charged his middle-aged protégé with becoming a medicine man, too. As a consequence, while Fat Crack worked, he had no glimmer about what the future might hold for Delia Chavez. He thought she and her mother would be away from the reservation for a matter of months, not years. He had no idea that he was helping send both of them into an exile that would last almost thirty years. And he had no hint that someday he—Fat Crack Ortiz—would be the one to bring Delia back home to the reservation.

With all that had happened in between, Fat Crack was hard-pressed to know whether or not he had done the right thing. If he hadn't fixed the Falcon that day, maybe Ellie and Delia never would have gone away in the first place. For sure, everything would have been different.

* * *

Brandon Walker took his tamales and tortillas and made his way to Basha's. When he had first visited the reservation, there had been two trading posts—the High Store, built on a hill, and the Low Store, not on a hill. You could buy milk and sodas and staples at the trading posts, but buying decent meat or finding fresh vegetables with an actual produce manager had been out of the question. This new store in Sells looked like a regular supermarket in Tucson—smaller, but much the same.

He made his way to the produce department and looked around. The selection was different from what he might have expected in town. For instance, Brandon didn't see any of his personal favorite—eggplant—but what was there seemed reasonably fresh. Across the aisle from the produce was a bank of shelves holding uncooked beans—navy beans, pinto beans, and the more exotic tepary beans, something that had been a staple in the Tohono O'odham food supply long before the arrival of the Spanish and their lard-laden *frijoles*.

A middle-aged woman emerged from a back room pushing a cart loaded with cardboard containers of bananas. The striking resemblance between her and Emma Orozco was enough to tell Brandon this was Andrea Tashquinth.

"Mrs. Tashquinth?" he asked, flashing the windowed wallet that identified Brandon Walker as a member of TLC. "Could I speak to you for a moment?"

Andrea Tashquinth eyed him suspiciously. "What about?" she asked.

"Your sister," he said. "Gabe Ortiz suggested I talk to you. So did your mother."

"I can't talk to you," she said. "I'm working."

Brandon hadn't expected a warm welcome, but this straight-out rejection surprised him. Before he could say anything more, however, Andrea had a sudden change of heart. "I'll be off at three," she said. "I'll talk to you then."

"Fine," Brandon told her. "I'll be waiting right outside."

As Andrea turned away and began unpacking the boxes of bananas, it occurred to Brandon that Fat Crack might be right. Maybe *I'itoi was* helping to solve this case after all.

While a records clerk ran background checks on the name Erik LaGrange, Detective Fellows turned back to Sue Lammers. "I'll have a deputy give you and your dog a ride home," he said. "If we need anything more, I'll be in touch."

"Thank you," she said gratefully. "I'd appreciate it. I'm still pretty shaky."

After flagging down a newly arrived deputy to take charge of Sue Lammers and Ranger, Brian headed for the crime scene. On the shoulder of the road, one of the crime techs was making casts of tire tracks. Ten yards off the road, someone else was taking photos. The detective approached the photographer and found a grisly jumble of bloodied body parts spilled out of several black plastic garbage bags. Stumps of a severed arm and leg showed signs of having been hacked apart at the joints. The head, detached at the neck, lay facedown beneath a clump of blooming prickly pear. And on the ribs and tiny breasts of the naked torso were scores of ugly marks that he recognized instantly as scabbed-over cigarette burns.

Brian had been in Homicide long enough to expect to be immune, but seeing not only the wanton slaughter but also signs of long-term torture caused those last few bites of burrito to rise dangerously in his throat.

"It's pretty rough," Ruben Gomez remarked as Brian turned away, swallowing hard.

The detective nodded. "Whoever did this wasn't interested in concealing the body."

"Just the opposite," Gomez agreed. "In fact, a freight-train engineer just called in a report on it as well. Dispatch told him we're already working the problem."

"Well, well," a brusque female voice commented from behind them. "Welcome to the dumping ground."

Brian and Deputy Gomez turned as associate medical examiner Fran Daly arrived on the scene. Dr. Daly was a sturdy woman with an unruly mop of cotton-white hair. Backlit in bright sunlight, her hair resembled a halo, but her vocabulary was distinctly non-angelic. She was known for showing up at crime scenes and autopsies alike in Western shirts, jeans, and various pairs of Tony Lama cowboy boots. Today her somewhat portly middle sported a wide leather belt with a silver buckle the size of a saucer.

"How's it going, Doc?" Brian asked.

"It was better before I got here," she said, taking in the scatter of dismembered human flesh without blanching. "Only one body, or more?" she asked.

"Just the one, as far as we can tell," Brian answered. "Female Hispanic, somewhere in her teens."

Fran Daly nodded. "Any idea how long she's been here?"

"The initial call came in a little before noon," Ruben Gomez told her. "A witness was out walking her dog and saw what she thought was someone illegally dumping garbage."

"It's illegal dumping all right," Dr. Daly agreed. "So it's not been all that long—an hour and a half or so?"

Brian nodded. "That would be about right."

His phone rang just then. "This is Shelley in Records," the caller told him. "I've got the info you wanted on Erik LaGrange and for the two phone numbers you asked about. Medicos for Mexico is on East Broadway, just west of Tucson Boulevard. It's closed on weekends. The second number is a private residence listed under the name of Professor Raymond Rice, who teaches architecture at the U of A. The number for Erik LaGrange has been disconnected, with calls being forwarded to Rice's number. I also checked with the DMV. I've got a driver's license for Erik LaGrange—not the same address as the one listed for Professor Rice. As far as a vehicle registered to Erik LaGrange? I came up empty there."

"So he's got no priors."

"Not even a parking ticket, as far as I can find."

"Good work, Shelley," Brian told her. "Now give me that address again."

Erik limped down the mountain with his injured ankle screaming at every step. As much as it hurt, Erik was forced to concede that maybe the ankle was broken. *Damn!* he muttered to himself. *Just what I need.*

It was hotter than he expected and he had already consumed the last of his water. Once he reached the trailhead, he could call someone to come pick him up. *Not Gayle, though. Not after last night.*

They had been lying in bed. They were *always* lying in bed, either at his house or hers. Given the reality of Tucson's social milieu and Gayle's standing in same, there weren't many places they could go in public without attracting attention. So they stayed home—his home or hers—ate take-out food, and screwed. Much later, one or the other of them would dress and go home.

"What's wrong?" she asked, tweaking one of the curls

of reddish-blond hair on his naked chest. "You're awfully quiet."

Erik didn't want to say what was wrong. They'd been going through a stormy period for the last several weeks. That happened fairly regularly, but things had been better the last couple of days, and he was reluctant to rock the boat. Gayle Stryker didn't like having her boat rocked.

What was wrong had its origin in a tiny blue envelope that had shown up in Erik's mail earlier that week—an envelope with a birth announcement inside. Ryan and Brianna Doyle had had a baby, a seven-and-a-half-pound boy they'd named Kyle.

Erik and Ryan had met in fifth grade at Hollinger Elementary, and they'd been friends ever since. Five years earlier, Erik had been best man when Ryan and Brianna were married at St. Philip's in the Hills. Receiving a birth announcement from a good friend shouldn't have been an earth-shattering experience, but it was.

Ryan's wedding had happened only weeks before Erik met up with Gayle Stryker, who promptly took over his life. Gayle *became* Erik's life. Since then he'd barely seen Ryan and Brianna. After neglecting them for so long, he was surprised he was still on their Christmas card list, to say nothing of the one for birth announcements. But seeing the picture of the wrinkly-faced, more or less ugly, round-headed baby had brought Erik's own life home to him in an entirely new way. *What the hell am I doing?*

In the beginning, once he got over being flattered and utterly dazzled by Gayle's beauty and attentions, he'd given himself a serious talking-to about the age difference between them. What did it matter if she was almost the same age his mother would have been, had Louise LaGrange lived, that is? Gayle was beautiful, she was rich, and she wanted him. What else counted? Erik had asked her more than once if she ever considered leaving her husband.

She'd laughed and said, "Every day and twice on Sunday," and let it go at that. She never spoke of getting a divorce. She never spoke of making any changes. She seemed perfectly content with the way things were—as if she didn't mind if she and Erik went on the same way indefinitely. And they had done exactly that—for more than five years.

Erik wondered sometimes about what would happen if Lawrence Stryker croaked. The man was pushing sixty-five. According to Gayle, he had lost all interest in sex, or at least all interest in sex with her. He took medication for high blood pressure, and there had been talk about his needing a pacemaker, although, as far as Erik knew, one had never been installed.

So, if Larry died, what then? Would Erik and Gayle's affair evolve into a more normal relationship? Or was normal not what Gayle had in mind?

That was how things stood right up until the day that damnable birth announcement arrived. Thirty-something women were supposed to be the ones with biological clocks, but suddenly Erik heard his own clock ticking loud and clear. He was thirty-five; Gayle sixty-two. Having kids had never been part of their equation, but still . . . Did he want to spend his life with someone almost twice his age? In the little cocoons where they spent their private time together, age didn't matter, but at work sometimes, there were things that struck him— music playing on someone's radio, for instance, or someone else cracking a joke—that made him realize he and Gayle came from different generations.

"Where are we going?" Erik said finally.

"Going?" she asked. "Well, now that we've had dinner and dessert, I'm going home."

"Not that," Erik said. "I mean, where are we going long-term?"

"Does it matter?" Gayle returned. "Seems to me we're doing just fine. What's wrong?"

"Wouldn't it be nice if you didn't *have* to get dressed and go home?" Erik asked. "If we could live together like normal people?"

"Like husband and wife, you mean?"

He nodded. "That, too."

Gayle's eyes blazed with immediate fury. "You've met someone, haven't you!"

"No," Erik said quickly. "Nothing like that. I swear to God."

"You're tired of me, then?"

"No. Of course not. You're wonderful—the best thing that ever happened to me."

But by then Gayle had already hopped out of bed. She pulled on clothing without taking her usual detour through the master bedroom's spacious shower.

"What, then?" she continued. "You probably want to go find some sweet little twat to have babies with! From what I've heard, having babies is vastly overrated."

Gayle's words bristled with so much hostility that Erik couldn't bring himself to say she was right. In the face of her fury he couldn't admit that having a regular life—with a home and a wife and a couple of kids, and maybe even a dog—was exactly what he wanted.

As Gayle strode down the hallway, buttoning her blouse, Erik went after her. "Come on," he said. "Why are you so upset?"

She rounded on him so suddenly that he almost

smashed into her. "*Why?*" she demanded. "If you're not smart enough to figure it out, I'm not going to tell you."

He caught up with her when she stopped in the kitchen long enough to slip on the high heels she had shucked off when she came in through the garage earlier in the afternoon.

"Please, Gayle," Erik pleaded, touching her shoulder. "Don't do this. It's all a misunderstanding."

She shrugged out from under his hand. "Misunderstanding?" she asked, glaring up at him. "I don't think so. I read you loud and clear!"

When they were in the bedroom—hers or his—she was always careful to keep the blinds closed and the lights properly dimmed. But out here in the kitchen with its bright fluorescent lighting and with anger distorting her features, the lines a team of skilled plastic surgeons usually kept at bay were clearly visible. Seeing them Erik realized suddenly that Gayle Stryker was old—old and shrill and very, very angry.

Once she sped out of the garage, Erik's first reaction was relief. This wasn't how he would have chosen to end their relationship, but ending it was probably a good idea—if he ever was going to have a chance at a "normal" life. But then, after the first shock wore off, Erik realized how much else would be ending as well—his love life, his job, his company car. Those were all irretrievably intermingled. His involvement with Gayle affected every aspect of his life. Walking away from her meant walking away from everything else.

When that realization hit him, he tried calling her cell phone—the one on a family-plan program that he and Gayle shared and where the bill never showed up at the offices of Medicos for Mexico. Erik called several times. She never answered, and he didn't leave a message.

Erik had spent the rest of the night trying to figure out how he would manage in a Gayle Stryker–free world. The future had looked pretty bleak and dismal to him in those black predawn hours. Now, reduced to almost crawling back down the mountain on his hands and knees, it looked even worse.

twelve

Brandon sat in the Suburban outside the super-market, watching people come and go, as he waited for Andrea Tashquinth to get off work. The more he thought about losing Fat Crack, the sadder he became. There had been many losses in Brandon Walker's life, and no matter how many times it happened, dealing with the loss never became any easier.

In giving Looks at Nothing's medicine pouch to Lani, Gabe Ortiz was passing a torch that possibly had been handed down from one medicine man to another stretching all the way back to that ancient medicine woman, *Kulani O'oks.*

Brandon was a born and bred *Mil-gahn.* Try as he might, he could never quite reconcile in his mind how Fat Crack Ortiz could be both a devout Christian Scientist and a powerful medicine man. Was the same thing true for Lani? How could she possibly return to the Tohono O'odham Nation as a full-fledged physician and also as a medicine woman? Yet neither Fat Crack nor Lani seemed to have any doubt that these two seemingly dia-metrically opposed ideas would someday become reality.

Brandon understood why Fat Crack had entrusted the medicine pouch to his old friend. He was saying good-bye. It meant Fat Crack knew he was dying. *And what exactly am I supposed to do about it?* Brandon wondered.

He pulled his cell phone out of his pocket. Much to his surprise, he had a full signal. He could call Lani right then if he wanted to, but should he? If that's what Fat Crack had wanted—if he expected Lani to hurry home to be with him—wouldn't he have said so?

In the end, Brandon put the phone back in his pocket and continued to mull over what had transpired. Why, for instance, was Fat Crack so troubled that Delia and Lani weren't friends?

Brandon had never given much thought to Delia. He knew she was the tribal attorney. He knew, too, that she had married Fat Crack's younger son, Leo. Wanda had told Diana something about a family squabble that had resulted in Leo and Delia's moving out of the Ortiz Compound and into what had once been Delia's aunt Julia's place in Little Tucson. Wanda had been heartbroken about it, especially considering that Delia was even then pregnant with this boy child who would be the first grandson to carry on the Ortiz name.

Thinking back on the pained expression on Fat Crack's face when he had mentioned Delia and Lani, Brandon wondered if perhaps the breach within the Ortiz family had something to do with the Walkers. Maybe that was the reason Fat Crack had wanted to be certain Looks at Nothing's medicine pouch went to Lani.

I'll be sure she gets it, Brandon vowed as he opened the glove box and placed the medicine pouch inside.

When he looked up again, Andrea Tashquinth was standing outside the supermarket's sliding door and surveying the parking lot. Brandon slammed the glove box shut and locked it. Then he opened the door to the Suburban, motioned Andrea inside, and went to work.

* * *

Larry Stryker woke up from his unintended nap and was surprised to see how much time had passed. The beer in the bottom of the bottle was too warm to drink. Looking at his watch, he sighed. Larry was tired. The morning heat had taken it out of him. Tomorrow he'd tell Al that he was through with golf for the summer. It was too damned hot to play.

For two cents he would have retreated to his room right then, undressed, and gone to bed. Still, tired as he was, he really did need to go downstairs and feed her. Whatever else Larry had in mind, he had no intention of starving the girl.

Had Gayle dropped by, he might have risen to the occasion and done something more creative, as he usually did on Saturday afternoons, but Gayle continued to be so besotted with Erik LaGrange that her showing up wasn't likely. To Gayle's credit, she didn't flaunt her boy toys around Larry, and he was grateful for that. He was also grateful for what few crumbs of attention she deigned to give him now and then.

He went into the kitchen and dropped a hamburger patty into a dirty frying pan. Tired as he was, he found himself looking forward to the feeding. What was this one's name again? He liked to call them by name occasionally, but in order to remember, he'd have to check in his most recent notebook. He kept a record of each girl's name there, along with a set of her photos.

Down in the basement, this one would smell the meat frying. She'd be expecting the food and dreading it at the same time, but today she had nothing to fear. Physically Larry wasn't up for anything more than watching her eat. He'd often let the girls go hungry for a while— twenty-four hours was just about right. When they were that famished, watching them eat was a real turn-on. He particularly liked the greedy way this one tore into her food. Even though he knew she didn't want it and would have preferred to starve herself to death, but when she was hungry enough, she couldn't help herself, either.

It intrigued him that all the girls seemed to have one thing in common: they were terribly self-conscious about eating in front of him. It was almost as though having him observe them eat made them forget how to perform the simple mechanical functions of chewing and swallowing. He wondered sometimes if their shyness was due to the fact that he was watching, or if it was because they were always naked when they ate—they were naked and he wasn't.

Once, before he began relying on the premade hamburger patties, one of them had choked on a chunk of gristle in the piece of meat he had given her. She had choked and gagged and finally spit it out, but he had forced her to eat it anyway. She had chewed and chewed and chewed for what seemed forever before she was finally able to choke it down. That was the ultimate power over someone—to know you could, if you wanted, force them to eat their own vomit.

That was actually what Larry liked most—having them fear him. The more his girls tried not to submit, the better he liked it. When he was with Gayle, she was the one who called the shots, but that was about her needs, not his. In the basement, he was the one in control, but even there Gayle held the ultimate veto power. She would arbitrarily change girls on him. Just when he had one trained the way he wanted, Gayle would take her away. Then he'd have to do without until she came up with a replacement. Fortunately there was always a new girl available. Gayle would make a few inquiries, and within days or weeks, a new one would appear, drawn from the plentiful stock to be found at one of the many detention centers served by Medicos for Mexico.

Larry wondered sometimes about that first girl in Mazatlán—the one Gayle had served to him with her limbs bound by Gayle's own brightly colored scarves. After her "session," the girl had been given money and food and sent on her way, but all that had happened while Larry was in the shower. Gayle told him she had helped the girl dress and had taken her home, but now, given what had happened to the ones who had followed in her footsteps, Larry doubted that was true. The way Daniella was starting out—Larry had no difficulty remembering her name—she most likely would have turned into a two-bit whore. Gayle had probably done the little slut an enormous favor by putting her out of her misery before she had a chance to grow up. As for the girls since then? For them, too, growing up had never been in the cards.

Carrying the plate of food—the hamburger patty, a spoonful of cold refried beans, and a chunk of stale tortilla—Larry went to the basement door and unlocked it with the key he always carried on his belt. As soon as the door opened, he knew something was different. The emptiness of the place blew up around him—along with a coppery telltale odor he recognized at once. Even before he started down the stairs, he knew what to expect. Still, he was astonished by the carnage Gayle had left in her wake.

Usually when this happened, Larry had done something wrong. Either he'd made some kind of blunder at work or done something Gayle didn't approve of, and this was her way of punishing him for it. She never told him in advance when she was going to rob him of his latest plaything, and she never did it while he was home. Gayle would come to the house, use her own keys to gain access, and then leave the mess for him to find—and clear away—on his own.

Shaking his head, Larry returned to the kitchen and dumped the food into the garbage. Then he went out to the garage for the power washer he would need to take the bloodstains off the basement's polished concrete floors and walls.

When she murdered Roseanne Orozco, Gayle Stryker had been cleaning up after her husband. One way or another, Larry had been cleaning up after Gayle ever since.

Gabe "Fat Crack" Ortiz sat in the warm sun and considered his life. By Tohono O'odham standards, he had lived to a ripe old age—seventy-two. More and more he was thinking about what Looks at Nothing had once told him.

"I have lost my sight," *S'ab Neid Pi Has* had told his new protégé as they raced toward Diana Ladd's Gates Pass home in Fat Crack's speeding tow truck. "I have not lost my vision."

Only lately had he begun to have a partial understanding of what had happened eight years earlier, when Delia's great-aunt Julia Joaquin had come to see him. As one of the movers and shakers in the village of Little Tucson, the old woman was ushered into the tribal chairman's office with appropriate ceremony. Fat Crack had greeted her formally and in their native language. He'd been prepared for a certain amount of small talk, but Julia got straight to the point.

"Do you remember my sister's daughter, Ellie Chavez?" Julia asked. "And her little girl, Delia?"

Fat Crack had closed his eyes and remembered that little girl with her luminous brown eyes, watching him from the shadows of Sister Justine's garage as he labored to put the dead Falcon back together. He remembered how, later on, he had heard that Ellie Chavez had finally divorced her husband about the same time she graduated from college. He had also heard rumors that she'd taken a rich Anglo woman to be her lover, but Gabe Ortiz paid little attention to gossip.

"I remember them both," he said. "I knew them when Ellie was leaving to go to school—left and didn't come back."

Julia frowned. "Things were bad between her and Manny. When one of the sisters from Topawa found a way for Ellie to go to college, she didn't want to miss the chance. I lost track of Ellie years ago, but I've stayed in touch with Delia. Her mother has a doctorate now and lives somewhere back east."

"And Delia?" Fat Crack asked. "The last I heard she was going to law school."

Julia Joaquin nodded. "She works for the BIA in Washington, D.C."

"I'm glad to hear it," Fat Crack said. "We need good Indian lawyers in Washington."

"I'm worried about her, though," Julia said. "I'm afraid something's wrong. She's married now, to that Philip Cachora."

"Philip Cachora?" Fat Crack repeated. "From Vamori?"

"From Vamori originally," Julia said. "He met Delia at some fancy party in Washington."

Gabe Ortiz closed his eyes and considered the odds against such a thing happening. The idea that two people born a few miles apart on the same Arizona Indian reservation would meet, fall in love, and marry in a big city on the far side of the continent seemed highly unlikely.

"Philip Cachora has been gone for a long time, too."

"Even longer than Delia," Julia Joaquin agreed. "He went off to Santa Fe to become an artist. And I guess he did, too."

"Why are you worried?" Fat Crack asked.

"She doesn't say anything, but her letters are different now," Julia said. "And since you're going to Washington . . ."

When she mentioned that, Fat Crack finally understood part of the reason for Julia Joaquin's visit to his office. Tohono O'odham tribal chairman Gabe Ortiz, along with leaders from several other reservations in the Western states, was due to attend an Indian gaming conference to be held in Washington, D.C., the following month.

"She might not appreciate my interference," Fat Crack said uneasily.

"I don't expect you to do anything," Julia said quickly. "But I thought if you could just see her, maybe you could tell me if she's okay."

And that's when he understood the rest of it. The tribal council was sending the tribal chairman on a mission to Washington. Julia Joaquin was sending a medicine man.

"All right," he said. "I'll see what I can do. How do I reach her?"

Julia reached in her pocket, pulled out a piece of paper, and handed it over. On it was a street address but no phone number.

That was why, a month later, late in the day, Fat Crack found himself standing on Kalorama Street in front of a three-story walk-up. The information operator had informed him that the telephone number for Philip Cachora was unlisted, leaving Fat Crack no choice but to show up unannounced on Delia and Philip's doorstep.

Approaching the door of the building, Fat Crack rang the bell next to their name and waited for several minutes. Finally, when he was about to walk away, a disembodied male voice spoke through an intercom. "Yes?"

If this was Philip Cachora, his voice was strangely slurred. "Is Delia here?" Fat Crack asked.

"Who wants to know?"

"My name is Gabe Ortiz—a friend of hers from back home."

"I don't remember her mentioning you."

"She might have known me as Fat Crack."

"Fat Crack?" Philip repeated slowly. "The guy with the tow truck?"

"That's right."

"Just a minute. I'll be right down."

Less than a minute later, the front door opened. A slight young man—a blond teenager—burst out of the doorway and then hurried down the street at a half-trot, shoving in his shirttail as he went. A full minute later, another figure appeared at the door—this one recognizably Tohono O'odham.

Philip Cachora was a burly man in his midforties. He exhibited all the obvious traits of an urban Indian gone to seed. He stepped outside the front door and pulled it closed behind him. When he let go of the door, Philip stumbled and faltered. He had to place one hand on the building's outside wall to steady himself. His breath reeked of beer. The distinctive odor of marijuana clung to his hair and clothing.

"Delia's not home," he muttered.

"When do you expect her?"

Reflexively, Philip glanced at his watch, then shrugged. "Don' know," he mumbled thickly. "After. She's at a meeting somewhere."

Philip Cachora had been away from the reservation for a long time, but time and distance had yet to strip him of his distinctively Tohono O'odham manner of speech. "Why'dya want her?"

There was more than a hint of belligerence in his voice. Fat Crack Ortiz had dealt with enough pissed-off drunks to read the signals and be wary. Philip was two decades younger and much heavier than him. That didn't make Philip tougher than Fat Crack, but it did make him dangerous.

Without having to be told, Fat Crack knew much of what was going on. It made him sad. All those years ago, Ellie Chavez had taken her young children and fled her abusive husband. By doing so she must have hoped to save them all. Despite Ellie's best efforts, her daughter had married a man much like her own father. No wonder her letters to Julia Joaquin had changed. She was probably too embarrassed to admit that she was repeating her mother's mistakes.

"I was thinking about offering her a job," Fat Crack replied.

In actual fact, he hadn't been thinking about it until the words burst unbidden from his mouth. He had known for months that Elias Segundo, the current tribal attorney, was thinking about retiring due to ill health. It wouldn't have been right to start a job search for his replacement before Elias was ready, but now . . .

Philip looked at Fat Crack speculatively. "What kind of job?"

Before Gabe Ortiz could answer, a shiny black Saab

nosed its way up to the curb and stopped in a passenger-loading zone. Leaving the car with its flashers blinking, an Indian woman wearing a smart red wool suit and matching high heels stepped out. Delia Cachora's long black hair was pulled back and fastened in a smooth bun at the base of her neck. She had grown into a strikingly attractive woman. What Fat Crack instantly recognized, however, were her wonderfully luminous eyes. Those hadn't changed.

"What's going on?" she asked, glancing apprehensively between the two men.

"Guy here wants to offer you a job," Philip muttered. "I'm going to buy myself a drink."

Delia was clearly embarrassed by her husband's behavior. "I'm sorry," she said, holding out her hand. "Things have been a little rough for Philip lately, but I must apologize, Mr.—"

"Don't apologize," Fat Crack said. "My name's Ortiz, Gabe Ortiz. You might remember me as Fat Crack."

It took Brian Fellows half an hour to get from the Fast Horse Ranch crime scene investigation to Professor Rice's foothills address. Brian drove up Pontotoc Road and stopped in front of a low-slung faux-adobe house with bright blue trim. A maroon four-wheel-drive Toyota Tacoma pickup truck with a matching camper shell sat parked on half the driveway in front of a closed two-car garage. Jotting down the license number, Brian called it in to Records. Within a minute Shelley had an answer for him. The Tacoma was registered to Medicos for Mexico. If this was Erik LaGrange's company vehicle, it might explain why there was no vehicle registered in his own name. It was also possible that Brian would find Erik LaGrange himself inside the house.

As Brian considered his next move, a woman at the house directly across the street came down her long graveled driveway hauling a wheeled garbage container behind her.

Brian got out of his car. At his approach, the woman placed both hands on her hips and regarded him suspiciously. "Can I help you?"

He offered her a glance at his identification wallet. "I'm curious about your neighbors, the ones who live here," he said, pointing.

"The Rices?" she asked. "Frieda and Ray are out of town right now. They're in Europe somewhere. They're not expected back until the beginning of fall semester."

"That's their truck, then?" Brian asked, pointing.

"Oh, no," the woman responded. "That belongs to their house-sitter. I don't know him except to see him on the street, but he seems like a very nice young man. Clean-cut. Quiet. Never causes any trouble. He seems to spend quite a bit of time with his mother. That's not something you see too often with most young people."

Brian paused long enough to write himself a note: "Check out LaGrange's mother."

When he looked back up, the woman was frowning. "There's nothing wrong, is there? I mean, he's not in any trouble or hurt or anything, is he?"

"No, ma'am," Brian said politely. "No trouble so far as we know. Just making a few routine inquiries. Thanks so much for your help."

Leaving his Crown Vic parked where it was, Detective Fellows walked up to the driveway, toward the Rices' front door. As he ambled past the parked pickup, Brian caught sight of a dark red smudge on the back bumper. He had been in homicide long enough to recognize something that looked suspiciously like blood. On the shady side of the car he paused and felt the tires. Enough heat lingered in the rubber for Brian to be reasonably sure the truck had been driven sometime during the day.

Getting warmer, Brian thought to himself. *And not just the tires, either.*

He checked to make sure his weapon was well within easy reach, then he walked up to the front door and rang the bell. While he waited for someone to answer, he examined the door and casing. Both were painted blue, but at arm level he spotted yet another suspicious smear.

Brian Fellows rang the bell again and waited for the better part of a minute before giving up and returning to the Crown Vic where, once again, he called in to the department. "I may be onto something," he told Lieutenant James Lytle, the weekend supervisor in Investigations. "I'll need a second detective out here—a detective and a warrant. Tell PeeWee I'm sorry to spoil his day off."

While he waited for PeeWee Segura to show up, Brian called home as well. "I'm still on that case," he told Kath when she answered. "It's just starting to heat up. No telling when I'll be home."

As an experienced officer for the Border Patrol, Kath Fellows knew all about the vagaries of law enforcement. "Fair enough," she told him. "I won't wait up."

thirteen

ndrea Tashquinth climbed into Brandon's Suburban and shut the door. "I don't know why Mother's doing this," she said. "Bringing it up after all this time won't do any good."

"Your mother's looking for closure," Brandon told her.

"Closure?" Andrea repeated bitterly. "What's the point? Roseanne died, and the cops always thought my father did it. They never arrested him. Nobody ever proved it, but it wrecked Daddy's life. People talked about him behind his back. He knew it. We all did." As she spoke, Andrea Tashquinth had been staring down at her lap. Now she looked up at Brandon defiantly.

"Mother told Sam—"

"Sam?" Brandon interrupted.

"My husband. He's the one who gave Mother a ride into town yesterday."

Brandon nodded, remembering the invisible son-in-law who had waited patiently outside their Gates Pass home for several long hours the previous day.

"Mother told him," Andrea resumed, "that you're doing this for free. I can't believe that's true. Mother doesn't have much money, Mr. Walker. She won't be able to pay you anything."

"As I told her yesterday, Ms. Tashquinth, your mother doesn't have to pay. Neither do you. TLC offers its services free to people like her. We take on old homicide cases and try to solve them. There's no charge—no financial charge, that is—but there is a cost," he added.

Andrea's dark eyes narrowed. "What's that?" she demanded.

"The cost is in pain for you, your mother, and for everyone else connected to your sister—the very real pain of bringing it up again. You may think you've forgotten all about it," he added, "but once you allow yourselves to remember, it'll be as real as if it happened yesterday."

Suddenly, amazingly, Andrea Tashquinth began to sob. "I know," she said. "It already is. I think about it every day because . . ." she added, "it's all my fault."

The story came out then in fits and starts. "I was almost two years older than Roseanne," Andrea said. "When I went to first grade, there weren't many jobs on the reservation and our parents were both migrant workers. They went away for months at a time. Whenever they were gone—to California or Washington or Oregon—Roseanne and I stayed at home with our grandmother—our father's mother—in *Ak Chin.*"

"Arroyo Mouth," Brandon Walker responded in English.

Andrea cast him a sidelong glance. She wasn't accustomed to *Mil-gahn* who spoke Tohono O'odham. Once again, just as it had with Andrea's mother the day before, Brandon's facility with the Desert People's native language allowed her to relax a little as she continued.

"When I went off to school on the bus that first day, Roseanne cried and cried. Our grandmother was a mean old woman, and Roseanne didn't want to be left alone with her. When I came home, I told Roseanne there were kids her age in another class, and she begged me to take her along. The next day, I told my grandmother that Roseanne was supposed to go, too. It was a lie, of course, but Grandmother didn't know any better. She let us go.

"When we got to school, everything was fine until Roseanne realized that she couldn't be in the same class with me. She got scared and started to cry. She cried so hard that finally the principal came. He was a big man—a huge man. He picked Roseanne up and carried her under his arm like a sack of potatoes. She kicked and screamed the whole way down the hall. I went after him and kept telling him to put her down, put her down, but he didn't. He carried her all the way back to his office. He threw her into a closet—a coat closet with no light inside it—and slammed the door. Then he made me go back to class. I heard her crying all the way down the hall.

"I didn't see her again until after school—until it was time for us to get on the bus. When she did, Roseanne's face was still wet like she had been crying the whole time. On the way home, I tried to get her to talk to me and tell me what happened. She wouldn't answer—wouldn't say a word. And she never talked again. Not to me, not to my parents, and especially not to anyone at school.

"She went to school because my father made her. She never answered questions in class or turned in papers. My parents took her to a bunch of doctors, here and in Phoenix, too, but they couldn't find anything wrong. When the doctors couldn't help her, my father even took her to a medicine man. He said she was retarded. There was nothing he could do—that's how she was."

Brandon Walker looked down at his own white skin and was suddenly ashamed. He felt a surge of anger toward that brutish grade school principal whose actions had so traumatized an innocent four-year-old girl that she had damned herself to a lifetime of silence.

The worthless son of a bitch! he thought. *Somebody should have thrown his ass in jail.*

"Two years later there was a new principal, a nice one," Andrea continued. "When the school secretary told him what had happened, he fixed it so Roseanne and I were in the same class. She was my shadow."

"*Ehkthag,*" Brandon said.

Andrea Tashquinth looked Brandon full in the face and smiled for the first time. "Yes," she agreed. "Roseanne was my *ehkthag.*"

"Whatever happened to the first principal?" Brandon asked.

Andrea shrugged. "Nothing," she said. "He left. Went somewhere else. When *Mil-gahn* do bad things on the reservation, they leave, but nothing ever happens to them. That's the way it is—the way it's always been."

After Philip staggered off, a humiliated Delia Cachora stood on the sidewalk looking at Fat Crack Ortiz, this ghost from her distant past. She had felt this same way the day her father had come to Ruth's house in Tempe to collect Eddie and take him back to the reservation.

When they arrived in Tempe, Ellie Chavez had planned to stay with Sister Justine's friend, Ruth Waldron, just that one night. They arrived late in the evening because it had taken so long to get the car running. Then they'd encountered a summer rainstorm that made the washes between Quijotoa and Casa Grande impassable. They'd had to wait for the water to go down.

When they finally stopped in front of the small frame house, they had passed through the worst of the storm, but a fitful rain still fell. It was late. Eddie had fallen sound asleep in the backseat. As soon as the car stopped, an outside light flashed on and a tall bony woman—the tallest *Mil-gahn* woman Delia had ever seen—emerged onto the porch. A cloud of mouthwatering fragrances drifted out of the house behind her, and Delia realized she was hungry.

Ellie stepped out of the Falcon. Taking Delia by the hand, they hurried up onto the porch and out of the rain. "Miss Waldron?" Ellie asked tentatively.

Ruth Waldron stretched out both hands in greeting. "You must be Ellie," she said. "Please call me Ruth." She turned to Delia, who wavered on the edge of the porch like a wild thing poised for flight. Ruth bent down until her face and Delia's were on the same level. "You must be Delia," she added with a toothy smile. "Now where's that brother of yours? Where's Eddie?"

Delia pointed to the car. "He's sleeping," she whispered.

"I'm sure you're all worn out," Ruth said kindly. "Sister Justine called and told me you were on your way. Go get Eddie and come in. Supper's waiting. By the time we finish eating, maybe the rain will be over so we can bring in your suitcases."

The next day, however, much to Delia's surprise, her mother didn't go apartment hunting after all. Instead, they stayed on with Ruth for the next four years—for as long as Ellie Chavez was in the undergraduate program at ASU. While Ellie was busy studying, Ruth Waldron, a phys ed teacher at two Tempe elementary schools, became Eddie and Delia's surrogate mother. She was good to the kids. She took them to ball games, to the zoo, and to the Arizona State Fair. She helped them with homework and attended PTA meetings when Ellie couldn't.

Delia loved school. At first she was far behind other kids in her class. She was lumped in with the slower ones and pretty much ignored, but with her own natural capabilities and with Ruth's nightly tutoring sessions at home, Delia soon bubbled to the top.

Neither Delia nor her brother saw their father again until four years later, the summer Eddie turned six and Delia twelve. Delia Chavez was within days of promotion to the eighth grade when, on a warm spring afternoon, she came home from the library with an armload of books and with her little brother in tow. As they approached the house, an unfamiliar pickup truck was parked in the front driveway. Manuel Chavez stood on the front porch, shouting at Ruth Waldron and at Ellie. Delia knew at once her father was just as drunk and angry as she remembered him.

"I want my son!" he yelled for all the neighborhood to hear. "You'd better give Eddie back to me before you turn him into an Anglo and a queer, too."

Eddie had been so young when they left Sells that he had no recollection of this man who claimed to be his father, but if this loud stranger wanted to take Eddie somewhere in a shiny pickup truck, the boy was eager to go.

While the children looked on, the argument raged back and forth. In the end Ellie agreed that Eddie would return to the reservation with his father.

To Delia, the whole thing was incomprehensible. It had taken the next several years for her to come to terms with what had happened that day on Ruth's front porch. How could her mother bear to send Eddie off with a horrible drunk who was a virtual stranger? How could she let him go without putting up a fight? It wasn't a matter of legal custody. As far as Delia knew, there had never been a divorce or a court order or any exchange of legal documents. Ellie simply handed Eddie over even though she must have known what the consequences would be. She must have guessed that once Manny drove away with her son, she would never get him back. He would disappear into the world of the reservation and into his father's family and be lost to her forever.

That was exactly what happened. Ellie and Ruth may have spoiled Eddie, but his Grandmother Chavez in Big Fields was far better—or worse—at spoiling. Eddie had grown up fat and lazy and every bit as much of a drunk as his father. When he graduated from eighth grade, he quit going to school, and Manny made no attempt to change his mind. Eddie contacted Delia only when he needed money—when he had wrecked his latest pickup or when he had been let out of jail and needed something to get by on until he could find a job for day wages.

As a twelve-year-old, Delia hadn't understood all the implications of what was being said on the porch, nor did she realize how much went unspoken beneath that flurry of angry words.

Delia's seventh-grade assessment of the situation was that her brother was a stupid, spoiled brat. That being the case, why had Manuel come to Tempe for Eddie and not for Delia? Why had he collected his crybaby son—someone who'd had to repeat kindergarten—and not his straight-A daughter? Why was Eddie worthy of being returned to the reservation when Delia was not?

Eventually, in high school, Delia understood more about the dynamics of the relationships involved. It took that long for her to grasp what was really going on between her mother and Ruth Waldron—a former Benedictine nun with strong connections to an old Boston family. Both women were exiles—Ellie from the reservation and Ruth from her convent and her disapproving family. Ellie and Ruth had been lovers almost from the beginning, from the night Ruth took the reservation refugees in off the street and welcomed them into her home.

Years after that, when Delia was in law school, she finally grasped the kinds of pressures her father could have brought to bear if Ellie hadn't given in to Manny's demands for Eddie. Lesbian mothers had no rights in those days. If Ellie had defied her husband, she'd have risked losing both children rather than just one. A legal fracas might also have cost her the postgraduate fellowship she'd been offered. And a public furor might have wrecked Ruth's career with the Tempe public schools as well. Gay and lesbian schoolteachers didn't start coming out of the closet until decades later.

To their credit, Ellie and Ruth were still together, all this time later. For years, during summer vacation, Ruth would come and stay with Ellie and Delia wherever they were. Now that Ruth was retired, she and Ellie lived comfortably together in a little house Ruth had inherited just outside Cambridge, Massachusetts. With her Ph.D. in education and her impeccable Native American credentials, Ellie Chavez had served a long stint with the BIA and was a much-sought-after consultant in the field of American Indian education, even though, after leaving the reservation that rainy August day, she had never returned to Sells, not even once.

Standing on the sidewalk in D.C., Delia Cachora was at a loss as to what she should do. She was delighted to see Fat Crack Ortiz and wanted to invite him up to their apartment, but after seeing the condition Philip was in, she worried that the apartment would be too much of a mess. Fat Crack solved the problem for both of them.

"If you'd give me a ride back to my hotel, perhaps we could talk there."

Delia was relieved to open the passenger door and let him in. When she handed the keys over to a parking valet, her 9000 blended in perfectly with other vehicles waiting in line at the Four Seasons.

Once they were seated in the lounge and had ordered drinks, Fat Crack grinned at her. "Accommodations for Indians are nicer around here than they were in the old days," he said. "At least when the Great White Father is paying the freight."

By then Delia had collected herself and she was able to smile back. "Yes," she said. "Things have changed."

Gabe Ortiz told her about his position with the tribe and explained how he'd come to Washington for an Indian gaming conference, but that still didn't make clear to Delia why he'd come looking for her.

"Did my mother's aunt Julia send you?" she asked.

Fat Crack searched her face in a way that made Delia feel he was peering into her soul. "Yes," he admitted finally. "Julia Joaquin did ask me to drop by. She's concerned about you. She wanted to know whether or not you're happy, but that's not why we're having this talk."

Delia felt a sudden rush of anger. She barely knew her busybody great-aunt. Had Delia passed Julia Joaquin on the street, she doubted she'd recognize her, yet Aunt Julia felt she could interfere in Delia's private affairs. It took a moment for Delia to realize Fat Crack had stopped talking and was waiting for her response.

"Why are we?" she asked finally.

"Have you ever thought about coming back to the reservation?" Fat Crack asked.

Delia shook her head. "Never," she said. "I like D.C. I love my job, and I haven't been near the reservation in years. Why would I want to go back there?"

"Your aunt tells me that you're very bright, that you're working as a lawyer for the BIA. What do you do there?"

"I study treaties," she said, relaxing a little. "My job is to try to make sure agreements that were supposed to last as long as the 'grass shall grow and rivers flow' continue to have meaning in the modern world. If a tribe signed a treaty about fishing rights a hundred years ago, one they haven't revised, then the treaty should still apply right now."

"Are you having any luck?"

"Some," Delia said. "Those *Mil-gahn* treaty writers were pretty damned tricky."

They both laughed at that.

"You mentioned fishing," Fat Crack resumed a moment later. "Does that mean you deal with mostly Northwest tribes?"

"No, they're from all over. Fishing rights. Timber rights. Mineral rights. Grazing."

"Gambling, too?"

"That's not usually mentioned, but we're maintaining that since the tribes are sovereign nations, it's implied."

"We're going to need a new tribal attorney," Gabe Ortiz said abruptly, without any additional preamble. "Elias Segundo is about to retire. I'm offering you the job."

Delia was dumbfounded. "Based on my aunt Julia's recommendation?" she asked. "Have you looked at my academic record, talked to my supervisors?"

"No," he said, after a moment. "I've done none of those things, but I can see you're your mother's daughter. That's good enough for me."

"You're serious, then?"

"Yes."

"Surely someone who's lived on the reservation all his life would be more qualified than I am."

"You'd be surprised," Fat Crack replied. "Or maybe you wouldn't. Young people on the reservation, especially the girls, haven't had the benefit of your education or experience."

Delia thought about that for a few moments—about all the girls whose mothers hadn't been able to do for their daughters what Ellie Chavez, with Ruth Waldron's help, had done for her.

"You want me to be a role model?"

"You would be," Fat Crack said. "You're one of the Tohono O'odham's lost girls. If you came home, maybe others would, too."

"My husband would never agree to go back," Delia told him finally. "This is where his business is—his gallery, his friends." She didn't add "and his drinking and drugging buddies," but she didn't have to. Fat Crack Ortiz already knew about that. He'd witnessed it with his own eyes.

"It might be good if Philip went home," Fat Crack suggested. "Reconnecting with your roots could be good for both of you."

It was one thing for Delia to agonize about her husband's difficulties. Having this relative stranger offer advice about them offended her. She put down her drink. "No," she said slowly. "I don't think it would. Philip will be fine, and so will I. He'll find his way." She stood up then. "Thanks so much for the offer, Mr. Ortiz. I really appreciate it, but I can't accept. Now, if you'll excuse me, I need to get home."

"Sure," Gabe said. "I understand."

As Delia walked away, she knew it was true. Fat Crack Ortiz understood far more than she wanted him to.

After spending most of the night awake, Lani didn't wake up until early afternoon. In the kitchen she made toast and a pot of coffee, then she settled in to study. For some reason she couldn't keep her eyes open. No matter how hard she tried, the words on the pages drifted into nonsense and her head drooped.

Sometime later, a ringing telephone startled her from a sound sleep. As she reached for the phone, she glanced at the clock. It was four o'clock in the afternoon.

"Lani?"

"Wanda?" Lani asked, struggling to recognize the woman's voice. "Is that you?"

"Yes," Wanda Ortiz said. "I went outside to check on him, Lani. Fat Crack's gone."

"Gone?" Lani took a deep breath and closed her eyes. There was no need to ask what "gone" meant. "I'm coming home," she said. "I'll call Mom and Dad first, then I'm on my way. I'll be there as soon as I can."

It took several hours to contact her various professors and make arrangements for her finals as well as for having her belongings packed and shipped home. Once that was accomplished, she called for airline reservations. The only flight available meant she wouldn't arrive in Phoenix until early afternoon the next day. Only after purchasing her ticket did Lani try calling her parents.

She knew from experience that when dealing with offspring, her dad was a far softer touch and more understanding than her mother. Diana was the tough one—the disciplinarian. Brandon was a pushover. From the time Lani was tiny, she had been smart enough to play both those ends against the middle.

She tried her dad's cell phone first, but he didn't answer. She hung up, but before she could dial again, her own phone rang.

"Lani," Diana said uncertainly. "Honey, I'm so sorry to have to tell you this. I just heard from Wanda Ortiz and—"

"It's all right, Mom," Lani interrupted. "I already heard. Wanda called me, too. I'm on my way. I'll be on the Northwest flight from Minneapolis that gets into Phoenix at one tomorrow afternoon. I'll catch the shuttle from there home."

Lani expected her mother to say she shouldn't come rushing home, but Diana surprised her. "Don't even think about the shuttle," she said. "Someone will be there to meet you."

"Thanks, Mom," Lani managed. They both heard the catch in her throat. "See you tomorrow."

fourteen

They say it happened long ago that the Tohono O'odham first came to the northern lands looking for new hunting grounds. Because it was very hot and dry, the first thing the hunters needed to find was water. In some mountains with very steep slopes they came upon a hollow shaded by mesquite trees, and in this hollow was a pool of water. There was a rock in the middle of the pool and on it sat a coyote.

When Coyote looked up and saw the hunters, at first he was very frightened because he didn't know what the hunters would do to him. Then he looked back into the pool and said in a very loud voice, "Stay down there. Don't come out and hurt these people."

This, nawoj, my friend, was back at a time when the Indians and the animals all still spoke the same language. When the hunters heard this, they were very puzzled because coyotes usually run away and hide somewhere.

The hunters stopped at the edge of the water and looked around, but they could see nothing. Finally, one very old man stepped nearer and asked Coyote why he was talking.

"Can't you see?" Coyote asked. "I'm talking to my

people who live in this pond. I do not want them to come out and kill you."

The hunters were surprised and told Coyote that they did not know his people lived in the water. Poor Coyote was trembling with fright but he answered bravely. "Oh, yes," he said. "Up here many coyotes live in the water except when they hunt." And then, looking back down into the water he said, "Do be quiet and let these people have some water."

And so, one by one, with Coyote watching, the hunters came to the pond and drank. After that, whenever Coyote saw the hunters coming, he would hurry to the pond. And there he would be, sitting on his rock, where the hunters first saw him.

And that, nawoj, is where the village of Ban Thak— Coyote Sitting—is to this day, near the rock where Coyote sat to guard his pond.

"Please tell me about your sister," Brandon said to Andrea.

"What do you want to know?"

"Everything. Was Roseanne smart?"

Andrea Tashquinth stared off into the middle distance. "I think she was smart," Andrea said finally. "When someone told a joke, she'd laugh along with everyone else. She never did any homework, but she could read. She loved reading books, especially the Bible. One of the nuns at Topawa told my parents there was a convent where she could go, a contemplative convent— where no one was allowed to speak. When our mother told Roseanne about it, she smiled and nodded. It was something she would have been good at and someplace where she would have fit in."

"Did she have boyfriends?"

Andrea shook her head adamantly. "No. Never. We

didn't hang around with boys the way some girls do. Our parents wouldn't let us. They wanted us to be good girls. They didn't want people to think we were too easy."

"But Roseanne was pregnant when she died," Brandon pointed out. "How do you think that happened?"

Andrea Tashquinth shrugged and didn't answer.

"You say Roseanne didn't have a boyfriend, and both you and your mother seem to think your father had nothing to do with it. Besides your father, then, were there any other men or boys who were around your house regularly? A visiting cousin or younger brother, perhaps?"

"No," Andrea answered. "Not that I remember."

"What do you remember, Ms. Tashquinth?" Brandon asked.

It was warm sitting in the Suburban with the hot afternoon sun beating down on the roof. Through the windshield, Brandon saw families with laughing children pile out of pickups, vans, and SUVs. They trailed in and out of the store, returning with carts piled high with groceries. Silence lingered for several long moments. Brandon Walker was content to keep quiet forever. Andrea was the one who blinked.

"It had to be at the hospital," she whispered finally. "I tried to tell Law and Order that at the time, but nobody was interested in what I had to say. Nobody listened."

"What hospital?"

"That one," Andrea said, gesturing with her head in the direction of the Indian Health Services Hospital just up the road. "That summer Roseanne got sick and had to have her appendix taken out. After she got out of the hospital, she was supposed to be better, but she wasn't. When school started that year, she was too sick to go. Finally, my mother took her to the doctor. He put her in the hospital for tests. When they let her out, Dad was supposed to go pick Roseanne up after work to bring her home. When he got there, she was already gone. Everyone assumed that she had just walked out of the hospital on her own. We never saw her again. The next week somebody found her body in an ice chest out along the road."

"You believe something happened to her while she was in the hospital the first time, for the surgery?" Brandon asked.

Andrea Tashquinth turned so she was looking Brandon square in the face. "I know something happened to her," she said fiercely. "I think my sister was raped."

"By whom?"

Andrea's diffidence returned. "I don't know. Someone who worked there, maybe? An orderly or a nurse. They had a few male nurses back then. Or maybe it was someone who was at the hospital visiting someone else."

"You told this to people at the time?"

"Tried to," Andrea said. "But I was sixteen. No one was interested in my opinions."

"Especially since they were all convinced that your father was the culprit."

"Yes," Andrea agreed.

"Did your parents or anyone else ever ask to see Roseanne's medical records?"

"I doubt it," Andrea said. "When I told them that I thought something had happened to Roseanne at the hospital, my parents didn't listen, either."

"What made you think that?" Brandon asked. "Did she say anything to you about it—communicate anything?"

"No. It was just a feeling I had. It was probably nothing."

Maybe not, Brandon Walker thought to himself as he jotted a reminder in his notebook.

That was one thing TLC had taught him. When you were doing cold-case investigations, you had to be willing to follow up on the dead leads everyone else had ignored.

By the time Erik reached Pontotoc Road, he looked as though he'd been through a war. His clothes were a mess. He was dusty, hot, thirsty, bloodied, and sweaty, and his ankle hurt like hell. He was sure now that it wasn't broken, but it was badly sprained. What he wanted to do was shower and then ice the damned thing, although this late in the game, icing was probably beside the point.

He was surprised to see a cop car with a single occupant parked in front of his house. Erik hobbled up to the vehicle.

"What's up?" he asked as the officer rolled down the window. "Is something wrong?"

The cop hustled out of the car. "My name's Detective Brian Fellows," he said, flashing a badge. "I'm an investigator for the Pima County Sheriff's Department. And you are?"

Erik glanced at his truck to see if it had been damaged in some way, but the Tacoma was fine and still parked where he'd left it. "I'm Erik LaGrange," he replied. "I live here. What's going on?"

"You seem to be hurt," the officer responded without really answering. "What happened?"

"I fell while I was up on the mountain."

"When was that?"

"A while ago. I don't know exactly. I'm on my way inside to shower and ice my ankle. You still haven't told me what's up."

Just then a second sheriff's department vehicle pulled up and parked. A second plainclothes officer stepped out and hurried over to Erik and Detective Fellows.

"Got it," the second cop said to the first one, who nodded. The meaningful glance that passed between them gave Erik an uneasy feeling. This wasn't just a routine neighborhood disturbance call. Something was going on—something out of the ordinary.

"This is my partner, Detective Hector Segura," Detective Fellows said. "This is Mr. LaGrange."

Instinctively, Erik held out his hand. Instead of taking it, Detective Segura reached into his jacket pocket and removed a folded paper, which he placed in Erik's outstretched hand. Erik unfolded the document and examined it. For what seemed like the longest time the words didn't penetrate, didn't register.

"A search warrant?" he stammered finally. "You want to search the house? My house? My car? How come? What the hell's happening here?"

"A young woman was found murdered in the desert near Vail this morning," Brian Fellows said easily. "Your business card was found among what we believe to be her effects."

"Somebody's dead? Near Vail? I haven't been anywhere near Vail in years. I know nothing about any dead girl. I have no idea why she would have had one of my business cards, but I work with a lot of people. Someone else could have given her one."

Erik heard the rising hysteria in his voice. He couldn't help that any more than he could quell a growing sense of panic. Obviously these two cops thought he had something to do with this poor murdered girl, but how could that be?

"Please, Mr. LaGrange. Don't get yourself all worked up."

Worked up? he thought. *What the hell am I supposed to do?*

When Erik spoke next, he made a concerted effort to sound calm and reasonable. "Look, you guys," he said. "There must be some kind of mistake. I had nothing to do with whatever happened. And what about probable cause? It's a long way from finding a business card to getting a search warrant. You can't just walk in here and—"

"Would you mind stepping this way, Mr. LaGrange?" the detective named Fellows asked, leading the way to the tailgate of Erik's Tacoma.

He was polite enough, so Erik voiced no objection.

"Take a look at that." Detective Fellows pointed to something on the bumper—a brown stain of some kind.

"I've never seen that before," Erik said. "What is it?"

"From my training and experience, I'd have to say it looks like blood," Detective Fellows said. "Do you mind if we open this up?"

"I . . ." Erik began.

"You'll find this vehicle specifically mentioned on the warrant," Fellows added. "Go ahead, Detective Segura."

Slipping on a latex glove, the other detective twisted the latch and raised the back door on the camper. Then he stood to one side, allowing all three of them to peer into the bed of the pickup. The smudge on the bumper had been baked brown in the sun. The pools of blood that lingered in the bed of the truck were still clearly red. Erik's knees gave way beneath him. One of the officers grasped him by the elbow and kept him upright.

"Easy," Detective Fellows said, leading him toward

one of two waiting Ford Crown Victorias. "You'd best take it easy for a while. Are you armed, Mr. LaGrange?"

"Armed?" Erik asked. "Are you kidding?"

"Sir, would you please lean up against my vehicle . . ." Detective Fellows said.

Not believing his senses, Erik did what he was told. He stood with his hands on the Crown Victoria's blistering hot hood and with his legs spread apart while the detective patted him down. Moments later, his backpack was removed and his hands were behind him, secured with some kind of plastic handcuff.

"You're not carrying any needles, are you? Or any illegal substances?" Detective Fellows asked the questions in an easy, conversational voice, but nothing in his tone could calm the quaking of Erik's heart or fill the terrible sinking feeling that was growing in the pit of his stomach.

"No," Erik said. "I've got nothing on me and nothing to hide."

"These are the keys to your house?" Fellows asked, removing Erik's key chain.

"Yes," he said. "The small one with the rectangular top is the key to the front door." He sure as hell didn't want these bozos breaking down the door.

Taking the key chain, Detective Fellows tossed it to the other cop, who caught it in midair, turned on his heel, and headed toward his house. As Segura hurried away, Fellows opened the back door to the Crown Victoria and motioned Erik inside. "Please have a seat, Mr. LaGrange."

"Wait a minute," he objected. "Are you placing me under arrest? Don't I get a lawyer or something?"

"Just have a seat," Detective Fellows said more firmly.

With the cop holding his head down to keep him from banging it on the top of the door, Erik slipped into the backseat. As he did so he caught sight of several of Professor Rice's neighbors and a bunch of openmouthed kids watching in amazement.

Shit! Erik thought. *This can't be happening.*

But it was. It surely was. At that very moment, the cop started reading him his rights, just as they did on that *Cops* show on TV. Only now, Erik LaGrange was the "bad boy" they had come for, and there was evidently nothing he could do to stop them.

With Erik LaGrange secure in the back of the Crown Vic, Brian Fellows headed toward the front door of the house, where he met PeeWee coming back out.

"What have we got?" Brian asked.

"Plenty," PeeWee said grimly. "I don't think this is where he killed her, but you can bet Erik's our guy, all right. I found a machete soaking in bloody water in the kitchen sink and what looks like bloody footprints on the living room carpet."

"We'd better call in CSI," Brian said.

"Already did," PeeWee told him. "They're on their way."

Brian stood for a moment scanning his notebook. Nowhere in Sue Lammers's statement was there any mention that the man unloading the body had walked with a limp.

But that was then, he said, putting his notebook away. *Whatever's wrong with LaGrange's leg could have happened later.*

Erik sat in the patrol car—at least he assumed that's what it was—and tried to decide what to do. Should he demand an attorney? On television, the guys who started squawking that they wanted an attorney were always the ones who were guilty and who knew their way around the law enforcement jungle.

But what should *Erik* do? He wasn't guilty. He still wasn't sure what had happened. They'd told him that a girl was dead, but who was she and how could she have anything to do with him? And how had all that blood—it really was blood—got in the back of his truck? The Tacoma's bed had been perfectly clean the last time he looked inside the camper shell. Erik had watched the guy vacuum it two days earlier, when he took it to the car wash at Speedway and Country Club. In fact, the vacuuming was the main reason he'd given the cleaning crew a nice tip.

And if he was going to call a lawyer, who the hell should it be? Before last night he wouldn't have hesitated. He'd have picked up the phone and called Rob Whistler. Rob was a good friend of Larry and Gayle Stryker. For the past three years, Rob had held a seat on the board of directors of Medicos for Mexico. As far as Erik knew, Rob had no dealings with criminal law, but he'd know someone who did. He'd have connections and know the right person to suggest.

But considering the situation between Erik and Gayle at the moment, Erik didn't think calling Rob was such a good idea. No, this was something Erik was going to have to figure out all by himself.

Just then the two cops returned from the house. As Erik watched them walk toward him, the grim set to their faces made the knot in his stomach grow even larger.

Detective Fellows leaned down and looked inside the car. "Let me ask you this, Mr. LaGrange. Do you own a machete?"

"Sure," Erik admitted at once. "I brought one back

from Mexico last year. I bought it from a dealer at one of the open-air markets. Why? What about it?"

"Where was this machete of yours the last time you saw it?" Detective Fellows asked. Despite the ominous words, his voice once again exuded nothing but kindness and sweet reason.

"In my bedroom," Erik said. "At the bottom of my underwear drawer."

"I see. And what time did you leave your house this morning?"

"I don't know. Early. Five-thirty or six. Why?"

"And where did you go?"

"Up Finger Rock Trail."

"Did you go by yourself or with someone?"

Even Erik could tell his story sounded lame. "By myself," he answered.

"Did anyone see you up there?" Fellows asked. "Anyone who could verify that they saw you there?"

Erik thought about the other hikers on the trail—the ones he had deliberately avoided because he was so upset over what had happened between him and Gayle.

"I saw a few people," he conceded, "but I doubt they saw me."

"Anyone from around here who might have seen you go?"

Erik shook his head. "You'd have to ask them. When I left the house, it was early on a Saturday. If anyone else was up by then, I didn't see them."

"And you left your truck here? How come?"

"The trailhead's not far up the road. I was going on a hike. Why ride when you can walk?"

"Does anyone else have keys to your vehicle or access to your home?" Fellows asked.

Erik shook his head and said nothing.

"What did you do yesterday?" the detective asked.

"I went to work."

"Until?"

He shrugged. "Five-thirty or six. I'm on salary. I don't have to punch in and out."

"What did you do after that?"

"I came home."

"Alone or with someone?" Fellows asked.

That was the moment when Erik LaGrange finally got a glimmer of just how much trouble he was in. If the murder had happened while he was with Gayle, she could give him an alibi—if she would, that is. But if she did that, it would blow the whistle to Larry, and everything about Erik LaGrange's private life would become public knowledge.

"You know," he said, "if you don't mind, maybe I'd better have an attorney present before I answer any more questions."

When Andrea got out of the Suburban and headed off across the parking lot, Brandon Walker glanced at his watch and was amazed to see how much time had passed. Prior to the interview, he had turned his cell phone on silent. Now, when he took it out and switched it back, he had a total of five missed calls. He scrolled through the list. Two from home, one from Lani, one from Davy, and another from the home of Gabriel Ortiz in Sells.

Without bothering to return any of the calls, Brandon put the Suburban in gear and headed for the Ortiz Compound on the far side of the highway. Seeing the number of cars parked around the three houses, Brandon knew before he ever went inside that Fat Crack Ortiz was no more.

That son of a bitch, Brandon muttered under his breath. *He told me he was going, but I didn't think it would be this soon.*

Fat Crack's boys, Leo and Richard, were already there. Brandon retrieved the cooler containing the homemade tamales and tortillas Wanda Ortiz had given him earlier. Knowing he was looking for their mother, the two sons nodded to Brandon as he passed. "She's inside," Baby Fat Crack said.

A woman Brandon recognized as Delia, Leo's wife, met him at the door and made as if to bar his way. "I brought back some tamales and tortillas," he explained. "Is Wanda here?"

He could tell that Delia Ortiz was getting ready to send him packing when Wanda called to her daughter-in-law from the living room. "It's all right, Delia," she said. "Let him come in."

Without a word, Delia took the proffered cooler and headed for the kitchen. Brandon found Wanda in the living room sitting alone on the couch.

"I'm so sorry," Brandon said.

"I know." Wanda sighed. "But it's all right. He was ready."

"Have you thought about a service?" Brandon asked after a pause.

Wanda nodded. "The funeral will be held at the gym at the high school at four o'clock Monday afternoon. The minister from the Presbyterian church will do the service. We plan to bury him at *Ban Thak*. The cemetery at Coyote Sitting is where Fat Crack's parents are buried and his aunt Rita as well."

"But a Presbyterian minister?" Brandon asked dubiously. "All this time I thought . . ."

"That Fat Crack was a Christian Scientist?" Wanda

returned, cutting Brandon off in midsentence. "That's right. He was, but Christian Scientists don't believe in funerals. I grew up a Presbyterian, and I do. Besides, the funeral's for me and the kids and for The People. What Fat Crack wanted or didn't want's got nothing to do with it."

"I see," Brandon said. And he did.

As he drove back home to Tucson sometime later, he was struck by something. Both Wanda Ortiz and Emma Orozco had spent years doing things the way their respective husbands had wanted them done, but once the menfolk were out of the way, neither of them was the least bit hesitant to do things her own way.

That's how it works, Brandon told himself philosophically. *I wonder what Diana will be up to once I'm gone.*

fifteen

Their long-established division of labor meant that Gayle disposed of the bodies and Larry cleaned up afterward, but he worried that he was getting too old to be doing such hard physical work. He had learned to duct-tape several layers of plastic tarp around the mattresses he used on the cot in the basement. One way or another, there were certain amounts of bodily fluids that got spilled on that cot. Larry had determined by trial and error that it was easier to get rid of ruined tarps than it was to ditch a fouled or bloodied mattress.

This time Gayle had gotten carried away with herself. Blood spatters were everywhere—on the floor, the walls, and even on the ceiling. In several places the layers of tarp had been cut clean through, leaving the mattress soaked with blood.

Larry decided to get rid of the mattress first. The cot was the size of an ordinary bunk bed, so the mattress was far smaller than a conventional single. Still, working alone, it was hell for him to wrestle the thing up the basement stairs, out through the back door, and into the bed of his old pickup. Then, since he was going to be using the backhoe anyway, he gathered up everything else that needed to go to the dump—the bloodied tarps, the filthy bedding, and—as an afterthought, the kitchen garbage. No sense having spoiled uneaten food sitting around smelling up the place.

Generations of Gayle's family had made use of The Flying C's private trash heap a mile and a half from the house. There a tin shed housed several pieces of essential garbage-dump equipment—including a backhoe and a front-end loader. Twice a year Larry had a mechanic from Catalina make a shed house call to keep the equipment in decent running order, because when Larry needed a trench dug—as he did now—there was no substitute for a backhoe.

Once finished with the task, Larry wiped his hands on his jeans and stood back to admire his handiwork. The trash heap looked as though it had gone undisturbed for years. And Larry trusted that would continue to be the case in perpetuity. Gayle, in her wisdom, had made arrangements to gift the property to the Nature Conservancy. Part of that arrangement was why The Flying C no longer functioned as a working ranch. Upon Gayle's death, the conditions of the gift mandated that all buildings on the property were to be blasted to oblivion, leveled by bulldozer, and then left to be reclaimed by the desert.

Tired but anxious, Larry returned to the house and began the real soap, water, and elbow-grease cleaning. He scrubbed the bed of the truck where the bloodied mattress had left a few dark smears. On aching knees, he used a scrub brush on the back porch and on the stairs. He scrubbed wherever he saw traces of blood and also where he couldn't. Finally he tackled the basement.

Cleaning that wasn't as difficult as it might have been. When they'd done the basement remodel, Larry had told the contractor he wanted a drain built directly into the polished concrete floor. Larry didn't know if the contractor had actually bought the story he'd made up about an overflowing washing machine, but the guy had been happy to install the system—the one Larry made good use of now as he sluiced blood off the ceiling, floor, and walls and let it flow straight down the drain. What could be simpler than that?

He had finished the job as well as he could and was wrapping up the cord on the power washer when he heard the back door open and close upstairs. He'd been so busy—so focused on the task at hand—that he hadn't bothered to lock the basement door as he usually did. For a moment Larry stood frozen to the spot, his breathing arrested and his heart pounding. Then he heard Gayle's voice.

"Yoo-hoo," she called. "Anybody home?"

Relief flooded through him. Once again Larry reveled in the thrill of getting away with something.

"Down here," he called back. "I'll be right up."

First encounters after Gayle went on one of her rampages were usually tense and prickly. Gayle always made it clear that Larry was the one who set her off, and most of the time Larry knew exactly what he'd done wrong. This time he was entirely mystified. He had no idea what he had done to annoy her, but the best thing to do was to face up to whatever it was and get it over with.

Hurrying upstairs, he found Gayle standing next to the bar in the living room, preparing to make herself a drink. Ever the gentleman, Larry took the empty glass from her hand. "I'll do that, sweetheart," he offered. "What would you like?"

"Macallan," she said. "Neat."

Gayle left Larry to work the bar while she crossed the room and settled on the couch. Slipping off her shoes, she tucked her legs up under her skirt. When Larry handed her the drink, she accepted it gratefully and favored him with a smile. "Thanks," she said.

Larry tried to be calm. He could tell from her drawn face that Gayle was tired and upset. He didn't quite trust her when she was in one of her moods. He took his own drink and retreated to the relative safety of his chair. From the far side of the room, he launched off into his stock apology.

"I have no idea what I did wrong," he began. "Whatever it was, I'm sorry."

To Larry's utter amazement, Gayle actually burst out laughing. "You didn't do anything wrong, silly," she said. She paused, took a delicate sip of her scotch and then smiled again. "And don't worry," she added. "I've already called Señora Duarte to let her know that we have another foster family available. She'll be sending a new girl up sometime in the next few days—certainly by the end of next week. You should know by now that I'd never leave my poor Larry in the lurch. Don't I always see to it that you're well taken care of?"

There was no arguing with that. "Yes, you do," Larry told her, with obvious relief flooding his voice. "And I'm very grateful. Cheers."

They sat quietly for the better part of a minute. Anyone seeing them there would have thought them to be what they were—a long-married couple sharing a relaxing moment at the end of an uneventful Saturday. It was a fiction Larry would have been happy to continue indefinitely, but he was sure Gayle had come to impart some kind of bad news. He hardly dared breathe while he waited to hear what it was.

"How's the room?" she asked, meaning how was the cleanup progressing.

"It's pretty well done," he told her. "The power washer I bought from Home Depot last year is a real miracle worker."

"Good," she said.

There was another long pause. Larry could do nothing but hold his breath and wait.

"You haven't heard from Erik today, have you?" Gayle asked casually.

"Erik?" Larry returned. "Good God, no! Why would I?"

"I thought he might call."

"Erik would never call me," Larry declared, "especially not on a weekend."

"He might try calling you today," Gayle said, thoughtfully sipping her drink. "I wanted to give you a heads-up. It's likely Erik will be facing some serious legal difficulties in the near future. He'll probably come to us looking for help."

Larry shook his head. "I can't imagine anything serious enough to make Erik come crawling to me for help."

"What about murder?" Gayle asked.

And then it all clicked into place. "You're setting him up?"

Gayle smiled again. "I'd say so."

"But why?" Larry began.

"Why? Because Erik LaGrange thought he could toss me out like yesterday's garbage. It turns out I wasn't quite done with him."

Hearing the lingering outrage in her voice, Larry Stryker was careful to keep his tone noncommittal. "Is there anything I can do to help?" he asked.

"I thought you'd never ask," Gayle said. She sounded genuinely grateful. "He'll bring up the affair. He'll claim I was with him last night and that we had a fight. I'll agree that's true, but I'll say that afterward I came here and spent the night with you—last night and this morning, too."

"But I had that damned golf tournament," Larry objected. "I was gone by five-thirty."

"Don't worry," Gayle said. "It'll be a Pima County case. Without Brandon Walker running the show, we can rest easy. Bill Forsythe won't let anybody push us around. If they do ask questions, we'll both acknowledge the affair. We'll also say that Erik learned last night he's about to be given a bad job review. He's getting even by putting us and Medicos in a bad light."

It all seemed plausible enough, but for Larry a smidgen of worry still lingered in the background. He needed reassurance. "You're sure it'll be all right?" he asked.

Gayle unfolded her legs, stood up, and crossed the room. When she reached Larry's chair, she bent down and gave him a long, inviting kiss. "It'll be just fine," she said soothingly. "Now what about something to eat? I'm starved."

Knowing food wasn't the only thing Gayle would need to satisfy her appetites, Larry stood up at once. "I'll get you another drink," he offered. "You sit here and relax. I'll rustle up some food."

Larry headed for the kitchen with a smile on his face.

"Davy?"

David Ladd sat in his office and wondered who was calling. In his corner office in one of Tucson's leading law firms he was usually referred to as Mr. Ladd. Lani was the only person who usually called him Davy, but the male voice wasn't Lani's. Hesitant, softly inflected words identified the caller as Tohono O'odham, but this wasn't someone whose voice he recognized.

"Yes," he said. "Who's calling?"

"It's Baby," Richard Ortiz said. "Baby Fat Crack. Mom wanted you to know about Dad."

"He's not . . ."

"He died this afternoon," Richard went on. "The funeral's Monday afternoon in Sells. Leo and I will be digging the grave at the cemetery in *Ban Thak* tomorrow, and we wondered if . . ."

David Ladd's heart constricted. He was Gabe Ortiz's godson, and Fat Crack's family was offering him the honor of helping dig the medicine man's grave at the same cemetery where he'd once helped dig the grave for his beloved Nana *Dahd*.

"Of course," David said at once. "What time?"

"Early," Richard said. "About six. Otherwise it'll be too hot. And that friend of yours," he added, "the one Dad liked so much, who was always hanging around with you . . ."

"You mean Brian Fellows?"

"Yes. That's the one. If he wants to come, too, he's welcome."

"I'll call him," David Ladd said. "I don't know about Brian, but I'll be there for sure."

Which was why, a few minutes later, when Diana Ladd called to ask if Davy could drive to Phoenix on Sunday to meet his sister's flight, he had to decline.

"Sorry, Mom," he told her. "My morning's already booked. I'll be out at *Ban Thak* digging the grave."

"I'm sure Dad will, too," Diana said. "I already told Wanda I'd come help cook."

"What about Candace and Tyler?" Davy asked. "Maybe they could meet the plane."

"You don't think Candace would mind?" Diana asked.

"I'll check with her," Davy said. "I'm sure she'll be happy to do it."

When he finally got off the phone, Davy sat for a long time, staring out at the traffic rushing past on Broadway. He was surprised at how much it hurt to realize that Gabe Ortiz was no more. Rita Antone's nephew had been an important and beloved part of David's life for as long as he could remember, and somehow he had assumed Fat Crack would always be there.

Now he wasn't.

Handcuffed in the backseat of the Crown Victoria, Erik rode through the sally port at the Pima County Jail and felt as if he were being driven through the gates of hell. How could this be happening? It wasn't possible. He'd done nothing. Surely this was some kind of bad dream, but he hadn't dreamed that a tow truck had hauled his Tacoma off to an impound lot. And it wasn't a dream that people had swarmed through his house and carried out cartons of supposed "evidence." Erik had been wide awake when all that happened.

Fellows stopped the vehicle, got out, and then came around to the side and unlocked the door before helping Erik climb out. He was led through the booking process like a sleepwalker. He'd been sitting on his hands, and they were numb. When it came time for fingerprints, his hands flopped loosely at the ends of his wrists as though they belonged on someone else's body. And when the booking officer lined Erik up for his obligatory mug shot, he suddenly realized why, in the mug-shot photos he'd seen, the poor stupes always looked dazed and completely bewildered. That was exactly how Erik La-Grange felt right then—bewildered.

Sometime later, dressed in an orange jumpsuit and

hobbling along on a pair of ill-fitting flip-flops, he was shoved into a cell the guard called a holding tank.

"When do I get to talk to an attorney?" Erik asked as the barred door locked behind him.

"Beats me," the guard replied. "I only work here, but it's Saturday night. If I was you, I wouldn't look for it to happen anytime before Monday morning.

Diana greeted Brandon at the front door with Damsel at her side. "I'm glad you're home," she said. "Are you all right?"

"I'm okay," he said, but it wasn't a convincing response.

"Dinner's almost ready," she said. "Are you going to want to eat or would you like a drink first? We could probably both use one of those."

Brandon nodded gratefully. "A beer would be great."

Diana headed for the refrigerator. Just then Damsel made a lunge for Fat Crack's medicine pouch and managed to snag it out of Brandon's hand. He rescued the pouch from the dog's mouth and laid it down on the kitchen counter as Diana returned with the beer.

"What's that?" Diana asked, scowling at the worn buckskin packet with its frayed fringe.

It surprised Brandon to think that in all the years he and Diana had been friends with Fat Crack and Wanda Ortiz, the medicine man had never once shown Diana his treasured pouch—the one that had come to him from Looks at Nothing. Now it belonged to their daughter, Lani.

"Fat Crack's *huashomi*," Brandon replied huskily. "He gave it to me this afternoon and told me it's for . . ." He paused and swallowed before continuing. "It's for Lani."

A glance at Brandon's bleak face told Diana how much he was hurting. She reached out and laid a comforting hand on her husband's forearm. "He must have known he was going," she said quietly. "I'm so sorry, Brandon, but there was nothing you could have done to change that, and nothing Lani could have done, either."

Brandon nodded, and then leaned over to hug her close. "I know," he said. "But it hurts like hell to lose an old friend," he said. "It really makes you feel your age."

Much later, when Diana and Brandon finally sat down to dinner, Brandon barely touched his food while Diana brought him up-to-date on the series of phone calls that had come in as the Ortiz family organized their resources and began planning the funeral.

"I'm so glad you took the tamales and tortillas back to Wanda," she said. "She's expecting a huge crowd at the feast house on Monday. She'll need them far more than we do. By the way, I canceled dinner with the kids for tomorrow. There's no way of knowing when you and David will finish up at the cemetery. Brian may even show up to help out at *Ban Thak*. I'll be at Wanda's helping with the cooking."

For the first time all evening, Brandon summoned the ghost of a smile. "Don't tell me you're going to try your hand at making tortillas? Heaven forbid!"

Grateful Brandon's mood had lifted enough so he could tease her, Diana teased right back. "Go ahead," she said. "Make fun of my tortilla-making abilities if you want. My tortillas may be ugly, but I'm great at washing pots and pans. Something tells me there'll be plenty of those."

It was almost ten o'clock when Brian Fellows dragged his weary butt home to the small house in Tucson's central area he and Kath had purchased for a song and then brought back from ruin with long hours of sweat equity. He found Kath asleep on the couch with an open library book facedown across her chest. When the hardwood floor creaked under his weight, she sat up briefly but then fell back onto the couch.

"Oh," she said. "It's you. What time is it?"

"Late. Once we booked the guy, I went back to the scene and hung out with the CSIs."

"You booked somebody? You mean you already caught the guy?"

Nodding, Brian collapsed into his leather. "Looks that way," he said. "But still . . ."

"Still what?"

"I don't have a good feeling about it."

Kath put down her book, got up, walked across the room to give Brian a peck on the cheek. "How come? And do you want something to eat?"

He nodded. "Now that you mention it, lunch was a very long time ago."

"Good. I made some chili colorado." Brian started to follow her into the kitchen. "Stay where you are," she told him. "I'll bring you a bowl."

Brian leaned back, closed his eyes, and listened as she "beeped" numbers into the microwave. He liked the tranquillity of the life they shared. It was far different from the world he'd grown up in, the constant uproar in the home of his flighty mother, her string of husbands and gentleman friends, and his two juvenile-delinquent half brothers.

"Incidentally," Kath said, returning to the doorway. "We're not going to Brandon and Diana's for dinner tomorrow night after all."

"How come?"

"Gabe Ortiz died today," Kath told him. "I thought about calling you on your cell phone, but I figured you'd be better off hearing the news after you got home."

"Damn!" Brian muttered. "What a shame! Fat Crack was a hell of a nice guy. He always treated Davy and me like we were special."

"Maybe you were," Kath said. "Davy called earlier to say you and he are invited to come to *Ban Thak* early tomorrow morning to help dig the grave. Six A.M. I told him that you were working a case, and I wasn't sure you could make it."

"I'll be there," Brian said at once. "It's an honor to be asked, and it would be bad form not to show up."

The microwave sounded in the kitchen, and the mouthwatering aroma of chili drifted into the room. Kath disappeared and returned moments later carrying a tray laden with a bowl of chili, silverware, and a glass of cold milk.

"The milk's to soothe the burn," she told him. "I went overboard on the chili. Now tell me about your case," she added, resuming her spot on the couch. "You've already got a suspect in custody. What's wrong with that?"

"It's just too easy," Brian replied. "The victim is a little Hispanic girl—maybe fourteen or fifteen—who was hacked to pieces and dumped out near Vail. No identification of any kind, but we're guessing from clothing left at the scene—clothing she wasn't wearing when she was murdered—that she's probably a UDA. Instead of an ID we found a guy's business card—tucked in among the victim's effects. The name on the card was Erik La-Grange and a phone number that turned out to be his home number was scribbled on the back.

"We located his house and went there to see if La-

Grange could help us ID her. Instead, I found what looked like blood on the bumper of his truck and more blood on the front-door jamb."

"Enough for a warrant?" Kath asked.

Brian nodded. "Once we gained access to his vehicle, we found lots of blood in his truck, and in the house we found bloody shoe prints in the hallway. There were shoes with blood on them in the bedroom closet and bloody clothes in a clothes hamper with the washing machine sitting right there next to it."

"Why didn't he stick them in the washer?" Kath asked.

"My thought exactly," Brian responded. "I sure as hell would have had it been me. But back to the scene, I put in a call to the department. About an hour or so later, while I was waiting for PeeWee Segura to show up with the warrant, a guy in his mid-thirties showed up who turns out to be Mr. LaGrange. He was bloody and looked like he'd been in a bar fight. He claimed he'd been off on a hike in the mountains all morning long and all by his little lonesome. Of course, nobody saw him hiking, so he's got no alibi, but still . . ."

Brian fell silent for a moment and savored the first bite of the piping-hot chili. Temperature wasn't the only thing that made his mouth sizzle.

"Does the name Medicos for Mexico ring a bell?" he asked after chasing the chili with a swallow of cold milk.

"Sure," Kath replied. "It's a charity that uses volunteers to provide free medical care for impoverished patients across the line in Mexico. The people who run it, Gayle and Larry Stryker, are big shots around town. He's a doctor, and she's practically the first lady of Tucson. Their pictures and names are in the paper all the time, mostly in the society pages. Why? What about them?"

"Erik LaGrange works for Medicos for Mexico. He's their development officer and reports to Mrs. Stryker."

"What happens now?"

"LaGrange won't talk to us without a lawyer. I'm hoping I can pull some strings and get one appointed tomorrow so we can interview him. The county attorney called a meeting tomorrow afternoon to speed up the process. With any luck the grave will be dug before that."

"He called a meeting on Sunday?" Kath objected. "That's our one day off together."

"I'm sorry," Brian told her. "When the county attorney says jump, grunts like PeeWee and me don't have much choice but to do it."

"I love it when elected officials remind us that we're public servants and need to be treated as such," Kath grumbled.

Brian Fellows took another drink of milk and then smiled at his wife. "That's one of the things I love about you, Kath. When I come home from work with tales of woe, I know I'm talking to someone who understands."

"Right," she told him. "Now finish your chili. If you're going to be at Coyote Sitting digging a grave at six tomorrow morning, you need some sleep."

Kath had the right idea. They went to bed soon after that, but Brian had a hard time falling asleep. When he did, he woke up time and again. He kept having the same dream over and over, one filled with black plastic garbage bags overflowing with bloodied body parts.

sixteen

Leo Ortiz snored the night away while Delia Ortiz tossed and turned. Years of living in the Anglo world left her ill suited to deal with death in the same undemonstrative way people handled it on the reservation. Leo and Baby Fat Crack had both loved their father and respected him, but they accepted his death with quiet fortitude and dealt with the logistics— getting a casket, making arrangements with a mortuary, and digging the grave—in the same unruffled fashion. Maybe that's one of the reasons Leo slept so peacefully. He hadn't been at war with his father. Delia had been. Guilt over the unresolved issues between her and Fat Crack kept Delia wide awake into the wee hours—that and the unrelenting kicking of the restless infant inside her womb.

Wanda Ortiz's reaction to her husband's death was much like that of her two sons. It had happened, and now she had things to do. Once the funeral and burial were over, all the attendees would show up at *Ban Thak* for the customary feast. Considering Fat Crack's standing in the community, not only as a former tribal chairman but also as the acknowledged *siwani*—chief medicine man—both events would be widely attended.

That required lots of food—and a good deal of organization. There were hundreds of tamales and tortillas to be made; vats of chili and beans to be cooked. To that end, Wanda Ortiz had summoned her daughter from Tucson, her two daughters-in-law, and any other able-bodied female relatives to appear at the family compound the next morning ready for a day's worth of nonstop cooking.

Before Delia had returned to the reservation seven years earlier, she had never made a single tamale or tortilla. Aunt Julia had tactfully suggested that it might be a good idea for her to learn; Delia had resisted. It reminded her of the fading poster that still hung in the hallway of Ruth's house outside Cambridge. It showed a photo of Israel's first and so far only female premier, Golda Meir. The caption under the photo said "But can she type?" That had been Delia's position as well. As tribal attorney, it didn't seem necessary for her to know how to make tortillas and tamales. In D.C., the lack of those skills had never been a problem.

She had been annoyed when tribal chairman Gabe Ortiz, at Aunt Julia's instigation, had shown up on her doorstep to offer unsolicited advice about her personal life. She'd been astonished when he offered her the job of tribal attorney, but she suspected that was only a thinly disguised smoke screen for her interfering auntie's private agenda—that Delia should dump Philip Cachora and come home to the reservation. Delia had turned the job down cold.

She had fallen hopelessly in love with Philip Cachora, and she was determined to keep him. She had met Philip at the grand opening of a show at the National Gallery, an exhibit of works by what they termed "Emerging Native American Artists." After growing up as an urban Indian, Delia was increasingly uncomfortable with the phrase *Native American*. Educated in the best private schools Ruth Waldron's Boston pedigree had wangled, Delia saw life through essentially Anglo eyes. For her, the words *Native American* conjured up pictures of loincloth-wearing savages.

She went to the gallery opening with her friend and roommate, Marcia Lomax, who worked for the Department of Justice. They went on a pair of free tickets given her by Delia's boss. They expected to show up, have a few drinks, nosh on the free food, and then go to a movie.

Delia and Marcia were standing and chatting in front of a massive full-length oil portrait of a handsome Indian man with much of his face obscured by a pair of mirrored sunglasses. He wore a tattered straw cowboy hat—a Resistol—and an equally tattered American flag wrapped around him like a toga. The piece was called *Promises*.

"Well, ladies," a pleasantly deep male voice said. "Have you figured out what it means?"

Delia turned from the portrait to the voice and did a double take. The painting seemed to have come to life, reflective sunglasses and all, although the straw hat had been replaced by a huge black felt Stetson and the flag by a designer tuxedo. As far as Delia was concerned, the affectation of wearing Ray•Bans inside meant two things—trouble and phony.

"I take it we're looking at a portrait of the artist as a young man?" Delia asked.

He pretended to wince. "Not that much younger, I hope. But yes, I'm him, or vice versa. The name's Philip Cachora. Where are you two from?"

"Justice," Marcia replied.

"BIA," Delia chimed in.

"I mean, where are you *from?*" Philip insisted. "Or is Justice the name of a little town somewhere in the middle of Tennessee or Missouri?"

"I work at the Department of Justice," Marcia answered. "I'm *from* Milwaukee."

Delia shook her head. "Forget it," she said. "Nobody's ever heard of where I'm from."

"Try me."

"Sells, Arizona," she said.

Philip Cachora's jaw dropped. "No shit!" he exclaimed. He tipped his hat. "If you'll pardon the expression."

"How about you?" Delia asked.

"Vamori," he said.

Delia and Marcia exchanged glances. "Okay," Delia said. "We give up. Where's that?"

"About twenty miles southwest of Sells, actually," he replied with a grin. "Obviously you're not up on Tohono O'odham geography. What's a nice Indian girl like you doing in a place like this?"

"I'm a lawyer," Delia answered. "For the BIA."

"Where's your family from?" he asked, moving in on Delia in a way that effectively edged Marcia out of the conversation. She shrugged and then obligingly strolled on through the exhibit, leaving Philip and Delia alone. "I mean, from what villages on the reservation?"

"My father came from Big Fields originally," Delia said. "My mother's family came from Little Tucson. That's all I know. I left the reservation when I was seven and haven't been back."

"That's a long time," he observed.

"Twenty years," she agreed. "What about you?"

"I wanted to be an artist. Halfway through high school I opted for a boarding school in Santa Fe. I've

been there ever since—in Santa Fe, not in boarding
school. Twenty years more or less, too, but who's counting? I make a good living. I paint Indians wearing flags
and sell them to guilt-ridden limousine liberals. One guy
who paid ten thousand bucks for a painting very much
like this one asked if I'd ever been on the warpath. I told
him I'd never been off it."

They both laughed at that. "And then," he added,
warming to the topic, "there are always a few rich babes
who figure if they buy one of my paintings they also
qualify for a roll in the hay. The trick is to pry them
loose from their money without getting dragged into
beddy-bye."

"You look more than capable of fending them off,"
Delia observed. She glanced down the gallery and caught
sight of Marcia standing near the doorway entrance into
another room, chatting with someone she knew.

"Do you have plans for dinner?" Philip asked.

"Yes," Delia said quickly. "My friend and I are
booked."

"What about tomorrow?"

"I think I'm busy then, too."

"Come on," he said. "I'm just a country bumpkin in
town for a day or two. Couldn't you find it in your heart
to show me a few sights? I mean, we're practically
neighbors."

It was a blatant pickup line, and Delia couldn't help
laughing. "I'll bet you use that one a lot," she said.

He grinned, an engaging, white-toothed grin. "It usually works, too," he said.

"Not this time," she told him. "Sorry." She ducked
away and caught up with Marcia.

"You escaped," Marcia said.

"Just barely," Delia returned. "It was a near thing."

But that wasn't the end of it. By three o'clock the next afternoon, a bouquet of red roses landed on Delia's desk at the BIA. She was both pleased and annoyed—flattered that Philip Cachora had gone to the trouble of tracking her down and dismayed because the nation's capital offered so little anonymity. An hour later her phone rang.

"What's your Indian name?" Philip asked as soon as she answered.

"I don't have one," she replied.

"How can you be Indian and not have an Indian name? I'm going to give you one," he added after a moment. "I think I'll call you *Moikchu*."

"What does that mean?" she asked.

"That's for me to know and you to find out," he told her with a laugh.

Delia's mother was the one who translated the word. *Moikchu* meant Soft One. When Delia first learned what it meant, she accepted the name as a compliment. It was only later, after everything had sorted itself out, that she wondered if the word couldn't also be used to mean soft in the head. Because when it came to Philip Cachora, she was certainly that.

"Now tell me," he continued, "are you really booked for dinner tonight, or were you just trying to get rid of me?"

"What time and where?" she asked, giving in. After all, for a twenty-seven-year-old struggling young professional, flowers and the offer of a free meal held some appeal.

She took a cab from her office in Interior to Philip Cachora's hotel, the Dupont Plaza. From there they walked the few blocks to the Iron Gate Restaurant on N Street NW. It was April and particularly balmy. With the air perfumed by hanging wisteria, they had an elegant romantic dinner at an outside table. When Delia fretted about the prices, Philip reassured her.

"Listen," he said. "I'm here on a grant. I'm on display as one of an endangered species—you know, Indian-artist-under-glass. This is all on somebody else's nickel. Have a ball. Order whatever you want."

Then he smiled across the table at her and asked, "What exactly does a smart lady lawyer do for the BIA?"

"I analyze treaties."

"No shit!" he exclaimed.

"No shit!" she shot back, mimicking his delivery.

"Looking for loopholes?" he asked. She nodded. "In whose favor?"

"In anybody's favor."

"And where do you live?"

"Are you saying whoever told you where my office was didn't also tell you where I live?"

"I'm from out of town." He grinned back at her. "My sources are good only up to a point."

She laughed aloud as a waiter refilled her champagne glass with bubbly that had clocked in at more than a hundred dollars a bottle. "If you must know, I live in Glover Park in a town house on Tunlaw Road—1849 Tunlaw Road. I live with a friend from law school, Marcia Lomax. You met her last night at the exhibit."

"Tunlaw Road," he repeated. "Sounds very upscale."

Delia smiled and shook her head. "Not really. Lots of students and young professionals, all of us struggling. The best thing about Tunlaw Road is the name. It's 'walnut' spelled backward. According to a legend I heard, nobody in the District was allowed to name a street after a tree, but somebody slipped that one past."

Philip raised his glass. "Here's to Tunlaw Road. I like it, too. I'm always in favor of slipping it to the Great White Father."

Dinner stretched far into the night. When it was time to go home, Philip invited her to his hotel. Delia shook her head and caught a cab, but on the way home she knew she was smitten. If he asked her out again, she'd go. If he invited her to his room again, she'd probably go there, too.

In the week and a half that followed, they'd had a great time together. She showed him the sights, his credit card provided the meals, and they availed themselves of the king-sized bed in his Dupont Plaza hotel room. Between times, Philip Cachora told Delia stories.

He was a charming and engaging storyteller. Ten years her senior, he had gone to both grade school and the first two years of high school on the reservation, at Topawa and Indian Oasis High School. He told her about going to rain dances and getting drunk on thick cactus-juice wine. He told her about his art and about some of the shows he'd been in. He told her about going to powwows around the country and trying to integrate what he saw there into his art.

Beguiled by his stories, Delia failed to question what he was editing out. Somehow, during that first evening and the whirlwind days that followed, he never mentioned a single one of his three ex-wives or why any of them had left him. And Delia never had the presence of mind to ask.

Gayle was glad Larry had been able to get it up with no difficulty. Once she took care of that item on her to-do list, Larry was out like a light, leaving Gayle free to slip out of bed and prowl around the familiar old house—the house of her childhood. Other than the relatively recent modifications in the basement, little else had changed. Much of the furniture was still the same high-quality and often re-covered highly serviceable stuff Great-Grandmother Madison had shipped by train from Ohio when she arrived at the ranch as a bride in 1901.

Sometime in the early seventies, Gayle's mother, Gretchen, had replaced the creaking 1950s-era appliances with all new Maytag-brand versions. Gretchen's once state-of-the-art appliances could now be considered museum pieces, but to Gayle's amazement, they continued to plug along. As far as she was concerned, they would never be replaced. When the time came, they'd be bulldozed right along with the house.

The ranch had been Gayle's father's domain and her mother's nightmare. He liked living there, while Gretchen preferred the social milieu of her own family's house in Tucson—the home that was Gayle's to this day. Had Winston lived, he would most likely have inherited that, just as Gayle had inherited the ranch. But Winston had died in the mid-1980s, and Gretchen, mourning her lost son, had soon followed. That left Gayle with both the ranch and the house in town and with her parents' model on how to conduct herself.

It was strange for Gayle to realize how much her marriage to Larry Stryker resembled that of her parents—her home in town and his miles away on the ranch. In private, Calvin and Gretchen had made no secret of their mutual loathing, but in public they had maintained a smilingly polite decorum that had held gossipmongers at bay for decades. In their respective lairs, Calvin had kept a steady string of dark-eyed and curvaceous housekeepers, while Gretchen had carried on secret liaisons with several of Tucson's highborn but decidedly "mannish" women. As for their children? Winston, permanently attached to his mother's apron strings, had avoided the ranch like the plague, while Gayle, adoring her father, had loathed the city.

It amused Gayle sometimes to wonder what a therapist would make of her incestuous relationship with her father. Supposedly she should have minded, but she didn't. Conventional wisdom said that she would grow up hating her father, but she hadn't done that, either. Gayle had resented her mother's mistreatment of Calvin and was glad to do what she could to cheer him up. Admittedly, she'd been jealous when a new housekeeper would show up, causing Calvin to absent himself temporarily from his daughter's bed. Gayle supposed that, to some extent, maybe what she did to Larry's girls—that wonderfully endless supply of lithe brown bodies—was a means of finding redress for the attentions Calvin's mistresses had stolen from her.

Here in this house, Gayle could see how the way she'd been raised had contributed to what she'd become—smart, pragmatic, unflappable. Both of her parents had provided outstanding role models about what to do when life turned out to be different from what you had expected. Irreconcilable differences plainly existed in her parents' separate households, but they were never mentioned. Neither was the word D-I-V-O-R-C-E. That simply wasn't done. If you made a bad choice, my dear, you pulled up your socks, stuck with it, and went looking for fun and entertainment wherever you liked—as long as you were discreet about it.

That was why Larry's actions with Roseanne Orozco had so infuriated Gayle. It had been anything but discreet, and it would surely have brought the whole world down around their ears if Gayle hadn't taken definitive action. The same thing almost happened again two years later, when one of Larry's old poker-playing buddies was caught sticking his dick where he shouldn't have. To save his sorry ass, he made a plea bargain that included shooting off his mouth about what had gone on in the hospital at Sells and had named names in the process—Larry's included. As a result, Larry and several other physicians were summarily drummed out of the Indian Health Service.

But what had first seemed total disaster turned out to be not that bad after all. A few calls to one or two of Gretchen's well-placed friends kept the story from making it into the local papers. Amazingly enough, arcane rules and regulations governing Indian Health Service physicians meant that lists of disciplined doctors were not made available to state or national medical associations, leaving Larry and the others free to practice medicine wherever they chose.

But by then Gayle no longer wanted to be married to a doctor. What had sounded like a great idea when she was in college had lost its allure. She didn't want to live with someone who had to be on call. She didn't like Larry's being out of her sight that much, either. As long as he didn't have brains enough to keep his pants zipped, she couldn't risk his going off to work at a hospital or clinic. The Easter weekend interlude at the beachfront hotel in Mazatlán had proved to Gayle Stryker just what she'd suspected about her husband's sexual preferences and had supplied her with the key to keeping Larry under her complete control.

Gayle had learned something about herself that afternoon as well. She'd been electrified by the girl's first involuntary whimper as she tried to shy away from the invading touch of that chilled beer bottle. The child had been helpless. She couldn't protect herself from what was coming, not from whatever Larry might want to do nor from what Gayle might want Larry to do. Gayle had felt that kind of power only once before in her life, but on the afternoon she had slaughtered Roseanne Orozco, it hadn't occurred to her that the heady stuff was something that could be duplicated. That afternoon, as Larry finally did it—when at Gayle's insistence he finally screwed up his courage and shoved the bottle home—Gayle had been thrilled. Hearing the cries, watching the girl writhe in agony had turned Gayle on in a way nothing else ever had.

That was when and why she had dreamed up Medicos for Mexico. Her parents, both of them, helped provide the initial seed money. Gretchen had written a check. Calvin had done his part by having the good grace to die and leave the ranch and a whole lot more to his daughter.

Over the years, running a cross-border charity had proved to be a gold mine. Yes, someone had to go out and raise money. That took work and skill, and Gayle was exceptionally good at schmoozing. But once those donated dollars flowed into the Medicos coffers, there was virtually no outside oversight—not from the public at large and not from the IRS. Medicos paid generous salaries to both Gayle and Larry. They paid their taxes on those without a whisper of complaint, but much of their lavish lifestyle was paid for in full or in part by monies gleaned from vaguely labeled items in the expense columns of the charity's books. Artful skimming also accounted for the almost finished mansion Gayle was having built, at no small expense, in a gated compound outside Cabo San Lucas.

Medicos for Mexico had provided Gayle and Larry Stryker with money, respectability, and standing in the community. It also supplied that unending stream of girls—those expendable little girls—Gayle needed to keep Larry firmly in line. Sometimes just watching what Larry did to them was enough to satisfy Gayle, but there were other times when the pressure was too much, when Gayle needed more than simply observing. Which is exactly what had happened today—the pressure had been too much.

Gayle went to the bar and poured herself a drink. Last night, setting Erik up to take a fall for killing the girl had seemed a far better idea than it did tonight. Gayle had done something she shouldn't have—she had allowed her emotions to get the best of her, thus creating a whole new set of problems. Now she'd have to figure out a way to deal with them. It was what she'd done in the past, and it was what she'd do again. The difficulty was, she wasn't entirely sure how.

It would take a day or two to handle the money issues, to empty the Medicos accounts and ship the money to Mexico—or the Cayman Islands. Certainly the money she had would stretch a whole lot further if she didn't have to split it two ways. That would mean sacrificing Larry, but so what?

He'd had a good run and enjoyed himself—probably more than he deserved—and he was every bit as expendable as Erik LaGrange.

seventeen

As time went on, the hunters brought their families along when they came north. With everyone hot and thirsty, it was a good deal of trouble to slip up to the pond to drink, all the while watching for the coyotes.

One day, an old wise man from the village said to the others, "I am going to drive the coyotes away, or else I will make them share their water with us." The old man went away and was gone for a week. When he returned, he was leading a baby coyote on a string. When they saw Baby Coyote on the string, the people of the village laughed and laughed. They laughed so loud and made so much noise that Coyote grew curious, wondering what all the noise and laughter was about. So he came out of his cave to see what was so funny.

Old Man led Baby Coyote a ways from the water and tied him to a tree. Then he told the children to go away and leave Baby Coyote alone. Soon Baby Coyote grew hungry and thirsty and lonely, and he began to cry.

Now the Mil-gahn—the Whites—will often walk away from other white men when they are hurt or injured or thirsty in the desert, but I'itoi's people would never do such a thing. This is as true of coyotes as it is of *the Indians who cannot deny a call for help. After Coyote and his mate listened to Baby Coyote cry for a while, finally they went to see who was in trouble. Mama Coyote went at once to find some food for the baby, but Mr. Coyote did not like the looks of that string that tethered Baby Coyote to the tree. The first thing Mr. Coyote did was chew the string in two.*

Just then Baby Coyote cried, "Look. Here they come."

Mr. Coyote looked and saw that the whole village had surrounded his water hole and the people were guarding it.

So the three coyotes ran away very fast, but even as he ran, Mr. Coyote laughed to think about how he had tricked the hunters and about how long he had kept the water from the hunters by sitting on that rock in the middle of the pool.

"Baby's here," Leo Ortiz whispered in his wife's ear. "Gotta go."

Delia blinked awake. It was barely sunrise. She heard the rumble of Richard Ortiz's Ford pickup outside the house.

"You'll be at Mom's later?" Leo asked.

Delia nodded, and Leo gave her blanket-covered belly an affectionate pat. "Don't let Mom and my sister work you too hard," he added. "And remember to sit down and put your feet up."

"I will," she said.

With Leo gone, Delia lay in bed and savored the fact that she didn't need to get up just yet. The baby, who had spent most of the night pummeling her ribs, seemed to be snoozing, too. She lay there and was grateful that, after all that had happened, not only were Richard and Leo brothers, they were also still friends.

* * *

Once they started dating, Philip Cachora had somehow parlayed his temporary grant status into a permanent gallery situation, where he was installed as resident artist. He said he had taken the position so he could stay close to Delia. It also gave him a somewhat regular paycheck regardless of whether or not he was producing and selling paintings. There were other benefits in the relationship as well, but Delia was oblivious to those.

The gallery job ended for reasons Delia never quite understood, and they moved into the combination studio/loft apartment on Kalorama Street, but Philip's paintings seemed to be losing their appeal as well as their patrons. Sales just weren't happening. At least the money wasn't there. Finally, insisting he had to do something, Philip bought a used van, loaded his unsold paintings into it, and took it on the road, heading off for a powwow in Montana. He returned home a month later with a credit-card balance full of hotel and meal charges and with most of his paintings still in the van.

A few nights later, Delia returned from work. On the living room coffee table she spied something that looked like a mushroom on a piece of clear plastic wrap.

"What's this?" she demanded, holding it up.

"Peyote," Philip answered, snatching it out of her hand. "Maybe you should try it sometime. It might make you less uptight. Besides, it's a religious thing."

"It's also illegal," Delia pointed out. "I don't want it in my apartment."

"It's your apartment now instead of ours?" he returned.

"It is if you look at who's paying the bills," she told him. The moment she said it, she was afraid she had gone too far.

Philip rounded on her in fury. "If you were a real Indian instead of such a stuck-up, straitlaced Bostonian, maybe you'd understand!"

Minutes after that, he was in the bathroom, puking his guts out. He slept on the couch in his studio that night. Much as Delia didn't want to admit it—especially to Marcia and others who had tried to warn her away from Philip in the first place—she knew it was the beginning of the end. She hung on for a time, hoping things would change and he would get better. That was why, a few months later, it hurt so much to realize that even Aunt Julia, more than two thousand miles away, somehow knew how bad things were and tried to help by sending Fat Crack Ortiz to the rescue. She responded to his offer of help by more or less telling him to take his job and shove it.

Two weeks later, she came home from work early with a migraine and walked in on a disaster that had been ten years in the making. There in the apartment she found Philip passed out in the company of a sixteen-year-old male prostitute. Delia turned around and stormed out of the apartment without waking either of them. She made her way back to her old neighborhood and checked into the Savoy. The next morning, she called in sick and made an appointment to see her ob-gyn, where she underwent a series of tests for sexually transmitted diseases. Then she went back to the hotel to await the results, which wouldn't be available until the following Monday.

She called no one, not even her mother. Especially not her mother. Instead, she sat in the hotel for the next eighteen hours, staring blindly at the traffic on Wisconsin Avenue and wondering whether or not Philip had contracted AIDS, and if he had, had he already passed it along to her? How long did it take to die of AIDS, she wondered, and how painful was it?

It wasn't until the sun was coming up the next morning that she found the strength to pick up the telephone and dial Santa Fe information. There were several Cachoras listed, and it took time to jot down all the numbers. When her office opened, she called in sick for a second time. Once it was eight o'clock New Mexico time, Delia dialed one of the numbers she'd been given.

She hadn't picked that number at random. Several of the Cachoras listed included male names. Delia skipped those, opting instead for M. A. Cachora with no address. That number had to belong to a single woman living alone. Not surprisingly, a woman answered. "Hello."

For a moment, the sound of the voice stunned Delia to silence. "Hello?" the woman repeated. "Is anyone there?"

"Ms. Cachora . . ." Delia began hesitantly.

"Yes. Who is this?"

Delia's voice trembled. So did her hand. She almost dropped the phone. "My name is Delia," she said finally. "I wondered if you happened to know someone named Philip Cachora."

"If we're talking about the same person," the other woman answered, "then he used to be my husband, the creep. What about him?"

"I married him, too," Delia managed. "I was wondering . . ." She stopped, unable to continue.

The woman on the other end of the line didn't make it any easier. "Wondering what?" she asked.

"If you'd tell me why . . ."

It was such a stupid thing to ask. Delia could barely believe she'd done it.

"Why what?" the woman demanded. "You mean why I divorced him? I'll tell you why—because he liked other people better than he liked me. Philip needs a home base, you see—a place to leave his paint and his easels and all that shit, but when he's out on the road, honey, he's also on the make. And he'll screw anything that walks. Male or female, it doesn't matter."

By the time the woman stopped speaking, Delia was sobbing uncontrollably into the phone.

"Oh, my God!" the woman exclaimed. "You just found out, didn't you!"

Still unable to speak, Delia nodded.

"I'm sorry," the woman continued. "I know how I felt the day I found out. I wanted to kill him. I should have killed him! If I had, this wouldn't be happening to somebody else, to you. Are you all right, honey? Do you have any friends there with you, someone you can talk to?"

"I'm all right," Delia managed. "I'll be okay."

"Yes, you will, but it'll take time. Years, probably. Where are you?"

"Washington," Delia answered. "Washington, D.C."

"I wish I knew somebody there I could have come talk to you. That son of a bitch! I'd tell you to sue his ass and take him for everything he's worth, but I already did that, so there's not much to take. When he left me, he was dead broke. I got the house and a garageful of paintings, which I've been selling, by the way. If you have a chance, at least try to pick up some of the art."

"He's not painting much anymore," Delia admitted.

"Drugs?"

It was as if the woman, this stranger halfway across the country, knew every sordid detail of Delia's life. "Yes," she whispered.

"Get out then," M. A. Cachora advised. "Get out and stay out. And go by the health department and have yourself tested. That stupid bastard is playing Russian roulette, and he isn't smart enough to figure it out."

"I already have," Delia said. "Been tested, that is. I get the results on Monday."

"Keep my number in case you need someone to talk to in the meantime. My name's Marcella, by the way. Call me anytime you need to talk."

"Thanks," Delia said. "I will."

But she didn't call Marcella back, and she didn't call any other numbers in Santa Fe, either. Delia had found out everything she needed to know.

She stayed on in the hotel all through the weekend. Somewhere along the way she finally realized she was hungry and ordered food from room service. Time moved in incredibly tiny increments. Occasionally she thought about calling her mother and Ruth, but she couldn't bring herself to do it. Ruth really liked Philip, and Delia didn't want to break the spell with a harsh dose of reality. With Ellie, it meant history repeating itself in a new generation.

When Delia returned to the doctor's office on Monday afternoon, her anxiety level was off the charts. When Dr. Hanley told her she was HIV-negative, the words hardly registered. She left the doctor's office in a daze and made her way to the nearest pay phone. It took a while to get the tribal chairman's number, but finally Fat Crack Ortiz came on the line.

"Yes?" he said.

"It's Delia," she said quickly. "Delia Cachora. Remember me?"

"Of course."

"I'm calling about your offer," she said. "Is the tribal attorney job still available?"

"Yes," Fat Crack answered. "As a matter of fact it is. Why?"

Delia paused and took a deep breath. "If you'll have me," she said, "I'd like to accept the position."

"Fine," he said. "I'm glad you're coming home. Your aunt Julia will be pleased."

For the five men who gathered in *Ban Thak* that Sunday morning, digging Fat Crack's grave was as much a time of remembrance as it was of physical labor. They arrived in four separate vehicles just as the sun cleared the jagged tops of the Tucson Mountains off to the east.

There was little left of the village—only the feast house, a tiny chapel, a few crumbling adobe houses, an equal number of mobile homes, and the parched-earth cemetery. Some of the graves were well tended, marked with headstones or crosses that were decorated with wreaths or vases of plastic flowers. Others moldered in obscurity, with the names of the dead long since obliterated from crosses that tipped precariously in one direction or the other.

Leo and Baby unloaded shovels, pry bars, and a wheelbarrow from the truck. Then they hauled the yellow-and-red watercooler over to the cemetery and perched it on a fence post so it would be close at hand when needed.

Long habit made it easy for the brothers to work without need of extraneous conversation. They had toiled together in their father's tow-truck and auto-repair business from the time they could each hold a wrench, and they had played in Four Winds, a modestly successful chicken-scratch band, from the time they were in high school. By the mid-nineties, people had teased them about being so *e wehem*—so together—that neither one of them would ever have room for a woman in his life. Then Delia Chavez Cachora appeared on the scene in her slick Saab 9000, and both Leo and Richard wanted her.

Baby Fat Crack, older than Leo by two years, remembered Delia from first grade at Indian Oasis School years earlier. Baby was shy and reticent, and his understated way of courting was to learn everything possible about her Saab. Leo solved the problem by making himself indispensable.

Delia's father, Manny, had been brutally attacked with a shovel. Although the medical community diagnosed his paralysis as a result of spinal-cord damage, Delia's aunt Julia claimed Manny had been stricken by Staying Sickness, one of a group of ailments specific to the Tohono O'odham people. Manny's particular strain, Turtle Sickness, resulted from a person's being rude.

Whatever had caused the paralysis, the result was the same. Manny Chavez was a hopeless invalid in need of constant care and supervision. Delia's brother, Eddie, spent most of his life timed-out on booze. Consequently, despite Delia's stormy history with her father, his care fell on her—and, because he volunteered for the task, on Leo Ortiz's broad shoulders as well. When Delia moved from her aunt's home into a house in what had formerly been the BIA compound in Sells, Leo was there, moving boxes and furniture and erecting a wooden wheelchair ramp so Manny could come to visit once he was finally released from the rehab facility in Tucson. Leo helped Delia find a suitable caregiver for her father, and he helped transport him back and forth to the hospital for various doctor's visits.

Leo's constancy and patient way of dealing with her

father and with her was so different from everything Delia knew from Philip that she couldn't help noticing— and falling in love. When the Saab's turbo hiccoughed and quit, Baby Fat Crack was the one who installed a replacement. And when the compressor for the air-conditioning went out, Baby fixed that as well, but somehow that all went right over Delia's head. She was too busy with other concerns. Had Baby come right out and said something, she might have realized how he felt about her. But it wasn't until after her divorce from Philip was final and she and Leo announced their engagement that the full implication of what had happened hit home—for all three of them.

The night before Leo and Delia's wedding, Fat Crack brought his two sons together and insisted that they sit down and share the Peace Smoke. Only then had they been able to move on and let bygones be bygones. After losing out on Delia, Baby had finally found himself a suitable bride. He and Christine already had one child— a little girl—with another on the way. Now, as the two sons labored together digging their father's grave, Fat Crack's spirit was still the glue that held them together— not only his sons, but his sons' children as well.

Brandon dropped Diana off outside Wanda's mobile home in Sells and then headed for *Ban Thak*. He arrived at the cemetery just after Davy and just before Brian. Brandon knew he was late. Baby and Leo had already dug down to knee level. Leo was down in the hole whaling away with a pickax while Baby stood on the surface leaning on a shovel.

He wiped his dusty hand off on his jeans before accepting Brandon's proffered handshake. "Thanks for having us," Brandon said.

Baby nodded. "Grab a shovel," he said. "We'll take turns."

The younger men worked faster, and although Brandon shoveled steadily and was a little winded, he had nonetheless accomplished almost as much when his turn was over. Standing on the sidelines, catching his breath and listening to the others joke and tease, he remembered what Fat Crack had told him once—that as a young child, Looks at Nothing had told Rita Antone she would be a bridge between the Anglo world and the Tohono O'odham. And it was true. Years after Rita's death, here were five men of different generations and races—Rita's great-nephews, Brandon Walker and his *Mil-gahn* sons, who weren't really his sons at all—working together in a blending of harmony and friendship that would have been unthinkable years earlier.

"Why so late?" Leo asked Brian. "Were you hanging around with that cute red-haired wife of yours?"

"I overslept," Brian admitted. "I was out late last night working a case and didn't set the alarm."

"What kind of case?" Davy asked.

"I'm sure it'll be on the news again today if you missed it last night," Brian said, making conversation. "Some guy hacked a little Mexican girl to pieces and tossed her out in the desert."

Brandon had stepped over to the fence to take a drink from the cooler, but the words stopped him. "What do you mean, hacked to pieces?" he asked.

Brian put down the pick and came out of the deepening hole while Davy went in to shovel up loosened dirt. Brian wiped his face and neck with a grimy hanky before answering.

"Just that. It was brutal. The murder weapon's most likely a machete. Her limbs were whacked off at the joints. A woman hiking near Vail yesterday morning found the body in bags strewn along the railroad tracks."

Brandon Walker's heart constricted. It was nothing scientific—nothing he could take to court or turn in on a written police report—but instinctively he sensed a connection between this new case and an old one, between this new dead girl and Roseanne Orozco from 1970.

"Why do you ask?" Brian continued.

Brandon Walker knew that his close connection to Brian Fellows had often been a detriment to Brian's career within the Pima County Sheriff's Department. The passage of time had made most of that go away, and Brandon didn't want to do anything that would jeopardize Brian's future by bringing their relationship back to the fore. He knew that if he and TLC were to solve a case that the Pima County Sheriff's Department had left hanging, Brian Fellows had better not be anywhere nearby when the shit hit the fan.

"There was another case like that a long time ago, a couple of years after I started working Homicide," Brandon said carefully. "It happened out here on the reservation. The victim's name was Roseanne Orozco. A highway worker found the body near Quijotoa. She'd been chopped to pieces and left in an ice chest. People called her the 'Girl in the Box.'"

"I remember hearing about that," Leo said. "I was just a kid. Grandma always used to tell us if we weren't good, we'd end up chopped to pieces and in a box the same way she was."

"Probably no connection," Brian said. "There wasn't any ice chest this time. This girl's body was in garbage bags and left out in the open in the desert. Besides," he added, "when did that homicide happen?"

"It must have been 1970 or so," Brandon answered.

That wasn't entirely true. Brandon had gone over his notes with care. He knew exactly when it was, but he wasn't about to say so. And since this was nothing but a hunch, he wasn't going to push it.

"There you go," Brian said. "The suspect we've got in custody wouldn't even have been in kindergarten in 1970. Unless he set out to be a serial killer very early on . . ."

eighteen

They say it happened long ago that an Indian man and his woman loved their baby very, very much.

The mother took very good care of her little one. She kept the baby with her all the time. Even when the woman went to work in the fields, she took her baby with her. She never left her in the care of someone else at home.

The other babies of the village grew strong and fat and cried and pulled things. But this baby never ever cried. All day she lay in her cradle and slept or smiled but never cried.

This Indian mother carefully arranged the ropes for her baby's nuhkuth, which, in the old days, was the soft cradle all Tohono O'odham mothers used to make to protect their precious babies. Over the ropes she put her softest blankets. She used extra ropes and extra blankets. When she took the baby to the field with her, she was so carefully wrapped that the nuhkuth looked like a big cocoon. And the mother always made sure that wherever she left her baby girl, it was nice and shady.

* * *

The grave was dug before it got hot. The five men drove into Sells, where they gratefully tucked into a breakfast of fresh tamales and paper-thin, hot-off-the-griddle tortillas. Brian and Davy stayed only long enough to eat, then they both headed back to Tucson. While mostly female visitors trooped in and out of the house to pay their respects to Wanda, Leo and Baby held court outside. They gathered visiting menfolk around Baby's baby—his blue 1983 Ford F-100 with its chromed-out valve covers and air cleaner and its oddball, low-powered 232 V6 engine. To a man they all marveled that anyone in his right mind would ever buy such an underpowered vehicle. Baby told them that the original owner, up in Phoenix, never drove it faster than thirty-five.

Tired of talking trucks and thinking Diana might be ready to head home, Brandon ventured inside to check. To his surprise, he found her busily wrapping corn husks around hunks of uncooked *masa* filled with meat.

"How soon before you'll be done?" he asked.

"Not for a while," she said. "Are you in a hurry?"

Brandon was, actually. Yesterday he had learned something concerning the Roseanne Orozco investigation that he was eager to follow up on today. He wanted to get started, but Diana, who spent most of her time in the solitary occupation of writing, seemed to be at home in the company of this group of industrious women.

"No," he said. "I'm fine. I'll wait outside with Leo and Baby and the others."

For a time Brandon watched a collection of children play makeshift soccer on the cleared dirt field between the compound's collection of houses and the mini-mart and auto-repair buildings along the highway. No doubt the kids had all been coached about the solemnity of the occasion, but childish natural exuberance could only be suppressed for so long. As they chased the ball back and forth, Brandon remembered when Lani was that age.

He had loved standing on the sidelines of her soccer matches, watching her jet-black ponytail plume out behind her as she raced up and down the field. Neither Tommy nor Quentin had been into sports. Besides, Brandon had been working too many hours when they were little. He had missed out completely on that part of their growing-up years, which probably accounted for his determination not to miss that time with Lani. He made it his business to be there for her—every game, every school program or play, every parent-teacher conference.

Brandon glanced at his watch and shook his head. If he'd known he'd be done in *Ban Thak* this early, he would have volunteered to collect Lani from the airport rather than sending Candace. Lani gave every evidence of adoring her nephew, but Brandon knew that the two-year-old—spoiled by both his doting mother and grandmother—could be annoying on his best days. With Fat Crack's death weighing heavily on her heart, Brandon suspected Lani wouldn't be up to dealing with Tyler's antics. Besides, Brandon regretted missing out on a few private hours with his daughter. Now that she was grown, father-daughter times when it was just the two of them were rare. As soon as Lani arrived home, she'd be drawn into the funeral preparations and events. It might be days before Brandon had some time alone with her.

One of the mothers broke up the soccer game by summoning the children to come eat. Left at loose ends, Brandon considered his options for a moment and then made up his mind. He went back into the kitchen, where Diana was still wrapping tamales.

"I'll be back in a while," he told her. "I need to run an errand."

"Where are you going?"

"To talk with Emma Orozco," he said.

Brandon Walker remembered Fat Crack telling him once that, as part of a grant from Arizona State University in the early nineties, all existing health records from the Indian Health Services hospital in Sells had been fed into computers. The study had been intended to learn how Tohono O'odham longevity compared with that of other ethnic populations. It was also a way of assessing and keeping track of which diseases on the reservation accounted for which deaths. That study—with records from as far back as the fifties—along with money from tribal casino operations, was one of the reasons the hospital at Sells now had its own kidney dialysis center.

The study also meant that records of Roseanne Orozco's appendectomy in July of 1970 should be only a few keystrokes away. But having the records available and being able to access them were two different things. Brandon knew that if he went to the hospital and asked, his request would be met with polite but implacable resistance. Whoever was in charge would take one look at his *Mil-gahn* face, smile respectfully, and tell him nothing like that existed. He hoped Emma Orozco wouldn't encounter the same difficulty.

Brandon drove to Andrea Tashquinth's place in Big Fields. It was a long, low adobe house that looked as though rooms had been added haphazardly over the years. When he drove up he heard two swamp coolers, one at either end of the house, humming away. A long-legged black mutt watched Brandon curiously but without objection as he stepped out of the car and knocked on what he hoped was the front door. Andrea herself an-

swered. "What do you want?" she asked. Some of her
initial hostility from the day before had returned.

"I'd like to speak to your mother," Brandon said. "Is
she here?"

"Yes, but she's very tired."

"I need her help . . ." Brandon began.

"Is it about Roseanne?" Emma Orozco called from
somewhere beyond the half-opened door and out of
Brandon's view.

"Yes," he said.

Andrea sighed and shook her head resignedly. "All
right," she said. "Wait here."

Brandon was neither surprised nor offended by not
being invited inside. Several minutes later Emma, leaning
on her walker, hobbled out of the house. "What is it?"
she asked. "Have you found something?"

"Not yet," Brandon told her, "but I'm working on it.
When I talked to Andrea yesterday, she mentioned that
shortly before her death, Roseanne had been hospitalized with appendicitis."

Emma nodded. "That's right."

"Do you remember the name of the physician who
took care of her?"

"No. It was a long time ago. Why do you want to
know?"

"Andrea said Roseanne was still sick after she got out
of the hospital."

Emma nodded again. "The doctor did some tests and
said she had an infection from the surgery. He gave her
something for it. Henry was supposed to bring her home
from the hospital, but she left before he got there. We
never saw her again."

"Mrs. Orozco, you told me on Friday that as far as
you knew, Roseanne didn't have a boyfriend. Correct?"

"Yes."

"And, because of Roseanne's condition—her inability to speak—she didn't exactly socialize."

"Yes."

"But she was pregnant when she was murdered. I'd like to track down her medical records. Then, if the autopsy results show how far along the pregnancy was when Roseanne was murdered—"

"You think she got pregnant while she was in the hospital?" Emma interrupted.

"It's possible," Brandon said. "Did anyone besides Andrea raise that issue at the time? Did she convince anyone at all to look into it?"

Emma pursed her lips and shook her head. "What do you want me to do?" she asked.

"Ride with me to the hospital," Brandon said. "Tell whoever's there that you've asked me to look into Roseanne's murder and that I need to see her medical records. They're usually confidential, but as her mother . . ."

Nodding, Emma turned and hobbled back to the door. Opening it, she called inside. "I'm going for a ride," she said. "I'll be back after."

Brian Fellows arrived at the Pima County Sheriff's Department well before the appointed time for the interview with Erik LaGrange. Brian had been told that as of that afternoon, Erik would be represented by a public defender named Earl Coulter, which meant nobody was doing LaGrange any favors. Coulter's nickname, the Snoozer, derived from his propensity for turning up at court still reeking of last night's booze and then dozing throughout the proceedings.

All the way into town, Brian had been thinking about

what Brandon Walker had said about the dead girl in the ice chest, the girl named Roseanne Orozco. The idea that there could be a connection between the two victims who had been murdered and dismembered more than thirty years apart seemed remote, but still . . . Brian was a cop who prided himself on keeping an open mind.

Once in his cubicle, he keyed Roseanne's name into his computer. Her case popped up along with all the other unsolved cold cases in Pima County. Only the basic facts had been summarized in the computer. To learn more, he'd need to examine the paper file. After requesting it from Records, Brian turned to what was available on yesterday's Jane Doe. *Although,* Brian corrected, *Juanita Doe would be more like it.*

PeeWee showed up dressed as though he'd come straight from church. "Anything new?" he asked, settling at his own desk.

"Not much," Brian returned. "LaGrange drew Earl Coulter as his public defender."

"All the better for us," PeeWee said with a grin. "What about the autopsy?"

"We won't have that until tomorrow."

"How come the ME can take weekends off and we can't?" PeeWee complained. Detective Segura wasn't known for maintaining a positive mental attitude.

"They've got refrigerators now," Brian answered. "Speaking of weekends off, the prosecutor's office is taking a pass on this meeting after all."

"They're the ones who set it up for today," PeeWee objected.

"Right," Brian said, "but right now it's just La-Grange, Coulter, and us."

"What a bunch of jerks," PeeWee grumbled.

When they entered the interview room, Earl Coulter

was already there. The airless, drab room reeked of beery breath and stale cigar smoke. "How's it going, Earl?" Brian asked.

"Can't complain," Earl said. Sporting an atrocious, food-spotted tie across his protruding gut, he made as if to stand before deciding it wasn't worth the effort. After rising an inch or two off his chair and holding out a pudgy hand, he settled back into his chair with a relieved wheeze.

A door opened and a guard escorted the prisoner into the room. The orange jail jumpsuit and fluorescent overhead lights combined to give Erik a sallow, sickly look. Brian could tell from looking at him that he'd slept very little. The lawyer made another abortive effort at rising. "Earl Coulter," he said to Erik. "Glad to make your acquaintance."

Barely acknowledging the greeting, Erik turned to Brian. "Look, Detective Fellows," he said. "Refusing to talk to you yesterday without having an attorney present was poor judgment on my part. I was so shocked by what was happening that asking for a lawyer was all I could think of, but this mess is some kind of awful mistake. I know there's been a murder. You told me yesterday that the victim is a girl, but I have no idea who she was or what happened to her. What I do know is that I had nothing to do with it. I want to help you find whoever's responsible."

"Really, Mr. LaGrange," Coulter began, but Erik brushed aside his attorney's objection.

"I said I want to help, and I do," Erik declared, looking directly at Brian. "Let's get on with it."

The fact that the suspect was ready to cooperate came as no surprise to Detective Fellows. A night in jail often produced remarkable changes of heart when it came to a suspect's willingness to talk. While PeeWee interrupted the proceedings long enough to announce on tape who was present, Brian removed his notebook from his pocket and consulted it.

"You stopped talking right about the time I asked you what you did after work Friday night. How about if we start there? Tell us about Friday."

"I came home," Brian said. "I picked up carry-out Mexican food from Lerua's after work and brought it home."

"By yourself?"

"I was with someone else. She wasn't with me when I got the food, but she came by the house later. That's the thing. I don't want to cause her any trouble." He paused, then added, "She's married. You won't drag her into any of this, will you?"

"That depends," Brian said carefully.

"On what?"

"On your telling us everything you can. We may need to check with her to verify that you've told us the truth and can corroborate your alibi."

"Mr. LaGrange . . ." Earl Coulter began again, but Erik wasn't listening.

"Her husband won't have to know?"

"We can be discreet," Brian said.

PeeWee Segura, standing behind the suspect, rolled his eyes at this blatant lie, but Erik was desperate and he bought it completely.

"Her name's Gayle Stryker," he said. "She and her husband, Larry Stryker, Dr. Lawrence Stryker, run Medicos for Mexico. Gayle's my boss. She and I have been . . . well, involved for some time."

"I take it her husband has no idea that the two of you are an item?"

"Right," Erik said. "At least I don't think he does."

"All right. The lady came to visit, the two of you had dinner together, and then what? Did she stay over?"

"No," Erik said. He paused, as if considering what to say next. "We had a fight. Gayle got mad and left early."

"What time?"

"I don't remember exactly. Maybe ten. Maybe later."

"What did you do then?"

"I went to bed. The next morning I got up and went for a hike. I was coming back from that yesterday afternoon when you found me."

"You have no idea how all that human blood ended up in the back of your pickup truck?" Brian asked.

"None at all. It wasn't there when I came home from work Friday afternoon."

"When you returned home from your hike, was your truck parked in the same place?"

"As far as I know. I couldn't swear, but it seemed like the same place."

"Who else has access to your vehicle?"

"No one."

"Is there an extra set of keys?" Brian asked.

"Yes."

"Where do you keep those?"

"In my briefcase."

"And that is?"

"At home. In the kitchen on the counter. I was carrying the food and the briefcase at the same time. I put them down on the counter."

"You still haven't told me how the blood might have gotten there. Are you suggesting someone gained access to your house, took your vehicle, used it during the course of a homicide, and then returned it to your driveway?" Brian asked. "Doesn't that seem a little far-fetched?"

Erik's face reddened. "It sounds ridiculous, but that has to be what happened."

"Who else has access to your house?" Brian repeated with apparent unconcern. "Do you have a cleaning lady, by any chance? Or does Mrs. Stryker have her own key?"

"No cleaning lady," Erik answered. "Gayle has a garage-door opener. She usually comes and goes through the garage."

Something about that rang a bell. Brian paged through his notebook until he found his interview with Erik's neighbor.

"Any other family members living here in town?" Brian asked. "Parents? Brother or sisters?"

"My mother died shortly after I was born. I have no idea if my father is dead or alive."

Which means, Brian thought, *the lady the neighbor saw Erik spending so much time with definitely wasn't his mother after all.*

"Are you a Diamondback fan?" Brian asked.

For a moment Erik seemed stunned, as though he thought the conversation had gone from discussing the murder to a casual "How-about-them-Cubs" bullshit session. "I guess so," he said.

"Do you have some of their gear?"

"Oh," Erik said. "Yes. A baseball cap, a sweatshirt, and a jacket. Medicos did a fund-raising event with them last year. Why?"

"What kind of tennis shoes do you wear?"

"Nikes."

"All right," Brian said. "That's it for now. How do we go about getting in touch with Mrs. Stryker?"

"But I thought you said you wouldn't drag her into this," Erik objected.

"I said we'd be discreet," Brian countered. "We need to talk to her to verify what you've told us so far. If you're telling the truth, I'm sure she won't mind vouching for you."

Erik looked uncomfortable.

Brian shrugged. "You can give us her phone number now, or we can track her down on our own tomorrow. Suit yourself."

Erik glanced uneasily at Earl Coulter, as if he was finally ready to take the attorney's advice. Unfortunately, Coulter wasn't listening. The Snoozer was sound asleep, his double chin resting on the awful tie.

As Erik was being led back to his cell, he tried to quell another attack of panic. Overnight he'd told himself things couldn't be all that bad, but in the interview room he had finally glimpsed the totality of what he was up against. A girl was dead—murdered. Her blood was in his truck and most likely on his clothing as well. His machete was the presumed murder weapon. It meant that someone somewhere was trying to frame him for a murder he hadn't committed. To make matters worse, Erik was stuck with a drunken attorney who was utterly useless.

Erik's only hope was that once Gayle knew the kind of trouble he was in, she'd forgive him and come to his rescue. That wasn't too much to ask, was it?

The guard took Erik as far as his cell and let him inside. As the bars clanged shut behind him, it sounded as though they were closing forever. He fell onto his cot. For the first time since his grandmother died, Erik La-Grange tried to pray.

nineteen

Brandon dropped Emma at the hospital's front entrance. By the time he had parked and come inside, Emma was seated at a desk where a young Tohono O'odham clerk sat before a keyboard.

Brandon's first instinct was to go to Emma and offer moral support. After a moment's thought, however, he decided against it. Emma's request would be better received without a *Mil-gahn* man peering over her shoulder. Brandon stationed himself by the door and tried to look unobtrusive. Not that it worked. Every person who went in or out gave him a serious once-over.

Emma's conversation was too soft-spoken for eavesdropping. Each time Emma spoke, the young woman would type briskly away. Then, after a frowning pause, she would shake her head. Brandon didn't have to hear what was being said to understand that.

Brandon was reconsidering his decision to stay out of it when the clerk typed in yet another request. This time, after the pause, she smiled and nodded. Seconds later, she reached over to a printer and removed several pieces of paper. After stapling them together, she handed them to Emma, who studied them briefly and stuffed them into her purse. She rose to her feet. With a nod of thanks, Emma swung her walker around and headed for the door.

Brandon leaped to open the door as Emma approached. "You got it?" he asked.

Looking at him, she shook her head almost imperceptibly, but she didn't answer aloud until they were outside the building.

"She's wrong," Emma said as she stamped along, banging her walker on the sidewalk.

"But I thought she gave you something," Brandon began. "I saw her hand you—"

"She says there's no record of anyone named Roseanne Orozco ever being admitted to the hospital," Emma said fiercely. "She said it was so long ago that maybe they lost the records, but it's not true. She found my record. It shows I was in the hospital three times—once when Andrea was born, once when Roseanne was born, and fifteen years ago for my hysterectomy."

Brandon helped Emma up onto the Suburban's running board. While she settled in, he stashed the walker behind the front seat. Once he was behind the wheel, he realized Emma was staring at him intently.

"Andrea's right," she said, nodding. "It was somebody at the hospital."

"We don't know that," Brandon cautioned. "Just because the records are missing . . ."

But Emma Orozco wasn't listening. "I could never understand it," she said. "They told me Roseanne was pregnant when she died, but I could never understand how that was possible. If she'd had a boyfriend, I would have known about him, or Andrea would have. But Roseanne didn't *talk*, Mr. Walker. Not to anyone. Not even to me or to her father."

Brandon had switched on the ignition. Rather than

pulling out of the parking lot, he sat with the engine idling while the air-conditioning gradually came on.

"But there were all those rumors," Emma added after a long pause.

"What rumors?"

"People said some of the doctors at the hospital . . ." Emma's voice faded away.

"Some of the doctors what?" Brandon asked.

"Did bad. You know, that they messed with their patients."

"What do you mean, messed with?" Brandon asked. "As in molested them?"

Emma nodded. "But it was a long time after Roseanne was gone. I wondered if it could have had something to do with her, but my husband . . ." She stopped and shrugged.

Brandon remembered what Andrea had said about the sins white men committed on the reservation going unpunished. This was clearly another case in point, and he understood where Emma was going.

"Since everyone but you seemed to have forgotten all about Roseanne, your husband didn't want you causing trouble and bringing it back up, right?"

Emma nodded again. "I shouldn't have listened to Henry," she said.

Brandon considered his next words carefully. "Mrs. Orozco . . ." he began.

"Emma," she corrected.

Brandon knew that being granted first-name status was a gift, and he accepted it as such. "Emma," he said, "I must caution you. This is all theoretical. We may be going nowhere with this. Still, it's a place to start. Given all that, are you sure you can't remember the name of Roseanne's doctor?"

Emma shook her head. "No," she said. "He was young, but all the doctors were young back then. I don't remember any of their names. They came for a few years and then left. Something about paying off college loans."

And keeping their butts out of Vietnam, Brandon thought. "It doesn't matter," he told her. "The hospital should have records of which doctors were there and for how long. Can you tell me exactly when Roseanne went into the hospital?"

"Early July, right after the rains started," Emma replied. "Henry and I drove into Tucson to get groceries. When we came home, we got stuck on the far side of the washes over by Ryan Field. It took a couple of hours for the water to go down enough so we could cross. Roseanne was feeling sick. Andrea took her over to the hospital, but they wouldn't do anything until we signed the papers. When we got home, it was almost too late. Her appendix burst. They told us she might die. Afterward, when she finally got home from the hospital, she was still sick.

"Did anyone at the hospital show a particular interest in your daughter?" Brandon asked. "We've talked about the doctors. What about someone else? An orderly, or maybe a male nurse?"

"No," Emma said. "I don't remember anyone like that at all."

"Was there anybody else who expressed an interest in her?" Brandon asked. "Someone from school, for example? Maybe one of her teachers."

"After her operation, Roseanne was still sick," Emma said. "When school started that year, she didn't go back."

Putting the Suburban in reverse, Brandon backed out of the parking place and headed back to Big Fields. For a while they rode in silence. In 1970, the investigators theorized that the father of Roseanne Orozco's baby might be responsible for her death, but when they learned their prime suspect—Roseanne's father—wasn't the baby's father, they let the investigation slide. Thirty-two years later, there were other tools that hadn't been invented or even thought of in 1970—tools that were capable of unlocking secrets that were decades old, but using them meant venturing into an emotional minefield.

They were almost back to Big Fields before Brandon Walker broached the subject. "Where is Roseanne buried?" he asked.

"Over there," Emma said, nodding in the direction of a small barbed-wire-enclosed cemetery near the far boundary of the village. "Her father's there, too. Why?"

"Do you mind showing me?"

"No."

Brandon parked the vehicle as close as possible to the battered iron gate that marked the cemetery's entrance. As he retrieved Emma's walker and helped her down to the ground, a collection of curious children gathered around. While Brandon opened the gate, Emma entered, holding her head high. She threaded unerringly through a collection of sagging crosses and simple headstones. Inside a small separately fenced plot were three headstones—two large ones on either side of a tiny white cross. Henry Orozco's name was carved into one of the large headstones. Roseanne's name was carved on the other. The cross between them had no name at all.

After examining the middle cross, Brandon looked questioningly at Emma. "Roseanne's baby?" he asked.

"Yes," she said quietly. "Roseanne couldn't name her, so we didn't either. They took the baby for the autopsy and kept it even after we buried Roseanne. When they finally released the baby's body, we put her here so she could be with her mother."

"The baby was a girl," Brandon said, thinking about what Fat Crack had said about the Tohono O'odham's lost girls. Roseanne Orozco and her daughter were two of them, right along with Lani and Delia. But that made sense. After all, hadn't Rita Antone and Fat Crack both taught him that among the Desert People all things in nature go in fours?

"Yes," Emma agreed.

The fact that the baby's remains had been separated from her mother's was more than Brandon Walker could have hoped for, but that didn't make asking the critical questions any easier. He wanted to be diplomatic and kind. Emma Orozco had been hurt enough.

"Was the baby embalmed?" he asked.

"I don't know. No one ever told us."

She spoke softly, carefully, but Brandon knew what both the questions and answers cost her. "Do you know about DNA?"

"You mean like at O.J.'s trial?" Emma returned. "Sure, I know about that."

"Yes," Brandon said. "Like with O.J., but DNA identification techniques have improved greatly since then."

"You want to dig up the baby?"

Emma's direct approach caught Brandon off-guard. "Yes," he said. "I'm thinking Law and Order may have been right back then. If we learn who the baby's father was . . ."

"Do what you need to do, Mr. Walker," Emma Orozco said. "If you need me to sign papers to make it happen, just let me know."

* * *

Diana had told Lani that Davy wouldn't be able to pick her up at Sky Harbor. Candace and Tyler would be coming in Davy's stead, but all through the long plane trip, Lani had hoped that either her brother or her dad would be there to pick her up.

It wasn't that Lani disliked Candace. It was just that, with Candace's upscale Midwest background, the two young women had virtually nothing in common—other than their mutual love for Lani's brother. On that single subject they were in total agreement.

When she saw Candace and Tyler waving at her from the far side of the security checkpoint, Lani's heart fell. She had tried without success to sleep on the plane. Now, bone-weary and still mourning, she was faced with riding home with someone who had once thought that Crack was somehow Fat Crack's last name. Davy and Lani knew the emptiness Fat Crack's absence would leave in both their lives. Candace had no clue.

Tyler, waving and grinning, gave every evidence of being delighted to see his auntie—right up until she was close enough to touch. At that point, he buried his head in his mother's shoulder and screamed bloody murder.

"How was your flight?" Candace asked, bouncing the child and trying to quiet him.

"All right," Lani said. "In terms of post-9/11 air travel, it went as well as possible."

"Sorry David couldn't make it," Candace said.

Lani winced. David was so much more formal than Davy, so much more serious. Davy was her brother. Who exactly was David?

"Gabe's sons asked him and your dad to come out to some village on the reservation and help dig the grave," Candace continued as they headed for the luggage carousels. "I don't know why they have to do things like that by hand. Back home, we had people with machines who dug graves. Nobody had to show up at cemeteries with picks and shovels."

Lani didn't hear the rest of Candace's complaint. For the remainder of the trip home, Lani was virtually impervious to Tyler's wails and screeches from his car-seat imprisonment in the back. Her feelings were no longer hurt. She was content.

Neither Davy Ladd nor Brandon Walker had driven to the airport to pick Lani up and bring her home, but both her father and her brother—the Boy with Two Mothers and Four Fathers—were at *Ban Thak,* doing what needed to be done.

And that, nawoj, she thought to herself, *is the way things ought to be.*

Alvin Miller was forty years old and had worked for the Pima County Sheriff's Department for more than half his life. He had started out doing an Eagle Scout volunteer project for the Latent Fingerprint Lab as a sixteen-year-old and had been there ever since, becoming the youngest person in the country to achieve full technician qualification with the Automated Fingerprint Identification System. With only a few community college credits to his name, all of his experience and most of his education had come the hard way—hands-on.

Alvin's unwavering loyalty to Sheriff Walker hadn't been lost on incoming Sheriff Forsythe. The new administration hadn't been tough enough to come right out and fire Miller, but Forsythe had done his underhanded best to run Alvin Miller out of Dodge. First he cut the fingerprint lab's budget and head count, thinking that tactic would persuade Alvin to pack up and go elsewhere. Instead, Alvin had worked more hours himself, many of them off the clock, until even Sheriff Forsythe could see that losing Miller's expertise would be a serious blow.

Late the previous evening, a CSI unit had come dragging back to the department with an armload of dishes, silverware, and other items taken from a crime scene related to Saturday's Vail homicide. The evidence had arrived too late in the shift to be processed on Saturday evening.

Alvin understood the sacrosanct pecking order inside the department. People with the least amount of seniority and experience were the ones who were stuck manning weekend shifts. Alvin, a lifelong bachelor with no family responsibilities, made it a practice to check in every Sunday morning to make sure whoever was minding the store didn't need assistance.

This morning, Sally Carmichael, his newest intern, called Alvin at home before he could call her. She seemed close to hyperventilating.

"What's the problem, Sally?" he asked. "You sound upset."

"I am upset," she told him. "I'm here by myself. Tom and Marlene left me a whole pile of stuff to be processed ASAP. Detective Fellows has already called twice, asking if I've done any work on it. I told him I'll try to get to it this afternoon, but I don't see how—"

"Don't worry," Alvin reassured her. "I'll come give you a hand."

In actual fact, Alvin was more than happy to do it. He still felt a proprietary interest in his AFIS equipment. No matter how well trained his people were, he was never quite as confident of anyone else's fingerprint enhancements as he was of his own.

Alvin came in, donned his lab jacket, checked the items in question out of the evidence room, and went to work. The CSI unit had brought in a number of prints they had lifted from the scene, but rather than paying attention to those, Alvin went looking for prints he could process himself from beginning to end. He started with the presumed murder weapon—the machete.

The evidence log reported that the machete had been found in a kitchen sink, soaking in soapy water. The soap had done some but not all of the work of removing the blood from the joint where the handle and blade came together and from the decorative carvings on the handle itself, but as far as usable fingerprints were concerned, the machete was clean as a whistle.

The plates and silverware were a gold mine by comparison. Working carefully and humming under his breath, Alvin dusted and retrieved what appeared to him to be two relatively perfect sets of prints. Once he had the prints lifted, he spent the better part of two hours going over each print and enhancing by hand the lines and whorls he found there so that the image fed into the machine would be as clear as possible.

"Do we have anything to compare these to?" Alvin asked when Sally peered at his work over his shoulder. He spoke without ever looking away from the print he was working on.

"The suspect's been booked," Sally told her boss.

"That means his prints are already in the system," Alvin said. "What about the victim's?"

"The autopsy's tomorrow sometime. We won't have her prints until after that."

"Some things can't be rushed," Alvin said. "When you entered the suspect's prints, did you get a hit?"

"No."

"Well," Alvin said. "Run me off a copy of his prints, and I'll take a look."

In a matter of minutes Sally returned. Alvin peered at the paper for only a matter of seconds before making up his mind. "Yup," he said. "The suspect's prints are on both sets of dishes. He probably served the meal and cleared up afterward. We'll put those aside for the time being. The ones we should concentrate on are the unknowns. If they belong to the victim and she's in the system, we may make a positive ID before the ME does. That would be a huge help to the detectives. The sooner they know who's dead, the sooner they find out who did it."

That was Alvin Miller's style—work, talk, and teach all at the same time. That was why people who moved on from his lab were always in demand.

It was almost noon before Alvin was finally satisfied enough with the second set of prints to put them into the machine for copying and transmitting. While the computer did its stuff, he walked back to his desk to retrieve a now-dead-cold cup of coffee. He had taken a single sip when Sally called him back.

"Hey, Mr. Miller," she called. "Come look at this."

Being referred to as Mr. Miller made Alvin feel old, but the excitement in Sally's voice was unmistakable. "Must be a hit, then," he said. "Whose is it?"

Wordlessly Carol handed him the printout. Alvin read it through.

"Holy shit!" he exclaimed. "We'd better get Detective Fellows on the horn right away."

Delia Chavez stood outside, patting balls of dough into tortillas and then tossing them onto a wood-fire-heated griddle. Her sister-in-law waited while the dough cooked, then turned them deftly with her fingers, let them cook on the other side, and then tossed them onto a waxed-paper-covered table to cool. Delia's tortilla-making deficit had been corrected first by her aunt Julia and later by her mother-in-law after Delia's return to the reservation.

She had come home grateful to have a job that allowed her to leave D.C. and Philip's betrayal far behind. But coming back to Arizona did something else—it brought her face-to-face with her father and his betrayal of her mother all those years earlier.

As far as Delia could see, Eddie was nothing but a worthless drunk; so was her father. Still bristling with anger at Philip, Delia had been more than ready to write both of them off. Then, when a seriously injured Manny was sent home from Tucson a virtually helpless cripple, Delia had no choice but to take charge of her father's life. She looked after him because she had to—because she was his daughter and there was no one else to do it.

"You shouldn't be so angry with him, you know," Aunt Julia said one day. She had come into Sells from Little Tucson and was patiently instructing Delia's clumsy computer-savvy fingers in the fine art of patting popover dough while Manny Chavez, visiting on his paid caregiver's day off, dozed in his wheelchair in the next room.

"You really need to forgive him," Aunt Julia continued. "Blaming your father for everything that happened is only hurting you and no one else. You're very smart, *ni ma'i*—niece, and a lawyer besides. Everything you learned in school should have taught you that it's wrong to see only one side of things."

Julia, Delia's mother's aunt, was the last person Delia expected to leap to Manny's defense.

"What other side is there?" Delia shot back angrily. "It *is* his fault. He's the one who beat my mother up. I saw him do it. If it's not his fault, whose is it, my mother's?"

"No," Julia said. "It wasn't Ellie's fault, either. She was too young to know what was what."

"Whose, then?" Delia persisted.

"If you want someone to blame," Aunt Julia said, "you should probably look to your grandmother, to my sister Guadalupe."

"Come on," Delia objected. "She died so long ago, I don't even remember her. How could you blame any of this on her?"

"Guadalupe knew what your mother was like. We all did, from the time she was little. It was wrong of my sister to arrange a marriage with Manny. Girls like that don't make good wives."

"Girls like what?" Delia demanded. "You mean girls like me—ones who are smart the way my mother was or who want to go to school to better themselves?"

"No," Aunt Julia said softly. "I mean girls who like girls."

That conversation had proved to be a watershed for Delia Cachora. For the first time she could see that the tragedy of her father's life wasn't so different from her own. Manny had married Ellie Francisco expecting one thing and had gotten another in the same way Delia's marriage to Philip had turned out to be far different from her own expectations.

From then on, Delia was able to be kinder to her father and far more patient in her dealings with him. Eventually she was able to forgive both her parents for the unwitting mistakes they had made along the way. She never forgave Philip, though. Unlike Manny Chavez and Ellie Francisco when they married, Philip Cachora had known exactly what he was doing.

twenty

But even with all the Indian mother's care, her baby seemed to grow smaller and smaller. When the cold days came, she slept more and more and smiled less often. And the mother, in those days, never smiled at all. She was afraid.

Then one morning, the parents found that their baby was not breathing.

So the mother wrapped the little one in her brightest blankets. And the father called for his neighbors to help him. The parents and their friends carried the baby to the mountains, where the dead are put in their rock homes.

They did not need much brush or many stones to cover such a little thing.

Now a good Indian does not show how he feels. Especially if one is sad, it must not be shown. Great Spirit—I'itoi—who is the Spirit of Goodness and Elder Brother of the Tohono O'odham—manages everything. So to feel very bad about anything is to oppose the Spirit of Goodness.

But this mother had eaten nothing all that day. In her throat there was something big and hard which she could not swallow. As she went up the mountain with *her friends, she kept stumbling. And this worried her husband. He was afraid she would let the water come in her eyes.*

PeeWee had gone home and Brian was at his desk trying to sort through his impressions of the LaGrange interview when his phone rang. "Brian? Glad you answered the phone."

Alvin Miller wasn't a great one for using proper titles, and Brian recognized his voice. "What's up?"

"AFIS just got a hit on one of the prints from yesterday's crime scene. I can fax it up to you or—"

"Hold on," Brian said. "I'll be right there."

He wasn't right there. The elevator took forever. "What have you got?" he asked as soon as Sally Carmichael unlocked the lab door for him to enter. "Is it the victim? Do we have a name?"

"Slow down," Alvin said. "One thing at a time. I've requested detailed information on the case in question. It should arrive in the next several minutes. AFIS only sends out an abbreviated version, but from what I've learned so far, the matching print was a single one found on the inside of a garbage bag containing dismembered human remains. It was found three years ago near a rest area along Interstate 8 on the far side of Gila Bend, halfway to the California border."

"Human remains?" Brian repeated. "What kind of human remains?"

"An unidentified female, thirteen to fifteen years of age."

"The case is still open?"

"That's right."

"Are you saying it's possible the victim here is actually the perpetrator in that other case?"

"I doubt that," Miller said. "I think it's more likely that you've stumbled into a serial homicide case. La-Grange may be involved, but I'm guessing so is somebody else. If I were you, I'd look for other cases with the same MO."

So Brian did just that. He went back up to his cubicle and logged on to the VICAP system. The Violent Criminal Apprehension Program, the brainchild of longtime L.A. homicide detective Pierce Brooks, was created back in the seventies, when the only way of finding similar crimes and perpetrators was to pore through mountains of newspaper files. Computers changed all that.

He keyed in the few details he knew: female victim, twelve to twenty years old, dismembered body. A few moments later, as he scrolled through the results of his search, what chilled him was the number of unsolved crimes that matched those criteria—forty-one in all, stretching through more than three decades. At the very end of the list, the earliest case in the database leaped out at him—Roseanne Orozco.

That was the name Brandon Walker had mentioned that morning as they dug Fat Crack's grave, the victim he had called the Girl in the Box. The coincidence was too much to ignore. It was highly unlikely that Erik La-Grange had already been a serial killer as a five-year-old. Still, Brian's instincts told him there had to be a connection. To find it, he needed information.

The Yuma County Sheriff's Department had been the investigating agency in the crime Alvin Miller had uncovered. Brian put in a request for information on that case, asking that it be faxed to him. He had already asked for Roseanne Orozco's file, but a weekend request for a paper file on a thirty-year-old case had yet to bubble to the top. Besides, since the homicide had occurred on the reservation, it seemed likely that much of the information on that case might still be located at the Law and Order office out in Sells.

He considered calling Brandon at home to ask if he remembered anything in particular about the case, but he thought better of it. Even though Brandon's involuntary exit from office was years in the past, Brian knew that involving the former sheriff in a current investigation was bound to have unpleasant repercussions for everyone concerned, most especially for Brian Fellows.

Brandon picked Diana up from the Ortiz place. As they drove home, she leaned back in the seat and closed her eyes. "Tired?" he asked.

"I'm not used to doing that much physical labor," she said. "If there isn't enough food to go around at the feast tomorrow, it won't be for lack of trying. If I ever look at another pile of *masa harina* or *masa trigo*, it'll be too soon. How about you? You were gone a long time."

He told her then about the situation with Emma Orozco and about how all record of Roseanne's stay in the hospital had somehow been misplaced or deleted. "Isn't that about when the husband of that teacher friend of yours was working on the reservation?"

"Larry Stryker?" Diana asked.

"Yeah. The guy who runs those free clinics down in Mexico."

"You mean Larry Stryker? Medicos for Mexico."

"Right. Maybe I should talk to him about this."

"About Roseanne Orozco? It happened more than thirty years ago, Brandon. She went in for an appendectomy. I doubt he'll remember the first thing about her."

"Roseanne happened to be an appendectomy patient who was murdered four months after undergoing surgery," Brandon replied. "The way I remember things, there weren't that many murderers in Pima County back then, let alone out on the reservation."

"Suit yourself," Diana said. "Their home number may be unlisted, but it's in my database."

"Good," he said. "That would be a big help."

Diana sighed and lapsed into silence. "What's wrong?" he asked several miles later. "I can smell the smoke."

"You're sure that's all it is?"

"All what is?"

"Your sudden interest in Larry Stryker. It's not because—well, you know."

"Because he and Gayle backed Bill Forsythe's election campaign?"

"Yes."

"Believe me," Brandon said, "if I thought Bill Forsythe himself could help me find Roseanne Orozco's killer, I'd be on my way to talk to him right this minute."

"Oh," Diana said. She sounded relieved.

When they got home, Lani was there. So were Davy and Candace and Tyler. It ended up being a hectic homecoming. The family gathering they had planned but canceled after Fat Crack's death ended up taking place after all. Davy and Brandon went off together to the Albertsons on Silverbell and Speedway Boulevard to pick up steaks and salad makings.

"I called to see if Kath and Brian could make it after all," Diana told Brandon a while later as he seasoned steaks at the kitchen counter. "Brian's still at work, so Kath took a pass."

"Too bad," Brandon said. "I always enjoy having everybody around."

Just then Tyler came streaking into the kitchen, hot on Damsel's trail. "Maybe you should take her outside while you grill the steaks," Diana suggested. "I wouldn't want her to hurt him."

"It looks like it's the other way around," Brandon muttered under his breath. "Come on, girl," he said to the dog. "Let's go outside and find you a little peace and quiet."

Taking the platter of uncooked steaks, Brandon retreated to the backyard with Damsel, where he turned on the grill. While waiting for it to heat up, Brandon sat down on one of the patio chairs. Damsel flopped down beside him.

"Tyler's a noisy little brat, isn't he?" Brandon asked.

Damsel replied by thumping her tail on the flagstone pavers.

"And you're a good dog. All you were trying to do was get out of his way."

A door opened on the far end of the patio. "Dad?" Lani said.

"Yup."

"Who are you talking to?"

"Damsel," Brandon replied sheepishly. Being caught talking to a dog seemed to him to be right up there next to senile. "We're out here commiserating."

"How come Tyler's so hyper?" Lani exclaimed.

"Tyler?" Brandon asked innocently. "'Hyper'? That may be your opinion, Damsel's opinion, and my opinion, but don't mention a word of it to your mother. She thinks the little rascal walks on water."

Gracefully, Lani folded her long slender legs. She sat down cross-legged next to Damsel and cradled the dog's head in her lap. This first quiet moment with his daughter found Brandon at a loss for words. It was a cool, clear night—downright chilly, in fact. Brandon had been sitting there thinking about going back inside for a sweater. Lani, on the other hand, wore a T-shirt and shorts. Her attire gave him a chance to exercise his fatherly prerogatives.

"It's cold out here," he said to her. "Shouldn't you wear something warmer than that?"

Lani rolled her eyes. "Compared to North Dakota, this feels like summer."

"Sorry," he said. "My blood must be thinner than yours."

They both fell silent while he stood up to put the steaks on the grill. "We should have called you about Fat Crack," Brandon said when he finished. "I had no idea things were as bad as they were. I don't think anyone else knew, either."

"I should have known," Lani said reproaching herself.

"But Fat Crack knew," Brandon told her. "If he had wanted you to be here with him, he could have had Wanda call you."

"What do you mean, he knew?" Lani demanded.

"Just a minute," Brandon said. He hurried into the house and returned a few moments later carrying Fat Crack's fringed leather pouch. Gently he placed it in Lani's hands.

"Looks at Nothing's *huashomi*," Lani whispered reverentially, clutching the frayed buckskin to her breast. "Why do you have it?"

"I saw Fat Crack early yesterday afternoon," Brandon said. "When it was time for me to leave, we smoked the Peace Smoke. Then he gave me this and asked that I give it to you."

"He knew he was dying," Lani murmured.

Brandon nodded. "And if he had told anyone . . ."

"They would have taken him to the hospital," Lani finished. Then she began to cry.

Brandon tried to kneel down beside her, but a knife of pain shot through his left knee. He settled for taking her hands and pulling her up so he could hold her in his arms. "And that would have been wrong," he said, rocking her like a baby. "You know Fat Crack would have hated that."

Lani leaned into her father's chest. "All I wanted was to talk to him one more time," she sobbed. "I wanted to ask him if there was anything else he thought I should know or . . ."

"Lani, Lani, Lani," Brandon murmured soothingly. "For the people left behind there's never a right time. We're greedy. We always want more. We're never ready to let go, but Fat Crack was ready."

"He told you that?"

"No, Lani," Brandon Walker said with a catch in his voice. "He didn't have to."

"Your ankles sure are swollen," Leo said to Delia as he crawled into bed beside her. "Are you okay?"

"I was on my feet a lot today," Delia said. "But I'm fine."

"How are things for tomorrow?"

"Everything's as ready as we can make it. Having the funeral at four will give the kids and buses a chance to leave the high school before everybody else starts showing up."

"Good thinking."

"You're not planning on going to work in the morning, are you?" Leo asked.

"I thought I'd put in half a day. Why?"

"You should take it easy," Leo said. "I'm worried about you and the baby."

"I'm fine," Delia said.

With that, she rolled over on her side and fell asleep.

* * *

It took time for the after-dinner hubbub to die down. Tyler, exhausted from his busy day, turned on the water-works in a foot-stomping red-faced temper tantrum that sent Davy and Candace scurrying home early. While Lani and Diana cleared away dishes and cleaned up the kitchen, Brandon retreated into his office and dialed Ralph Ames's number in Seattle.

"Sorry to bother you on a Sunday night," Brandon said once Ralph came on the line. "But something's come up. I'm working the Orozco case. When Roseanne's homicide was first investigated, the top theory was that the father of her unborn baby would be the culprit. Since she had no known boyfriend, everybody thought it was a case of incest and that her father, Henry Orozco, was responsible."

"For both the baby and the murder?" Ralph asked.

"Right," Brandon replied. "But a blood test on the fetus eventually ruled Henry out as the father. The case went cold without turning up any other suspects."

"It doesn't sound like anyone was trying very hard," Ralph Ames observed.

"She was an Indian," Brandon said. "And the murder happened in 1970. Indian homicides weren't exactly a priority in those days, but now I'm thinking the cops back then may have been right. I've located the fetus's grave site. The grandmother is willing to let us exhume the remains, but before I dig them up, I want to be sure DNA testing is authorized."

"Expensive but authorized," Ralph assured him. "Hedda Brinker's philosophy was to spare no expense. How far along was the fetus?"

"About four months," Brandon said. "You think that's too young for a DNA match?"

"Iffy but possible," Ames said. "Where's the grave located?"

"On the reservation. At a village called Big Fields."

"Even with the grandmother's permission, you'll probably need a court order."

Brandon thought about standing in the hot sun earlier that morning digging Fat Crack's grave. That had been simple enough. They showed up at *Ban Thak* with picks and shovels and dug away, but that had been to bury someone, not to dig them up. Brandon didn't know all the Tohono O'odham taboos concerning the handling of the dead, but he suspected there were some.

"We'll probably need a court order and a medicine man," Brandon replied.

"Do you know any?" Ralph Ames asked. "A medicine man, that is."

Brandon paused before answering. "The one I did know died yesterday."

"Surely there are others," Ames returned.

There's my daughter, Brandon Walker wanted to say. But something kept the words from escaping his lips. If he said that to Ralph Ames—a sophisticated urban attorney in his Brooks Brothers suit and Pink's tie—there was a chance Ames would dismiss Brandon as some kind of superstitious nutcase. *But by not saying it,* Brandon argued with himself, *aren't I denying what Lani believes and everything Fat Crack believed as well?*

"Well," Ralph continued, "if you can find another one to do the job, hire him and pay the going rate. In the meantime, tomorrow morning I'll get on the horn and find out where to send samples of the remains once you have them. After more than thirty years, we're going to be dealing with tiny remains and badly degraded DNA.

One lab may be better than another. I want to use the right place first time out."

In a matter of seconds, Ralph Ames had switched from discussing medicine men to DNA testing—effortlessly negotiating the same treacherous philosophical chasm Lani crossed daily as she moved between the worlds of superstition and belief and the teachings of modern science.

No wonder Hedda Brinker put him in charge, Brandon thought. *Here's a guy who isn't afraid of using every available tool.*

When Brandon got up from his desk, he had to stand for a long moment leaning against the wood and resting his arthritic hip before his leg would actually hold his weight. He had only clambered down into Fat Crack's grave a couple of times, and he hadn't worked all that hard, but his body was telling him otherwise.

He limped over to the door and switched off the light. "Getting old is hell," he muttered under his breath as he started back down the hall to the kitchen.

Which is the same thing, he thought, *that Fat Crack told me yesterday.*

By the time Brandon emerged from his office, the kitchen was clean, Diana had taken herself to bed, and Lani was sitting outside on one of the patio chairs, staring up at the sky. "Didn't the stars used to be brighter?" she asked. "Or is that just how it seems?"

"They used to be brighter," Brandon agreed. "As the lights in and around Tucson expand, they reflect off moisture in the sky, making it lighter. Stargazing is better on the other side of the pass."

He sat down next to her. As his eyes adjusted to the ambient light overhead, he realized Lani was sitting with Fat Crack's medicine pouch resting in her lap.

"I really wanted to talk to him," she said.

"I know," Brandon said.

"I feel like he abandoned me, and that he did it on purpose."

"Lani, if he'd done things the way you wanted him to, if he had abandoned his beliefs and accepted the kind of medical care you wanted him to have, he wouldn't have been true to himself."

"I know that," Lani said. "I guess."

She wished she could have told Fat Crack about the strange woman's dissolving face and the skull that had appeared in her crystals and obliterated the medicine man's features, but she knew better than to try talking to her father about it. This didn't seem like something Brandon Walker could understand or accept.

They both fell silent. While they sat quietly, what must have been a dozen Harleys came roaring up the road toward Gates Pass. The sound of their noisy engines reverberated off the cliff faces on either side of the road as they hurtled past. The echoes lingered on long after the motorcycles had crossed the pass and started down the other side.

Brandon was cold, but Lani, still sitting in her T-shirt and shorts, gave no hint of being chilly. "Are you tired?" he asked finally.

"A little," Lani admitted. "I didn't get much sleep last night."

"Maybe you should try," Brandon suggested. "Between the funeral and the feast tomorrow, it's going to be a long day."

"What do you think about Candace?" Lani asked suddenly.

"Candace? What about her?"

"Do you think she's happy here?"

Brandon shrugged. "I've never given it much thought. She seems happy to me. Why?"

Lani shook her head. "I don't know. It's just that she's so different from Davy. And the way she lets Tyler do whatever he wants to."

Brandon nodded. That he had noticed. "I agree Tyler's spoiled, but you have to remember his mother isn't raising him the same way you and Davy were raised. I sometimes think that little boy could use a good healthy dose of Rita Antone. She'd straighten him out in ten minutes flat."

Lani laughed at that. Nana *Dahd* had died on Lani's seventh birthday. She vividly remembered the old Indian woman and her many lessons, all of them taught gently, but with the firm expectation that Lani would behave politely and respectfully.

"Maybe that's where you come in, Lani," Brandon said, rising and taking his aching hip and knee into the house. "You're the closest thing we have to Nana *Dahd* around here. Isn't that the way it works with the Desert People? Don't aunts and uncles do the disciplining?"

Lani laughed. "That's what I've heard, too. The only problem is, Tyler Ladd isn't a Tohono O'odham kid, and I'm not sure his mom would want me to turn him into one."

Picking up Fat Crack's leather pouch and clutching it to her, Lani Walker followed her father into the house.

twenty-one

Brandon and Diana were both sleeping soundly the next morning when Damsel went nuts. "What's up, Damn Dog?" Brandon mumbled sleepily. Just then the doorbell rang. "I'll get it," he told Diana as he hopped out of bed and pulled on clothing.

He and Damsel reached the front door together as the doorbell rang again. Brandon used the security peephole to see who it was. Emma Orozco stood there, leaning on her walker. In the background her son-in-law, Sam Tashquinth, was hauling something unwieldy out of the back of his pickup and lugging it toward the gate. As he entered, Brandon saw Sam's load was swathed in plastic garbage bags that had been duct-taped together.

Shutting Damsel inside, Brandon stepped out on the porch. "Good morning, Emma," he said. "What can I do for you?"

"Bring it," Emma said to her son-in-law, pointing to a spot next to her on the porch.

With a relieved sigh, Sam Tashquinth dropped his burden where she had indicated, while the old woman turned back to Brandon. "She's here," Emma said. "Roseanne's baby."

"You dug her up?"

Emma shrugged. "To ask permission we'd have to go before the tribal council. It would take too long. After dark last night, Sam and my grandson did it."

In terms of speed, taking shovels in hand without waiting for permission got the job done. In terms of establishing a chain of evidence, Emma's self-appointed grave robbing was entirely wrong. Had Brandon been a sworn police officer, his reaction would have been tempered by evidentiary considerations. As part of TLC, he was conflicted by the need to get results for survivors while, at the same time, being able to hold someone accountable in a court of law.

"Thank you," he said. "I'm sure it was a difficult decision."

"I want you to find Roseanne's killer," Emma said determinedly. "Even if he's dead, I want to know he can't ever do this again."

"Yes," Brandon said. "I couldn't agree more."

"Do you want me to leave it here, Mr. Walker?" Sam Tashquinth asked.

"My Suburban's in the garage. We'll put it there. I'll go get the key." He turned to Emma. "Would you like to come inside? My wife would be glad to make coffee . . . "

"No," Emma said at once. "Thank you. We should go. Sam has to get to work."

Brandon hurried inside. Diana was in the kitchen making coffee. "What's up?" she asked.

"Emma's out on the porch. They dug up Roseanne's baby's coffin. It's on the porch, too."

"They dug up the baby?" Diana looked appalled. "Why?"

Brandon removed the car keys from their pegboard

hook. "We're hoping DNA can identify the baby's father—and help us find Roseanne's killer."

"What should I do?" Diana asked, collecting herself. "Invite them in? Offer coffee?"

"No," Brandon said. "Emma told me they have to go back to Sells as soon as we load the casket into the Suburban."

When he went to help, Brandon was surprised by the weight of the casket. It was heavy enough that it took both men to heft it into the Suburban. The fetus itself would have been tiny. "Why such a big casket?" Brandon asked as he shut the luggage doors.

Sam Tashquinth shrugged philosophically. "I asked that. Emma said the man at the mortuary told them it was the only size they had."

And one they could charge more for, too, Brandon thought.

Once they were finished, Sam stepped away from the Suburban, vigorously rubbing both hands on his jeans. The Indian man was clearly relieved to have the casket out of his possession, and Brandon could see why. Even without taking Tohono O'odham taboos into consideration, the idea of driving around with a corpse in the back of his vehicle wasn't Brandon's idea of a good time, either.

The barking dog woke Lani. She came out to the kitchen to find her mother unloading the dishwasher. She looked upset.

"What's going on?" Lani asked.

"Somebody just dropped a dead baby off on the front porch. Your father is loading it into the Suburban."

"A dead baby? For Dad?" Lani was mystified. "How come?"

"It's a case Dad's working on for TLC—a girl from the reservation who was pregnant when she was killed some thirty years ago. Dad's hoping that modern DNA testing can shed some light on the case."

"He really is working for that volunteer cold-case group?"

Diana nodded. "It's been good for him—given him back a sense of purpose, but I don't think he expected to have a casket turn up on the doorstep at six o'clock in the morning. Come to think of it, neither did I."

After pouring three cups of coffee, Diana took hers and headed for her office. Lani and Damsel waited until Brandon came in from outside to wash his hands. Lani handed him his coffee, then, calling Damsel, she headed for the door. "Let's sit outside in the sun," she said. "Mom told me about the case you're working on, but I'd like to hear it from you."

Out on the patio, Brandon told Lani about Roseanne Orozco and what had happened to her. Lani had been the same age as Roseanne when she had lived through her own harrowing experience at the hands of Mitch Johnson. Hearing the story of another Tohono O'odham girl, one who had not survived a similarly savage attack, left Lani feeling half sick. It also explained why her father was so deeply involved.

They had drunk that first pot of coffee and the better part of a second before Diana joined them on the patio. "I'm done answering e-mail," she said. "Can I interest anybody in breakfast?"

Brandon nodded. "Sounds good," he said, "but first I need to call Ralph Ames and find out what he wants me to do about our early-morning guest."

As he headed for his office, Lani turned to her mother.

"You're right," she said. "Dad really is happy to be working again."

Ralph Ames answered on the second ring. "You're up and around early," he said.

"Well," Brandon replied, "I've got some good news and some bad news. The good news is, I have Roseanne Orozco's baby."

"Good," Ames returned. "We should be able to start the DNA testing right away. I've found a place here in Seattle that may be able to get results on fetal remains. What's the bad news?"

"I've got the whole body," Brandon replied. "Coffin and all. The grandmother had it dug up overnight and delivered it to my doorstep bright and early this morning."

Ralph Ames paused for a moment. "I guess that means we don't have to worry about going through the tribal council."

"You could say that," Brandon agreed. "But whoever's doing the testing won't want us to ship them a loaded coffin."

"Right. Let me give them a call and get right back to you," Ames said.

The phone rang again a few minutes later. "Here's the deal," Ralph told him. "The customer relations lady at Genelex tells me we'll need heart tissue. Was the baby embalmed?"

"I asked that. The grandmother doesn't know."

"It's evidently more difficult to get results from embalmed tissue," Ralph told him. "But they'll be glad to try. Where do you want the kit sent?"

"Kit?" Brandon asked.

"A nonstandard tissue-collection kit," Ralph said.

"They'll FedEx it to whoever's obtaining the sample for us."

"I suppose that's better than shipping a coffin across the country," Brandon returned.

"They want the sample collection to be done by an official agency, preferably a medical examiner's office. How's your track record with your local ME?"

"It wasn't bad years ago," Brandon said, "but times have changed. I've been out of the game for a while. My showing up at the morgue with a thirty-two-year-old corpse in the back of my car is likely to go over like a pregnant pole-vaulter."

Ralph chuckled. "See what happens," he said. "If you can't find anyone willing to do the job, let me know."

"Sure thing," Brandon said. "I'd best get started."

Larry Stryker's back hurt. He'd done a lot of unaccustomed physical labor over the weekend. He was getting too old to wrestle mattresses around by himself, but he'd managed. He'd done it. The basement room was ready again—ready and waiting.

Disappointed that Gayle had slipped away without staying the night, he dragged his aching body out of bed and staggered into the bathroom to get ready for work. He kept a radio there so he could listen to news while he showered and dressed. Today the lead story was about the murder of an unidentified female homicide victim whose body had been found near Vail on Saturday morning. An unnamed suspect had been arrested in connection with the case. The victim, estimated to be in her mid- to late teens, was thought to be Hispanic in origin.

Standing in front of the mirror, razor in hand, Larry smiled at his steamy reflection and experienced that incredible rush that always flooded through him at times like these. His most recent girl was dead, and Erik La-Grange was in jail, but for Larry nothing at all had changed. Except for one thing: Once news of Erik La-Grange's identity leaked to the press, Medicos for Mexico would be overrun with reporters. Bearing that in mind, Larry chose that day's clothing with care. If his photo was going to be in the papers or on television, he wanted to look his best.

During the hour-long drive into town, a few shadows of doubt crept into his thoughts. Always before, through years of disposing of bodies, Gayle had done so in ways that had never led back to Gayle or Larry or Medicos for Mexico. This was different. Was it possible that fury over Erik's betrayal had carried Gayle a step too far? Was she losing her touch? Still, despite his misgivings, Larry knew from what Gayle had said the night before that maintaining a united front was essential. And since Larry's name topped the Medicos for Mexico organization chart, he would have to be there to answer questions about their jailed employee.

That was Larry's part of the job. His reward for hanging tough would come at the end of the week, when Graciella Duarte sent him the next occupant for the room downstairs. In the meantime, he'd have to remember to buy another mattress for the cot and a few more plastic tarps.

Kath was gone by the time Brian woke up, which wasn't a good sign. She usually kissed him good-bye when she left for an early shift. When he went into the kitchen and found she hadn't made coffee, either, he knew he was in trouble. They generally managed only one day off together each week. Kath didn't take kindly to being cheated out of it—even if the reason was work-related. Especially if it was work-related.

At least we'll be together at the funeral this afternoon and the feast tonight, Brian told himself. *Maybe that'll get me out of the doghouse.*

Haunted by his mother's scattershot approach to love and marriage, Brian had entered into his union with Kath determined to make it work. It was a challenge to combine law enforcement careers with two different agencies in the same household. As for having kids? That was too complicated even to consider.

He showered and dressed. An hour later, he was sitting in his cubicle poring over faxes of information from the other similar cases he had located on Sunday. For several of them, he had only cursory reports, but the details were surprisingly familiar. The bodies, so far all unidentified, had been strewn in the desert—just the way this Saturday's victim had been. In two others—one near Sierra Blanca, Texas, and one near El Centro, California—the dismembered remains had been stuffed into Rubbermaid trash containers. He was reading through one from Yuma County—the one where AFIS had picked up that single fingerprint—when a clerk dropped off Roseanne Orozco's dusty paper file. Her case, dredged out of the archives, seemed eerily similar to the others.

The Papago Tribal Police, as they were then called, had been the primary investigative agency. Having played a secondary role, Pima County didn't have extensive involvement. The Orozco file was painfully thin, but the facts were clear. Roseanne's dismembered body had been found by highway workers collecting trash along Highway 86 west of Sells. The body had been hacked to pieces and stuffed into a Coleman cooler. An autopsy had revealed that the fifteen-year-old homicide victim had been pregnant at the time of her death. For some reason, Henry Orozco, the girl's father, was initially considered to be a prime suspect both in terms of Roseanne's death and as the father of her unborn child. When a blood test excluded him as the baby's father, he was dropped as an official suspect in the murder investigation as well. Within weeks of Roseanne's death, new entries in the file ceased completely as the investigation was left to go dormant.

Even so, Brian thought, *Brandon remembered her the moment I brought it up. Why? There was no mention of Brandon Walker's name in the file. His signature didn't appear on any of the reports. Still, it was a case that stuck with him decades later.*

Brian reached for his phone and dialed the Walker place in Gates Pass. Lani answered. "Hi, Brian," she said. "You missed a great dinner last night."

"I know," he said. "Had to work. Sorry. Is your dad around?"

"No. He left a little while ago. Do you have his cell-phone number?"

"I do," Brian said. "Thanks." But before he had a chance to dial, PeeWee arrived and settled at his own desk. "What are you up to?" he asked.

Wanting his conversation with Brandon Walker to be private, Brian put down the phone. He had been sorting the faxed case files into two separate stacks: scattered remains versus contained remains. He added Roseanne Orozco's file to the second stack and passed the piles along to Detective Segura. "Anyone for a serial killer?" he asked.

While PeeWee scanned the material, Brian walked down the hall. Returning minutes later with coffee, he found PeeWee engrossed in the files.

"You may be right about these being related," PeeWee

said, tapping the stack of faxes that dealt with containerized remains. "These may be connected, too, but this one?" He tapped the Orozco file, which he had pushed to one side. "LaGrange is too young for this one, but I'll check his credit card transactions to see if we can put him in the vicinity for any of the others."

PeeWee took a thoughtful sip of his coffee. "You picked all this stuff off the computer in a matter of hours. How come you're the first investigator to make the connection?"

"Because I'm smarter than the average bear?" Brian asked with a laugh. "No, it's the same old thing. Nobody else found it because nobody else was looking. I'm guessing these are all throwaway kids. They went missing and nobody even bothered to file a missing persons report."

"And without some relative keeping the heat on . . ." PeeWee added.

They both knew why active cases went cold. Time passed and nothing happened. With no grieving relatives maintaining pressure, the respective investigative agencies finally stopped looking.

"Somebody's applying pressure now," Brian said. "You and me. So let's get cracking. I'll call Yuma and talk to the detectives over there. The Vail autopsy is scheduled for ten. Who's going to do that?"

"I'll flip you for it," PeeWee said, tossing a coin in the air. "Heads you go. Tails I do."

The coin came up heads. "Too bad, buddy." PeeWee grinned. "This is one damned autopsy I'm happy to miss."

Brandon drove to the back side of Kino Community Hospital and pulled up in front of the Pima County medical examiner's office. He had come here often enough in the distant past, back when what he still considered the "new" hospital first opened. It had been years now since he'd had any official business with the ME's office. He wondered what kind of reception he should expect when he showed up with a nonroutine corpse and a nonroutine request for a DNA sample.

Brandon walked through one door into a locked entry. While waiting to be buzzed in through a security door, he studied a reader board that listed the names of staff doctors and field investigators. Of those, he recognized only one—associate medical examiner Dr. Frances Daly. Brandon remembered Fran Daly as a brash young woman fresh out of school and just starting her first job. At the time, female MEs had been rare. No one had thought Fran Daly would last, but she had—lasted and thrived. She had moved up through the ranks and was now second in command.

"Yes?" a voice asked over an intercom. "May I help you?"

Brandon knew to start at the top, or close to it. "I'm here to see Dr. Daly," he said.

"Do you have an appointment?"

"No. I'm a friend. Name's Brandon Walker." The disembodied voice sounded too young to remember that someone named Brandon Walker had once been sheriff of Pima County.

The lock buzzed. Brandon let himself inside. In the old days he had come into the place via this back door—the official cop entrance—but the office had seemed larger then. Now it was cluttered with a collection of apparently new and old desktop computers that covered every available surface. Behind the counter stood a young woman about Lani's age. Her face was marred by a series of piercings—lips, nose, and chin. The gold and silver studs stuck in her flesh made Brandon's heart flood with gratitude that Lani had so far avoided body piercings—at least ones her father could see.

"I'll see if Dr. Daly is available," the young receptionist said. "What's your name again?"

"Walker," he repeated patiently. "Brandon Walker."

He half expected to be left cooling his heels. Instead, bare moments later, Fran Daly burst into the outer office. If anything, her colorful cowboy shirt was more outrageous than ones she'd worn years before. Her snakeskin boots were far more expensive than those she had worn in the old days.

"Why, Sheriff Walker," she said, flashing him a gap-toothed smile and giving his hand a powerful shake. "It's been years. How good to see you again! What can we do for you?"

The young woman had returned to her place behind the counter and was watching the meeting with undisguised interest. Although gratified by Dr. Daly's enthusiastic greeting, Brandon wasn't eager to discuss the corpse in his car within the young clerk's earshot.

"Good to see you, too," he said. "But if you don't mind, I'd like to discuss this in private."

"Of course." She ushered him out of the lobby and into a corridor that stretched deep into the interior of the building.

"It's good you caught me when you did," she said. "I have an autopsy scheduled in a few minutes. If I'd started that, I'd have missed you. We're shorthanded at the moment. A number of our people are in the reserves and have been called up for active duty. I hope to God their skills won't be needed as much as some people think."

Although Brandon had dealt with Fran Daly in the past, this was the first time he had ever ventured into her private domain. The room had no outside windows, but it was a surprisingly cheerful place, painted with colors that weren't on any officially approved palette for decorating drab governmental facilities. One wall was dominated by a glass-fronted case full of rodeo-related trophies that dated from the late seventies and recounted Fran's riding and roping prowess. Looking from the trophies to Fran Daly, Brandon saw her manner of dress in a whole new light.

"I had no idea you were into rodeo," he said.

"It's one of those things I never got over. I still compete occasionally, but it gets harder all the time." She sat at a battered wooden desk and motioned Brandon into a chair. "Now, what can I do for you?"

"I've got a problem," he said. "There's a coffin in my car, a coffin containing whatever's left of a fetus from thirty-two years ago. It's been buried out on the reservation between then and now."

Fran Daly was suddenly all business and all interest. "What's the deal?"

"We're attempting to identify the father."

"With decomposed DNA," Fran said, nodding. "Was the body embalmed or not?"

"I don't know," Brandon said. "The mother was murdered. The fetus was examined in hopes of identifying the father and perhaps the perpetrator. The grandmother has no idea what was done to the body prior to its being returned to the reservation for burial."

"What's your connection to all this?" Fran asked.

"The case was never solved. The murdered girl's mother—the baby's grandmother—has asked an organization I'm affiliated with to see if we can find out what happened."

"I've heard of that," Fran said. "What's it called—T. L. Something?"

"Right," Brandon supplied. "TLC—The Last Chance. Emma Orozco, the grandmother, came to TLC for help. She also had the coffin exhumed and brought it to me."

"In other words, this isn't an official Pima County case," Fran said.

"That's right. It's cold and not being actively investigated by anyone but me."

"Given that, I doubt I could devote any time or people to this. Plus, if the tissue was embalmed, obtaining definitive results may not be possible. Besides, DNA testing is expensive."

"A company in Washington State will do the actual testing," Brandon interjected. "I'm asking you to attempt to collect a non-standard tissue sample. If you'll agree to try, I'll have Genelex send you a collection kit."

For a moment, Fran Daly sat with her fingers templed under her chin. Finally she made up her mind. "Where's the coffin now?" she asked.

"Out front," Brandon said. "In the back of my Suburban."

Fran sighed. "Bring it around to the side door. I'll have one of my assistants check it in."

"Much appreciated. Should the collection kit be sent to your attention?"

Fran Daly nodded. "Yes, but we'll only work on this as time permits. One thing for sure, though: If you're looking to establish a chain of evidence . . ."

"How about we go for results first and worry about the chain of evidence later?" Brandon asked.

"You bet," Fran replied with a smile. "As far as I'm concerned, you're still the boss."

twenty-two

Brian's initial call to Yuma didn't go well. It took hardly any time at all for him to figure out Lieutenant Jimmy Detloff of the Yuma County Sheriff's Department was a jerk.

"That hacked-up UDA?" he returned when Brian inquired about the girl whose body had been found in a trash bag not far from a rest area on Interstate 8. "Why are you asking about her?" Detloff continued. "That case happened years ago."

"We have reason to believe it's happened again," Brian returned. "AFIS got a hit. A fingerprint on a new case matches one from the garbage bag your victim was found in."

"Oh," Detloff said. "I remember that now. Our new little fingerprint gal was really proud of herself for finding it. We'd just gotten our AFIS computer up and running. She was all hot to trot to put that one print into the system. Didn't do any good. Nothing came of it at the time."

It has now, you creep, Brian thought. He said, "What did you come up with?"

"On that case?" Detloff said. "Not much."

"You never identified any suspects?"

"Are you kidding? We never identified the victim, to say nothing of a suspect. Like I said, she was a UDA. They die like flies around here, especially in the summer, and who cares? If we tried to track down what happened to every damned wetback who ends up in the wrong place at the wrong time, we'd never get anything else done. End of story."

A creep and a bigot! Brian thought. "Not quite the end," he said. "If you don't mind, I'd appreciate having a faxed copy of the file—including the autopsy results—as soon as you can send it to me. I have the AFIS summary, but I need the rest."

Detloff sighed. "That'll take time. I'm not sure when I'll be able to get around to it. I have other cases to deal with—current cases."

"I'm sure you do," Brian said. There was no sense pissing him off. "Whenever you get around to it will be fine."

He gave Detloff the fax number, but as soon as the line was clear, he punched redial. When he reached the Yuma County Sheriff's Department, he asked to speak to the fingerprint lab.

"Deborah Howard," a woman answered.

"My name is Detective Brian Fellows with the Pima County Sheriff's Department . . ."

"You wouldn't happen to be calling about that AFIS hit, are you?" she interrupted.

"As a matter of fact, I am."

"That's so cool. It was one of my first cases when I came to work here three years ago, and I was the one who found the print inside the bag. It was the first one I personally enhanced and entered in the system."

"I was just talking to Lieutenant Detloff—"

"Oh, him," Deborah said. She didn't say anything derisive, but she didn't have to. Her tone of voice said it all. "What's up with him?"

"I asked him to fax me a copy of that homicide file," Brian said carefully. "My guess is it'll be a long time coming."

"Right," Deborah agreed. "Don't hold your breath. Is there any way I can help?"

"Maybe so," Brian said. "Other than the trash bag, was any other physical evidence found with the victim?"

"Hang on," Deborah said. "Let me check." A few minutes later when she came back on the line, she sounded excited. "I just checked with the evidence clerk. A bag of clothing was found near the body. Detloff is a complete ditz. None of the clothing was ever checked for prints."

"Can you do that?"

"You'd better believe it," Deborah Howard said. "If I find any, I'll put them into AFIS right away. And if you'll give me your numbers, Detective Fellows, I'll call you with any updates. And if Lieutenant Detloff doesn't deliver that report in a timely fashion, let me know. I may be nothing but Detloff's 'little fingerprint gal,' but I have plenty of friends in other units in this department. Not going across desks and through channels doesn't scare me. If Detloff doesn't send you that report, I will."

Brian Fellows was smiling when he hung up the phone for the second time. Yes, Detloff was a jackass who had managed to annoy a key member of his own department, leaving her terminally pissed. From where Brian was sitting, that was perfectly fine.

When Brandon Walker left the ME's office, it was only mid-morning. He knew he and Diana would have to leave the house by one o'clock in order to be in Sells before the funeral, but there was enough time to squeeze in one more stop on his way home.

The Medicos for Mexico office was located on the north side of East Broadway in what had once been an auto dealership. An upscale resale furniture store had taken over the showroom space. Medicos's suite of offices had been carved out by remodeling the service bays. Brandon parked near the front door and walked into the building.

The receptionist in the spacious lobby turned out to be a young blond woman with a spectacular figure, pouty lips, and no visible signs of body piercing.

"Can I help you?" she asked. Her cool appraising glance was one step short of hostile.

"My name's Brandon Walker," he told her. "Is Dr. Stryker in?"

Evidently the former sheriff's name carried no ink here, either. In response she folded both arms across her chest—not a good sign. "Do you have an appointment?" she demanded.

"No," Brandon admitted. "No, I don't."

"What's this about?"

"It's a private matter," Brandon reassured her carefully. "Larry and I are longtime acquaintances. We've met occasionally, on a social basis. I was in the neighborhood this morning and thought I'd drop by. You might tell him I'm Diana Ladd's husband."

"One moment," the receptionist replied skeptically. "I'll see if he can meet with you."

The Medicos lobby was accented with huge hunks of original modern art. The artists had probably found their inspiration somewhere in the interior of Mexico. The signatures scrawled in the lower corners hinted that the artists themselves probably hailed from south of the border as well.

Brandon settled into a good-looking but relatively uncomfortable chair and wondered if Diana had been right to question his motives. Did he really think Larry Stryker could provide pertinent information about Roseanne Orozco, or was he here to tweak the son of a bitch because he felt like it—because he could and because hassling Stryker would give Brandon a little of his own back?

The receptionist's voice roused Brandon from his reverie. "Dr. Stryker will see you now," she said.

Larry Stryker sat at a large rosewood desk. Behind him was a matching wall of built-in bookshelves laden with books. A carefully folded copy of the *Wall Street Journal* lay in solitary splendor on an expanse of otherwise pristine polished wood. If a computer lurked somewhere in his office, it wasn't readily visible.

Larry may have been dressed to the nines, but Brandon was startled to see how much he had aged since their last encounter at the Man and Woman of the Year event two years earlier. Stryker no longer sported a full shock of white hair. It was much thinner now. His once strong facial features seemed blurred and blunted in a way that made Brandon suspect an overreliance on drugs or booze. When he stood up to greet his visitor, he seemed thinner as well.

Them's the breaks, Brandon thought. *He's not that much older than I am, but he's probably thinking I look older, too.*

"Good to see you again, Brandon," Stryker said heartily. "To what do I owe this honor? How's the family? We hear about Diana's success often."

But not about mine, Brandon thought. Larry Stryker

may not have spoken the barb aloud, but Brandon Walker heard it loud and clear.

"Yes," he replied, maintaining Larry's phony hail-fellow-well-met tone. "She's doing great, isn't she? And everybody else is fine as well."

"Good, good. Have a seat," Stryker continued. "And your daughter? Beautiful girl. What's her name again?"

"Lani."

"Wasn't she going to work with us one of these summers?"

"That's what her mother had in mind," Brandon said. "Turns out Lani made other plans."

"Kids do that, don't they," Stryker agreed amiably. "Now to what do I owe the pleasure of this visit?"

Taking his time, Brandon opened his wallet and extracted one of his TLC business cards. "Actually," he said, handing the card across the desk, "I'm working a case."

"A case?" Stryker repeated. "Really? I was under the impression you'd retired. What are you, some kind of private investigator?"

"You might call it that," Brandon agreed. "I've followed your footsteps into the world of nonprofits."

"A nonprofit private eye?" Stryker asked. He pulled on a pair of reading glasses and examined the card closely. His hands were liberally sprinkled with liver spots. Brandon stole a look at the backs of his own hands. He had a few of those spots, too, but not nearly as many.

"So TLC stands for The Last Chance," Stryker observed. "What does that mean?"

Brandon nodded. "We're a voluntary consortium that investigates cold cases—ones law enforcement agencies no longer have the time or resources to handle. Usually we're called in by grieving relatives who are looking for closure. The case I'm dealing with now is an unsolved homicide that happened out on the reservation more than thirty years ago. The victim was a teenager named Roseanne Orozco. I believe she was a patient at the hospital at Sells shortly before her death. I wondered if you might remember anything about her."

There was only the smallest of pauses before Lawrence Stryker answered—a pause that wasn't long enough to encompass more than thirty years of remembering and one punctuated by the involuntary bobbing of Stryker's prominent Adam's apple.

"No," he said, with a frown meant to pass as concentration. "I don't recall anyone by that name."

In that one electric moment, all of Brandon's old hunting instincts came into play. Larry Stryker was lying. The man knew *exactly* who Roseanne Orozco was, but, for whatever reason, he didn't want to admit it. Once a lie surfaces in an interrogation, it's time to push for more information. Even so, a yellow caution light began blinking at the back of Brandon's head. He was little more than a private citizen, but he was investigating a very real murder—one in which Larry Stryker might well turn out to be a suspect. That being the case, what the hell was Brandon Walker doing questioning him on his own? Good sense dictated that he walk away from the interview. Force of habit kept him where he was.

"Unusual case," Brandon said casually. "Roseanne was fine as a toddler and she seems to have developed normally right up until she went to kindergarten. She came home from her first day at school and never spoke again—not even to members of her family."

"Oh, yes," Stryker said quickly. "I guess I do remember now. The mute girl. She was evaluated countless times. No one could find anything physically wrong with her. There must have been some kind of trauma involved, but I don't think anyone ever figured out exactly what it was. And now that you mention it, I do remember that, shortly before her death, she was hospitalized for surgery—appendicitis, I believe. Later on she was back in the hospital for tests of some kind. It seems to me that there was a mixup about who was picking her up once she was released. She left the hospital on her own and never made it home. Instead, she turned up dead out along the highway."

Stryker shook his head and clicked his tongue. "Tragic case all around. I believe her father was suspected of having had something to do with her . . . her condition."

"Her pregnancy?" Brandon asked.

Stryker nodded. Brandon was struck by the fact that, although Larry Stryker had first claimed to have no knowledge of Roseanne Orozco, he was now exhibiting almost total recall—one lie compounded by another.

"Yes," Brandon agreed. "Henry Orozco was a suspect initially, but a blood test eventually proved he wasn't the baby's father. Roseanne's killer was never caught."

"You're trying to solve the case after all these years?" Brandon nodded. "That's the idea."

"Why now?"

"Because Roseanne Orozco's mother still wants to know who killed her daughter."

"What does any of that have to do with me?" Stryker asked.

It was Brandon's turn to ask a question. "How long were you out on the reservation?"

"Seven years and a little bit," Stryker answered. "Why?"

"That's several years longer than most doctors stay on at Sells, isn't it?"

"I suppose so," Stryker answered. "Usually people don't stay any longer than what it takes to pay off their student loans. Once they're debt-free, they head for the hills—for the cities, rather."

"But not you?"

"No. I really liked the people out there, but eventually it just wasn't practical to stay any longer. Even so, my wife and I came away from the reservation with an abiding interest in taking modern medical services to the impoverished peoples of the world. Under the aegis of Medicos for Mexico, we've been doing just that ever since."

"I know you have," Brandon agreed. "And it's very commendable. But getting back to Roseanne Orozco. Now that you remember who she was, do you happen to recall the name of her attending physician?"

"My dear man," Stryker said. "As you yourself pointed out a little while ago, this all happened many years ago. Of course I don't remember something as inconsequential as that. There were always three or four doctors on staff at Sells at any given time, all of us living in the hospital housing compound. We traded cases back and forth all the time. It could have been any one of us, or a combination of more than one. I really don't see what the point is . . ."

Brandon couldn't fail to notice that Stryker, who had gone from knowing nothing to knowing virtually everything about Roseanne Orozco, was now unable to recall this final, crucial detail. If he was lying, did that mean he was the killer? The possibility sent a clutch of fear deep in the pit of Brandon's stomach. Whatever else Larry might be, he was also a "friend of the family." He knew where Diana and Brandon lived. He knew Lani's name, and he knew where she lived, too.

With a supreme effort, Brandon kept his tone easy and conversational. "I'm trying to get a sense of what was going on in Roseanne's life during the months leading up to her death," Brandon explained carefully. "I'm sure it was a difficult time for her. Is it possible she may have found a way to communicate her troubles to her personal physician, someone she might have expected to help?"

An almost imperceptible change had occurred in Lawrence Stryker's countenance as the discussion continued. That one brief moment of uncertainty had passed and he was back in control.

"Well," he answered after a moment's hesitation. "If you wanted to find out who was assigned to be Roseanne Orozco's physician, you could drive out to the hospital at Sells and have them check their records. But again, even if you locate her doctor, I doubt he'll remember much about her, not after all these years."

"I already checked the records," Brandon said.

"And?" Again there was a slight waffling—a damning hint of hesitation.

"Nothing," Brandon said, shrugging. "Roseanne Orozco's records are missing. There are other records from around that time, but hers are nowhere to be found."

"Probably a clerical error of some kind," Larry Stryker said smoothly. "It's not easy finding decent clerical help anywhere anymore, but particularly out on the reservation. No doubt it's hiding right in plain sight, but when you're working with computers, even the smallest misspelling can make a record totally irretrievable."

"Right," Brandon agreed. "I know just what you mean. Garbage in and garbage out." He stood up. "I guess I'd better be going. You've been most kind to give me all this time when I didn't even call ahead for an appointment."

"No problem," Larry Stryker said at once. "And no need to stand on ceremony where appointments are concerned. After all, any friend of Gayle's is a friend of mine."

It was the last thing Brandon Walker wanted to hear from Larry Stryker about then. If he did turn out to be a killer—the very last thing.

After Walker left, Larry stayed at his desk awash in the familiar rush as adrenaline turned fear to pleasure. Once again he was out there, walking on the edge. It was nothing but a coincidence that ex-Sheriff Walker had shown up asking questions about Roseanne Orozco, still . . . There was something subtly different about Brandon Walker's appearance—something that had changed since the night of the Man and Woman of the Year Gala.

Larry waited until he was sure his guest had exited the lobby, then he dialed Gayle's extension. "You'll never guess who was just here," he said.

Gayle's answer was impatient. "I don't have time to play games, Larry. Tell me."

"Brandon Walker."

"What did he want?" Gayle asked.

"He was fishing for information about Roseanne Orozco."

There was a pause—a slight pause and maybe even a slightly in-drawn breath—before Gayle answered. "So?"

"So why's he bringing this up now?" Larry asked. "What does it mean? Should we be worried?"

"What it means is you should settle down," Gayle told him smoothly. "You sound utterly panic-stricken."

You talk a good game, Larry thought to himself, *but you sound a little upset, too.*

* * *

For a long time after she'd finished talking to Larry, Gayle sat at her desk, thinking her way through the problem. She had tried to sound calm in the face of Larry's concern, but Gayle knew he was right, and this meant trouble. After all these years, why in the world would Brandon Walker start asking questions about Roseanne? That was ancient history.

"Don't worry about Brandon Walker," she had assured Larry. "He's out of it. He can't hurt us. No one's going to pay attention to anything he says."

"But he's working for somebody else, an organization that starts with a *T*, gave me a card, but I can't . . . Oh, yes. Here it is. The Last Chance. It's a group of do-gooders who go around solving cold cases. He's working at Roseanne's mother's—"

"What exactly did he ask you?" Gayle asked. She spoke slowly, trying to make Larry settle down and focus.

"Who the attending physician was when Roseanne was admitted for her emergency appendectomy."

"Did he ask you anything about what happened to her later?"

Larry paused. "No, not that I remember."

"See there? I'm sure it's nothing."

But with Larry off the phone, Gayle knew that wasn't true. This was something, and it wasn't good. She had already run up the flag to Bill Forsythe with her claim that Erik LaGrange was doing his best to discredit both Gayle and her husband. That might have worked with Sheriff Forsythe, but it wouldn't wash with Brandon Walker.

In his current state, Larry was in danger of crumbling like a house of cards as soon as a detective or a reporter asked him a single question. That made Gayle's husband a liability she could ill afford. He would have to be dealt with. So would Brandon Walker. After all, Walker wasn't a police officer anymore. He had no more protection than anybody else, and no more legal clout, either. Not only that, Gayle knew where he lived. The question was, could Gayle come up with some kind of elegant solution that would deal with both Larry and Brandon at the same time? To do that, she needed to think. She picked up her phone and dialed the receptionist. Gayle had meant to fire the little man-stealing bitch first thing this morning, but with so many other things on her mind, she hadn't quite gotten around to it.

"Denise," Gayle said as civilly as she could manage, "I'll have to cancel my luncheon at Canyon Ranch this morning. Could you please call Ron Farrell, the manager out there, and let him know? His number's in the database."

Outside, Brandon sat in the Suburban, savoring the warmth of the smooth leather seat and trying to come to terms with what he had done. By barging in on Stryker and asking questions, it was possible he had put his whole family at risk—himself, Diana, Lani. And for what? For Emma Orozco?

Not really, he told himself in disgust. *I did it because I wanted my old life back—because I wanted to be useful. I wanted to be a hero. But now that my damned ego has jeopardized my whole family, what the hell should I do now?*

He used his cell phone to call Ralph Ames. "What's up?" Ralph asked.

"I may have found Roseanne's killer," Brandon said carefully. "But there's a problem—a big problem. The guy knows me, he knows my family, and he knows where we live. I'm going to need some backup on this, Ralph. If this is our guy, we've got to nail him now—or I'll never sleep again."

Ralph Ames processed the information and went into his problem-solving mode. "Who is he?" Ralph asked. "Let's see what our reference librarians can dig up on him. What's his name?"

"Stryker," Brandon answered. "S-T-R-Y-K-E-R, Dr. Lawrence. Wife's name is Gayle. He was out on the reservation working as a doctor at the same time my wife was teaching there. Gayle and Diana taught there together. This isn't definite, but I suspect Larry Stryker was Roseanne's attending physician at the time she was hospitalized. I also know that later on—years later—there was a scandal on the reservation about doctors abusing their patients. He may have had something to do with that, but it was all a long time ago. Since then, Stryker and his wife have turned into big deals here in Tucson. They run a nonprofit organization called Medicos for Mexico."

"In other words, we may find lots of material," Ralph said.

"That's right," Brandon returned. "I'm looking for the proverbial needle in the haystack, and first I need you to find the haystack."

"I'll get right on it," Ralph told him. "You do what you can to keep everyone out of harm's way. In the meantime, I'll see about getting you some help. Once we're set, I'll be back in touch."

"Thanks," Brandon said. "I appreciate it."

Brian was within minutes of heading out to Kino Hospital for the autopsy when Homicide Captain Julio Hernandez stopped by his desk. "What's up?" Brian asked.

"The Big Guy wants to see you."

The Big Guy was none other than Sheriff William Forsythe. In all his years with the Pima County Sheriff's Department, Detective Brian Fellows had never before been summoned for a personal audience with the top gun. He blinked in surprise.

"Sheriff Forsythe wants to see me?" Brian asked stupidly.

Hernandez nodded. "ASAP."

Feeling like a grade school student being sent to the principal's office, Brian made his way to the administrative wing of the building where, after giving his name to a receptionist, he was nodded into Bill Forsythe's spacious office. The sheriff was on the phone. Frowning, he motioned for Brian to have a chair.

"Sure," the sheriff said into the phone. "Of course. I know just what you mean, and I'll take care of it. Don't worry about a thing."

Forsythe put down the phone and then glowered across his desk at Brian. "Thanks for coming, Detective Fellows," he said. "I was just looking over the paperwork from yesterday, and I came across your interview with Erik LaGrange."

"Is there a problem?" Brian asked.

"I'll say there's a problem," Forsythe growled. "Do you know who LaGrange works for?"

"Yes," Brian answered. "Medicos for Mexico. It says so right there in the report."

"And Medicos for Mexico is run by . . . ?"

Brian bristled at the condescending, pop-quiz nature of Forsythe's dressing-down, but he tried not to let it show. "Dr. Lawrence and Gayle Stryker," he answered carefully.

"Do you have any idea how influential these people are in this community?" Forsythe demanded. "You don't drag people like them through a homicide investigation just for the hell of it."

"Gayle Stryker was having an affair with the guy who's our prime suspect," Brian interjected. "He claims she's the only one who can give us an accounting of where he was and what he was doing the night before the murder."

Forsythe pounced on Brian's words. "Yes," he said. "The *night before*, but not the *day of* the murder. I've looked at the preliminary ME report. Fran Daly estimates time of death as sometime Saturday morning. La-Grange told you himself that the woman left his house the previous evening. That means, Detective Fellows, that Mrs. Stryker's being with LaGrange on Friday night has nothing whatsoever to do with whether or not the dirtbag has an alibi."

"But—"

"No buts, mister," Forsythe interrupted. "I'm giving you the word, and I'm giving you an order. Back off! If you even so much as call Gayle Stryker and ask her a single question, I'll have your ears and your badge. Is that understood?"

"Yes, sir."

"Good," Forsythe grumbled irritably. "Now get going."

twenty-three

The dead baby was so small that they could not place her kneeling as the Desert People place their dead. So they laid the little girl on her bright blankets and very carefully covered her with branches of shegoi—creosote bush and kui—mesquite. Then they picked up the big rocks.

By then the mother could not see. She was looking at the sun. She did not want to be a weak Indian, but she could not watch as they threw the rocks on the little mound of brush. She turned and started down the mountain toward the village. She walked fast and stumbled often.

When the woman reached her house, the first thing she saw was one of the cradles which she had made for her baby. The cradle was swinging from the branches of a mesquite tree. For this nuhkuth she had used a brown blanket. She snatched the cradle down. She folded the blanket and pressed it against that thing inside her which hurt so much. Then she went away from the house because she did not want to be there when the others came back.

The trail led down to the water among the cotton-

woods. The woman could not see where she was going,
but she did not care.

There were many trees down by the water, but most
of the leaves had come off because summer was gone.
And it was almost dark because Tash—the sun—had al-
ready set.

The woman was still holding the brown cradle blan-
ket close against her breast when she seemed to hear a
baby's weak voice. She looked and just beyond the wa-
ter she saw a tiny brown cradle swinging from the low
branches of a tree.

Brian Fellows arrived at the ME's office still smarting
from his encounter with Sheriff Forsythe. By the time he
got there, the victim's fingerprints had already been
taken and forwarded to the lab, but even with that out of
the way, the rest of the autopsy seemed to take forever.
Dr. Daly's work was thorough and unhurried. One by
one she noted the numerous individual wounds—evidence of long-term physical and sexual abuse that had
resulted in visible damage as well as internal bleeding
and scarring.

"This isn't something that went on for a day or two
and then stopped," the ME said. "The extent of the
scabbing and scarring would be consistent with weeks
or maybe even months of torture. You're dealing with a
monster here, Mr. Fellows, a real sicko. If I were you, I'd
get him off the streets pronto."

To Brian's way of thinking, "sicko" hardly covered it,
especially if any of those other cases turned out to be related. "I already figured that out," he said. "What about
defensive wounds?"

"Didn't find any," Dr. Daly returned. "See that?" She

pointed to a still-visible indentation on what remained of one pathetically thin wrist.

Brian nodded.

"Chafing like that would be consistent with her being bound or chained for long periods of time," Dr. Daly explained. "I'd say we're finding no defensive wounds because she wasn't able to defend herself."

"Are you saying she was alive when the final assault began?"

Fran Daly nodded grimly. "Hopefully not for long," she said.

Two hours later, Brian left and went straight back to his office, where he discovered PeeWee was among the missing. Tackling the pile of sorted files, Brian hit the phone and began contacting the various agencies involved, requesting complete autopsy reports on each of the victims. Brian wasn't at all surprised to find nothing in his in-box from Jimmy Detloff. Before he could make an end-run call to Deborah Howard, however, PeeWee burst into their shared cubicle. "How'd it go?" he asked.

"Mixed bag," Brian answered. "Forsythe bitched me out personally and told me we should lay off the Strykers. His contention is that the time of death makes Gayle Stryker's involvement with LaGrange beside the point. Plus, they're pillars of the community."

"And the autopsy?" PeeWee asked.

Brian sighed. "You lucked out big-time. Dodging it was the right thing to do. That poor kid went through hell before she died, and hell lasted for a very long time. The more I think about LaGrange, the less I think he's capable of doing what was done to her. He strikes me as too much of a wimp."

"Maybe you're right, but what about that matching

fingerprint?" PeeWee returned. "The one from his house that AFIS connected to the Yuma County case?"

"What if LaGrange didn't do it, but knows about it and knows who did?" Brian asked.

PeeWee thought about that. "If it was me and knowing the kind of nutcase the killer is, I'd be scared to death—afraid the killer would turn on me next."

"Bingo," Brian returned.

"Want to go talk to him again?"

"Not right this minute," Brian said. "We'll let him stew in his own juices awhile longer. When we do get around to him, he'll be even more up for talking than he was yesterday."

Donna, the Homicide Unit's head clerk, tapped on their cubicle wall. "Mail call," she announced, handing over a large interoffice envelope. "Faxes, actually. They came in a few minutes ago, all of them labeled 'urgent.'"

"From Jimmy Detloff?" Brian asked.

"No," Donna said. "They're from someone named Deborah Howard. Is she a detective over there in Yuma County?"

"Deborah Howard isn't a detective," Brian replied, "but she probably ought to be."

Erik LaGrange lay on his cot and breathed the fetid air while time slowed to a standstill. After two nights of virtually no sleep, he had finally dropped off on Sunday night despite the steady din from the other cells and the disturbing presence of lights that dimmed but never went out completely.

Sometime toward morning, though, he had been awakened by a terrible groaning coming at him from somewhere down the barred corridor. The moaning rose and fell, with no particular message of either pain or sorrow—

a steady keening wail of hopelessness. Whatever was wrong with that person—mental or physical—there was no fixing it, just as there was no fixing what was happening to Erik.

He understood now that he was lost. Despite his earnest prayers, no one—not Gayle and certainly not God—would come to his rescue. Erik had done nothing wrong, but whoever was after him had convinced the cops he was guilty of murder, and those two hotshot detectives wouldn't rest until they'd nailed him for it.

Saturday morning he'd been worried about losing his job. On Monday he kept trying to get his mind around the fact that he would probably lose his freedom—maybe even his life.

When a guard showed up and unlocked Erik's cell in the early afternoon, his spirits soared. "Are they letting me out?" he asked.

The guard's hatchet-nosed face broke into a smile that revealed more than one missing tooth. "Sure, buddy," he said, applying a pair of handcuffs. "You'll be out in no time."

"Really. Will they give me back my clothes?"

The guard's jack-o'-lantern grin cracked into a hoot of laughter. "That's a good one."

He led Erik as far as the barred entrance at the far end of the cell-lined corridor. After he pushed a keypad, the door was unlocked by an invisible hand. As they walked to the far end of an empty corridor, the guard spoke into his radio. "Hey, Conrad. Get this. Our guy thinks he's got one of those Get-out-of-jail-free cards. Wants to know if we're going to give him back his clothes."

The unseen recipient of this information laughed, too. Meanwhile, the guard turned serious. "It's a bail hearing," he explained. "Those are pretty much come-as-you-are."

When Erik was led into the courtroom, Earl Coulter, wearing the same awful tie, appeared at his side. The proceedings were so amazingly short that Earl didn't have time to fall asleep. In a matter of minutes a judge had agreed with the prosecutor's claim that there was ample evidence that Erik LaGrange should be bound over for trial. When asked how he pleaded, Erik had to be nudged in the ribs before he choked out, "Not guilty." There was never a question of bail.

As Erik waited with the other prisoners to be returned to his cell block, he looked at them. Studying their faces, tattoos, and surly expressions, he tried to understand how it was that he was now one of them. Whoever they were, whatever they had done, these men, and others just like them or worse, were likely to be Erik's companions for the rest of his life.

With that realization, a black pall of despair engulfed him. He saw no way out.

Delia Ortiz had barely slept all night. She'd been on her feet so much the previous day that her back was killing her. When she finally did sleep, she dreamed about the baby. It was always the same. The baby was born. She knew he was alive because she'd heard him cry, but when she asked the nurse to show him to her and let her hold him, the woman shook her head. "No," she said, speaking in the style of the Tohono O'odham, "not right now. After."

Every time Delia dozed off, the dream reappeared. Each version was slightly different. Sometimes Fat Crack and Wanda were in the room. Sometimes Aunt Julia was there, although Aunt Julia had been dead now for two years. Sometimes only she and Leo were there with the doctors and nurses, but the basic part of the story was always the same. Delia would ask for the baby, only to be told no, she couldn't have him. Each time the dream reached that point, she would awaken, panting for breath and with her heart pounding in her throat.

It was almost sunrise when Delia finally drifted into a deep, dreamless slumber. She was so sound asleep, she didn't notice when Leo crept out of bed. Planning to stop by the office on her way to Wanda's house, she had set the alarm for seven, but when she finally awakened, it was nearly eleven. Leo had turned off her alarm. At first Delia was annoyed with Leo for letting her sleep, but when she discovered how much her back still hurt, she decided he was probably right. She had needed the rest far more than she needed to stop by her office.

She lay in the room that had once belonged to Aunt Julia and thought about how her friends from D.C. would laugh if they saw her in this tiny house. In yuppie D.C., Aunt Julia's place would have been considered less than a hovel. But coming from Great-aunt Julia, the adobe-walled house was an inheritance Delia treasured.

The baby was disturbingly still, and Delia began to worry. Maybe the dream was right. Maybe this baby, too, had perished in her womb. Then, after several anxious minutes, he awoke from his nap and landed a solid kick in Delia's ribs. Relieved, she rolled herself up onto the edge of the bed and looked down at her bare feet. Her ankles were still swollen, but not as badly as last night. She'd have to remember to take Leo's advice and stay off her feet as much as possible.

She took her time getting dressed. At this late stage of pregnancy, Delia didn't have much choice when it came to maternity clothing. She had to settle for the stuffy, too-warm maroon dress that had been fine during the winter but was bound to be too hot this afternoon and tonight at the feast house at *Ban Thak,* but at least, for the graveside part of the services, Delia would be seated next to Wanda in one of the chairs under the canopy. By then she'd be ready for shade and a chair.

It was almost noon when she drove into the Ortiz compound and spotted a flashy bright red convertible parked next to her mother-in-law's door. Delia knew at once whose it was. Leo had spent months reconditioning Diana Ladd's stupid Buick.

"Great," Delia muttered to herself. "I should have known she'd be here first."

Except it turned out Diana wasn't there after all. Lani was the one who answered the door.

"I'm so sorry," Lani said when she saw Delia. It wasn't clear if the girl was saying she was sorry Fat Crack was dead, or if she was apologizing for something else. And it didn't matter.

"Yes," Delia said, forcing herself to be civil. "It's too bad, isn't it."

Coming home to the house in Gates Pass about noon, Brandon noticed at once that Diana's Invicta convertible was missing from the garage. He was struck with a momentary stab of fear. If Diana and Lani weren't home, where were they? Inside, though, he found Diana safely tucked away in the office with her nose buried in her computer. Damsel lay at her feet.

"Where's Lani?" Brandon asked.

"On her way to Sells," Diana answered. "She wanted to spend some time with Wanda before the funeral starts, and she's delivering our flowers in person."

Diana's blasé answer was totally at odds with Brandon's gut-roiling concerns. It set his teeth on edge. "You let her take the Invicta?" he objected.

The perfectly reconditioned 1960 Buick Invicta, a bright Tampico Red convertible with its powerful engine, was Diana's special baby. She'd bought it from the widow of the original owner, who'd unloaded it at a charity auction. After paying far too much for what was little more than a wrecked hulk, she'd had the sorry spiderweb-laden husk of a convertible trucked back to Arizona from San Diego and delivered to the Ortiz brothers' garage at Sells. Leo, who had spent a lifetime keeping decrepit old cars and trucks limping along, had been overjoyed at the prospect of bringing a once-splashy classic back to pristine condition. He'd even hired an old upholsterer in Nogales, Sonora, who, for a price, had replicated the Invicta's signature red-and-white Cordaveen imitation-leather interior.

Once Leo had delivered her reconditioned prize into Diana's waiting hands, she seldom let anyone else drive it—Brandon included. When she went into town to run errands, she'd slap on a scarf and take off, turning heads wherever she went. Brandon was astonished that Diana had turned Lani loose with that 325-horsepower engine. And to drive it to the reservation? That defied belief.

"She tried starting the Camry," Diana explained. "It wouldn't turn over. She was going to jump it, but I told her not to bother. We're taking the Suburban, right?"

"She'd better not wreck the damned thing," Brandon grunted. It was easier for him to complain about the Buick than it was to bring up what was really bothering him—Larry Stryker.

Diana laughed his grousing aside. "Come on," she said. "Don't be paranoid. She's only ever wrecked one car."

"That may be true," Brandon agreed, "but the girl

was born with a lead foot, and that 401-cubic-inch engine was made to fly."

In that moment they both thought back to a night several years earlier when Lani, a few days past her eighteenth birthday, had totaled her Toyota pickup. Returning from visiting a friend near Three Points, she had lost control of the vehicle on a tight curve at the top of Gates Pass. Miraculously, even though her vehicle had sailed off a cliff, it had landed upright and stayed there.

When the dust finally cleared, Lani realized she wasn't hurt. Not wanting to suffer the indignity of being driven home by one of her father's former deputies, she'd asked the tow-truck driver for a lift. With the smashed remains of her car chained to the bed of the tow truck, she had arrived home at almost 2 A.M. and awakened her parents out of a sound sleep.

That night, when he saw the wreckage, Brandon was so overwhelmed with gratitude that she was still alive that he said almost nothing. The next day, though, he had visited the scene of the accident on his own. When he saw the cliff and the tracks her speeding Toyota pickup had sliced through the dry grass as it plowed off the roadway, he had felt sick to his stomach. Had Lani been thrown from the car, she would have been smashed to pieces on surrounding mounds of boulders and rocks. Her seat belt and exploding air bag had saved her life. Rather than dying or ending up in a hospital trauma unit, she'd walked away from the accident with nothing but a few cuts and bruises, one of which had left a tiny scar on the side of her left cheek.

After leaving the scene, Brandon returned to the house and raised hell with Lani, railing at her—as only fathers can—about her irresponsibility and thoughtlessness. She paid her traffic fine as well as her increased car insurance premiums without a murmur of complaint. Although three years had passed without any further incidents, Brandon was petrified that Diana's powerful Buick would prove too much of a temptation. *On the other hand,* he thought, *if anyone tries coming after Lani when she's driving the Invicta, they'll have a hell of a time catching up.*

"How soon do you want to go?" Diana asked, changing the subject.

Brandon glanced at his watch. "Give me half an hour," he said.

Still thinking about Lani and the convertible, he retreated to his own office, where a mess awaited him. TLC's research librarians had been hard at work and turned up a prodigious amount of material. They had been in the process of faxing him multiple multipaged documents when his laser printer went nuts and started shooting sheets of paper in every direction. In fact, his laser printer was still in the process of whirring out one multipaged fax after another, sending the pages into a scattered jumble in the middle of the floor.

"I know I said I wanted a haystack," Brandon sighed, looking at the mess. "But this is ridiculous."

As Brian Fellows read through the autopsy results on the Yuma County case, the hair on his arms stood on end. It was scarily similar: evidence of vicious, long-term sexual abuse and torture resulting in internal damage and scarring. Marks on the remains indicated they had been severed with a sharp object, possibly a butcher knife.

"I think we're onto something," Brian told PeeWee. "We need copies of all the other autopsies immediately, if not sooner."

"Which cases?"

"Let's start with El Centro, California, and Sierra

Blanca, Texas," Brian suggested. "If we can connect the dots between some of them—say, Yuma's, ours, and one or two others—we may be able to pick up more later on. Whoever this guy is, he's been doing his thing with impunity for a long time. I want us to be the ones who bring him in." Stretching to ease his aching desk-bound shoulders, Brian glanced at his watch. "Damn!" he muttered.

"What's wrong?" PeeWee asked.

"I've gotta go. I told Kath I'd be home by now. A friend of ours died over the weekend. We're due at the funeral this afternoon at four."

"Get going, then," PeeWee told him. "I'll handle things here."

twenty-four

The Baboquivari High School gym was filled to overflowing. Not only were the bleachers packed, so were the lines of folding chairs that covered the entire floor of the gym. An open casket, surrounded by lush banks of flowers, lay on a makeshift podium as the Desert People came to pay their last respects.

Gabe "Fat Crack" Ortiz was someone who had left an indelible mark on his community. Years of running the car-repair/tow-truck operation with his two sons had given him a position of prominence on the reservation that had eventually vaulted him into the political arena, first as a tribal council representative from Sells and later as the tribal chairman. And the fact that he was Looks at Nothing's hand-chosen successor had augmented his influence.

The Reverend Jeremy Moon, the Korean-born pastor of Sells First Presbyterian Church, was a relative newcomer to the United States as well as to the Tohono O'odham Nation. He had been drafted into doing the service as a favor for Wanda Ortiz. During the pastor's remarks, he kept referring to Gabriel Ortiz, making it clear that the Reverend Moon had never met Fat Crack and knew precious little about him.

Feeling miserable, Delia Ortiz sat in the front row between Leo and Wanda. She was sure every person in the room knew the details of her very public disagreements with her late father-in-law. Still, regardless of Delia's relationship with Fat Crack, she knew the man deserved better than this embarrassing excuse of a eulogy delivered by someone whose words didn't come close to honoring a man the community had known and respected.

When the Reverend Moon finally finished, he looked around the room. "Would anyone care to make additional comments about Mr. Ortiz?"

Delia hadn't planned on speaking at the funeral. For one thing, Wanda hadn't asked her to, although, as tribal attorney, Delia was—next to Fat Crack himself—the most prominent member of the family. While the Reverend Moon looked expectantly around the room, Delia was surprised to find herself rising to her feet and moving forward. As she made her way up the steps, she stumbled and would have fallen. Baby, Fat Crack's older son—the one she had rejected—reached out a steadying hand and caught her.

By the time she reached the lectern and turned to face the audience, her knees were wobbly. Her nervousness wasn't due to being unaccustomed to public speaking. She had been doing that for years. What worried her was speaking in front of this large assembly of her own people who were, in many ways, as alien to her as Fat Crack was to the Reverend Moon.

Not sure how to begin, Delia glanced down at the front row in time to see both her husband and Baby smiling at her and nodding encouragingly. Those two nods, offered in unison, made it possible for her to speak.

"I'm here today," she began, "because *Gigh Tahpani*

saved my life, not once but twice." There was a subtle shift in the audience. Delia's was the first reference to the beloved Fat Crack, as opposed to some stranger named Gabriel Ortiz. Sensing that the audience appreciated what she had said, Delia took a deep breath and continued.

"When I was seven, our family situation was bad. My parents were having problems, and my mother needed to get away to go to school in Tempe. The nuns at Topawa helped by offering us the use of a broken-down car, one that wasn't running. Fat Crack came in that old tow truck of his. It took all day long, but he got the car running again.

"Leaving the reservation that day was what made it possible for my mother to get her education and for me to get mine. Years later, I was living in Washington, D.C., and I was having troubles with my husband—the same kind of troubles my parents once had. One day, when I barely knew where to turn, Fat Crack showed up and offered me a job—here at home, back on the reservation. When he first offered me the job, I told him no, but as many of you know from personal experience, telling my father-in-law no and making it stick were two very different things.

"When I came back, my aunt Julia despaired that I'd ever find myself a nice man to marry. Wanda told me that by then, she and Fat Crack had reached much the same conclusions about their two sons, Baby and Leo, who were both confirmed bachelors. I sometimes wonder if Fat Crack didn't shake a few feathers at us or do the Peace Smoke, because Baby and Christine are married now; so are Leo and I."

A wave of gentle but approving laughter washed around the room. When it died down, Delia resumed.

"*Gigh Tahpani* was a medicine man. He didn't really want the job, but he took it. He was careful about it and serious. Over the years he and I had our disagreements, but he was a good man—an honorable man. I will miss him every day from now on."

To the sound of polite applause, Delia stepped down from the podium. As she returned to her seat, Leo reached out and patted her knee appreciatively. At the same time, Lani Walker stepped up to the lectern. Lani was everything Delia wasn't right then. Lani was young and slim and lovely. Delia felt old, fat, pregnant, and very, very jealous. What right did Lani have to stand up in public and pretend that she, too, was a member of the Ortiz family?

"My name is Lani Walker. When I was a baby, Wanda Ortiz saved my life. Later, when I was adopted, *Gigh Tahpani* and Wanda became my godparents."

Delia had heard the story of the Ant-Bit Child and how Wanda and Gabe Ortiz had helped arrange the baby's unorthodox adoption when Lani's own blood relatives, regarding the child as a dangerous object, had refused to take her. No doubt many of the people in the gym that afternoon remembered the story as well, but none of them stirred. They listened with rapt attention.

"Later," Lani continued, "when I needed a medicine man, Fat Crack stayed beside me during a very difficult time. Like Delia, I'm glad so many people came here today to honor him and, again like Delia, I will miss him forever."

Delia watched as Lani returned to her seat in the second row, looking poised and lovely and totally at ease. There was nothing Lani had said with which Delia could find fault. She had made no inappropriate claims of kinship, nor had she wallowed in a public display of grief, but the very fact that she had spoken at all still rankled. For a few moments, Delia herself had glimpsed part of what made Lani special—the very thing that Fat Crack had valued about her, and yet . . .

As applause for Lani's comments died away and someone else made his way to the lectern, Leo touched Delia's knee. "Are you all right?" he whispered.

Delia nodded, but for some reason she was unable to speak. In spite of herself, she was beginning to see how her father-in-law had exerted the same kind of influence on Lani's life as he had on Delia's. Maybe Lani did have the right to be at the funeral, speaking and grieving. Maybe Delia herself was wrong.

"I'm okay," she said, but by then she was giving way to tears. As the next speaker began, Delia leaned on Leo's shoulder and let him comfort her.

"Shhh," he whispered. "It's all right." But Delia wasn't convinced. She suspected that by shedding tears in public she had let her father-in-law down one last time. With Fat Crack dead, there would be no way for Delia to redress the wrong she had done him.

By the time the mile-long funeral cortege reached the cemetery at *Ban Thak,* the sun had already dropped behind the crest of *Ioligam.* People crowded into the dusty cemetery, stumbling over crumbled headstones and crooked crosses and standing on what must have been graves themselves as they strained to hear whatever words the Reverend Moon had to say this time.

After the casket had been lowered into the ground and properly covered with new blankets fresh from JC Penney, the crowd remained transfixed while Leo and Richard helped their mother drop the first shovelful of earth onto the casket. One at a time, each of the children took their separate turns. After that, while the menfolk worked at filling the grave, women and children headed toward the feast house, where the smells of wood smoke from cooking fires filled the warm desert twilight.

With people lining up outside, Wanda took her place at the door to the feast house and offered a short blessing. "Thank you, Lord, that in this time of sorrow you offer us food that we may remember to live. Amen."

Then she flung wide the feast-house door and let the first group enter.

From where Brian stood, the line seemed to stretch forever. Every fifteen or twenty minutes, a group of forty or fifty people would be allowed inside. Only when that group had finished eating and left was the next group admitted. Brian had come home late. He and Kath had arrived at the high school gym just after the service started. Now he and Brandon Walker stood near the end of the line. With both their wives helping cook and serve, there was no sense rushing.

"There are lots of people," Brian observed. "It's hard to imagine they won't run out of food or dishes."

Brandon had been to plenty of Tohono O'odham feasts, but this was by far the largest he'd ever seen. He nodded. "The old miracle of the loaves and fishes all over again," he said.

The two men stood slightly apart from the rest of the line. Had Leo or Baby been with them, Brian and Brandon would have been included in some of the easy laughter and lighthearted banter from other people waiting in line. Without Ortiz relatives to run interference, the two Anglos were left alone—*Mil-gahn* outsiders in an essentially Indian world.

"Brian, I've got to talk to you," Brandon began.

A cell phone chirped farther up the line. The crowd paused and waited. The idea of a cell phone ringing while people waited to eat food cooked over a wood-stove struck Brandon's funny bone. Years earlier, when hard-wired telephone lines had been difficult to come by on the reservation, phones had been a rare commodity outside the villages of Sells and Topawa. Now, though, with revenue-raising cell-tower sites dotting reservation lands, cell phones had proliferated.

Finally, as general talk and laughter resumed, Brandon broached a subject he'd been waiting to bring up. "I understand you made an arrest in that case," he said casually. "The one from over the weekend. I heard a snippet on the radio earlier, but since I haven't had a chance to look at the paper, I'm short on details."

"We did," Brian agreed. "And the guy's been bound over for trial."

"You don't seem too happy about it," Brandon observed.

"Arresting him may have been premature," Brian said. "I suspect there's a whole lot more to the story than we know so far."

"You and PeeWee are both good detectives," the older man said encouragingly. "You'll get to the bottom of it."

Brian accepted Brandon's praise gratefully. He wasn't getting strokes like that from Sheriff Forsythe. "By the way," he added, "I did look at that file you mentioned the other day."

Brandon's heart leaped, but he tried not to show it—tried not to sound too eager. "Roseanne Orozco's file?" he asked.

Brian nodded. "I have to admit, that case does bear an uncanny resemblance to this new one, but I doubt they're related," he said. "For our guy to be the perp, he would have started killing people when he was five."

"Right," Brandon agreed. "That's not too likely. I think I—"

He was interrupted by the arrival of Davy and Candace, who had emerged from the feast house as the group at the head of the line was ushered inside. Tyler, whimpering and whining in typical two-year-old fashion, clung tightly to his father's shoulder.

"The kid's run out of steam," Davy explained. "We have to get going."

"How are our womenfolk holding up in there?" Brandon asked.

Davy grinned. "Fine," he said. "They're washing dishes like mad."

"What about the food, Ty?" Brandon asked. "Was it good? Did you leave any for Grandpa?"

For an answer, Tyler Walker Ladd shook his head and buried his face in his father's neck. Candace, standing off to one side, beckoned impatiently and then headed for the car. Davy nodded in acknowledgment, sighed in resignation, and followed.

"She keeps him on a pretty tight leash," Brian said.

"True, but what do you expect?" Brandon agreed. "She's a woman, isn't she?"

Another cell phone chirped. This time it was Brian's turn to dig his phone out of his pocket. Not wanting to listen in, Brandon contented himself with wondering whether or not he should say anything about his own suspicions. What did he have to go on other than a sense Larry Stryker had been lying? He had nothing concrete to offer that would cover Brian's back if Sheriff Forsythe came gunning for him. *And until you do,* Brandon told himself, *shut the hell up.*

Brian clicked off his phone. "Damn!" he muttered.

"What's the matter?" Brandon asked.

Brian Fellows turned to his old mentor with a face full of anguish. "PeeWee and I were going to interview our suspect again this afternoon, but things came up. I was worried about being late for the funeral, so we put the interview off until tomorrow. Now it's too late."

"What do you mean, it's too late?"

"Our suspect just tried to off himself, but he botched the job and is on life support at Saint Mary's," Brian said. "PeeWee thinks we should be there if he wakes up—or if he doesn't."

Brandon understood. More than once the same thing had happened to him when a suspect had committed suicide before answering the critical question that might have filled in the missing pieces of some puzzle. "Sorry about that," he said.

"Thanks," Brian replied. "I'd better go."

It was hot inside the cooking portion of the feast house. As the evening dragged on, tempers ran short. "How many more groups?" Wanda Ortiz asked, surveying the dwindling stacks of tamales and tortillas.

"At least three more," Kath Fellows answered, "not counting this one."

Wanda shook her head. "Maybe we won't run out of food," she said, "but it's going to be close." She glanced at Delia, who had been manning the serving line for most of the evening. "You look tired. Sit down and put your feet up for a few minutes."

Delia glanced toward the sink, where Diana Ladd and Lani had been doing KP duty all evening long. Other people had offered to spell them, but they had refused all offers. They claimed to be doing fine and were more than happy to keep on doing it. Even now, hours into the event, they were still talking and laughing. Despite the tragic occasion, working together in the hot kitchen provided its own salutary remedy.

Not wanting to be outdone in the dutiful department, Delia shook her head. "I'm fine," she told her mother-in-law. "You're the one who should sit down."

By then the new set of guests had their plates and were streaming into the serving line. When a discreet knock sounded on the exit door, Wanda opened it to find Brian standing outside.

"I have to go in to work," he called to Kath, who stood in the serving line doling out thick red chili. "Can you come now?"

Kath made no move to leave her station. "Does it look like I can come now?" she asked.

Lani, who had heard the exchange, pulled her soapy hand from the dishwater and dashed over to Brian. She gave him a brief but enthusiastic hug. "Long time no see," she told him. "But don't worry about Kath. Leave her here with us. I'll see to it that she gets home. Promise."

"You're sure?" Brian asked. "It's out of your way."

"I don't mind," Lani said.

"Is that all right with you, Kath?"

"Sure," Kath Fellows told her husband. "It's fine. Get out of here now. You're holding up production."

The whole day and most of the evening passed without Gayle's being able to sort out what to do about Larry and Brandon Walker. Frustrated and tired, she finally went to bed in the upstairs bedroom of her El Encanto home. She switched on the television set just as that night's edition of the *Ten O'Clock News* came on. KOLD-TV's "Breaking News" headline stunned her.

"This afternoon Erik LaGrange, former director for development for Medicos for Mexico, one of Tucson's premier nonprofits, was charged with first-degree murder in the death of an unidentified teenage girl whose dismembered body was found near Vail on Saturday. We've just received word from the Pima County Sheriff's Department that this evening, shortly before nine o'clock, LaGrange attempted suicide in his Pima County Jail cell. He's been taken to Saint Mary's Hospital, where he is listed in guarded condition."

Gayle's joy knew no bounds. This was nothing short of a miracle—a gift from a god Gayle Stryker hadn't, until now, believed in. If Erik died, what could be better? When it came to assumptions of guilt, nothing quite compared with committing suicide—or even attempting it. And if he lived? No problem. Gayle Stryker was a master at the art of spin. She knew that the very act of saying something loud enough and long enough could make it true, even if it wasn't. She had told Bill Forsythe earlier about the unsatisfactory job-performance review looming in Erik's future. Now she had a chance to turn that job review into a motive for murder.

After looking up KOLD-TV's phone number in the book, Gayle dialed the "Breaking News" number and asked to speak to the news director. While the weatherman was doing his gig, Gayle Stryker was speaking to a blundering young woman who was obviously out of her league.

"My name is Gayle Stryker," she said firmly. "I'm the chief operations officer for Medicos for Mexico. I'm concerned about the headline story you ran a few minutes ago. I'd like to make a public statement."

The assistant news director mumbled and fumbled and tried to put her off. She evidently had no idea who Gayle

Stryker was. Or maybe she just didn't believe that the woman speaking on her phone was actually who she claimed to be, but Gayle refused to be dissuaded.

"Put Gary Fisher on the line," she ordered, referring to the station's nighttime news anchor and hunk. "I've done lots of charity events with Gary. He knows me personally."

Which is how, after the end of the sports segment, KOLD's *Ten O'Clock News* filched a little time out of Monday evening's David Letterman show. While the camera focused on one of the station's stock photos of Gayle Stryker, her voice came through loud and clear.

"At Medicos for Mexico it has recently come to our attention that our former director of development, Erik LaGrange, may have been using his position of trust with us in order to entice young women to enter this country illegally. It is suspected that he may have had something to do with the murder of one of those poor girls. My husband and I are both appalled and disheartened that he might be capable of such heinous actions, and we can only express our terrible sorrow and regret that anyone connected to Medicos for Mexico—someone we regarded as a trusted employee—could have used our organization's good name to camouflage such evil."

All in all, it was a masterful performance. Afterward she was sorry she hadn't thought to turn on the VCR. Most of the time when she appeared on a news broadcast, she simply asked the station to send her a copy.

In this instance, that would probably be a bad idea.

A little before eleven, Diana Ladd went looking for her husband, who was outside leaning on Leo's truck. "Uncle," she said. "I'm not as young as I used to be. Do you mind taking me home?"

"Are you kidding?" Brandon grinned. "I thought you'd never ask. Where's Lani?"

"She and Kath are staying on to help clean up."

Brandon was torn. Should he say something about Larry Stryker or not? Confide his fears in Diana and worry her, too, or count on the presence of other people to protect Lani?

As they headed toward the Suburban, Brandon noticed that Lani had left the Buick's top down in *Ban Thak*'s dusty parking lot. "Why did she do that?" he grumbled, masking his real concerns. "The interior's going to be filthy."

"Don't hassle her about it," Diana cautioned. "I'll have it detailed tomorrow."

Diana fell asleep before they ever reached the highway. As far as Brandon was concerned, that was just as well. He had been tired while he waited all those hours at the feast house, but now that they were going home, he felt the adrenaline kicking in. He was eager to go to his study and see what the TLC reference librarians had sent him.

He had parked inside the garage and turned off the engine before Diana roused herself. "Sorry to conk out on you," she said. "I'm wiped out and on my way to bed. What about you?"

"I'll stop in my office for a few minutes," he told her. "TLC sent me some faxes earlier. I didn't have a chance to glance at them."

Diana shook her head. "I forgot," she said, climbing out of the car.

"Forgot what?" Brandon asked.

318 • J. A. Jance

"How you are when you're on a case. Totally focused. And immune to sleep."

"I sleep," he said.

"Not as much as I do," she told him. "And not as much as you should." She reached up and kissed him as she went past. "Good night."

Brandon fed Damsel and used playing ball with her as an excuse to check out the yard and the exterior of the house. Finally, reassured nothing was amiss, he went into his office. Earlier, when his printer had been acting up, Brandon had only taken time to scrape the scattered papers into a pile. Now, sitting down to sort them, he discovered there was a rudimentary order to them. He laid them out like a game of bridge, matching faxes and page numbers rather than suits of cards.

Once he had the material organized, he grabbed a highlighter and started to read, all the while keeping his ear cocked for the sound of the Buick's big tires crunching the graveled driveway.

twenty-five

The woman dropped her own cradle blanket and ran to the nuhkuth *from which the baby's voice had come. She took the cradle in her arms, but her arms held only some dry brown leaves that were swinging from a spider's thread.*

Then the woman heard another baby cry. This cry came from among some low bushes, but when she reached the place, there were only more dry leaves. The leaves were curled into tiny cradles, but the cradles were all empty.

The woman stood, puzzled. From left and right and all around, she heard the cries of little babies, but when she looked she found only more dead leaves. And the leaves were thick under her feet. The noise of the dead leaves was almost as loud as the cries of the babies.

The woman put her hands over her face.

The last group of diners had been herded through the feast house before the cooks and servers finally sat down to eat. There weren't enough tamales or tortillas to go around, but by then they were all too tired to eat very much anyway. Then they tackled the cleanup.

Once the big pots and pans had been washed and

dried, Leo and Baby loaded them into the back of a pickup truck. When they had finished loading, Leo popped his head back in the door and saw Delia sitting with her feet up. "Do you want to ride home with us?" he asked.

Wanda cut him off. "Leave Delia here," she ordered. "You two have all that stuff to unload. I'll drop Delia off on the way. She'll be home sooner if I take her."

"Is that all right with you, Delia?" Leo asked.

Delia nodded. "Whatever gets me home and in bed the fastest is what I want to do."

Leo and Baby left a few minutes later as the women began the final wiping down of tables and sinks and sweeping the floor. Delia was half asleep when a sudden gush of water brought her fully awake. She was astounded to find herself sitting in the middle of a growing puddle.

"Your water!" Wanda exclaimed. "It broke. The baby's coming."

Delia heard only that much before her body was doubled over by a powerful spasm. It started at her rib cage, front and back, and then rolled down and through her body like a marauding truck, leaving her gasping for breath and clinging to the bench with both hands to keep from falling.

The next face Delia saw was Lani's, right in front of hers, barely inches away. Lani's mouth was moving, but at first Delia heard nothing. Finally a few of the words came through. Something about "hospital." And something about "walk." And then the contraction ended.

"I'm all right now," Delia said. "I can walk." She tried to stand, with her clothes dripping around her. As soon as she did, another contraction hit. She dropped back down on the bench as though her legs had been lopped from under her.

When Delia came around again, Lani's face was once more in front of hers. ". . . car . . ." she was saying urgently. Then, with Lani Walker at one elbow and Christine at the other, Delia felt herself being lifted off the bench and propelled out of the feast house. Just outside the door sat Diana Ladd's huge convertible with the top down and the engine running. Kath was behind the wheel. She got out to help Lani lever Delia through the passenger-side back door and into the backseat. Delia was lying flat when the next spasm hit.

She saw the worried look on Lani's face and heard her say ". . . not make it . . ." Then she heard nothing more. When the contraction overcame her, Delia no longer cared if she was standing up or lying down.

When she came to herself again, the space above her was filled with stars. Somehow she was moving through or maybe under them. *I must be dead,* she thought. *The baby and I are on our way to heaven.* But then Lani's face obliterated the stars. This time she held a long, pencil-thin flashlight between her teeth. Her long hair whipped around her face. That was when Delia finally understood that she was in the backseat of an open convertible. As they bounced along over a rough dirt road, she realized Lani was there in the backseat with her. Before Delia could make sense of any of that or say a single word, she was overwhelmed by another powerful spasm.

I'm not dead, Delia told herself. *I just wish I was.*

Kneeling between the Invicta's front and back seats, Lani tried to keep her face in front of Delia's. "Breathe," she urged. "Pant like a dog. It'll help you deal with the contractions."

If Delia had ever heard of Lamaze, none of it was accessible. The contractions were coming too hard and fast. By the time Kath slowed for the intersection with Highway 86, Lani knew they'd never make it to the hospital in Sells in time. "We'll have to stop," Lani called to Kath. "Soon!"

Wanda had offered to let them use her pickup, but Lani had nixed that idea. Putting a woman in labor in the bed of a pickup seemed like a bad idea, but the backseat of Diana's Invicta was only marginally better.

"Should we put the top up?" Kath had asked once Delia was lying in the backseat.

Lani shook her head. "No time," she said. "Let's go."

Now, as Kath put the Buick in park along the shoulder of the road, she asked, "Have you ever delivered a baby before?"

"No," Lani returned. "But it's probably pretty self-explanatory."

Seconds after they parked, Wanda pulled her Dodge Ram pickup up beside them. She jockeyed it around until her headlights blazed in through the Buick's door, lighting the scene. In the brilliant glare of Wanda's high beams, Lani saw the unmistakably wet and shiny glow of a baby's emerging head.

Steeling herself for the task, she reached out and grabbed the baby's head, easing it forward. "Do you have anything sharp?" she asked. "We're going to need to cut the cord, and we'll need a string to tie it with."

"There's a Leatherman in my purse," Kath replied.

"Bring it."

Moments later Lani Walker held a squalling, slippery infant in her arms. Wanda Ortiz was there, too, holding a handful of clean towels—extras she'd brought along just in case they needed them at the feast house. While Wanda wiped off the baby boy, Lani's fumbling fingers tied the rubbery umbilical cord with a piece of hem snipped from one of Wanda's towels. Then she cut it with Kath's Leatherman. Lani had just finished that when Wanda handed the baby back to her. Quiet now, he lay in her arms wrapped in the soft folds of an immense flannel shirt.

Lani looked down at him. In that moment she understood why Fat Crack and Nana *Dahd* had so patiently answered all her questions. It was so she—Lani—would have those same answers to pass along to someone else.

"Did you ever teach Baby or Leo the things you teach me?" she had asked Fat Crack once as he showed her how to collect and dry *wiw*—the wild tobacco used in the Peace Smoke.

He shook his head. "No," he said after a while. "They're not interested."

"Why not?"

"I don't know. Maybe if I had been a medicine man the whole time they were growing up, it might have been different. By the time Looks at Nothing showed up and started teaching me, Baby and Leo were already too old and didn't want to learn."

"Weren't you too old then, too?"

"That's what I thought," Fat Crack chuckled. "But not according to Looks at Nothing. I guess he was right."

"What about me? Am I too old?"

"No, *Kulani O'oks,*" Fat Crack said softly. "You're just right. Aunt Rita knew the moment she saw you that you were special—that she could pass along whatever she knew to you for safekeeping. I've learned the same thing, but the gifts we've given you aren't yours alone, Little One. They are treasures for you to know and keep and then pass along when you find someone who's worthy."

Looking down at that tiny baby—his fists clenched, his eyes pinched shut against the glaring headlights—Lani Walker knew who this child was. Leo and Baby hadn't been interested in learning the lore and traditions their father had wanted to teach his sons, but this child—this baby boy—would be, and Lani would be there to pass it along.

"Is he all right?" Delia asked.

In reply, Lani turned to her and smiled. "He's perfect," she said, handing the baby to his mother. "Beautiful and perfect. What are you going to name him?"

"Gabriel Manuel," Delia Ortiz said. "After his two grandfathers."

Lani heard a strange whirring sound. "Get out of the way," Kath ordered. "I'm raising the top. We'll need to turn up the heat long enough to take this mother and baby to the hospital, where they belong."

Time dragged by moment by moment as a worried Brandon Walker tried to concentrate on the pages of faxed material.

Ralph Ames's researchers had been incredibly thorough in finding out all there was to know about Lawrence Stryker and his wife as well. The material detailed their respective childhoods—Larry's growing up in impoverished circumstances in L.A. to Gayle's high-society, old-money background both in Tucson and on her father's family ranch northeast of Marana. There were old articles detailing Lawrence's fourth-place standing in his graduating class at Emory University Medical School and newer ones about him and Gayle being named Tucson's Man and Woman of the Year. There were literally dozens of articles that told about the founding of Medicos for Mexico and about Larry's and Gayle's unstinting and heroic efforts to make life better for those less fortunate. There was even a copy of Bill Forsythe's public disclosure forms—the same forms Brandon had seen years earlier—with their names front and center on the campaign donor list.

With all that mound of material, it wasn't until well after midnight that Brandon found the needle—the one thing he'd been looking for. It was there in the form of a tiny article culled from a congressional committee doing oversight on the BIA's Indian Health Service. It spoke about the appallingly large number of poorly trained and/or unethical physicians who for years had been allowed to practice nonstandard medicine on Indian reservations all over the country. Only a few physicians were mentioned by name. Dr. Lawrence Stryker's name was listed in a group of doctors who had been dismissed following allegations of sexual impropriety.

There were no further details—no discussion of who had lodged the charges or when the events took place, but now Brandon Walker had a pretty clear suspicion of why Larry Stryker had left his position at Sells. Neither Emma Orozco nor Andrea Tashquinth had mentioned Larry Stryker's name in that connection. They might have had their suspicions but very little reason to bring them up. Stryker was *Mil-gahn;* they were Indians. Based on past experience, they would have had no expectation that people in authority would listen. In fact, no one *had* been listening back then. But Brandon Walker was listening now. He was hearing them loud and clear.

It was all strictly circumstantial. Still, Brandon was convinced Larry Stryker had molested Roseanne Orozco. When the girl turned up pregnant, Stryker got rid of her. What could be simpler than that? Blame it on Roseanne's poor father. Blame it on anybody. Meanwhile the good doctor went off to live his exemplary do-gooder life. Supposing Brandon's suspicions were correct, what the hell was he going to do about it?

The DNA sample collection kit would arrive in Tucson tomorrow morning. Once the material had been collected and sent back to Washington State, Brandon had no idea how long it would take for Genelex to get results, or even if results were possible. What Brandon did know was that, if DNA testing yielded results, he would need something for a match.

"I guess I'll be going back to see Dr. Stryker first thing tomorrow morning, Damsel girl," Brandon said, speaking to the dog, who had remained in the knee-well of his desk the entire time.

Having once been spoken to, Damsel stood up and stretched. "Out?" Brandon asked. Obligingly, Damsel headed for the door.

He had let the dog back in and had apprehensively checked the yard one last time when the phone rang. The sound of it electrified him. Late-night calls were usually bad news. Fighting a wave of panic, he leaped to answer. "Hello!"

"Dad?" Lani asked.

"Where are you?" he demanded, his voice fueled now by a rush of relief. "Are you all right?"

"I'm at the hospital in Sells, and yes, I'm fine."

"Are you hurt? Is anyone else hurt?"

"Nobody's hurt," Lani answered, "but there's a slight problem."

"Don't tell me! You wrecked your mother's Buick!"

"It's not wrecked," Lani corrected. "But there's a problem. Delia's water broke while we were still at *Ban Thak*. Kath and I tried to get her to the hospital in time, but we didn't make it. Gabriel Ortiz was born in the backseat. The car will have to be cleaned. It's a mess."

"What is it, Brandon?" Diana Ladd asked from behind her husband's shoulder. "Is it Lani? Is she all right?"

Brandon Walker suddenly felt like laughing out loud. "She's fine," he said, handing her the phone. "Perfectly fine, but you may want to talk to her. It sounds like our daughter has been practicing medicine without a license and playing midwife—in the backseat of your Invicta."

A phalanx of media people were ranged around the entrance of St. Mary's Hospital when Brian arrived there. He had to shoulder his way through them in order to get inside. When he reached the ICU waiting room, PeeWee Segura was there.

"How's it look?" Brian asked.

PeeWee shook his head. "Not good. From what I hear, the guy's brain-dead. They'll probably end up pulling the plug."

"Shit!" Brian muttered. "Why wasn't he on a suicide watch?"

"Not our job, Brian baby. Not our job."

Brian glanced around the room. There were several different groups of people, each of them huddled in its own private hell of shared misery. "Anybody else here for LaGrange?"

"Nope. When it comes to next of kin, you and I are about it," PeeWee said.

"What about Gayle Stryker? If Erik and Gayle Stryker were as close as he claimed, why isn't she here?"

"Funny you should mention her," PeeWee said. "She was on the news a little while ago."

"Doing what?" Brian asked.

"Throwing poor old Erik to the wolves, saying how sorry she and Doc Stryker are that their employee could do such a terrible thing, blah, blah, blah, blah."

"In other words, she's doing damage control to pull Medicos' reputation out of the fire."

"You got it."

The door at the far end of the waiting room opened. A bull-necked man in a T-shirt, cutoffs, and sandals burst into the room. He spoke briefly to the clerk at the reception desk, who nodded toward Brian and PeeWee. Leaving her, he hurried over to the two detectives.

"My name's Ryan Doyle," he said, holding out his hand. "Erik and I have been friends since grade school. Who are you?"

PeeWee and Brian produced their respective IDs. When he realized who they were, Ryan Doyle's whole body was transformed. His fists knotted. His muscled neck bulged. His face reddened with anger. "Jesus Christ!" he exclaimed furiously. "You must be the ones who arrested him!"

"That's right," Brian said mildly. "We are."

"Well, you're dead wrong about Erik. Him hurt a little girl? Not ever. He wouldn't do such a thing, never in a million years. I just heard about it tonight, on the news. We didn't know anything about it—that he'd been arrested, nothing. Why the hell didn't he call us? Brianna and I would have tried to help. We would have been there for him."

Suddenly, all the fight went out of the man. Ryan Doyle slumped heavily onto a nearby couch and buried his face in his hands.

Brian sat down next to him. "I'm sorry, Mr. Doyle. I'm sure all this is a terrible shock to you . . ."

Ryan raised his head and looked around the room. "And where's she?" he demanded. "Where's the bitch?"

"Who?" Brian asked.

"Gayle Stryker," Ryan muttered bitterly. "Who do you think?"

"You knew about Erik's relationship with Mrs. Stryker?"

"Relationship? Bullshit! The word *relationship* implies a two-way street, something that goes in both directions. Gayle was playing with him, using him, leading him along. Bree and I both tried to warn him about her. Bree said when Gayle was done with him, she'd drop him like a hot potato. Erik didn't believe it. For the longest time—for years, even—he was convinced that someday, somehow, Gayle would leave her husband for him."

"*Was* convinced?" Brian put in. "You mean he wasn't anymore?"

Ryan sighed and shook his head. "I'm not sure. Bree and I just had a baby—a boy. Erik and I talked on the phone. He was congratulating me, saying how lucky I was to have a wife and baby. It's not that he said anything specific, but I could tell it really got to him. I told him, 'You know, Erik, you could have this, too,' and he said, 'I know. Maybe I will.'"

"When was this?" Brian asked. "When did you have this conversation?"

"I don't know. A couple of weeks ago. Why?"

Brian was thinking about what Erik had told them. He had claimed that he had done nothing, that someone was framing him for murder. Brian had heard similar stories for years from punks complaining they were being framed, but maybe this time it was true.

A doctor entered the waiting room through the swinging doors and made straight for where the three men were sitting. "Has the sheriff's department had any luck locating next of kin?" he asked.

The question was addressed to PeeWee Segura, and he was the one who answered. "We're still working on it, but I haven't heard if we've made any progress."

"Erik doesn't have any next of kin," Ryan Doyle interjected. "His mother died when he was a baby. His father walked out and left him to be raised by his grandmother. She's been dead for years. Why?"

The doctor peered down at Ryan Doyle over the top of a pair of reading glasses. "And you are?"

"My name's Doyle, Ryan Doyle. Erik and I have been friends since grade school. I came as soon as I heard."

The doctor held out his hand. His name was on the badge he wore, but he introduced himself nonetheless. "I'm Mr. LaGrange's physician, Fred Ransom. You're fairly certain he has no relatives—no brothers, no sisters, no aunts or uncles?"

Ryan shook his head. "There's no one, no one at all, but you still haven't told us why you need to know."

The doctor took a step back and considered before he answered. "I'm sorry to have to tell you this, Mr. Doyle," he said at last. "It doesn't look good for your friend. His brain was denied oxygen for too long."

"You mean Erik is going to die?"

"He's on life support," the doctor said. "That's what's keeping him alive. If he had relatives, I'd need to consult with them before . . . well, before doing what's necessary."

Ryan Doyle closed his eyes for a moment, as if processing that information. Brian thought briefly that he might break down. Instead, he stiffened his massive shoulders and straightened his back. "What about his organs?" he asked.

"Excuse me?" the doctor said.

"Erik signed up to be an organ donor," Ryan said. "We both did it when we first started driving. It should be on his driver's license."

"I'm afraid Mr. LaGrange's driver's license wasn't made available to us when he was admitted . . ."

Ryan Doyle wheeled back on Brian. "His license isn't here because he was in jail, right?"

Brian nodded. "Yes, but—"

Ryan took a deep breath. "Look," he said. "When we were in high school, Pueblo High School, one of our pals needed a kidney. Robby Martin was on dialysis and waiting for a kidney to become available when he caught an infection and died. Erik and I made a pact at Robby's funeral that we would always be organ donors. We thought if we died, maybe some other kid might be saved. If you check in his wallet, you'll find it there. I swear to you, Erik would want to donate his organs. At least let him have that shred of dignity. Please."

Dr. Ransom looked from Ryan to the two detectives. PeeWee was the one who broke formation. "I'm not sure if it's possible," he said, "but hold on. I'll go outside and make a few calls."

twenty-six

When it came to the *Ten O'Clock News,* Larry Stryker preferred watching KVOA to KOLD. Erik LaGrange's suicide attempt was the lead story on Channel 4, just as it had been on Channel 7. Larry was intrigued. If Erik actually succumbed to his injuries, it was possible the authorities would lay the blame for Saturday's homicide at Erik's door and that would be the end of it. Case closed. Larry and Gayle would be off the hook.

Wanting to discuss the situation with his wife, Larry went so far as to pick up the phone and dial through to the house in Tucson. The call went straight to voice mail, however. By the time Gayle's voice-mail greeting ended, Larry had reconsidered. Yes, Gayle had said she was setting Erik LaGrange up for this latest death. Yes, she was pissed that Erik had given her her walking papers, but that didn't mean she'd be pleased that he was dead.

No, Larry decided, ending the call without leaving a message. *Better to let sleeping dogs lie.*

Larry Stryker turned off the television set before Jay Leno ever came on and he missed his wife's solo end-of-news performance on the other channel. Feeling incredibly relieved, Larry toddled off to bed and slept better than he would have expected. Yes, Brandon Walker had come around asking questions about Roseanne Orozco, but Gayle was probably right about that, just as she was about everything else. There was no evidence left that would hold up in court as far as he could see. Difficult and challenging as his wife might be at times, Larry was lucky to have her.

At three o'clock in the morning Brian Fellows finally headed home. It had required time and effort, but a decision that might have taken days to settle had been handled in a matter of hours. Erik LaGrange's organ-donor card had indeed been located among his personal effects. When made aware of the situation, Sheriff Forsythe had taken an uncharacteristic pass, leaving the ME's office to make a final determination.

When Brian left the hospital, it was with the understanding that Ryan Doyle would remain at Erik's side until blood- and tissue-typing had all been accomplished and it was time to turn off the respirator. Under similar circumstances, many people would have simply walked away. Brian couldn't help being touched as well as a little surprised by Ryan's level of commitment. Brian had been quick to write Erik off as a total loser. If he could inspire that kind of friendship, maybe Brian's initial assessment was somewhat off the mark. Not only that, Ryan's absolute contempt for Gayle Stryker set little alarm bells jangling in Brian's head. Erik had proclaimed his innocence, saying he was being framed. Committing suicide made Erik's claim of innocence less plausible. But what if it was true?

What was absolutely clear was the presence of that one unidentified fingerprint—the one with the AFIS match to the homicide in Yuma. True, Erik LaGrange could no longer tell investigators who else might have been in his house, but there was one other person who might be able to—Gayle Stryker. Even though Sheriff Forsythe had ordered Brian to leave Gayle Stryker out of the equation, Brian made up his mind on the drive home that, come tomorrow morning, he was going to track the lady down and ask her a question or two.

As late as it was, Brian drove home expecting to find his wife sound asleep. Instead, lights were on all over the house. Kath was just stepping out of the shower.

"Why are you still up?" he asked, kissing her hello. "I was sure you'd be in bed by now."

"In bed? Are you kidding? I just got home. Lani dropped me off a few minutes ago."

"Why so late? Car trouble?"

Kath laughed. "Hardly. Before we left *Ban Thak,* one of Fat Crack's daughters-in-law went into labor. We tried to get Delia to the hospital in Sells, but she ended up having her baby in Diana's car."

"What'd she have?"

"A little boy. He's fine; so is she. We took them to Sells and checked them into the hospital after the fact. Delia told us they're going to name the baby Gabriel after Fat Crack. And the middle name . . . Oh, I don't remember it right now. I must be too tired. The second name comes from Delia's family—from her father, I believe, the boy's other grandfather."

"Manny, by any chance?" Brian asked.

"Right. Manuel, but how come you know that?"

"You should, too," Brian said. "Delia's father, Manny Chavez, is the guy you found that time out on the reservation. The one Quentin whacked over the head with a shovel."

Kath's jaw dropped. "That guy was Delia's father?"

Brian nodded.

"I didn't know that, or if I did, I'd forgotten," Kath said. "But then I'm a latecomer to the game. You've known these people all your life."

"That may be true," Brian said, giving his wife a hug. "Luckily for them, though, you're the one who's always around in a pinch."

"I didn't do anything," Kath said. "All I did was drive. Lani did everything else."

"Lani?" Brian asked in surprise. "Are you saying she knows how to deliver a baby?"

"She does now," Kath said. "And so do I."

By ten o'clock the next morning, Brandon Walker's Suburban was parked outside the Medicos for Mexico office on East Broadway. He knew what he wanted, but he wasn't quite sure how to go about getting it.

Brandon was groggy from lack of sleep. He had evidently strained his arm the other day when they were working on Fat Crack's grave. The pain had kept him awake overnight, and it was bothering him still.

Out of practice as far as being in stake-out mode, Brandon relieved his boredom by walking across the street to the Circle K for a cup of coffee and to pick up a vending-machine newspaper. Much of the front page was occupied by an article about the homicide suspect who had attempted suicide in his Pima County Jail cell the night before. A small inset article toward the bottom showed a photo of two people Brandon recognized, Dr. Lawrence and Gayle Stryker, beaming out of the paper—Larry in a tux and Gayle in a body-skimming little black dress.

Settling back into the Suburban, Brandon scanned

through the article, learning in the process that the prisoner was the man arrested on suspicion of murdering the
teenager whose dismembered body had been found near
Vail on Saturday. That meant this was Brian's case, Brandon surmised, and the suspect had been a long-term employee of Medicos for Mexico, the locally based charity
founded by Dr. Lawrence and Gayle Stryker.

The Strykers. Recognition surged through Brandon
like an electric shock. The Strykers' proximity to those
two separate but similar cases—murdered and dismembered girls found thirty-two years apart—was too close
to be considered a harmless coincidence.

Brandon was reaching for his phone to call Brian
when it rang. "Good morning," Ralph Ames said.
"How's it going?"

"I'm on the trail of Larry Stryker's DNA," Brandon
said.

"How do you propose to do that?" Ralph asked.

"It's not illegal, but it's better that you don't know,"
Brandon said with a halfhearted chuckle.

"Don't ask/don't tell?" Ralph asked.

"Something like that. Now what's the deal with getting me some backup?"

"I was thinking about calling the Pima County Sheriff's Department," Ralph Ames said. "But then I was going through my copy of the paperwork Research sent
you. I saw that the Strykers were some of your oppo-
nent's big-time campaign donors. I decided against it."

"I could have told you that," Brandon said.

"But I did talk to Geet Farrell," Ralph Ames added.
"He's tied up until midafternoon, but he'll be there this
evening. He'll call as soon as he gets to town. Is that all
right?"

While Brandon watched, a pearlescent white Lexus,

covered in a layer of dust, pulled into the back parking lot and stopped in a shaded parking place marked RE-SERVED next to a much cleaner but otherwise identical Lexus sedan.

"It'll have to be," Brandon said. "I've gotta go."

As Larry Stryker stepped from his vehicle, Brandon battled to rein in his emotions. He had come here hoping to collect DNA evidence that would link Larry Stryker to Roseanne Orozco's long-ago murder. Now he was faced with the very real possibility that the man might be a still-active serial killer.

Hoping his face didn't betray him, Brandon stepped out of the Suburban. "Hey, Larry," he said as casually as possible. "How's it going?"

Stryker, once again impeccably dressed, stopped in his tracks and regarded Brandon warily. "You again," he said. "What now?"

"I have a couple more questions—about the same thing we discussed yesterday," Brandon responded breezily. "No big deal, but I thought it might be better if we did it in private. How about having a cup of coffee somewhere? Just a few minutes of your time."

Dr. Stryker was clearly torn. He looked longingly at the door to his office, as if wishing himself inside. "Sure," he said at last, "as long as it doesn't take too long. My car or yours?"

"Let's go in mine," Brandon said.

Not wanting to risk going somewhere that would serve coffee in real cups, Brandon had already plotted a course to the nearest Burger King—at Speedway and Campbell. Chatting amiably about Diana and Gayle's long-term friendship, he drove to the fast-food joint's drive-up order station. "How do you take it?" he asked.

"Cream, no sugar," Larry said.

"Did you hear that?" he asked the invisible attendant. "We'll take two of those."

Once the cups of coffee were safely in the Suburban's cup holders, Brandon drove into the parking lot and shut off the engine.

"Okay," Larry said. He picked up his cup and took a tentative sip. "What's all this about?"

"Roseanne Orozco," Brandon returned.

"Look, Brandon, we talked about this yesterday. As I told you then, I barely remember the girl. There's nothing more I can tell you."

Brandon waited long enough for Larry to raise the cup to his lips for a second sip. "Were you the father of Roseanne's baby?" Brandon asked.

Larry Stryker's response to that unexpected question was as classic as it was revealing. He choked. He coughed. Coffee splattered his tie. When he put his cup down, Brandon was gratified to notice that his hand was shaking.

"What the hell gives you the right to ask such a crass question?" Larry Stryker demanded in outrage.

Brandon shrugged. "Well," he insisted mildly, "were you?"

Larry reached for the door handle and shoved the door open. "I won't even dignify that accusation with a response." He stepped down onto the pavement and stood there, his face distorted with outrage.

"Come on, Larry," Brandon said. "Get in. I'll give you a ride back to your office."

"The hell you will. I'd rather walk." With that, he slammed the door shut and stamped away, leaving Brandon with exactly what he wanted—the coffee cup and what he hoped was a fully retrievable sample of Dr. Lawrence Stryker's DNA.

But Brandon also had a problem. He had definitely tipped his hand. Larry Stryker was onto him. Geet Farrell wouldn't arrive a moment too soon.

Brian had dragged himself into the office late that morning. Around eleven-thirty, as he headed for the break room for coffee, his cell phone rang. "Hey, Brandon," he said cheerfully after checking caller ID. "How's the local midwife? According to Kath, Lani did herself proud last night."

"She was still sleeping when I left the house," Brandon replied. "She was pretty jazzed when she got home last night. I didn't think we'd ever get her to shut up and go to bed."

Brian laughed. "I had the same problem with Kath. She was way too wound up to sleep."

The truth was, Kath had come home from helping deliver Delia Ortiz's baby with a whole lot more on her mind than talking. Brian had awakened that morning with the distinct impression that Kath Fellows had made up her mind to go off the pill and think about starting a family.

"What's up?" Brian asked.

"I need to talk to you," Brandon said urgently. "ASAP. Given my history with the department, it's probably better for you if I don't show up there. Could we meet for lunch?"

There was undeniable urgency in Brandon Walker's voice. "Where?" Brian asked.

"How about the Old Pueblo Grill?"

Brian knew that particular central-area watering hole was far enough off the law enforcement beaten track that there was little danger of the two of them being seen together. "I'll see you soon," he said.

On his way out, Brian stopped by the cubicle. Fortunately, PeeWee was away from his desk, so Brian didn't have to lie about where he was going or what he was going to do. As a kid he had sometimes fantasized about growing up and working a case with Brandon Walker—the man who was the closest thing to a father Brian had ever known. But now that it was happening and his dream was finally coming true, Brian couldn't tell anyone about it, not even PeeWee. Instead, he had to race off to meet Brandon in secret, as if they were a pair of undercover agents.

Walking into the Old Pueblo Grill, he spotted Brandon sitting under an umbrella at a tall outdoor table in the far corner of the patio. A copy of that morning's *Arizona Daily Sun* was spread out in front of him.

"What's up?" Brian asked, hiking himself up onto one of the stools.

Wordlessly, Brandon Walker pushed the newspaper in Brian's direction. It was folded to reveal the front-page article about Erik LaGrange's attempted suicide. Brian knew that, as of two hours earlier, LaGrange's suicide was a fait accompli rather than a mere attempt. A heavy circle of blue ink surrounded a photo of Dr. Lawrence and Gayle Stryker.

Brian nodded. "The suspect's dead. He was declared brain-dead last night. His organs are being harvested this morning."

"He worked for Gayle and Larry Stryker."

It was a statement, not a question. Brian nodded again. "What about them?" he asked.

"What if I told you there's a good chance Larry Stryker was the father of Roseanne Orozco's baby?"

The question took Brian by surprise. Before he could respond, a waitress appeared at the table and dropped off Brandon's iced tea. "Can I get you something?" she asked.

"I'll have the same," Brian said, nodding toward the tea. "Can you prove it?" he asked as soon as the waitress walked away.

"I think so," Brandon said seriously. He picked up a paper bag and handed it over. "There's a Burger King coffee cup in there—complete with some of Larry Stryker's DNA. I'm hoping the ME will be able to collect enough DNA from Roseanne's fetus for us to get a match."

Stunned, Brian set the bag down without looking inside. "Even if it's true and he was the father of her child, it doesn't prove that he killed her."

"No, but it gives him plenty of motive for wanting to get rid of her."

Brian nodded while he considered the implications. The deaths of Brandon's cold-case victim, the Girl in the Box, and the dismembered girl from Vail might indeed be connected. The same could be true of the girl whose remains had been found near Yuma.

Brian took a deep breath. "We've discovered that there are several other cases with similar MOs, cases that may or may not be related," he said. "We're talking about homicides that have been spaced over a long period of time and spread over a wide geographical area but with distinct similarities—most notably with dismembered remains."

Brandon Walker sat up straighter. "Cases in addition to Roseanne's and to this latest one?"

Brian nodded. "That's right. At the moment there's only one case with a definite link. A fingerprint we found in Erik LaGrange's house matches a print found at the scene of a Yuma County cold case. The print was on the inside of a garbage bag."

It was Brandon Walker's turn to be stunned. "In other words, there's a chance Stryker's been doing this ever since Roseanne Orozco died?"

"Somebody's been doing it for years," Brian said grimly. "And he's been getting away with it." He picked up the Burger King bag and looked at it with renewed interest. "You say Stryker handled this cup?"

"Yes. So did I."

"Before it goes to the ME's office, I'll take it to Al Miller and have him lift some prints. If any of them match the one from Yuma . . ." He stopped cold.

"What?" Brandon asked.

"There were latent prints in that old Orozco file . . ." the detective said.

". . . that probably haven't been entered into AFIS," Brandon finished.

"They will be soon," Brian Fellows declared. "If we get a hit, we pick up Stryker and *voilà*. There you have it—cold case solved."

The waitress showed up with Brian's tea. "Can I take your order?" she asked.

Brandon waved her away. "There may be a problem with that," he said, leaning across the table and dropping his voice.

"What kind of problem?"

"I've already blown my cover as far as Stryker is concerned. When I talked to him earlier, I let him know I was onto him about Roseanne. When I brought her up, he almost choked to death on his coffee. I know I shouldn't have done it, Brian, but I couldn't help it. I wanted to make him squirm and he did, but now I'm afraid he may come after me or Diana or Lani."

"Where are they?" Brian asked.

"Lani and Diana? At home. At least that's where they were when I left them."

"I've got a few connections in the Patrol division," Brian said. "I'll put in a word for the deputies to keep an eye on your place."

Brandon let out his breath in gratitude. "Thanks, Brian. I appreciate it."

"But do you really think he'll come after you?" Brian asked. "If I were Larry Stryker and thought people were closing in, I'd head for the border."

"You're right," Brandon said. "They have all kinds of connections in Mexico. Once he makes it across the border, we've lost him."

Brian nodded. "Especially if this turns into a death-penalty case," he said. "Mexico won't extradite anybody who's likely to go on trial for a capital crime."

And Lani and Diana won't ever be safe, Brandon thought. Making up his mind, he stood up and slapped a five-dollar bill down on the table. "Come on."

With that, Brandon headed for the patio exit. Brian Fellows padded after him, carrying the Burger King bag. "Where are you going?"

"Medicos for Mexico."

"Why? What we've been talking about sounds good to us, but so far it's pure speculation. We don't have anything that gives us probable cause."

Brandon Walker stopped short. "See there, Brian? That's the difference between you and me. You're a cop. Cops have to worry about little details like probable cause, so go get it. Take that damned coffee cup to Alvin Miller and see if he can give you enough probable cause for a warrant. As for me? I'm retired. These days Brandon Walker is nothing but an ordinary private citizen. I have absolutely no intention of arresting the guy—couldn't do it if I wanted to. So I don't need probable cause, but I'll tell you this: I'm going to stick to Larry Stryker like flies on shit. If he makes a move in the direction of Mexico, I'll be there to slow him down."

Brandon was already unlocking the Suburban. "Do you have a gun?" Brian asked.

Brandon nodded and patted his underarm holster. "Took it out of my gun safe and cleaned it just this morning."

"What about a vest?" Brian asked.

"I don't have one," Brandon Walker said. "Turned mine in when I retired."

Brian was already unbuttoning his shirt. "Take mine," he said. "I'll pick up my other one when I go back to the department."

"But . . ." Brandon began.

"No buts," Brian told him. "If I let you go without a vest and something happens to you, Diana will kill me, and I wouldn't blame her."

Gayle Stryker was at her desk, talking to her private banker and moving funds around when Larry stumbled into her office. His face was red, his tie askew. His white shirt was spotted with what looked like a spray of coffee. He was hyperventilating. "I've gotta talk to you," he gasped.

"I'll call you back," she said into the phone, and then put down the receiver. "Larry, what's the matter? You look like hell. Don't you know there are reporters out there?"

"Brandon Walker's the matter," Larry stammered. "I just talked to him. I swear, he knows all about Roseanne Orozco. Yes, I saw the media people camped out outside the front lobby. Why the hell do you think I came in through the delivery door? What are we going to do?"

"I handed Denise a written statement to give to the press. If you want to read it . . ."

"I don't give a rat's ass about that," Larry interrupted impatiently. "What are we going to do about Brandon Walker?"

"Come on, Larry." Gayle kept her demeanor calm. Larry was upset, and she didn't want to make things worse. "What do you mean, Walker knows about Roseanne? What did he say?"

"He came right out and asked me if I was the father of her child. How could he possibly know to ask me that? Nobody else ever figured it out. Why would he?"

"You're right," Gayle said. "This does sound serious."

"What should we do?"

"I think it's time we headed south," she said quietly.

"Permanently?" he asked.

She nodded. "I was just on the phone checking the money situation. We'll be fine. If we leave now—today—by the time anyone figures it out, it'll be too late. Once we're across the border, we're home free. There are no legal problems in Mexico that can't be fixed with the right amount of money put into the right hands."

"But what about the house? What if someone goes through it and comes across the room in the basement? I've cleaned it as well as possible, but there's always a chance . . ."

"I'll take care of the house, Larry," she assured him. "You know very well that it's always been my intention to take care of the house. Is there anything you want from there, anything you want to take along with us?"

He paused and seemed to consider. "No," he answered at last. "There's nothing I want."

"Good," she said. "I'll call for a jet to take us to Cabo. By contract we have to give them eight hours' advance notice, but they may well have a plane available to pick us up sooner than that. I have some errands to run, then I'll head out to the ranch and take care of things there. You hold down the fort here, but keep a low profile. Don't talk to the media. Don't grant any interviews."

For several long seconds, Larry appeared to be seized with indecision. Gayle was afraid he hadn't heard a word she'd said.

Finally he nodded. "All right." Then, making what seemed to be a supreme effort to pull himself together, he added, "You're sure you won't need my help out at the ranch?"

She smiled at him then. Things always worked more smoothly when she was the one who came up with the plan and all Larry had to do was follow orders.

"I can handle it," she said.

"But you will be careful," he cautioned. "That stuff can be very dangerous."

"You know me," she said. "I'm always careful."

twenty-seven

Feeling all his sixty-plus years, Larry left Gayle's office and went to his own. He shut the door and locked it. Then he called out to reception and said he was not to be disturbed.

He hadn't exactly told Gayle the truth. He *did* want something from the house. If he had known he was leaving today, he would have brought his notebooks to work. They would have fit in his briefcase. Now, because he hadn't wanted to admit to Gayle that the notebooks even existed, he was faced with the prospect of leaving them behind. If Gayle destroyed them along with the rest of the house, fine, but if anyone happened to stumble across them . . .

In terms of treasure, Larry's prize didn't amount to much—a series of cheap photo albums he'd picked up from Walgreens over the years. What he valued was the collection of photos he kept inside—dated Polaroid shots of each of his girls, pictures that graphically chronicled each of their individual journeys. When he was between girls—as he was now—he often consoled himself by revisiting his past exploits. Browsing through the pictures was a balm to him, but in someone else's hands . . . Regardless of what he had told Gayle, he had to go get them. If she caught him there, he'd make up some excuse, but the notebooks had to be in his personal possession when he stepped onto the jet.

Unable to sit still, Larry paced back and forth in his office. The incident with Brandon Walker had unnerved him. Eventually he would feel the rush of relief, but right now he was mired in fear. Periodically he glanced out the window. Since Gayle had told him to stay put, he couldn't leave before she did. Unfortunately, her Lexus remained in its place.

Hoping for relief, he forced himself to sit down and try to relax. He used the remote to turn on his Bose radio, tuned, as it always was, to KUAT, where they were playing Mozart—his favorite, the Piano Concerto no. 22 in E-flat Major. Lost in the music, he actually managed to doze for a while.

When he awakened, the news was coming on. The opening item caught Larry's attention: "Media relations officer Ted Garner has just confirmed that a prisoner found hanging in his Pima County Jail cell last night has died as a result of what the medical examiner's office is calling self-inflicted injuries. Erik LaGrange, longtime development officer for Tucson-based Medicos for Mexico, was booked into the jail in connection with the death of a teenage girl whose dismembered body was found near Vail on Saturday. In a court appearance yesterday afternoon, LaGrange had pleaded innocent to all charges."

The newscaster went on to other topics, but Larry Stryker was no longer listening. Gayle had finished with Erik LaGrange, and now he was dead. Welcome as that outcome might be, it left Larry with a disturbing question rattling around in his head. It wasn't the first time he'd asked it.

What happens if she's ever finished with me?

* * *

Lani woke up late. She poured some coffee and then went looking for her mother. Diana was in her office, fingers flying over her laptop's keyboard. "Where's Dad?" Lani asked.

"Beats me," Diana said. "He was out of here early. I'm sure it has something to do with the case he's working on. How are you feeling?"

"Fine," Lani said. "Can I have your car keys? I left a mess in your car last night. I want to take it into town and have it detailed."

"You don't have to do that," Diana said. "It wasn't your fault."

"Please," Lani said.

Diana smiled. "Sure," she said. "You know where to take it?"

"You still use that same place on South Fourth?"

"Smitty's," Diana said with a nod. "Come pick me up afterward. We'll have lunch, just us girls."

Staring at the bloodstains that now marred the red-and-white imitation-leather seats, Smitty Coltharp plucked fitfully at the end of his foot-long ponytail. "My land, girl," he said. "Your mama loves this car so much, I'm surprised she didn't kill you. There's dust in there an inch thick, and what on earth were you doing in that backseat?"

"A friend of mine," Lani said, "a friend of the family, actually—was having a baby."

"Whoa!" Smitty said. "Sorry I asked."

"Do you think you can clean it?"

He shook his head mournfully. "We'll see," he said. "But it's gonna cost you. You go inside out of the sun and sit tight. I'll let you know when I'm finished."

Lani did as she was told. The office came complete

with grimy plastic chairs, a scarred wooden desk, and a collection of dog-eared magazines. Next to a coffeepot filled with an inch-thick layer of what could have been year-old coffee sat a newspaper folded to reveal a more-than-half-completed *New York Times* crossword puzzle. Looking around for the remainder of the paper, she found the rest of the *Sun,* virtually unread, tossed in a trash can. Glancing at the front page, her eye was drawn to the picture of a man and a woman in the lower right-hand corner.

Gasping with recognition, Lani almost dropped the paper. The woman's face was one she knew—the same one that had obliterated Fat Crack's face in the photo and in Lani's dream; the same face that had, in seconds, morphed into a featureless skull. Now, just seeing that face smiling at her out of the newspaper photo filled Lani with a terrible dread.

Who is this woman? Lani wondered. *What's the matter with her?*

Looks at Nothing's crystals had tried to warn her about this woman. So had Fat Crack in her dream. Trying to quell a rising sense of fear, Lani forced herself to read the article, which told her almost nothing. A murder suspect named Erik LaGrange had attempted suicide in his Pima County Jail cell the previous evening. The man and woman in the photo, Dr. Lawrence and Gayle Stryker, founders of an organization called Medicos for Mexico, had been the suspect's employers.

Those three words finally rang a bell—Medicos for Mexico. That was the volunteer medical organization her mother had suggested Lani work for rather than going with Doctors Without Borders. Lani struggled to remember what her mother had said about the people who had been friends years earlier back when both women were still on the reservation. *But why is this woman so dangerous?* Lani asked herself. *And what does she have to do with me?*

Not able to summon any answers on her own, she picked up Smitty's phone and called her mother. "Who is Gayle Stryker?" Lani asked when Diana answered.

"She and her husband are old friends of mine," Diana said. "You've met them, haven't you?"

"Not that I remember," Lani said. "But I saw their picture in the paper this morning."

"So did I," Diana said. "I'm sure they're really broken up over what's happened to that nice young man who worked for them."

"You knew him?" Lani asked. "The man who was in jail?"

"I met him a couple of years ago," Diana said. "At a banquet in the Strykers' honor."

As Lani listened to her mother's answers, she knew that what Diana was saying wasn't enough. There was something more. Maybe Diana didn't even know the problem existed, but Lani had to find out what it was. She tried to frame her questions in a way that would unmask the difficulty.

"Have you seen them recently?" Lani asked.

"Not for years," Diana said. "Your father may have, though. He didn't say for sure, but I know he was thinking about it."

"About seeing the Strykers?"

"Well, one of them, anyway," Diana said. "Years ago, Larry Stryker was one of the doctors at the hospital in Sells. He was working there when that girl whose case Dad's working on was murdered. Dad was going to try to see Larry yesterday to see if he could find out who her attending physician was at the time she was hospitalized."

Lani's body was suddenly strung so tight she could barely breathe. Even without Looks at Nothing's crystals, before Lani's eyes the flesh was sloughing off Gayle Stryker's photograph, leaving behind nothing but a gaping skull.

"Did he?" she asked, trying to keep the quiver out of her voice. "Do you know if Dad saw him . . . or her?"

"I have no idea," Diana answered. "Things were so hectic yesterday with the funeral and everything, I never got around to asking him. Why do you need to know?"

"I was just wondering," Lani answered lamely. "I saw the picture and remembered they were friends of yours."

"You're right," Diana said. "They are. How's the car?"

"Smitty's working on it," Lani said.

"Good," her mother told her. "If anybody can get those stains out, Smitty's the guy."

Lani put the phone down and then stared out at the traffic going past on South Fourth. All her life she had heard stories about how, on the day Nana *Dahd* needed Looks at Nothing's help, she had sent her nephew, Fat Crack Ortiz, to fetch him.

The Gadsden Purchase of 1852 had divided the ancient lands of the Tohono O'odham, leaving part of the tribe in Mexico and the rest in the United States. *S'ab Neid Pi Has,* a wiry old medicine man, had lived in a Tohono O'odham village just south of the border. Fat Crack had agreed to go on what he was convinced would be a fool's errand. He drove as far as The Gate— an unsupervised and unregulated border crossing on the reservation—that allowed tribal members access to friends and relations on either side of the international border.

Because Looks at Nothing's village had no telephone

access, Fat Crack expected to have to park on the United States side of the border and then hitchhike or walk to the medicine man's village. Instead, and much to his surprise, he found the blind old man resting in the shade of a mesquite tree patiently awaiting Fat Crack's arrival. Somehow, without having to be told, he had sensed Nana *Dahd*'s need of him and had made his way to The Gate fully expecting that someone would arrive to take him to her.

Lani understood there were mysterious ways of knowing things—just as Fat Crack had known she would someday be a doctor, and as Lani herself knew Fat Crack's new grandchild, Gabriel, would be a willing student of all the things Nana *Dahd* and Fat Crack had taught Lani.

Now, studying the photo, Lani's vision kept the skull eerily superimposed over the woman's face. In the process Lani suddenly could see something she hadn't known before. Gayle Stryker was evil—in the same way Andrew Philip Carlisle and Mitch Johnson had been evil. Lani couldn't quite discern what Gayle Stryker had to do with the Girl in the Box, but she knew it was Fat Crack who had brought Brandon Walker and the dead girl's mother together. If Fat Crack had been the instrument of drawing Gayle Stryker—this Dangerous Object—into their lives, that meant that *I'itoi,* Elder Brother himself, was the real moving force behind all their actions.

Once *I'itoi* had brought Andrew Carlisle and Mitch Johnson to the reservation for one purpose and one purpose only: so the evil *Ohbs* could be destroyed. This had to be the same thing. Once again Lani picked up Smitty's telephone. Wanting to warn her father of this possible danger, she dialed his cell-phone number. When the voice-mail prompt came on, Lani hung up. She couldn't figure out how to leave that message.

And so, sitting in Smitty Coltharp's grimy office waiting for her mother's Buick to be finished, Lani did what Tohono O'odham *siwani*s always do. She began to sing under her breath, letting the words flow out, knowing as she did so that she was singing for power. Once the words of protection took wing, she repeated the four stanzas the required four times because, as Fat Crack and Nana *Dahd* had taught her, all things in nature go in fours.

Smitty came in a while later. "Car's ready," he said. "Good as new." He examined Lani's face. "Are you all right?" he asked. "You look upset."

"No," she told him. "I'm fine."

But that wasn't true. Dolores Lanita Walker wasn't fine at all.

Once Larry left her office, it took time for Gayle to pull things together. The call to CitationShares was prompt and courteous, but not nearly fast enough to suit her. She waited on the line, drumming a pencil impatiently on her desk while the Owner Services representative checked aircraft availability. Finally the young woman came back on the line.

"All right, Mrs. Stryker," she said. "We can have a CJ-1 at the Tucson Airport executive terminal by six P.M. this evening to take you to Cabo San Lucas. You're familiar with the airport facilities there?"

Gayle breathed a sigh of relief. "Yes," she said. "We've flown in and out of there several times. And a six o'clock departure will be fine."

"How many passengers will there be?"

"Only one this time," Gayle said. "I'll be flying by myself. My husband won't be able to join me until later. He'll call for a plane once his schedule smooths out."

"Will there be any special luggage requirements—golf clubs, that kind of thing?"

"No," Gayle said. "This is work, not play. I'll have several suitcases and briefcases, but no golf equipment."

"Any special catering requirements?"

"I'll be busy this afternoon, and I'm already missing lunch. How about some cold lobster and a nice Caesar salad to go with the white wine you already have on board."

"Will you need us to send a town car to pick you up?"

"No, I'll drive myself to the airport, but I will need a pickup at the other end."

"What about hotel arrangements?"

"You've got my profile," Gayle said. "The usual will be just fine."

As soon as she was off the phone with CitationShares, Gayle dialed Larry's extension. Larry came on the line almost immediately. He still sounded upset. "Is something wrong?" he asked.

"Oh, no," Gayle said smoothly. "Everything's fine. The plane is set."

"Good. What time?"

"It'll be at the Tucson International executive terminal at eight," she answered.

"Will there be enough time for you to do what needs to be done?" Larry asked.

"Plenty of time." Her answer was confident and reassuring. "Besides, what if we're a few minutes late? The jet isn't leaving without us. See you at the airport about a quarter to."

* * *

As Brian headed back to the department, he called Pee-Wee from the car. "Where the hell have you been?" Brian's partner asked irritably. "You walk out for a cup of coffee. Next thing I know, you've disappeared off the face of the earth."

"Trust me, PeeWee, I'm working. I was meeting with an informant." In the current climate, that was by far the best way to refer to Brandon Walker. Every detective had his own private stable of informants. Partners might share almost everything else, but not informants. "Now I need a favor," Brian added.

"What?"

"You remember that old file we dredged up—the one from 1970?"

"Sure. Roseanne Orozco. I've got it right here. Why?"

"As I recall, there were several sheets of latent prints in the paper file. Can you see any record that they've been entered into AFIS?"

Brian waited and listened while PeeWee thumbed through the paperwork. "Nope," he said. "No sign that they have."

"I want you to hand-carry them down to Alvin Miller. Tell him we need those old prints fed into the AFIS ASAP."

"Are you saying the Orozco case is about to go active again?"

"I hope so," Brian returned.

"Goddamn it, Brian, if you're holding out on me . . ."

"I'm not holding out," Brian countered. "When I know for sure, you'll be the first to hear."

Leaving Old Pueblo Grill, Brandon switched his phone ringer off silent before he headed back to the Medicos for Mexico office. The cell phone's readout reported one missed call, but it wasn't from anyone he recognized.

In the Medicos parking lot the two matching LS 430s still sat in their respective reserved and shaded spots. The front of the building was awash in media vehicles. Right that minute, media scrutiny was something Brandon fervently wished to avoid. Rather than pulling into the lot, he drove around the block and parked in a residential neighborhood that backed up onto the businesses that lined East Broadway.

It was hard to maintain his concentration. This last week in April, early-afternoon temperatures had soared into the midnineties. The air-conditioning unit in the Suburban was excellent, but idling in Tucson with the AC running was a good way to screw up the engine. Brandon found himself wishing he'd brought along the iced tea he'd left behind on the table at the Old Pueblo Grill.

Sitting and waiting and watching nothing happen gave Brandon time to reflect. Brian was right. Doing this on his own and without backup was stupid, but as long as Brandon kept Larry Stryker under surveillance, the man wouldn't be on the loose and able to pose a threat to Diana or Lani.

Was Larry a serial killer? If the answer to that question was yes, then what were the chances he was armed? As a sworn law enforcement officer, Brandon would have had access to gun-licensing records. He would have known if Larry Stryker had a legal weapon but not an illegal one. As a TLC operative, Brandon wasn't privy to any of that information. What if he observed the Strykers making a headlong run for the border? What would Brandon do then? Call for reinforcements? From Bill Forsythe? As Ralph Ames had quickly grasped, that was a no-brainer, unless Alvin Miller came up with the right kind of print information . . .

At the rear of Medicos for Mexico a metal door marked DELIVERIES ONLY opened. Gayle Stryker hurried across the parking lot, unlocking one of the Lexus sedans as she went. Intent on avoiding the reporters camped out front, she quickly started the car and sped out the back way.

It would have been simple to follow her, but Brandon was torn. Should he go after her, or wait for his real prey—Larry Stryker? Had Brandon Walker been blessed with a partner right then—one with another vehicle—it would have been possible for him to follow Gayle while his partner kept an eye on Larry's activities. Forced to choose, Brandon opted to stay where he was.

His cell phone rang. Brandon leaped to answer, hoping Brian would be calling with some news. "Hi," Diana said. "The car's clean and Lani's on her way home from Smitty's. We're going to come back into town for lunch. I'm sure she's dying for Mexican food. We're going to Karichimaka. Care to join us?"

"I'm busy right now," Brandon told her. "I'll have to pass."

"You won't get a better offer," Diana told him with a laugh.

Brandon knew it was true, but the best part about missing lunch with his wife and daughter was knowing Diana and Lani would be out together—in public. That was better than their being home alone and trusting their safety to a passing deputy. Lani and Diana were safe, leaving Brandon free to keep watch on Larry Stryker.

It doesn't get any better than that.

*   *   *

Gayle went by her house and picked up a few essentials—including her loaded Davis Industries P-380, which she slipped into her jacket pocket. After hastily stuffing two suitcases, she loaded those, along with three empty briefcases, into the back of the Lexus.

Then she began her circuit of three separate banks, visiting each in turn, going through the safe-deposit boxes and removing everything of value she found there. She'd learned it was wise to have close banking relationships with several different banks, and the loot she'd managed to squirrel away in all of them over the years was quite impressive. The problem was, she couldn't simply waltz into a bank and waltz right back out again. She was an important customer in every one of them. The people who worked there—managers and tellers alike—wanted to visit with her and chat her up. One or two even expressed careful sympathy over the "unfortunate" situation with Mr. LaGrange.

Gayle tried to keep things light. More than that, she tried to keep things moving. When leaving a vault, she attempted to carry her briefcase with the same casual indifference she'd used when carrying it in. That wasn't easy, since loaded briefcases were far heavier than empties.

Finally, when the safe-deposit boxes were cleaned out and the Lexus fully loaded, Gayle headed for The Flying C. She wouldn't have gone at all except, unlike Larry, there were a few items she wanted from the ranch. Some of the artwork was too valuable to just abandon. She'd put the pieces she wanted in the backseat and drop them off at her storage unit on the way to the airport.

As she headed north, Gayle called the office. When Denise answered, she was crying.

"What's wrong?" Gayle asked.

"Haven't you heard?" Denise sobbed.

"Heard what?"

"About Erik?"

"What about him?"

"He's dead, Mrs. Stryker. One of the reporters just told me. He committed suicide in jail. I can't believe it! I just can't believe it!"

You'd better believe it, bitch, Gayle thought. *If he hadn't been sniffing after you, maybe he'd still be alive.* That's not what she said. "What terrible news. Does Dr. Stryker know?"

"I haven't told him, but someone else might have."

"Put me through to him, then," Gayle said.

"What about the reporters? They want to talk to either you or Dr. Stryker."

"I already handed you a copy of our standard no-comment response, Denise," Gayle said firmly. "All you give them is that. Do *not* answer questions. Is that clear?"

"Yes." Denise sniffled.

"Now put me through to my husband."

"Hold on, then," Denise told her. "I'll have to knock on his door. He has DND selected on his extension."

Denise Lindsay came back on the line a minute or so later. "He's not there," she said.

"What do you mean, he's not there?" Gayle demanded. "Maybe he's in the rest room."

"He's not," Denise said. "I checked. His car's not in the parking lot either. He left without telling me. He must have gone out the back way."

Gayle was upset, but she didn't allow any of that concern into her voice. "That's all right, then," she said. "I'll try his cell."

She did—immediately—but he didn't pick up, not the

first time or the second or the third. *That son of a bitch!* she muttered. *I told him to stay put. What the hell is that damned fool up to?*

When Gayle hit the first traffic tieup on Oracle, she shot over to the freeway. She preferred to take the long way around rather than sitting stuck in stalled traffic.

twenty-eight

Minutes after Gayle left the Medicos lot, Brandon spotted her husband. Larry Stryker opened the delivery door and furtively checked to see if anyone was looking before hotfooting it across to his Lexus. Brandon put the Suburban in gear and waited to see what would happen. When Larry peeled out through the back entrance, Brandon had to execute a U-turn in order to follow him. He was doing just that when his phone rang.

"It's me," Brian said.

"What's the word from Alvin Miller?"

"Not good," Brian answered.

"What do you mean?"

"Not what we expected," Brian said. "Larry Stryker isn't our guy. None of the Orozco prints match any of the ones on the Burger King cup. But one of the Orozco prints does match one of the unidentified prints we picked up from LaGrange's house. Ditto for Yuma County."

Brandon processed that information in stunned silence. He had invested so much belief and emotion into the idea that Larry Stryker was a serial killer, he couldn't quite let it go.

"That leaves us only one viable suspect," Brian continued. "It has to be someone who was present in 1970 when Roseanne was killed and who was at LaGrange's house on Saturday night."

"Gayle Stryker!" Brandon breathed.

"You've got it," Brian agreed. "Either her alone or both of them together. I'd love to have a set of her prints, but there aren't any official ones on file—at least none that Alvin can find that are officially identified as hers. I can't go for a warrant without something more specific, but I don't need a warrant to talk to the lady. If I just happened to hand her something and—"

"Damn!" Brandon muttered.

"What's the matter?"

"She's gone. She left the Medicos office a few minutes ago. I'm following Larry west on Broadway."

"PeeWee's pulling DMV info on all the Medicos company vehicles. While he's at it, I'll have him pull licensing information on Gayle and Larry. Once he has that, we'll come straight there. Who knows? Maybe we'll get lucky and she'll come back to the office."

"That would be nice," Brandon said, but he didn't sound hopeful.

"What are you up to again?" Brian asked.

Brandon wasn't eager to say, but he did. "I'm following Larry Stryker through downtown and out toward the freeway. He came racing out of the office a couple of minutes ago, threw a briefcase in his car, and took off."

"You're following him alone?" Brian asked.

"Looks like," Brandon said.

Brian Fellows sighed. "Okay," he said. "Stick with him. PeeWee and I will leave here in just a couple of minutes. Once we're under way, I'll call so you can let us know your location."

"Got it," Brandon said. "And Brian?"

"What?"

"Having backup is an excellent idea. Thanks."

"You're welcome," Brian said. "But do me a big favor."

"What's that?"

"Keep your vest on."

"I hear you," Brandon said. "And I will."

It was only a little past two, but already northbound traffic was building up. From Miracle Mile on, Oracle was gridlocked. Over and over, Larry had to wait through two full cycles of a light before he could clear a single intersection. The lines of traffic barely moved. Time, on the other hand, seemed to streak by. It was only a matter of hours until they would be out of the country and, if Gayle was right, relatively safe from prosecution. Still, Larry worried. He didn't want to be late.

What had happened? For years—for longer than most people stayed married—he and Gayle had maintained an unconventional but relatively untroubled lifestyle. She had allowed him his indulgences, and he had allowed Gayle hers. Last week, everything was fine. This week, the world was falling apart—and all because of a totally unremarkable girl named Roseanne Orozco, someone he barely remembered. She was the ultimate cause of everything coming undone—Roseanne and a jerk of an ex-sheriff named Brandon Walker. What gave that asshole the right to meddle in Larry's private affairs? Wasn't that why they'd helped un-elect him—so he couldn't do that anymore?

Larry inched his way through another light, crossing River Road just as the light turned red overhead, but squeezing through didn't do any good. A hundred yards beyond the light, traffic stopped cold again, waiting for a light to change so far ahead that it wasn't yet visible.

He glanced at the clock on the dash. Another ten minutes had passed, but he was nowhere near the Tucson city limit. It was just as well they were leaving. The traffic back and forth to the ranch was getting worse every year. Larry Stryker was tired of having to fight his way through it morning and night, coming and going. Didn't these people understand he was in a hurry? He had to get out to the ranch and back into town before Gayle did.

Somewhere north of River Road, Larry looked off to the east, toward the spot where he knew Erik LaGrange had lived, and he was struck by a fit of doubt. Gayle had sacrificed that little shit without so much as a backward glance. What if . . . ?

Plucking his cell phone out of his pocket, he scrolled down until he found the number for CitationShares. "This is Larry Stryker," he said when an Owner Services rep came on the line. "I just wanted to reconfirm our flight for tonight."

"Your wife's flight from Tucson to Cabo San Lucas?" the rep asked.

"That's right," Larry said. "That's the one."

"It's scheduled to depart at six P.M.," the clerk told him.

Larry caught his breath. "Did you say six?" he asked. "I understood it wasn't leaving until eight."

"No, it's definitely departing at six. The itinerary calls for one passenger, Mrs. Stryker, leaving for Cabo San Lucas at six P.M. Do you need me to change that, or are you ready to arrange your own departure?"

Larry could barely speak. "No," he said. "That's fine."

He ended the call, then pounded the steering wheel with both fists. "That bitch!" he shouted at the top of his lungs. "That incredible bitch! She's planning to take off and leave me holding the bag!"

By the time he was stopped at the next light, though, Larry had reconsidered. He picked up his phone and hit redial. "This is Dr. Stryker again," he said. "You're right. I do need to make my own flight arrangements. I'd like to leave tonight—as soon as you can get a plane here."

"Departing from Tucson International?" the reservations clerk asked.

"No. I'll be at home, north of the city. I'd rather leave from the FBO at Pinal Air Park."

"Will you also be going to Cabo San Lucas?"

"No," he said after a moment's pause. "I'll be going to Mexico City."

"And only one passenger?"

"That's right," he told her. "Only one. But I'd like a Bravo or an Excel—something big enough so I can make it in one shot."

"You realize this will be considered simultaneous use. I can't guarantee you a plane until I check availability. Do you want to stay on the line?"

"Yes," Larry said. He almost added "please," but he managed to stifle himself. The wait was interminable.

"All right," the rep said brightly, coming back on the line. "There weren't any Excels, but I can have a Bravo there at nine-thirty. So that's one passenger departing from Pinal Air Park."

"Wonderful," he said.

"Any special catering requirements?" she asked.

"Scotch," he told her, letting out his breath. "And plenty of ice."

"Cars? A hotel?"

"Have a car meet me at the executive terminal in

Mexico City," he said. "I'll decide on the hotel on the way."

Brandon's arm was bothering him again. He had forgotten about it for a while, but now it was aching like crazy. And the Suburban's air conditioner didn't seem to be pumping out enough cool air. *Nerves,* he told himself. And it was true. When his cell phone rang a few minutes later, Brandon jumped as though he'd been shot.

"Where are you?" Brian asked.

"Stuck in traffic northbound on Oracle at Orange Grove," Brandon replied. "At least he's not on I-19 headed for Nogales."

"If he's going north on Oracle, Stryker's most likely going to his ranch," Brian put in. "It's The Flying C on the far side of the Tortolitas. That's the address listed on his driver's license—101 Flying C Ranch Road. Are you having any difficulty maintaining visual contact?"

"Are you kidding? We're crawling along at such a snail's pace I could walk fast enough to catch up, but I'm also in the Suburban. I'm five or six car lengths back. I'm high enough to see him, but I doubt he can see me. How about you?"

"PeeWee and I just left the department. With all the construction at I-19 and I-10, we're taking surface streets. It may take us a while. Do you want us to use the siren?"

"Don't bother," Brandon said. "Traffic's too heavy for that. I'll keep you posted, but give me that home address again, just in case. I'll key it into my GPS. That way, if I do end up losing him, I'll still have some idea where he's headed."

After ending the call, he started messing around with the GPS controls. The obligatory warning came on, telling him not to make adjustments to the system while the car was in motion, but there was no danger of that. The Suburban was stopped cold at a traffic signal. As soon as the GPS system had located the address and mapped it, Brandon called Brian back.

"Wait a minute," he said. "The Flying C is off Highway 79. It's in Pinal County, not Pima. What's going to happen if Bill Forsythe finds out you've strayed into another jurisdiction?"

"We're just going to ask a pair of suspects a few questions," Brian said. "No big deal."

But Brandon knew that once Sheriff Forsythe heard what was going on, there would be hell to pay.

The lunchtime rush was mostly over. Diana and Lani sat at a table in the far corner of the room while Lani picked at her food.

"I never saw a Mexican combination plate you didn't devour on sight," Diana said to her daughter. "Is something wrong?"

Lani looked at her mother—her *Mil-gahn* mother—and shook her head. Lani still didn't understand the terrible dread she was feeling—dread brought on by that vision of the flesh disappearing from Gayle Stryker's face. And if Lani couldn't understand it, there was no way she could explain it to her mother.

"I'm worried about Dad," she hedged at last.

"Don't be," Diana said with absolute confidence. "Your father's a big boy. He can take care of himself."

Not without help, Lani thought. She pushed her plate away and gave her mother what she hoped was a convincing smile. "I'm full," she said. "Let's go home."

She wanted to be back home—back in her room with the door closed. There, at least, she'd be able to sit on the floor with her legs crossed, hold Looks at Nothing's crystals in her hands, and sing the song that had come to her earlier. As a medicine woman, it was all she knew to do. As a daughter, it was the best help she could offer.

Staying at a discreet distance, Brandon followed Larry's LS 430 through Catalina, past Saddle Brook, and then off onto Highway 79 at Oracle Junction. When Larry slowed and signaled for a left-hand turn at Flying C Ranch Road, Brandon took his foot off the gas and then drove by with his face averted in case Larry happened to look in his rearview mirror. Brandon continued on up the highway another half mile or so before pulling another U-turn and parking on the shoulder.

Taking out his phone, he called Brian. "Where are you?" Brandon asked.

"Just past Oracle and Orange Grove," the detective returned. "Traffic is the pits. We finally had to put on the lights and siren."

"Don't worry," Brandon said. "Everything's cool. Larry just pulled off Highway 79 onto Flying C Ranch Road. My GPS says that's a dead end, so he'll have to come back out eventually. I'm parked up the road a few hundred yards. When he comes back out, I'll see him, but he won't see me."

"Sounds good," Brian said.

"I've been thinking about all this while I've been driving," Brandon added. "Larry was all upset when I brought up the possibility of his being the father of Roseanne Orozco's baby. I'd talked to him about Roseanne yesterday. He kept his cool then, but the paternity issue threw him into a blind panic. If you and Pee-Wee can apply the screws . . ."

"With pleasure," Brian returned. "We'll see what we can do."

"Okay," Brandon told him. "I'll hang tight. See you when you get here."

Larry's phone rang again as he drove up Flying C Ranch Road. When he checked the readout and saw that it was Gayle, he didn't answer that time, either. Obviously she knew now that he had left the office and was trying to track him down. Too bad!

He was still shaken by the phone calls to Citation-Shares, still astonished that she would betray him like that. He had always worried it *might* happen, though he had never really thought it *would*, though now it had. Gayle had turned on him, just as she had turned on Erik LaGrange, but with one big difference: Larry had figured out what was up in time to get his own damned plane. Gayle was on her way out of town; so was he.

When he drove into the yard, Gayle's Lexus was nowhere to be seen. He had half expected that she might have beaten him here and he'd arrive to find the ranch house already reduced to rubble, but it wasn't. *She probably lied to me about that, too,* he thought bitterly. *She probably never planned to blow it up at all.*

That was an appalling possibility. What if somebody stumbled into the basement room with its restraints and shackles and the rest of his equipment? He stopped the car. For a space of time he was too shaken to get out. He had cleaned things up as best he could, but he knew enough about current crime scene investigation to realize that tricky alternate-light sources could locate blood droplets that were invisible to the naked eye.

What should he do? If Gayle wasn't going to destroy the evidence against him, should he try to do it himself?

No, he decided finally. *Get the notebooks and get the hell out. Go wait at the airport. No one will ever think to look for me there . . . not at Pinal Air Park.*

So Larry Stryker hurried into the house and on into the study. He'd had a wall safe installed there, behind one of the big oil paintings. And because Gayle had no idea the safe existed, it had been the right place for him to keep his notebooks.

He was upset enough that his hand shook as he worked the combination. It took three tries before he got it right. Swinging the door open, he grabbed up the notebooks. He shoved them into the open briefcase on his desk and slapped the lid shut. He turned back to the safe to close it and return the painting to its place.

"What do you think you're doing?" Gayle asked.

He hadn't heard the car or her. The sound of her voice scared him to death. A chill ran up his spine. The painting fell from his hand, splitting the heavy gilt frame as it smashed onto the Saltillo floor. This couldn't be happening. Larry led a charmed life. He wasn't supposed to get caught.

"Nothing," he said, turning to face her. That's when he saw the gun—a chrome-plated pistol—that was pointed straight at his chest. It wasn't a very large weapon, but it seemed to grow in size. He stared at it until the gaping mouth of the pistol was all he could see. "I came to see if you needed any help," he added lamely.

She smiled and shook her head, but she didn't move the gun. It stayed pointed at him.

"I never knew about that safe," she said quietly. "What do you keep in it?"

"Odds and ends. Nothing important. Put down the gun, Gayle. Shouldn't we get to work?"

"Did you have money in there?" she demanded. "Were you hiding money from me?"

"Of course not!" he declared. Flustered, he felt his face turn red. "Nothing of the kind."

"Then open the briefcase," she ordered. "Show me."

As he carried on his end of the conversation, Larry Stryker was trying to grapple with this new reality. There was no question about whether or not she would pull the trigger. Of the two of them, Gayle was the natural-born killer. He had known that about her for more than thirty years. He had always supposed he was immune. But he wasn't. His only hope was to fight back.

So he stepped toward the desk and made as if to comply. Instead of opening the briefcase, he picked it up and heaved it at her. She dodged out of the way of the flying briefcase, and her first shot missed him completely. The second one didn't. The bullet hit him square in the chest and flung him backward. It took forever for him to slide down the wall. He watched her, expecting her to fire again. She simply disappeared from view as he slid behind the desk.

"Gayle," he called. "Don't leave me like this. Please."

She didn't answer. The last thing Larry Stryker heard was the sound of the study door slamming shut behind her.

In twenty-six years of driving gravel trucks, Amos Brubaker had never had an accident—not even a fender bender. This, his last load of the day, was headed for another new development on the far side of Saddle Brook. The gravel pit was in the riverbed west of I-10 and southeast of Marana. According to the map, it should have been easier for him to get where he was going by backtracking as far as Rillito and going east there. Mileagewise, that would have been closer, but that was the sad truth about Tucson-area traffic. Amos was actually better off going miles out of his way, taking the freeway as far as north Red Rock, cutting over there to Highway 79, and approaching his drop-off point from the opposite direction.

Amos was doing that now, sailing along on the straightaway at slightly over the 65-miles-per-hour legal limit. He slowed slightly when he saw a green Suburban parked on the right-hand shoulder. These days DPS sometimes used stealth vehicles rather than clearly marked patrol cars to police Arizona's highways. But the Suburban turned out to be just that, a Suburban with a single occupant—a man—sitting in it. His hazard lights weren't on. He didn't look like someone having car trouble or trying to flag someone down, so Amos put his foot back on the gas pedal and kept going.

Just then some dim-bulb babe in a Lexus went tearing past him doing at least eighty-five. She'd barely gone around the front fender of his Mack truck when she slammed on her brakes and turned off on a dirt road. Amos flipped her a bird as he went past. What the hell was the matter with drivers today—and not just women drivers, either? If she was planning on turning right, couldn't she have stayed behind him for that last quarter of a mile? Did bimbos like her have even the vaguest idea of how much blacktop was needed to stop a loaded gravel truck? That was another problem with driving these days. Everybody was in too much of a hurry.

Amos was coming up on Oracle Junction. He reached the place where the straightaway ended. Beyond that point the road narrowed slightly and was far more curvy. Amos eased back to a real 65. He saw the car ahead of him—a pale yellow vehicle of some kind—approaching in the opposite lane, but he didn't worry about it—didn't consider it at all. He saw the approaching car and assumed whoever was in it saw him, too. Bright red Mack gravel trucks are hard to miss.

But then, when he was almost on top of the car—a Honda—it turned left directly in front of him. He saw now that the pale yellow Honda was driven by a woman—a gray-haired woman about the same age as Amos. At the very last moment, she glanced up and saw the truck. In that electric instant, he saw the look of horror flash across her face; saw her lips form themselves into a surprised O; saw her eyes open wide, shocked and disbelieving.

Looking for a way to avoid hitting her, Amos checked the left lane, but now there was another car in that lane, a cop car with flashing lights that was speeding toward both the Honda and Amos's truck. By then, the Honda was fully astraddle the right-hand lane, directly in the path of the speeding Mack truck. Amos Brubaker had split seconds to make his decision. Between T-boning the seemingly stationary Honda or crashing head-on into an oncoming vehicle, the woman's Honda presented the least lethal choice.

Almost standing on the brake pedal, Amos clung to the wheel and tried to keep the truck and its add-on trailer on the road. He had dodged enough—or maybe she had sped up enough—that instead of hitting her dead-on, he clipped her right quarter panel. Instead of being flattened under the truck's front bumper, the Honda spun away. When it hit the soft shoulder on the side of the road, it flipped and flew end over end before finally coming to rest, leaning at an angle, against a barbed-wire fence.

Amos felt the impact and saw the car go whirling away. For the barest of moments, he thought he had made it—thought he was home free, then he felt a sickening lurch behind him. He looked in the rearview mirror long enough to see the trailer swing back across the centerline. In that awful moment he knew what was going to happen. The heavy load of gravel would pull him over. As the wheels of the tractor left the ground, all Amos Brubaker could do was hold on for dear life. Hold on and pray.

twenty-nine

Brian Fellows had heard the expression "watching a train wreck," but he had never understood the implications until that very moment. It seemed to happen in slow motion. Not wanting to alert Larry Stryker, he had shut off the siren as they entered Oracle Junction. Once they were on Highway 79, he saw the approaching gravel truck. He saw the little yellow Honda. When the Honda's brake lights came on, Brian assumed that the vehicle was preparing to turn, but when the turn signal didn't come on, there was no way to tell which way the Honda was going. Then, to Brian's gut-wrenching dismay, the Honda turned directly into the path of the truck. And through it all, there was nothing—not one thing—Brian could do to stop it.

"My God!" PeeWee shouted. "Look out!"

And Brian was looking. He was searching desperately for some safe haven, somewhere to pull off the road and get the hell out of the way. He saw the speeding tractor slam into the side of the Honda. With one tire bouncing high in the air above them all, the out-of-control Honda spun through the air while the truck careened straight toward them. Trying to dodge out of the way, Brian wrenched the wheel to the right. He managed to miss the bouncing tire and the Honda, but the maneuver sent the Crown Victoria pitching off the steep shoulder and directly into a concrete-bridge abutment, where it slammed to a stop.

For the briefest moment, Brian's vision was obscured by what turned out to be his deployed air bag. When he could see again, the fully loaded gravel truck and trailer were skidding on their sides along both lanes of roadway, spilling mounds of gravel and raising clouds of dust.

Brian turned to PeeWee. "Are you okay?"

PeeWee nodded, rubbing his collarbone. "I think so," he said. "You?"

Brian tried the door. The frame was evidently jammed. His door wouldn't open. Neither would PeeWee's. They ended up having to shove their way through the shattered safety glass in the windshield.

"You go," PeeWee said when the hole was wide enough for Brian to slip through. "I'll radio for help."

When Brian hit the ground, the Mack truck tractor lay on its side, wheels still spinning, with its signature bulldog hood ornament buried in the broken remains of a crushed mesquite tree. As Brian watched, the shaken truck driver scrambled out through a window opening and crawled across the door. Gripping the running board, he slipped over the side and then dropped the last few feet to the ground.

As soon as the man landed, he took off at a dead run. At first, Brian had no idea where he was going. Only when he looked beyond where the driver was headed did Brian see the wreckage of the smashed yellow Honda. It lay at the bottom of a steep wash, leaning up against several strands of barbed-wire fence. The truck driver ran to the edge of the wash and scrambled down the side. By the time Brian reached him, he was pulling desperately on the driver's-side door handle.

"We've got to help her," the man was saying. "We've got to get her out of there."

But that door wouldn't budge, either. Peering through the window, Brian saw the still form of a woman. She was flopped over against the door with blood seeping from a deep cut on her head. When he pounded on the window beside her, she didn't move.

Leaving Brian behind, the truck driver raced around to the far side of the vehicle, clambered over the fence, and shoved. To Brian's surprise, the Honda wavered for a moment and then tipped back onto its three remaining tires. Brian had to step back to get out of the way. With what seemed superhuman strength, the truck driver wrenched open the passenger door. He stood to one side, panting with exertion, while Brian scrambled inside. The woman still hadn't moved. Brian felt for a pulse and found one—weak and fast, but there.

He clambered back outside. "Well?" the driver demanded. "Is she okay?"

Without answering, Brian turned back toward the wreckage of the Crown Vic. "She's still alive," he shouted at PeeWee, "but only just. Get on the horn. Tell them we'll need a medevac helicopter out here. On the double."

Brian turned back toward the truck driver, but the man was no longer standing. Pale and weak as a kitten, he had dropped to his knees and was quietly puking into the dirt.

Parked on the shoulder, Brandon saw the big red gravel truck bearing down on him from behind and the white car come out to pass. As they roared past him, the passing vehicle was on the far side of the truck. He didn't see it again until the truck braked as the other vehicle slowed to turn off on Flying C Ranch Road. That was when he recognized the white car for what it was— Gayle Stryker's Lexus. Why was she coming from the north?

Brandon had picked up his phone to call Brian when he saw an explosion of dust a mile or so farther south toward Oracle Junction. Dust like that had to mean that the speeding gravel truck had somehow come to grief, but that wasn't Brandon's concern. What worried him was that Brian didn't answer his phone. After three rings, the cell phone went to voice mail, giving Brandon no choice but to leave a message.

"It's me. You're not going to believe it. Gayle Stryker just showed up from the north and turned into the ranch. I don't know where you are, but get a move on. I need you here now."

He waited several minutes, thinking that surely Brian would call him back. Finally, impatient, he punched redial. Again, the cell phone rang several times. "Pick up, for God's sake!" Brandon grumbled.

"Hello?" Brian said at last.

"Where the hell are you? Did you get my message?"

"What message?"

"I called a few minutes ago. Gayle Stryker showed up. She and Larry are both here at the ranch."

"There's been an accident," Brian said. "My phone ended up under the car seat. I didn't find it until it started ringing."

"What accident?" Brandon stopped. "Wait a minute," he added. "Somebody's coming down the road. It's a white vehicle, so it may be . . ." He squinted into the sunlight. "Yes, it's definitely a Lexus. I can't tell which one, and I don't know how many passengers—if they're both in there or if it's only one of them. The vehicle's almost back to the highway. If there was ever a time for backup, this is it."

"That's what I'm trying to tell you. There's been a wreck," Brian said. "A bad one, just short of the junction."

"But . . ." Brandon slipped the Suburban into gear and moved forward. The Lexus had pulled up to the intersection now and was turning right onto the highway. "He's coming out now, turning your way and heading for Tucson."

"He won't get past here," Brian said. "A gravel truck tipped over and spilled its load on top of a culvert. The road's completely blocked in both directions."

"Can't you and PeeWee get through?"

"Negative on that," Brian returned. "We managed to get out of the way, but we hit a bridge abutment. PeeWee and I aren't going anywhere. Neither is our vehicle."

Brandon rounded a curve and saw the field of wreckage up ahead. A few other Tucson-bound cars were already stopped. As he watched, the Lexus swung off onto the shoulder and then turned.

"Stryker's just this side of your position," Brandon shouted into the phone. "He's pulling a U-ey."

"I'm on foot, but I'm on my way," Brian told him.

But Brandon soon realized that having Brian on his way wasn't nearly good enough. Once the Lexus was back on the highway, it would start gaining speed. Brandon did the only thing he could. Using the Suburban's bulk, he drove toward the much smaller LS 430, forcing it off the highway and onto the shoulder. Only then, with the two vehicles sitting nose to nose, did Brandon see there was only one person in the Lexus. The driver wasn't Larry Stryker after all—it was Gayle.

She honked at him furiously and motioned him out of her way. When he didn't budge, she backed up, hit the gas, and tried to swing around him. He blocked her again. That time a stricken look of recognition crossed her face when she finally realized who he was. There was barely a moment of hesitation between her recognizing him and the appearance of the gun. She held it out the window and fired three rounds in rapid succession.

Brandon threw himself across the front seat and hoped that the Suburban's engine block and dashboard would offer enough cover. He lay there with his ears ringing and wondered if she would fire again. Not wanting to be hit by spraying glass, Brandon rolled down the automatic window with the touch of a button while plucking his Walther out of its holster.

When he heard the squeal of rubber on pavement, he realized Gayle was once again trying to push past him. He raised up in time to see the front side panel of the Lexus surge by. With her on the far side of the moving vehicle, Brandon knew it would be difficult for her to return fire. Leaning out the window and holding the Walther in both hands, he fired two separate shots. Hitting the right rear tire was no big thing. It was so close and presented such a large target that even a beginner could have hit that one. As that tire exploded, though, the car began to fishtail. Hitting the second tire dead-on was sheer luck.

But when Brandon Walker turned back to the steering wheel, he knew he wasn't home free. A cloud of steam engulfed the Suburban's whole front end.

"Damn!" he exclaimed. "She shot the hell out of my radiator."

Even so, Brandon plunged the gearshift into reverse and turned around. He had no idea how far he could drive before the Suburban overheated and the engine seized up, but with Brian and PeeWee stuck on the far side of the gravel truck, he had to try.

Once the vehicle was moving forward, the steam cloud swept back under the Suburban enough so Brandon could see to drive. He came around the last curve before the straightaway hoping that, driving with two flat rear tires, she would have lost control and gone off the road. No such luck. A mile or so ahead of him he saw Gayle's crippled Lexus. It wasn't moving fast, but it was moving, moving and turning—turning left, back onto Flying C Ranch Road.

By the time Brandon reached the turnoff, the temperature gauge was already at the top of the red. There wasn't much time. Just where Flying C Ranch Road left the highway was a cattle guard. Brandon pulled onto it at an angle so the Suburban straddled the whole metal grate. He rolled up all the windows, set the emergency brake, and put the transmission in "park" before shutting off the engine. When he got out, he locked the doors and set the alarm for good measure. The smell of hot metal hurt him. He had loved that old Suburban. The engine was probably doomed, but it would make one hell of a good roadblock.

Common sense dictated that Brandon stay with his vehicle, but that's what everyone would expect him to do—be the old guy, know his limitations, sit on his duff and wait for the cavalry—the young guys—to ride to his rescue. By then, though, Brandon Walker was far too pumped up to stop. Besides, this was personal. Gayle Stryker had tried to take him out. He was determined to return the favor.

Looking off across the desert, he saw a swath of green trees. The screen of trees probably meant that the ranch buildings were tucked in among them. No doubt Gayle and Larry Stryker were concealed in among those trees, too. They would expect him and his reinforcements to come driving up the road. They wouldn't expect someone to show up alone, on foot, walking through the desert. So that's what Brandon did—he walked.

As he moved along, he popped a new clip into the Walther. He had fired only two shots, but he wanted a full load of ammunition at his disposal if and when he needed it. Wanting to tell Brian what was happening, he reached for his cell phone, but it wasn't there. In all the excitement, he must have dropped it somewhere in the Suburban. He could have gone back for it, but that would have taken too much time. Instead, he kept going.

Behind him, he heard the faintest wail of a siren. Maybe Brian had managed to summon help after all. If that was the case, using the Suburban as a roadblock hadn't been such a smart idea after all. It might keep the Strykers from getting back on the highway, but it would sure as hell keep backup from getting through as well.

Great planning, Brandon told himself grimly. *Hell of a good plan!*

"Come on, PeeWee," Brian shouted at his partner. "Brandon needs help."

Clambering up and over a mountain of spilled gravel, he saw the two cars—Brandon's dark green Suburban and a white sedan—sitting nose to nose. Brian set off at a gallop, but even as he did so, he knew that with him on foot, they were too far away—much too far.

Loping down the highway, Brian heard the sickening sounds of gunfire. Pop. Pop. Pop. He tried not to think about what that meant. He kept running, juggling his cell phone as he went.

"Nine one one. What are you reporting?"

"Shots fired," Brian gasped into the phone. "Officer needs assistance."

He saw a cloud of steam billowing from under the Suburban's hood. He saw the Lexus take off. He heard more shots and saw puffs of smoke as Brandon returned fire. The Lexus wavered and slowed, but it didn't stop. Brian kept running, but he wasn't close to making up the distance when Brandon shoved the steaming Suburban into reverse, turned, and took off after the Lexus.

Brian stopped then. There was no use running anymore. He would never catch them. He stood doubled over, breathing heavily.

"Sir," a tiny voice whispered to him from very far away. "Are you still there? Sir?"

He looked down. His cell phone was still clutched in his doubled fist. "Yes," he gasped. "I'm here."

"What is your position? Are you at the scene of the gravel-truck rollover?"

"Yes. No. I'm on Highway 79, but I'm a quarter mile or more north of the gravel truck. I'm Detective Brian Fellows of the Pima County Sheriff's Department. An armed homicide suspect is fleeing northbound on Highway 79. A private citizen—a private investigator—is in pursuit."

"A DPS unit is on its way, coming southbound from Red Rock. It should be there in a few minutes."

"Good," Brian managed. "Maybe he can intercept them, but remember to tell him 'Shots fired.' The guy in the Lexus should be considered armed and dangerous."

Two more southbound vehicles went past, but Brian made no effort to flag them down. Instead, he started back toward the gravel truck—toward PeeWee and the Crown Vic's police radio. With that he'd have a better idea of what was going on.

It was only a matter of two or three minutes until he heard the wail of a distant siren. At first Brian wasn't sure if it was from emergency vehicles arriving at the gravel truck from the other direction or the DPS unit responding from Red Rock. As it came closer and closer, though, he realized it was coming toward him from the north, and it didn't turn off. When Brian saw the flashing lights, he realized that the State Patrol officer must have disregarded his request to intercept the fleeing Lexus.

Brian Fellows stepped onto the pavement and waved frantically. The cruiser screeched to a stop. The passenger-side window rolled down and a female officer peered out at him. "What's the problem?" she asked.

"Didn't you get the call?" Brian demanded. "I sent word for you to intercept a pair of homicide suspects fleeing north in a Lexus."

"You're Detective Fellows, then?" she asked, which meant she had gotten the message. Why the hell had she ignored it? Brian nodded.

"I'm Officer Downs," she said, unlocking the door. "Get in. I never saw any Lexus."

"What about a Suburban, then?" he asked as he clambered into the vehicle. "A green Suburban driven by a private detective. It would have been smoking. I think the suspect nailed the radiator to put it out of commission."

Officer Downs was already turning her vehicle around. "Oh," she said. "I saw that."

"The Suburban?"

She nodded.

"Where?"

"A mile or two back. It was parked along the road, but I was responding to everything else. Fasten your seat belt, please," she added, and took off.

As they drove, Brian tried to give her some background. Two minutes later they reached Flying C Ranch Road. When Brian saw the Suburban parked crookedly astraddle the cattle guard, his heart fell. He jumped out of the cruiser and raced up to the Suburban, more than half expecting to find Brandon Walker's body slumped in the front seat. It wasn't. The vehicle was empty—locked and empty.

Brian was turning back to Officer Downs, who had joined him by the Suburban, when a volley of gunshots came from somewhere up Flying C Ranch Road. "Did you hear that?" he demanded. "They must be somewhere up there."

But Officer Downs was already heading back to her vehicle. She popped open the trunk and returned carrying a pair of wire cutters. Next to the cattle guard was a gate held shut with a padlocked chain. In moments she cut through the chain and the gate swung open. "You wearing a vest?" she asked.

"Yes."

"Good. Me, too."

Together they leaped back into her cruiser. Brian's foot was still on the ground as Officer Downs pulled out.

Brandon darted through the trees—a grove of magnificent tough old eucalyptus—grateful for the cooling shade and the protective cover they offered. The screen was only six or seven trees thick. Nearing the far side, Brandon realized he was out of breath. He hadn't thought he was moving that fast, but he slowed and tried to catch his breath—tried to stop sounding like an over-worked steam engine.

Pausing under the trees, he could see that he was approaching the ranch and outbuildings from behind. There in front of him—parked side by side—were two matching Lexus sedans. Doors and trunks to both vehicles were wide open, and Gayle was hurriedly transferring luggage and other items from one to the other.

There was no sign of Larry and no sign of Gayle's weapon. Brandon stopped behind the nearest tree. "Drop your weapon," he ordered. "Place both hands on the vehicle."

Gayle Stryker stopped what she was doing, stood still, and turned toward him, but he could tell from the way her eyes scanned the trees that she hadn't seen him—had no idea where he was.

"I said, drop your weapon!"

"What if I said no?" Her response was cool and defiant, but the bravado didn't quite work. Her voice cracked slightly on that last word, and Brandon heard it.

"Give it up, Gayle. One way or the other, you're not leaving here."

"You never had any idea who you were dealing with, Brandon Walker. And you never will."

The exchange of words must have been enough to give away his position. Putting her right hand in her blazer pocket, she charged, coming straight for the tree trunk that sheltered him. Her hand never came out of the pocket, but he heard a single slug slam into the far side of the eucalyptus.

Then he fired, too. One, two, three, four, five separate shots. His years of range practice paid off. The deadly pattern appeared like spots of bright red paint on her chest.

The barrage of bullets stopped her forward motion. Swaying, she looked down at her chest in surprise and then fell face-first into the dirt.

Brandon smelled cordite mixed with eucalyptus and the combination somehow made him think of his mother's old cold remedy. He knew he needed to stay hidden in case someone else came out of the house, but he was having a hard time remembering all that—keeping it straight. Brandon heard the siren again. It seemed closer now—closer and louder, but there was a pain in Brandon's chest that was worse than anything he'd ever felt.

Damn, he thought as he crumpled slowly to the ground. *I didn't think I was hit, but she must've got me after all.*

With Officer Downs at the wheel, the patrol car screamed into the yard of The Flying C. Brian saw the two Lexus sedans parked side by side, with all the doors and with both trunks open, but there was no sign of movement, no sign of life.

"There," Officer Downs said, pointing. "Someone's on the ground."

Brian reached Gayle Stryker's body first. He saw at a glance that she was dead. Then he looked around for Brandon. It took only a few seconds to find him, but for Brian those seconds lasted forever. Finally he spotted him. "Here he is!" Brian shouted. "I think he's been shot."

Together Officer Downs and Brian raced to Brandon Walker's side. He wasn't breathing. There was no pulse. But there was no blood, either—no sign of any wounds other than a gash on his head from where he had scraped his head on the rough tree bark as he fell.

"He's not shot," Officer Downs surmised. "I think he's had a heart attack. Get that vest off him. I've got a defibrillator in the car. I'll be right back."

She returned moments later carrying a bag of equipment. "I've been through the training," she said as she knelt next to Brandon's still body, "but I've never used one of these things in the field before."

"Let's hope it works," Brian Fellows told her. "Let's hope to God it works!"

thirty

Then, after a time, the woman heard someone speaking very, very softly. She knew without looking that it was I'itoi—Elder Brother—who was speaking to her.

I'itoi said: The babies are here, my sister. They are the babies who have left their mothers, just as your baby has left you, to live with me. These tiny brown curled leaves are the cradles in which the little ones go to sleep when they are tired. These babies who have left their mothers are very happy with me. And they do not like you to feel as you do. That is why they are crying now in their tiny brown leaf-cradles. Are you different from all the mothers?"

And the woman raised her head from her hands and smiled. And from all around her came the sound of babies laughing.

Then the woman took her own brown cradle blanket and went back to the village.

She found the neighbor women busy in her home. The ground was swept and cleaned. The fire was burning under the cooking olla.

A friend called out to her not to go too close to the fire; the smoke would make her eyes bad. But an old In-

dian woman who looked at her sharply said, "She has talked to I'itoi."

And always after this the woman's eyes seemed to be looking a great way off. Sometimes you see eyes like that, big and quiet but looking beyond—farther and farther. Then you will know, that person has talked to I'itoi.

When Brandon Walker finally opened his eyes, it took time for him to make sense of his surroundings. He was alone in a dimly lit room that seemed to be filled with a collection of humming medical equipment. Pinned to the pillow beside him was a cord with a button on it, a call button, he reasoned.

He was about to push it when Diana came into the room. Her hair was pulled back in a ragged ponytail. She wore no makeup. Her face was lined with weariness. She looked more haggard than he had ever seen her, but when she saw him looking up at her, her face brightened while her eyes glistened with sudden tears.

"You're awake," she said, reaching for his hand and gripping it tightly in her own, squeezing it until his knuckles ground together.

Brandon tried to speak, but something prevented it.

"It's the tube," she explained. "You can't talk until they take it out."

He freed his hand from hers and then made a writing motion. Diana searched until she found pencil and paper. When she handed it to him, he scrawled a single question mark onto the paper.

"You had a heart attack," she said. "Brian found you—Brian and a DPS officer named Cassie Downs, who happened to have a defibrillator in her patrol car. She managed to get your heart going again. Fortunately, there was a helicopter there to pick up someone from the gravel-truck accident. The woman in the Honda didn't make it. The medevac chopper picked you up instead and brought you here."

Brandon took the paper from Diana's hand. He pointed to the question mark a second time.

"You mean, where's 'here'?" she asked.

Brandon nodded impatiently.

"You're at Tucson Medical Center," she said. "You've had triple bypass surgery. Damn Dr. Browder, anyway. He was always going on about your hip and your knee. Why the hell didn't he say something about your heart?" With that, Diana Ladd burst into tears.

The next time Brandon opened his eyes, he was in a different room altogether. Through drawn blinds he could tell that it was daylight outside. When he felt his face, the tube was gone. Minutes later, the door swung open. Brandon expected Diana or Lani to appear at his bedside. Instead, Brian Fellows sank silently onto the chair beside the bed.

"I'm awake," Brandon said, causing Brian to jump. "And thirsty as hell. Is there any water around here?"

A water glass with a straw in it sat on the table. Brian had spent years caring for his invalid mother. With a practiced hand, he helped Brandon take a drink. "Not too much," he cautioned.

"Where am I?"

"ICU," Brian replied. "Family visitors only," he said. "Diana told them I'm family." He turned away, sniffled briefly, and wiped his eyes before turning back.

Brandon reached out and grasped the younger man's hand. "You always have been," he said.

They were both quiet for a few seconds, until Brandon let go. "What happened?" he asked.

"You had a heart attack."

"Not to me," Brandon Walker said gruffly. "The Strykers."

"They're dead," Brian said. "Both of them. Gayle had a private jet reserved to fly to Mexico that night. From what we've been able to learn, she was leaving on her own, but Larry must have figured out what she was up to, and she shot him. If it hadn't been for you sitting on Larry Stryker's butt, chances are one or both of them might have gotten away."

"Are you saying they were both involved in Roseanne Orozco's murder?"

Brian Fellows sighed heavily and nodded. "That and a whole lot more," he said. "I'll tell you all about it sometime, but not now. Later. When you're better."

Lani Walker sat on the hardbacked chair in the waiting room, holding tight to Looks at Nothing's precious crystals. During the past two days, she had spent hours in the waiting room outside the cardiac ICU. It seemed like a lifetime. Lani had learned more than she'd ever wanted to know about what it felt like to be in a hospital waiting room—waiting. With this new, unwanted knowledge, she vowed that someday, when she was the person coming through the door in her surgical scrubs, she would remember how it felt to be one of the people here—sitting in this awful purgatory, trapped somewhere between despair and hope.

Her mother had been here most of the time, and Davy a lot of it. Brian Fellows, however, off work on what was being termed "administrative leave," was a constant presence. Through the long, lonely hours, he had—without meaning to, without knowing quite why—spilled his guts to Lani, telling her about Larry Stryker's appalling notebooks and about the awful toll Gayle and Larry Stryker had taken in their long reign of terror. DNA and a series of long unexamined fingerprint cold-case evidence had now linked the two of them to fourteen separate cases. Unfortunately, the notebooks held pictures of several more girls than that, dead teenage girls who had yet to be identified.

When he finished, he expected Lani to be as torn up about it as he was. Lani merely nodded. "I knew she was evil," she said.

"How did you know?" Brian asked.

Lani shrugged. "Fat Crack told me," she said, knowing somehow that it was an answer Brian could understand and accept.

"But all those poor girls," Brian continued. The pictures he had seen haunted him in a way nothing else ever had. "Nobody reported them missing," he said. "No one went looking for them. Once someone really started working the cases, it didn't take much time to sort it out. Bottom line? Nobody cared."

Lani reached out and took Brian's hand in hers. "That's not true," she said. "Somebody did too care about them—you and Dad. Those murdered girls may never have had their day in court, but at least they had their day."

"Yes," Brian Fellows said sadly. "That's the best we could give them—a day of the dead."

When Brandon opened his eyes next, Diana sat dozing in the chair. Knowing how stressed and tired she had to be, he said nothing and let her sleep. Tentatively raising his hand, he managed to reach the water glass on his own. When he did so, he noticed a single red rosebud sitting in a vase.

Eventually Diana woke up. "Good morning," he said, smiling at her. "I'll bet you're tired."

"A little," she admitted. "How long have you been awake?"

"Not long," he fibbed. "Only a few minutes. Thanks for the flower."

Diana looked at the rosebud and then back to her husband. "That's not from me," she said. "It's from Emma Orozco. She wanted to say thank you, but only relatives are allowed in the ICU."

"If you see her again," Brandon Walker said, "give her a message for me. Tell Emma both Fat Crack Ortiz and I say she's welcome."

Here's a glimpse at J. A. Jance's
next thrilling novel of suspense featuring
J. P. Beaumont

Long Time Gone

Available in hardcover from
William Morrow

prologue

By standing on her tiptoes on a kitchen chair, five-year-old Bonnie could just see out over the sill of the window in the tiny daylight basement apartment where she lived with her parents. The sun had finally burned through the low gray clouds, and now splashes of sunlight cast a crazy-quilt pattern across the rain-dampened grass of the yard and the cracked concrete of the crumbling sidewalk and driveway. Sunlit spring afternoons were rare in Western Washington, and Bonnie longed to be outside, but she didn't dare, not with Mama and Daddy gone.

When they went away on those long Saturday afternoons, they'd tell her that she'd better stay inside and be good until they got home, or else . . . Bonnie knew what "or else" meant. If they found Bonnie had been outside while they were off drinking beer and smoking cigarettes, Daddy would take off his belt and light into her. Or Mama would go outside and cut a switch from the weeping willow tree and use that on Bonnie's bare legs or the thin, raggedy panties that covered her equally thin behind.

The outside door was unlocked. Bonnie could have gone up the stairs and let herself out if she had wanted to. She would have loved to run barefoot through the grass, chasing the butterflies that drifted in and out of Mimi's garden or to play a solitary game of hop-scotch on the smooth surface of her neighbor's driveway. But she didn't. No matter how well she tried to hide what she had done, Mama always seemed to know exactly when Bonnie was telling fibs.

So Bonnie stayed where she was, watching and waiting, sometimes shifting her weight from side to side and holding onto the window sill to help keep her balance. Then something interesting happened. A big car came creeping up Mimi's driveway. Her driveway was far nicer than theirs. It was smooth and clean with no gaping cracks where grass and weeds and dandelions squeezed through.

The car stopped a few feet from Bonnie's window perch. It looked new and shiny, and it was red. Not fire engine red, but a funny kind of red Bonnie had never seen before. She watched as a man got out, a big man wearing the kind of dress-up clothing Daddy never wore, not even on holy days when Mama made him go to church. The man slammed the car door shut. He hurried over to the steps and pounded on the back door. After a while, Bonnie's friend Mimi opened the door and stepped out onto the porch and stood with her back to the screen door.

During the week when Mimi went to work, she wore dresses and heels and had her hair pulled into a bun at the back of her neck. Today, though, her long dark hair was in a ponytail which made her look much younger. She wore light green pedal-pushers with a matching top along with white sandals. Even from where she stood, Bonnie could see the bright red polish that Mimi wore on her toenails. Mimi had even offered to paint Bonnie's toenails once but Daddy had said, "No. Absolutely not." And Mama had said Bonnie was too young for nail polish. So all Bonnie could do was look at Mimi's brightly colored toes and wait to grow up.

Since Saturday was housecleaning day, Mimi wore a flowery, full-length apron. As she talked to the man on her porch, Mimi crossed her arms under the bottom of the apron as though her arms were cold and covering them with the cloth of the apron might help warm them.

Bonnie couldn't hear any of the conversation, but from the bright red splotches of color on her friend's cheeks Bonnie knew that Mimi was angry. So was the man. He waved his arms. His face turned red. And every time he stopped talking, all Mimi did was shake her head. Whatever the man wanted, Mimi's answer was no.

One of the car doors opened and another woman stepped out. This one looked familiar. Bonnie thought she might have seen the woman before, coming to the house with a vase of flowers or maybe a covered dish for supper. Although Bonnie had never seen Mimi's mother, Bonnie knew the woman was old and sick and couldn't get out of bed. Mimi worked in an office all day. The rest of the time she was at home taking care of her mother.

As the second woman walked toward the porch, she opened her purse, reached inside, and pulled something out. Only when the sun glinted off the blade did Bonnie realize it was a knife. That seemed odd. Most of the women Bonnie knew used their purses to carry lipstick and hankies and compacts and change purses. Never a knife.

Why a knife? What was going on?

The woman stepped up onto the porch beside the man. She looked angry, too. Bonnie wondered what was wrong. Why were those two people yelling at Mimi?

Bonnie didn't have to hear the words to know they were saying mean and nasty things. At last Mimi turned and started to go inside. That's when the man reached out and grabbed her. Catching her by the arm, he pulled her off the back porch.

Bonnie watched in horror as Mimi fell all the way to the sidewalk where she lay still for a moment, as though the force of the fall had knocked the wind out of her. Bonnie knew how that felt. The same thing had happened to her when she had fallen out of the apple tree.

Then, instead of helping Mimi up, the man dropped on top of her with his knee in her stomach. There was a brief struggle. The man seemed to be hitting her. The woman was standing in the way, so Bonnie couldn't see everything that happened. She wanted to scream out at him, "Stop! Stop! You're hurting her." But her voice froze in her throat. The words wouldn't come.

At last the woman reached down and helped the man up. The two of them stood there for a moment, looking down at Mimi. Even from where she was standing, Bonnie could see that the man's hands were bloody. So was his shirt. After a moment, the man and woman hurried into the house, closing the door behind them and leaving Mimi lying on the sidewalk.

For a time Bonnie didn't move. She didn't know what to do. She might have run upstairs and told their landlady, but Mrs. Fritz was a cranky old woman. Mama had made it clear that she didn't like children and that Bonnie was never, under any circumstances, to go upstairs and bother her. But still, Bonnie couldn't just stand there and do nothing. At last she jumped down from the chair, ran up the stairs, and hurried out the door.

If the afternoon sun was warm on her body, Bonnie didn't feel it. She raced across their driveway and the narrow strip of grass that separated their backyard from Mimi's. A few feet away, she stopped and stared in horror. There was blood—bright red blood—everywhere. Mimi's flowery apron was drenched in it. Blood spilled onto the cement driveway and pooled beneath her. The handle of a kitchen knife that looked just like Mama's stuck out of her stomach.

"Mimi," Bonnie gasped when she was finally able to speak. "Are you okay?"

Slowly Mimi turned her head and looked at Bonnie. Her eyes searched aimlessly. It was as though she was seeing Bonnie from a very long distance away and was having trouble finding where to look. Mimi opened her mouth and tried to speak, but at first no words came out.

"Please," Mimi began finally, but she couldn't go on. Her lips moved, but Bonnie couldn't hear what she was saying. The horrified child dropped to her knees, hoping to lean near enough to hear and to understand what was needed. Mimi reached out, but instead of taking Bonnie's hand, she pushed her away. "Go," she whispered urgently. "Please go!"

Just then the back door opened. The woman hurried out onto the porch. "Who the hell are you, you little shit?" she demanded staring down at Bonnie. "What the hell are you doing here?"

Bonnie struggled to her feet and dodged backward just as the woman lunged toward her. Fortunately the woman's high-heeled shoe caught on the edge of the driveway and sank into the muddy grass. It was enough to allow Bonnie to dodge out of the way.

"You come back here!" the woman ordered.

But Bonnie saw the blood—Mimi's blood—on the woman's hands. Bonnie shook her head and kept backing away.

Just then Mimi made a strange sound, a gurgling sound. The woman looked down at her briefly. Then she glanced at Mimi's back door and again at Bonnie who was still backing away across the yard as fast as her short little legs would carry her.

"You'd better get the hell out of here then," the woman snarled. "And if you say a word about this to anyone, he'll do the same thing to you, understand?"

At that, Bonnie turned and fled. She ran as fast as she could, past the door into the apartment and around to the back of the house where she ducked into her favorite hiding place, a small passage between a crumbling tool shed and an overgrown hedge. She crouched there in the mud gasping for breath while her heart thumped wildly in her chest. She cried for a while, but then, afraid the man and woman might be looking for her and hear her sobs, she fell quiet and listened—for what seemed like a long, long time. At last she heard the sound of car doors slamming. Moments later, the big red car nosed slowly past the front of the house. Only then did Bonnie creep out of her hiding place.

She tiptoed around the end of the house, back to the side yards and to the place where she had seen Mimi lying in a pool of her own blood. Mimi was gone, and so was the blood. The sidewalk at the bottom of the porch was wet as though someone had hosed it off.

For a few moments, Bonnie stood staring at Mimi's back door, wondering if Mimi was inside and if she was okay. But Bonnie didn't go up the steps and knock on the door. It was getting late. Her parents would be home soon. She didn't want them to find her outside.

She hurried back into the downstairs apartment. Once she was inside, she looked down and saw that her dress was splattered with mud—mud and blood. Mimi's blood. If Mama saw that, she'd want to know how it got there. Next would come the switch or the belt. Bonnie was convinced that if she told anyone what had happened—even Mama and Daddy, she was sure the man who had hurt Mimi would find out about it and come looking for her.

So Bonnie took her dress off. She washed her hands and face and knees, and then she changed into a clean dress. She rolled up the ruined one as small as she could make it. She was standing in the kitchen, looking for a place to hide it, when she heard the sound of her parents' car pulling up outside. Desperate, she shoved the dress as far as she could into the space between the back of the refrigerator and the wall.

Seconds later, Mama and Daddy came in the door. They were laughing and smiling and having a good time. Daddy came over, picked Bonnie up, and swung her around the room.

"There you are," he said. "Have you been a good girl?"

"Yes, Daddy," she told him. "I've been a very good girl."

He put her back down on the floor and pulled a Tootsie-Roll out of his shirt pocket. "That's for being good then," he said.

Tootsie-Rolls were by far Bonnie's favorite candy. Instead of tearing the paper off and biting into it, she held the paper wrapped candy in her hand and stared at it.

"What do you say?" Mama asked.

"Thank you," Bonnie murmured.

"Well," Daddy asked. "Are you going to eat it or not?"

So she did. Under her parents' watchful eyes, Bonnie unwrapped the candy and managed to choke down that

Tootsie-Roll. It was the last one she ever ate. From then on, the very idea of that soft, chewy chocolate reminded her of something that was too awful to think about or remember.

Over the years Bonnie forgot all about her friend Mimi lying there in the spreading pool of her own blood, but she never forgot that the very act of biting into a Tootsie-Roll had the power to make her physically sick.